PRAISE FOR M. K. WREN'S
CONAN FLAGG MYSTERIES

Curiosity Didn't Kill the Cat
"Conan Flagg is an appealing sleuth . . . and there's atmosphere in the Oregon Beach resort and plenty of excitement."
—King Features

Wake Up, Darlin' Corey
"A nice job, written with compassion and buttressed with some sharp observations."
—*The New York Times Book Review*

Oh, Bury Me Not
"Something different, a detective story set in western ranch country with cowboy characters . . . Suspenseful and a challenge."
—*Publishers Weekly*

Nothing's Certain But Death
"Conan Flagg's many fans will enjoy his latest involvements. As always, this series is top fare."
—*The Columbus Dispatch*

DEAD MATTER

M. K. Wren

BALLANTINE BOOKS • NEW YORK

All rights reserved under International and Pan-American Copyright Conventions. Published in the United States of America by Ballantine Books, a division of Random House, Inc., New York, and simultaneously in Canada by Random House of Canada Limited, Toronto.

Library of Congress Catalog Card Number: 93-90077

ISBN: 0-345-37821-0

Manufactured in the United States of America

First Edition: July 1993

CHAPTER 1

Miss Beatrice Dobie pushed open the dormer window and inhaled deeply, convinced she could smell the spindrift in the morning air. That was unlikely, since her house—which she liked to call her cottage, as neatly kept in middle age as she was—stood on the flank of Hollis Heights three hundred feet above the surf.

She looked south where, along a shallow curve of summer-pale beach, the houses of Holliday Beach formed a random rampart, casting triangular shadows across the sand, the apexes of shadow roofs pointing west toward the blue-green Pacific Ocean.

It was going to be hot today. A relative term on the Oregon coast, of course. Here *hot* was anything over seventy degrees. And already, at eight in the morning, the beach was dotted with people. Saturday. August. Miss Dobie sighed. By January she'd be complaining about the dearth of customers at the bookshop, but now she took solace in the thought that Labor Day—and the end of the tourist season—was only ten days away.

Miss Dobie abruptly turned from the window, pulled off her quilted robe, and tossed it on the water bed as she crossed to the closet. She didn't have time now to think about Labor Day. Not on *this* day.

She was ready except for her dress and shoes, and she knew exactly what she would wear: the silk shirtwaist that was the same color as her auburn hair with its purposeful curl and not a hint of gray. She wasn't willing to attempt anything to alter the sagging jowls that made her face ever squarer, but in this day and age, she could certainly do something about gray hair.

She frowned at the dress, so conservative, so staid, and wondered if Savanna Barany would come to the autographing, wondered what Savanna would wear. Something décolleté, no doubt; something bright and slightly exotic. Miss Dobie sighed again. There had been a time when she had worn décolleté, bright, slightly exotic clothes.

Of course, Savanna might not come. There were rumors that she and her husband weren't on the best of terms. But with people like Savanna Barany and Ravin Gould, there were always rumors.

"Ravvvin," Miss Dobie whispered. "Like the first two syllables of *ravenous*." She'd heard him say that on more than one television talk show. Family name. Something like that.

She slipped the dress over her head, careful not to disturb her hair. But what if Savanna *did* attend the autographing? Miss Dobie had alerted the Portland television stations. After all, that was the purpose of this shindig: publicity. The Holliday Beach Book Shop, which had been moldering for half a century in dowdy obscurity, was hosting Ravin Gould, one of America's top ten best-selling authors. And just possibly, Savanna Barany, at one time billed as the sexiest woman in the world.

Of course, there was a secondary purpose: money. Miss Dobie's mouth tightened into a horizontal line as she thought of the three hundred copies of *The Diamond Stud* waiting at the bookshop. Three hundred copies of a book that retailed at $22.00 a copy. That wholesaled at $13.20. Plus freight. For the Holliday Beach Book Shop, that was a *major* investment.

She stepped into a pair of white pumps, her best ones, checked her reflection in the mirror on the closet door to be sure her slip wasn't showing, then crossed to the dresser to pick up her good white purse.

And a copy of *The Diamond Stud*.

The jacket was of satiny black paper with a female figure outlined in hot-pressed gold. Where the navel might be, was a stylized diamond. The title was crowded at the bottom of the jacket in red letters. At the top, the author's name glittered in solid gold: James Ravin Gould.

She studied the photograph on the back. Definitely a handsome man, with a hint of—well, sexiness about him. She wondered if other people were as surprised as she had been to discover how *short* this handsome, sexy man was. He couldn't be more than five six. And it was curious how much this photograph reminded her of Mr. Flagg. Conan Joseph Flagg and Ravin Gould were about the same age, and Miss Dobie was old enough to consider anything under forty-five young. Both men had black hair and dark skin, and a certain lean intensity in their faces. But Mr. Flagg was a head taller, and his eyes were black and slightly tilted—that was the Nez Percé coming to the fore—while Ravin Gould's eyes were a pale, rather unpleasant gray-green.

And what was behind those eyes . . .

That was hard to decipher. She'd only talked to the man once, although he'd been in Holliday Beach over a month. But in a way, she did know him. She had read *The Diamond Stud* and found it rife with gratuitous sex and violence. That didn't surprise her. Gould had made his reputation on sensationalism. But there was an undercurrent of something she couldn't quite pin down, something that made it a relief that she didn't know him better and wasn't likely to. Something that made any comparison between Ravin Gould and Conan Flagg a travesty.

Her breath caught, and she closed her eyes.

Thank God Mr. Flagg was in Cornwall and wasn't due back until the day after Labor Day.

He *was* her employer, after all, and she was well aware that he considered Ravin Gould books literary garbage. He

might recognize the right of any individual to read anything
he or she chose, but he also maintained his right *not* to provide shelf space for a Ravin Gould book.

Miss Dobie put down a momentary queasiness. Mr. Flagg
had left the bookshop in her hands—as he did nearly every
summer, when hordes of tourists mushroomed Holliday
Beach's population from two thousand to twenty thousand—
and even if he considered the shop a hobby of sorts or an
obligation to the maintenance of civilization, she staunchly
considered it a business, and always hoped to make it a *prof-
itable* business. She couldn't overlook an opportunity like
this. Ravin Gould was, after all, one of Holliday Beach's few
claims to fame: Gould had been born and spent the first
twelve years of his life here.

She squared her shoulders and checked her watch. Eight-
thirty. She wouldn't open the bookshop until ten, but first
she had to pick up the sign Gwen Loftstern had made, the
coffee urn at the Grange, the cookies at the bakery; she had
to decorate the refreshment table and call Tina Burbank to
make sure she didn't oversleep; she had to feed Meg and
hope the cat would stay out from under people's feet today.

Beatrice Dobie forgot to lock her front door as she marched
out to the red Porsche in her driveway. It was going to be a
fantastic day. But still . . .

She said another silent prayer of thanks.

Mr. Flagg wouldn't be home for ten days.

CHAPTER 2

At least he had a window seat out of Denver. Conan Flagg looked down from thirty thousand feet on titanic folds of rock etched in snow golden in the dawn. His eyes ached with sleeplessness, and his decision to come home ten days early had long ago begun to seem irrational. At the moment, he wasn't even sure what day it was.

Yesterday—or the day before yesterday?—after weeks of leisurely exploration of England's west coast from Solway Firth to Land's End, he had walked along a beach in Cornwall and felt a restlessness he didn't understand until he stood looking out at the blue-gray roil of the Atlantic Ocean and found himself desolate with homesickness for his own ocean. It was all one sea, he knew, whatever the names given its various parts by the human beings who lived on its shores. Still, he longed for the ocean named Pacific on a clear day, and he longed particularly for the few square miles of the Pacific he could see from his house, the few square miles he called his own.

At that point, his impatience had made sense, but in the grinding hours since he left Heathrow, he began to doubt his sanity. His impatience not only cost him lost sleep—he'd

never learned to sleep upright or in the presence of strangers—
it condemned him to a night flight from New York and a
three-hour layover in the noisy caverns of Denver's airport.

But the sun had time to catch up with him there, and when
at last he resumed his homeward journey, northwest across
the Rockies and the enigmatic reaches of the Basin and Range
country beyond, when at last his plane crossed the cloud-
veiled Cascade Mountains and he saw Mount Hood, magnificent in summer snow, looming beyond the wing tip as
the plane descended toward the green tapestry of the Willamette Valley, he began to believe it was all worthwhile.

But Portland International Airport was still three hours
from the coast, counting the time it took to get out of the
airport and maneuver the clogged freeways of Oregon's larg-
est city. Finally he left the last suburb behind and drove
west, too tired to leash the black Jaguar XK-E to the speed
limit. With the top down so the hot, humid wind beat at
his skin, he faced the bastion of the Coast Range, gentled
by forests of fir and spruce and hemlock, and he waited
for the moment when at the crest of those hills he would
feel the temperature drop, the air turn sweet under the influence of the Pacific Ocean, still thirty miles away, but
reaching out to him in cool welcome.

And now he was sure it was all worthwhile.

At length, he reached the junction with Highway 101, the
Coast Highway, drove south a few more miles, and just past
the sign that read HOLLIDAY BEACH POP. 2001, he caught a
glimpse of the razor-line horizon of the sea beyond the new
shopping mall.

The mall had the architectural originality of a potato shed,
but the same could be said of most of the buildings in Holliday Beach. Here there was none of the charm of antiquity
in which he had steeped himself for the last six weeks. This
village was a product of the Depression, and its architectural
traditions were necessity, availability of materials, and re-
calcitrant individualism, out of which any charm Holliday
Beach possessed arose perversely and against all odds.

Conan puttered behind a caravan of campers down Highway 101, Holliday Beach's main street, anticipating what he

would see when he reached what he considered its true center. On the west side of the highway, paralleling it and separated from it by a concrete curbing, he would see a block-long parking lane wide enough for cars to park on both sides, while two cars might barely pass in the middle. Facing the lane, he would see a row of shops, most of them sided in grayed cedar shingles, splashes of color provided by geranium-filled planter boxes.

And dominating the block from its position between the mom-and-pop grocery and the Chowder House Restaurant, he would see the Holliday Beach Book Shop, a long, shambling, two-story building, topped by three mismatched dormers; a building that had acquired, by virtue of age and the weathering of countless sou'westers, its own stolid charm. There were occasions when Conan regarded the bookshop as his albatross, yet it never occurred to him to rid himself of it. It was also—he admitted on other occasions—his *raison d'être*.

Still, the bookshop wasn't his objective now. At the moment, his only objective was home and the beach. But since he had to pass the bookshop to reach his house, he decided he might as well stop to let Miss Dobie know he had returned.

Yet the closer he came to the bookshop, the slower the traffic moved. Inching along in the fuming wake of a Winnebago, he had ample time to notice that the old Day store had a new occupant. SHE SELLS SEA SHELLS, the sign over the door proclaimed. No doubt shells raped from tropical beaches. A few more feet, and he sighed at the first hint of the approaching political season: placards planted among the weeds in front of the empty Higgins building. One of them briefly held his attention: EARL KLEBER FOR COUNTY SHERIFF. Kleber was chief of the Holliday Beach Police Department, and Conan was surprised that he would take on the incumbent, Gifford Wills, who was well entrenched in Taft County's political good-ol'-boys network. Conan hadn't thought of Kleber as a tilter at windmills.

The Winnebago spewed more smoke in Conan's face as it lurched forward another two yards, and he began swearing methodically. Yes, it was the height of the tourist season, but this was absurd. Finally he saw the Hollis Street sign just ahead and signaled for a right turn. When he reached Hollis, he had only to dogleg into the parking lane. . . .

And he found himself snared in a one-block gridlock.

In five frustrating minutes, he made it only as far as the grocery store, and there he was forced to stop altogether, unable to move in any direction. The sidewalk was mobbed with pedestrians—tourists, most of them, although he recognized a few natives—all converging on the bookshop. Double-parked outside the main entrance near the south end of the shop was a van marked with red, white, and blue stripes and the words KEEN-TV CHANNEL 3—THE EYES OF PORTLAND. One man was unloading equipment, while a second stood on the sidewalk talking with a stringently petite woman in a white dress whose dark hair seemed immune to the wind.

Shelly Gage. Few people in western Oregon wouldn't recognize her; they saw her daily on the evening newscasts and on her morning show. But Conan had met her more than once in person, and her persistence in demanding an interview with him had not endeared her to him.

But why was she here now?

He looked around at the cars and campers entrapping the XK-E and saw that none of them was likely to move in the near future. He pulled the emergency brake and left the car to join the crowd surging around the bookshop's north entrance.

"Mr. Flagg! You made it after all."

He smiled and sidled past portly Mrs. Iona Higgins, wondering what it was he had made.

"Conan! How was England?" That from a tall black woman. Kara Arno taught physical education at Holliday Beach High School and served as living proof of the efficacy of fitness.

"England was fine, Kara," he said absently. "How's Dan?"

She laughed. "Up in the air. As usual."

"Hey, Mr. Flagg!" Hiram Hitchcock, stooped and knuckly. "I was meanin' to talk to you 'bout that roof soon as you got back." Then Mrs. Hopkins, the wife of the Methodist minister, with her dour husband in tow. Then the Daimler sisters, Adalie and Coraline. "Nice to see you home, Mr. Flagg, and just in time."

Not, he thought, if he couldn't reach the door of his own shop.

But he did, finally. The doorway angled across the northeast corner of the building, with a wooden stoop filling out the truncated corner. He reached it just as Mrs. Hollis, well over ninety years old, stumbled on the stoop. Conan caught her twiglike arm, and she gave him a nod that might have indicated thanks, but probably only indicated recognition. He shouted, "Mrs. Hollis, what's going *on* here?"

"What?" She tilted her supposedly good ear toward him, and when he repeated the question, she replied, "Well, it's Rev'rend Good! Heard it on the radio. Didn't know he wrote a book, though."

With his hand still at her elbow, Conan pushed his way into the shop. "What's the name of the book?"

It was like entering a crowded cave. Or maybe the Black Hole of Calcutta. Conan took off his dark glasses, but it didn't seem to help.

"Can't rightly remember," Mrs. Hollis shouted over the hubbub of voices. "Somethin' about *The Blinding God*."

But before he could question that, Mrs. Hollis slipped away to be swallowed up in the crowd. Conan maneuvered into a spot against the shelves on the east wall where he could let his eyes adjust to the twilight, his ears adjust to the high decibel level in a place usually as quiet as a library, and where he could let his jet-lagged, sleep-deprived mind adjust to a scene that was, quite simply, incredible. The Holliday Beach Book Shop had never held a crowd of this magnitude, and he wondered if the aged floor joists would support the weight.

Reverend Good, one of the most venal of the televangelists? *The Blinding God?* Conan felt an incipient headache behind his eyes.

"Never seen anything like it, have you, Conan?"

Conan was washed in the fragrance of young Scotch as
Dr. Maurice Spenser—who liked people to call him Doc—
leaned close to ask that question. Slight and stooped, he was
wearing his brown suit today, and he seemed entirely sober.
He always did. But at sixty-eight, he looked eighty-eight, his
skin netted with broken veins, his gray eyes swimming behind the thick lenses of plastic-framed glasses.

"No, Doc, I definitely have never seen anything like it."

And where the hell was Miss Dobie?

Over the din of voices, he heard the clang of the old cash
register and knew that's where he'd find Beatrice Dobie. But
getting to her was another matter. The register was near the
south end of the building, and at least a hundred sardine-
packed people stood between him and that clang. He thought
of Meg, the blue point Siamese whom some regarded as the
shop's true owner, and wondered where she was hiding.

He began working his way along the wall toward the center
of the shop. The crowd seemed most densely packed there,
and eventually he reached a point where he could look over
and between heads to see what held everyone so spellbound.

A folding table had been set up in the alcove formed by
two jutting bookshelves. The table was stacked with black-
jacketed, hardbound books, and above it, suspended from
the ceiling, hung a sign painted in red and black on a sheet
of mat board:

HOLLIDAY BEACH'S OWN RAVIN GOULD!
BEST-SELLING AUTHOR OF *THE DIAMOND STUD*!

Conan might have laughed at the malapropism arising from
Mrs. Hollis's faulty hearing, but at the moment, Ravin Gould
and *The Diamond Stud* made no more sense than Reverend
Good and *The Blinding God*.

Ravin Gould? Here? In Conan Flagg's bookshop?

Two women turned away from the table, clutching black-
jacketed books, and before the next customers moved in,
Conan saw him.

Ravin Gould. Here. In Conan Flagg's bookshop.

Conan was on the verge of charging through the crowd,

impelled by righteous rage, but it was at that moment that he saw *her*.

Savanna Barany.

Oh, yes, there she was in the fair, subtly voluptuous flesh, perched on a stool behind and to one side of Ravin Gould.

And now Conan knew where Meg was. He should've anticipated that far from seeking a place to hide, Meg would seek the one place where she'd be the center of attention—on Savanna Barany's lap, stretched out luxuriously along the lady's thigh.

But for once, Meg was upstaged. She seemed no more than a whimsical accessory, her white to gray fur contrasting with Savanna's peasant blouse and full skirt of deep blue-green. Peacock blue, it was probably called, and no other color could more perfectly complement her coppery hair. It was arranged in a Gibson pile cascading from the crown of her head to sweep her bare shoulders. Curling wisps brushed her cheeks like silken whispers, and when she smiled, her face seemed luminescent.

Conan had seen that face hundreds of times in magazines, newspapers, on screens both large and small. It occurred to him that he hadn't seen it so often recently, but he remembered exactly when he first saw it: seven years ago in New York in a musical called *Blitz*, her vehicle to instant fame. It was a face out of another century, a perfect oval with a small mouth indulgently curved, and lavender-blue eyes so large, they gave that face a childlike aspect, yet were heavy-lidded, capable of seduction. She sat with her long dancer's legs crossed, one hand stroking Meg, the other braced on the edge of the stool. It was an extraordinarily sensual pose, and Conan recognized in it a self-aware calculation. Or perhaps it was art.

She turned to speak to the tall, saturnine man standing beside her, and Conan sighed. "What is *she* doing here?"

A whiskey-scented laugh reminded Conan that he'd asked the question aloud and that Doc Spenser was still with him. Doc said, "Well, she's married to Jimmy Gould, after all. Didn't you know that?"

"Jimmy?" Conan glanced at Doc, but didn't have a chance to ask more. KEEN-TV was invading from the south door.

"We need some space around the table," Shelly Gage said, smiling sleekly, as the camera and sound men waded in, and space was made without complaint, with only excited murmurs, despite the crush of bodies pressing closer. Conan's headache was no longer incipient as he flattened himself against the bookshelves and watched Shelly introduce herself to Savanna and Gould. Gould took her hand, lavished on it a kiss, with a smoldering look into her eyes. Savanna's smile faded.

Abruptly the camera lights went on, and the glare made a small stage of the alcove. The tall man with the saturnine face stepped back into the corner out of center stage, while the cameraman positioned himself in front of the table, panned from the sign above it down to Savanna Barany—on whom he lingered a long time—then to Ravin Gould, then to Shelly, who stood at the end of the table, her mike and smile ready. "The quaint coastal village of Holliday Beach is bursting with excitement today. The old Holliday Beach Book Shop—a landmark here—is hosting best-selling author Ravin Gould, and with him . . ." A pause for dramatic effect, then, ". . . his lovely wife, Savanna Barany!"

Savanna leaned toward the camera and blew her unseen viewers a kiss, upstaging her husband as effortlessly as she did Meg, and the crowd in the bookshop responded with applause and whistles.

Ravin Gould's gray-green eyes were cold as he flashed a smile and reached for Shelly's mike, then laid his hand on Savanna's knee in a patently proprietory gesture, ignoring Meg's hissing show of teeth. "Eat your hearts out, guys!"

The erstwhile studio audience laughed, and Shelly retrieved the mike to ask, "Mr. Gould, what brings you to this quaint little village?"

"Well, Shelly, this is my hometown, you know. I was born and spent twelve years of my life in Holliday Beach."

"You've come back to rediscover your roots, so to speak?"

A confiding laugh. "That title's been taken. But it's true in a way. I'm finishing my next book here. *Odyssey.* Yes, I know that title's been taken, too. It's what you might call an autobiographical novel.''

Shelly looked earnestly quizzical. ''Then it's really *your* life story?''

''Well, not the *whole* story, I hope. I plan to add a lot to my life story before I die. Let's just say it's based on some of my experiences.''

''Including your childhood here in this quaint little village?''

''Oh, yes. And it wasn't always so damned quaint.''

Conan smiled at that barb as Shelly countered, ''Do you mean this book is going to be a sort of exposé?''

Gould shrugged, teeth white against his tan in a sardonic grin. ''It just might be, Shelly, and if you don't think anything interesting happened in this quaint little village, you're dead wrong. It's all in the book. Everybody's there.'' And he singsonged sarcastically, ''Doctor, lawyer, po-lice chief.''

He seemed to be looking directly at Conan with that, and Conan felt a chill. What in hell was Gould talking about?

''Excuse me . . . let me through . . . I've got to get *through*!''

There was a moment of confusion on the alcove stage as a young woman with golden hair elbowed her way through the crowd, her blue eyes wide with what Conan could only call fear.

He recognized her; he'd known her since she was a cheerleader at the high school. Angela MacGill. Angela *Kleber* MacGill, oldest of Police Chief Earl Kleber's two daughters. She carried a manila envelope, and she was so intent on Gould that she seemed oblivious to the cameras and lights or even the rapt crowd. She reached the table, offered the envelope with shaking hands, leaned over to whisper urgently to Gould, but he cut her off with ''Damn it, I'll talk to you later! Can't you see—''

''But it's *Cady*! Ravin, you've got to get *out* of here!''

He surged to his feet. ''Shut up, Angie!'' Then to Shelly, ''Goddamn it, stop that camera!''

Startled, Shelly signaled the cameraman with a finger across her throat at the same moment a shriek of alarm followed by a sputtering roar sounded from outside the north door. There was an uneasy stirring in the crowd, then Meg catapulted out of Savanna's lap as pandemonium erupted.

Screams and shouts catalyzed a stampede away from the door, and the cameraman staggered and fell, a display rack toppled, paperbacks scattering to be kicked aside like autumn leaves on a sidewalk; a crash of crockery punctuated the melee, and Conan held on to Doc to keep him on his feet, while the sputtering roar rose to a nerve-rending crescendo.

And Cady MacGill strode onto the stage, a latter-day, black Irish Paul Bunyan in a plaid shirt, red suspenders supporting Levi's cut and frayed at the ankle, his caulked boots shaking the floor. Six foot five and well over two hundred pounds of solid, supple muscle, his enormous hands gripping a thirty-six-inch Husqvarna chain saw that vibrated with braying menace, Cady bellowed, "Gould, I'm gonna cut off your balls so you won't *ever* sleep with another man's wife again!"

Gould kicked the table over, sending black-jacketed books avalanching, and crouched behind it. Savanna, Shelly, and the tall man huddled in the corner, and Cady swung the chain saw high, demolishing the sign above the table. The torn remnants whipped about like demented birds. From behind his barrier, Gould cursed with the vitriol of a longshoreman, while Cady matched him with a logger's repertoire at twice the volume, and the chain saw revved to an earsplitting pitch as the spinning blade sliced through the supports of the bookshelf at the north side of the alcove. Splinters, books, and a confetti of shredded pages made a sudden blizzard.

And Conan crossed a threshold from annoyance to anger. He elbowed his way toward center stage, noting peripherally that the cameraman had recovered his footing and was still taping, that in the debris around the table, an orange purse had fallen open, disgorging its contents, including a small, chrome-plated automatic.

"Cady! You damned fool, put that saw down!"

Cady turned, the lethal blade slicing within a few inches of Conan's belt, and Conan stopped abruptly, his headache escalating with the pounding of his heart. He had known

Cady MacGill as long as he'd known Angie—who, he noticed, had disappeared when her husband arrived—but it occurred to him now that perhaps he didn't know Cady as well as he thought he did. Cady's beard-shadowed face was warped with rage, black brows drawn over eyes blue-hot.

Then he pulled the saw back. "Conan?" Briefly his baleful face reverted to the eternal chagrin of adolescence. But his rage rebounded as he shouted, "I got business with this bastard!"

And Conan shouted back, "Not in *my* bookshop, you don't! Turn off that damned saw, Cady!"

The saw spewed on, poised in Cady's big, capable hands, and he didn't move, not so much as the blink of an eye. Nor did Conan.

But at length, Cady faced Gould, who still peered over the top of his table barrier. Cady's mouth curled in a sneer of contempt, and with an eloquently negligent motion, he turned off the saw.

The silence was profound. Ears ringing, Conan held out his hand, open. "Give me the saw, Cady." And when Cady seemed ready to protest, "You've made one hell of a mess here, and you're going to pay for every book you've damaged! Meanwhile, *I'll* keep the saw."

Cady looked around at the chaos he had created, vaguely amazed, then he grimaced, thrust the saw, blade toward the floor, at Conan. "I'll pay for it—every damned cent."

Conan nearly dropped the saw. It weighed at least ten pounds more than he expected. He got a better grip on the bar and said, "I'll keep this in my office until you—"

But Cady wasn't listening. "Gould, you stay away from my wife! You hear?" And with that, he thudded to the north door and vanished.

Ravin Gould, red-faced, veins throbbing in his forehead, sprang up from behind the table. And, incredibly, Shelly was there, mike in hand, asking, "Mr. Gould, would you care to comment on—"

"You *bitch*!" And with a glance at the cameraman, who was still recording, "You put one second of that tape on the air, and I'll sue the hell out of you!" Then he vaulted over the table. "Byron! Savanna! Come on, we're getting *out* of this dump!" And when Savanna, who was kneeling at the moment, didn't seem to respond quickly enough to suit him, Gould grabbed her arm. "Come *on*, you dumb broad!"

Conan's hands tightened on the saw, and he saw in Savanna Barany's eyes a fathomless loathing in the split second before Gould pulled her toward the north door, with the tall man he called Byron a pace behind, and Shelly and her minions in hot pursuit.

Conan found himself the focus of a multitude of eyes. Squinting through his headache, he announced, "The Holliday Beach Book Shop is *closed*. As of now!" With the chain saw in hand, he made his way through the debris of splintered wood, shredded books, and, as he passed the refreshment table, a gravel of broken cups, to the cash register, where Miss Dobie, wide-eyed and pale, still manned her post. He only glanced at her, then turned to the door on the west wall behind the counter, went inside, and closed the door gently.

And in this soundproofed sanctuary, where the walls were hung with a few of his favorite paintings, the floor graced with a scarlet Kirman, he placed the chain saw atop the stacks of mail on his desk. He went to the stereo to put on a tape, then sank into the chair behind the desk. He found a pack of cigarettes in a drawer, lit one, and closed his eyes to absorb the somber cadences of Chopin's "Raindrop" prelude.

He was thinking about a beach in Cornwall.

Then he heard a rustling of papers on his desk and opened his eyes to meet Meg's sapphire gaze. "How are you, Duchess?" She ignored him, meticulously examining the red-enameled motor housing of the chain saw. She always made a point of ignoring him for a day or so when he returned from a long absence. He didn't push her.

It was fifteen minutes later when the office door opened. Miss Dobie paused there and loosed one of her long, expressive sighs.

"The shop is locked up, Mr. Flagg."

Conan walked past her and crossed to the entrance without looking around at the shambles of his once orderly, if slightly musty, albatross and *raison d'être*.

CHAPTER 3

A block south of the Holliday Beach Book Shop, Highway 101 met Day Street, which began at that juncture and ended only two blocks to the west at a small, paved beach access. The house south of the access seemed from that perspective a forbidding arrangement of shingled slabs weathered to silver, the garage door stained a matching gray, the front entrance set deep in a niche as if a portcullis might at any moment be lowered. But from the beach, the house presented an array of reflective spans of glass that made sea and sky integral to its design. The west wall of every room was composed, floor to ceiling, of windows, from the kitchen at the north end, with its angled glass bay, and above it, Conan's bedroom, where the wall of glass included a sliding door opening onto a deck; then a span of windows forty feet long and thirty feet high for the living room; and at the south end, the library, and above it, the guest bedroom. There was no lawn, no plantings that weren't native. A cluster of jack pines hid the small patio that opened off the south wall of the library, and the house was backed into a steep hill shrouded with pine. Below the living room deck, there was only room for a salal-covered bank and a seawall that turned all but the highest winter waves. When the house was built, some of the natives dubbed it Flagg's Folly, in part because of its risky proximity to the sea, but Conan contended that one man's folly is another man's castle. And this was *his* castle, every inch of it designed to his specifications, every object in it there by his choice: his castle and his haven.

Yet when he parked the XK-E in the garage next to the Vanagon, he didn't go into the house but straight to the beach, stripping off his tie and jacket as he crossed the access. Above him, gulls flew into the wind, casting shadows on the sand. He waved at them as if they were long-lost friends.

At the moment, he could overlook the tepid summer surf and the myriad footprints made by the strolling, jogging, lounging, wading, kite-flying, shouting, squealing, Frisbee-tossing crowds with whom he had no choice but to share the beach. The summer people. He tried not to begrudge them their pleasures, but as he walked along the scalloped tracks of the waves, it didn't bother him that the northwest wind blew cold and incessantly, and the water, chilled by the up-welling that surged to the surface along the coast every summer, was frigid. Ten days until Labor Day, and then could winter be far behind? Winter would whip these languid waves into magnificent fury and empty this beach of people by the expedient of drowning it at every high tide.

And he was amply satisfied now with the summer sea. Here he could put the alarums and excursions at the book-shop into perspective and finally even laugh at them.

When he reached that point, he turned and began slogging through the soft, pale summer sand toward his house. Home. He was home now, and it was indeed worthwhile.

By four-thirty he had unpacked his suitcases and the gifts he had purchased on his trip, caught up on six issues of the weekly *Holliday Beach Guardian*, refreshed himself with a long soak in the Jacuzzi, and now he stood on the living room deck with the wind whipping at the black cotton caftan he treasured because of its comfortable practicality, as had the desert merchant from whom he had bought it years ago in Cairo. The sun glared in searing white reflections off the sea, and on the horizon, a train of fog moved constantly south under its impetus.

He took a puff on his cigarette, let the wind catch the smoke, surprised to find that a melody was playing in his mind's ear: the theme song from *Blitz*, "I Never Asked for Forever." And—inevitably, perhaps—an image shimmered in his mind's eye: the image of Savanna Barany. He found himself wondering what she was like beyond the beauty and extraordinary talent. Was there more to Savanna Barany? Was she intelligent and curious? Was she capable of empathy and laughter?

He didn't know, and it was unlikely he ever would. Yet he had to admit he *wanted* to know. A face and body of such silky perfection and intense vitality seemed to ignite questions like static electricity.

Finally he finished his cigarette and, with a rueful laugh, put such vagaries out of his mind. He checked his watch, then left the deck and went to the kitchen to search the contents of the freezer, where he found a boxed entrée, Chicken à la Something. He microwaved it, poured a glass of Elk Cove Vineyards Pinot Noir Blanc, and carried his repast down the hallway behind the wooden screen that divided it from the living room and on to the library, a room with three walls occupied by books and paintings, the fourth occupied by glass and sea. He settled in the Eames chaise, found the remote for the television, and turned it on. The evening news had just begun on Channel 3: KEEN-TV.

Conan wondered if Shelly Gage's employers had been intimidated into silence by Gould's threat of a lawsuit. Shelly wasn't in her usual seat beside the male anchor. Conan ate his passably palatable chicken and sipped his wine through political scandals, wars, toxic spills, droughts, and drug busts—and he always winced at hearing that word, however effective as slang, in the formal context of a news report. Finally, when he had almost decided that KEEN-TV had indeed been intimidated, there was Shelly on the alcove stage at the bookshop, and there was Ravin Gould, tanned and worldly, and there was Savanna Barany, bright hair fired by the lights.

And a few seconds later, there was Cady MacGill and his roaring chain saw. Most of Cady's dialogue with Gould, red-faced behind his table barrier, had been bleeped out, and all but the last ten seconds of Cady's confrontation with one Coven Fledd, owner of the Holliday Beach Book Shop (a landmark in the quaint little village), had been edited out. "The perpetrator of the alleged assault," the substitute female anchor added, "has been identified as Cady MacGill, a local logger. A spokesperson for the Holliday Beach Police Department said they've put out an APB for him." A cut to Sergeant Billy Todd saying, "He'll turn up, don't worry." Then a shot outside the bookshop of Gould hurrying Savanna into a glaring yellow Ferrari, and the female anchor concluded, "Mr. Gould had no comment on the incident."

Conan smiled as he turned off the television. At least, no comment that could be aired under FCC obscenity rules. He rose to take the remains of his meal to the kitchen, but the ring of the phone diverted him to the desk on the south wall. He snatched up the receiver. "Yes?"

"Conan? This is Shelly Gage."

"How did you get this number, Shelly? It's supposedly unlisted."

"Reporters have their sources. Did you see the newscast?"

"I saw it."

She laughed. "And loved it, I can tell. Anyway, the reason I'm calling is to invite you to take me out tonight."

Conan bit back a less than delighted response, and Shelly explained, "I have an invitation from Ravin Gould to what he called a little informal gathering at his beach house. Well, it's not really his. He's renting. Just calls it his."

"Why would Gould invite you to a gathering, formal or otherwise?"

"It was when I followed him out to his car. Maybe his agent whispered in his ear about how many KEEN stories the network picks up. He's fence-mending, Conan. Ravin understands PR very well."

"No doubt. But what *I* don't understand is why you're stretching Gould's invitation to include me."

"Conan, you're *perfect*. I can't wait to see Ravin's face when I walk in with the owner of that *dump*—who just happens to be the owner of the biggest ranch in the state *and* a millionaire *and* a licensed PI."

"You're showing off, Shelly, and you haven't got your facts straight. I'm only majority stockholder at the Ten-Mile, and I am not a millionaire, and it is not the biggest ranch in the state."

"Just second biggest? Well, you *are* a PI. It's on record. And you're the man who saved Ravin from the mad logger. By the way, that woman who came in right before MacGill— is she his wife?"

"Yes."

"What was in that envelope?"

"Probably the plans for the superconductor."

"Sure. *Was* she sleeping with Ravin?"

"Somehow I just don't consider that any of my business."

"Or mine? Okay. Look, all I ask is a couple of hours of your time. No interview, no questions. I promise."

"Damn it, Shelly—"

"Just think about the look on Ravin's face. . . ."

Conan sighed, but he wasn't thinking about Gould's expression. He was thinking about Savanna Barany. At least, this was one way to get to meet her, to perhaps assuage his curiosity to some small degree.

"And, Conan, at least this is one way to get to meet—"

"All right, Shelly. I'll pick you up . . . when?"

"Eight-thirty. But I have my car. I'll meet you at Ravin's house. It's the last house on Dunlin Beach Road. You know, south of Sitka Bay."

"I know. You got on first-name terms with Gould damned fast."

"That's just the California coming out. He claims to be a native Oregonian, but he lives mostly in San Francisco. And Honolulu. And New York. He has a condominium in Portland, though, just to keep up his claim to Oregon. Anyway, he first-names everybody."

"Especially young and attractive women?"

"Hey, why do you think I want you along as my escort?"

At that, Conan laughed. "Don't count on *me* for protection."

"I never count on anyone for that. Okay, I'll see you at eight-thirty. And thanks, Conan. You're a sweetheart."

Before Conan could respond, she hung up. As he cradled the receiver, his eye was caught by the painting in the corner farthest from the light. *The Knight*. A life-size figure in equivocal armor that was both obdurate bronze, and bone and muscle. The head was helmet and skull at once, and in one hand, it offered the rose of love and the butterfly of hope, while the other hand held the waiting shackles.

Conan had often used that painting as a sort of litmus test. If people found it morbid, they never had an opportunity to see it again.

Disturbing, he could accept. And at the moment, that juxtaposition of rose and butterfly and shackles seemed to fix itself in his mind like a melody that wouldn't leave him in peace.

CHAPTER 4

The sun had set, and at the horizon a wash of red—the pinkish red of smoke from slash fires in the Coast Range—was mirrored on the surface of Sitka Bay, a marine estuary all but cut off from the sea by Shearwater Spit. Conan smiled as he drove south on Highway 101 past that splendid expanse of life-rich water. That it had not become a fouled pond for human recreation was due in part to his efforts. But his smile faded as he considered the cost of that victory.

And the victory had been only partial. Sitka Bay had been spared the housing development that threatened it, but Baysea Properties had pursued its plans for a destination resort, and now Baysea Resort occupied a square mile of land between 101 and the beach, offering luxurious rooms, two restaurants, tennis courts, golf course, swimming pool, an airfield, a helicopter shuttle to Portland, and car rental service. But at least *this* destination was a mile beyond Sitka Bay and didn't impinge on its shores, and Conan didn't have to look at it now.

At the south end of the bay, he turned right onto Dunlin Beach Road, threaded along the top of basalt cliffs, then turned left where the road divided and a sign pointed to Dun-

lin Beach. It was a barely graveled road that paralleled the
beach behind a buffer of beachfront lots. He geared down to
accommodate the ruts, occasionally passing driveways hinting at the existence of houses hidden in thickets of jack pine
and rhododendron that after half a mile gave way to salal and
beach grass as the road neared its dead end.

The house west of the turnaround terminating Dunlin
Beach Road presented a sienna-stained cedar facade unbroken except for the inset porch where a pair of lights glowed.
The grounds were landscaped in bark chips and stray pines,
and three cars were parked at the edge of the gravel in front
of the house: Gould's yellow Ferrari, a silver-gray Buick, and
a blue Nova. The latter was occupied, as Conan discovered
when he parked behind it. Shelly Gage got out and waited
for him, made a show of checking her watch. "You're a
minute late." Then she added soberly, "Thanks for coming,
Conan."

He offered his arm. "Shall we go see the look on *Ravin's*
face?"

But at the crackle of tires on gravel, he turned, squinting
into a glare of headlights. The car passed them and came to
a stop in front of the Ferrari. When the dust settled, Conan
noted that it was a new, white Buick with Oregon plates. It
was so much a clone of the gray Buick, he decided both were
rentals. The woman who got out of the car and hurried toward the house seemed startled when she met Shelly and
Conan as they started up the flagstone walk.

"Oh," she said—more a gasp than a word—as she studied
them over the top of swoop-framed glasses. Conan guessed
she was at least fifty, and perhaps that many pounds over-
weight, the excess distributed to her bosom and hips and not
disguised by an unfettered floral-print dress. Her short, curly
hair wasn't quite as auburn as Miss Dobie's, but probably
owed as much to her beautician. She smiled and said in a
Lauren Bacall voice laced with a New York accent, "You're
Shelly Gage. I saw you this evening on TV. And you . . ."
She shifted her inquiring gaze to Conan. "Weren't you at
this morning's debacle, too?"

Conan laughed at that. "Yes, I was. Were you?"

She shook her head as they continued up the walk to the porch. "No, but Ravin gave us a play-by-play this afternoon. That autographing will probably end up in one of his books eventually. But don't worry, you'll never recognize it." When she reached the porch she turned and added, "I'm Marian Rosenthal. Publicity director at Harkness, Cronin and Company. Ravin's publisher."

"Conan Flagg." He took her offered hand for a firm, brief handshake. "I own the bookshop that was the site of the debacle."

Marian Rosenthal's eyes widened, and Shelly put in, "Conan was the one who took the chain saw away from that logger."

"Shelly, Cady *gave* me the saw," Conan said irritably.

Marian responded with a laugh. "Either way, even Ravin admitted that took guts." She pressed the doorbell to the right of the double doors. Conan heard a distant chime, but nothing more. Marian pressed the doorbell again. Waited. And rang again.

After the third chime, both doors abruptly swung back, and Ravin Gould, in white pants and a white shirt, open to the waist, long sleeves cut with dashing fullness, a red silk handkerchief thrust nonchalantly into the pocket, greeted them with a flashing smile and open arms. That he found it necessary to look up at all three of them apparently didn't bother him. He had the panache of a prince in voluntary exile.

And Shelly was doomed to disappointment. If Gould was surprised at seeing Conan, he didn't show it. And Shelly, now that she was actually confronted with the look on Gould's face, seemed mesmerized as he focused on her and said, "Welcome to Casa Dement!"

Then he included Conan and Marian in his ebullient "Come in!" and waved them into a small foyer two steps above a living room decorated in beige and muted pinks with accents of maroon and cobalt blue. There was a fireplace on the left wall veneered in pale sandstone, and facing it, a couch with a settee at right angles at the west end, both upholstered in beige corduroy and piled with pink, maroon, and cobalt pillows. A blond oak coffee table supported a bouquet of white orchids and ginger. The room was empty, but on the lighted deck beyond the west windows, Conan saw two of the other guests. And the hostess.

"What'll you have, Shelly?" Gould asked, taking her arm as he led the way to the bar on the north wall. "I've got the makings for almost anything, but unfortunately not the bartender."

"Just Perrier and a twist. I have to drive back to Portland tonight."

"That's a hell of a note." Gould went behind the bar and filled a glass with ice. "I was hoping to get to know you better, Shelly." He poured the Perrier, but his eyes were on Shelly, and Conan saw a flush in her cheeks that wasn't rouge. Marian leaned on the bar, watching Gould with an ambiguous half-smile.

Shelly said lightly, "I was hoping to get to know *you* better. In an interview, maybe?"

"All things are possible, Shelly. We'll talk about it later. Okay?"

"Okay." Then she glanced at Conan. "Ravin, you haven't been properly introduced. This is Conan Flagg, the man who—"

"Saved me from a fate worse than death—getting my balls cut off? I owe you, Conan. You know, that MacGill bastard reminded me of my old man. He was a logger, too. But not that damned *big* a logger. Hell, I never saw MacGill before in my life, and he comes after me with that monster balls saw." Gould cut a slice of lime, squeezed it, and dropped it into the Perrier, his eyes seeking Shelly's confidentially. "But I run into a lot of weirdos. The price of fame, I guess."

Shelly nodded in sympathy, but her reporter's instincts hadn't entirely deserted her. "Or the price of sleeping with a certain very big logger's wife?"

Gould only laughed. "Angie just types my revised drafts. Marian, what can I do for you?" Then in an aside to Shelly, "As if I didn't know. Marian's a *publicist*. That's what they call them these days."

Marian played to his straight line with "What did they call us in the old days, Ravin? And I'll have a gin and tonic."

While he opened a bottle of Tanqueray, he said, "Well, it had something to do with snake oil." Marian managed a smile, and Gould explained to Shelly, "The only reason Marian ventured into the wilds of Orygawn is to convince me that writers don't need to write. Our purpose in life is to exhaust ourselves flying from city to city, scarfing down microwaved literary luncheons, fending off mobs of autograph seekers, and enduring talk show hosts who take pride in *never* reading a book by an author they interview. Oh—" He folded his hands in mocking prayer. "With the exception, I'm sure, of your lovely self."

Shelly addressed her response to Conan. "You know, Conan, I think this man is almost as full of Irish blarney as you are."

"Irish?" Gould stared at Conan until he decided that was a joke and called for a laugh. He was still laughing when he gave Marian her drink.

Conan's attention was caught by that otherwise unnoteworthy action only because of Marian's sudden intake of breath. She was staring at the hand with which Gould offered the glass. His left hand. It seemed to be the ring on his fourth finger that fixed her attention and sent a rush of color into her face. The ring was a wide band of turquoise inlaid with gold in an odd pattern of thick curves.

Gould reached under the counter for another glass, and, apparently oblivious to Marian's reaction, asked, "Conan, what'll you have?"

"Bourbon rocks, thanks."

"Coming up," Gould said as he tossed ice into a faceted rocks glass, then half filled it from a bottle of Jack Daniel's. He slid the glass across the bar to Conan, then put another glass on the bar and opened a fifth labeled Bruichladdich Islay Single Malt Scotch Whiskey. Perhaps noticing Conan's raised eyebrow, he said, "This'll put hair where it belongs. First time I got my hands on a bottle of Bruichladdich was twenty years ago in Tijuana. Didn't exactly pay for it—not in those days—but I decided then if I ever got rich, this would be my poison of choice. Can't even buy the stuff in Oregon. Have to import my own.'' He filled his glass, then gestured toward the deck. ''Might as well see the last of the sunset.''

There was little left of the sunset, and the artificial light washing the deck made the sky seem darker. Beyond the deck, across a lawn perhaps thirty feet wide, Conan saw the railing and top step of a stairway descending to the beach, where the surf murmured lazily. A man and a woman sat at a round, rattan table near the door. The man was the one with the saturnine face who had been at the bookshop this morning. At first, Conan judged him to be in his fifties, but his thin hair and the fragile texture of his skin made that estimate questionable.

Defying etiquette, Gould began the introductions with this man: Byron Lasky, head of the Lasky Literary Agency in New York, Gould's agent since his second book, *Hot Snow*. Lasky rose, a little stiffly, offered his hand to Shelly and Conan in turn, his smile warming as he took Marian's hand. ''Marian, we thought you were lost.''

She shrugged. ''I just lost track of the time. Justine, you look marvelous. I told you that hot tub would work wonders.''

The tall, slender woman at Lasky's left laughed, and she and Marian exchanged brushing kisses near their cheeks before Marian seated herself in the empty chair beside her.

''Justine Lasky,'' Gould said with a mocking bow. ''Byron's better half and business partner. The power behind the throne.''

Justine's smile faltered, but she said nothing beyond a polite recognition of Shelly and Conan, the cool edge sharpened by an upper-class British accent. She wore a dress of red linen, its full sleeves and square neckline decorated with white embroidery, and her black hair was swept back in shining curves held by a pair of gold combs of Mayan design. The effect was exotic, but she had the face for it: high cheekbones and heavy-lidded eyes that were not the black Conan expected, but a pale gray.

Conan thought Gould was saving Savanna for last to enhance the effect on the local yokels. Throughout the intro-

ductions, she lounged against the deck railing, the essence
of summer in slacks and a loose, sheer blouse of clear yellow,
her hair unconfined, caught in the wind. But when Gould
concluded his introductions to the Laskys, he seemed to feel
his obligations were fulfilled. He pulled a chair out from the
table for Shelly.

Savanna put on a smile and crossed to the table. "Ms.
Gage, it's a relief to meet you again under more pleasant
circumstances."

Shelly popped up from the chair, seemed on the verge of
a curtsy. "Me, too. I mean, relieved for the more pleasant
circumstances. By the way, is there anything to the rumor
that you might do a movie of *Blitz*?"

Savanna tensed, but kept her smile. "Not at this time."

"That's too bad. I heard Booth Kettering was—"

"Oh, Booth has so many projects going now." Then she
turned to Conan, extended her hand, and her smile turned
ingenuously, subtly seductive. "I'm glad you came, Conan."

Her hand was warm and light in his, and he wondered why
he seemed to be getting the full treatment, but couldn't deny
its efficacy. He read in her magnificent eyes, more violet than
blue now, a lively curiosity, an ironic awareness of her effect
on him, and an equivocal cast of melancholy. He said,
"Thank you," and could think of nothing else to add. It
didn't matter; he had lost her attention.

The wind hadn't slackened with the twilight, and Shelly
shivered, rubbing her bare arms. "I wasn't planning on an
evening at the beach when I left Portland this morning."

At that, Gould turned solicitous. "You need a sweater or
something. Go get one of yours, Savanna. Or maybe that red
shawl thing."

Savanna stared at him incredulously, and Shelly put in,
"Oh, no, please don't bother. I'm fine. Really."

"Well, *I'm* not," Marian said as she rose, breaking the
taut silence. "I didn't bring a fur coat. Thought it was summer. I'm going in."

That set an exodus in motion, and once inside the living
room, the guests gravitated toward the canapés and hors
d'oeuvres arrayed around a mound of caviar on the narrow

brass and glass table backed to the couch. While Gould played bartender, Savanna went to the stereo by the fireplace. The voice that filled the room a few minutes later was husky and capable of poignant breaks, but Conan knew the power in it, knew it could fill a theatre to the last row and could probably shatter glass. It was the voice of Savanna Barany, and the song was "I Never Asked for Forever."

As she approached the table where Conan and Shelly were sampling elegant tidbits, she looked at him, recognizing his smile of appreciation with a brief smile of her own.

Shelly said, "Oh, I *love* that song. It went gold, didn't it?"

Savanna nodded. "Yes, it did. My first—"

"Damn it, Savanna," Gould cut in, "I've heard that stupid tape till I can lip-synch every word."

She picked up a tiny cracker, loaded it with caviar, and coolly ignored her husband. "Conan, have some of this. It's beluga."

"Thanks, but where I come from, fish eggs are used for bait."

She laughed. "What a waste." And drifted toward the bar. "Any more of that champagne left, Ravin?"

He found a tulip glass behind the bar and, in filling it, emptied the bottle, made a show of dropping it in a wastebasket with a solid thump. "One down—but who's counting?"

"Not you, darling. Not if you're talking about fifths of Bruichladdich." And with that barb, she walked around the settee to stand in front of the fireplace. "Justine, that dress is gorgeous. Where did you find it?"

Justine Lasky was sitting with her husband on the settee. She held a martini in a graceful, manicured hand, while his glass seemed to contain nothing more than Perrier. Justine said, "Actually, I found this dress in Cancún three years ago." She sent Lasky a rueful smile. "That was the last vacation we took."

Savanna shook her head. "Byron, you've got to let go now and then. I mean, you're going to work yourself to death."

"Letting go isn't always feasible," Lasky responded with

a stiff smile, a smile that faded as he looked over at Gould, who was pouring himself another Scotch. "Ravin, I've *got* to talk to you about that Bantam contract. You can't keep putting me off."

Gould came out from behind the bar, went to the couch where Shelly sat alone at the end nearest the settee, and sank into the cushions next to her, ignoring the length of couch left unoccupied. "Byron, *you* take care of the Bantam contract. That's why I pay you your ten percent pound of flesh. *I've* got work to do. Tonight . . . well, all work and no play, you know." And he rested his arm on the back of the couch behind Shelly, who responded with a doubtful glance as she shifted a few inches toward the end of the couch. Savanna watched her husband over the rim of her glass, her narrowed eyes failing to conceal a chill resentment.

Conan saw Marian Rosenthal, a small plate in hand, standing at the windows looking out toward the carmined horizon. He took his glass and joined her. "Is this your first trip to the Oregon coast?"

"Yes. Sure beats hell out of the California beaches, doesn't it?"

"Don't tell the Californians that. Besides, this is our dry week. Stick around a few days and the monsoons will hit."

Marian laughed, a throaty laugh that was loud enough to be unpleasant, yet wasn't. "Well, I guess I'll miss that. Byron and Justine and I are going back to New York Monday."

"You're traveling with them?"

"Yes. Mixing business with pleasure. Known them for years, but we don't seem to have time to see much of each other in New York. What are those lights out there on the horizon?"

"Fishing boats."

"Well, if some of them brought this smoked salmon—" she popped a canapé into her mouth "—they have my eternal gratitude."

"Actually, fishermen very seldom catch smoked salmon."

She laughed again. "They don't catch lobster tails where I come from, either. Jacob and I have a place at the beach on Long Island. He calls it the farm. Not that he ever raised anything on it except horses, but it was nice when the kids were growing up."

"How many kids do you have?" Conan asked politely.

After an odd hesitation, she said, "Well, there's Deborah, who followed in her father's footsteps into corporate law. David's a stockbroker. They're both married and have produced four grandchildren altogether, and yes, I have pictures in my purse, but no, I won't bore you with them. You married?"

"No."

"Never been married?"

Conan shrugged. "Once."

"And it's none of my business." Her brown eyes glinted over her swoop-framed glasses.

Conan answered that with a noncommittal smile as he tuned in on the conversation around the fireplace. Rather, the monologue. Gould was holding forth with ". . . pitch-black and raining like hell, and there I was in this alley, crouched in a doorway. I didn't figure there was anybody anywhere near. Just me and the rats. Then this big black buck came staggering off the street. Stoned out of his mind and bigger than that damned logger. Me, I'm trying to pass for invisible, but there was a light over the door, and he saw me. Took one look and let out a roar. Primal bellow. Says, 'You motherfucker, that's *my* place!' " Gould paused for effect, but apparently Shelly, who had shifted farther toward the end of the couch, was the only member of his audience whose reaction concerned him. She made no comment, nor did the Laskys. Conan could see Justine's face in profile as she faced Gould. Her fixed expression made it obvious that she had heard the story before.

Savanna still stood by the fireplace, watching without listening, while Gould went on, "Well, I figured I was dead meat. That bastard headed for me like a Mack truck. Then I saw something move. Looked like a pile of garbage up against the wall between me and this black buck, and all of a sudden a two-by-four shot out just in time to catch the black guy's feet. Damn, he went down like a boulder, and this wizened little man came up out of the garbage and hollered, 'A bolt of lightning! Praise the Lord, I saw it! A bolt of lightning done come out of heaven and struck this man down!' '' Gould laughed, a little too hard, then concluded, "And that black bastard *believed* him. Took out of that alley praying for mercy."

Conan glanced at Marian, saw her call up a bemused smile. He asked, "Does that have any basis in fact?"

"Probably. With Ravin's tales, it doesn't really matter."

"You've known him a long time."

"Since his second book. Harkness did his first one, too, but nobody in the publicity department even knew his name till *Hot Snow*. I was arranging author's tours then. Ravin and I got on fine. I'm motherly enough not to be a threat to him. He still likes to have me with him on his tours."

"Isn't it unusual for a publicity director to nurse authors through tours?"

"*Very* unusual. But these days, whatever Ravin wants, he *gets*."

Conan sensed an edge of bitterness in that. He asked, "Are you setting up tours for *Stud* now?"

"No, not now. *Stud*'s been out six months at least. Tours aren't worth a damn this late in the game."

"*Odyssey*, then? When will it be published?"

"I don't know. He hasn't even finished it yet. Not the spring list, for sure. Maybe next fall. Of course, there's no guarantee we'll get it. Ravin never signs a contract for a book until he has a finished manuscript. I'm just assuming we'll do *Odyssey* on the basis of past history. He's been loyal to Harkness since his first book, and Harkness has been loyal— and very generous—to him since his second hit the best-seller lists."

Gould had launched into another tale, and his glass was again empty. Savanna's glass was empty, too, but she didn't seem to notice, looking on like a stranger, while her husband shifted even closer to Shelly. Justine Lasky glanced at her watch, leaned toward her husband to speak into his ear, and he nodded, but made no move to rise.

Conan asked, "Marian, how long have the Laskys been Gould's agents?"

"Well, Byron's been his agent since *Hot Snow*. That was— what?—sixteen years ago. Byron and Justine didn't get married until about four years later. Second marriage for her. Her first husband was a professor at Columbia. Got hit by a cab just outside their apartment. Anyway, when she and Byron got married, she was a senior editor at Champlain Communications Group. But they fired her. They were idiots to let her go—she was the best they had—but they'd just been conglomerated, and the new management wanted fresh blood. She started working with Byron then, and now they have one of the top agencies in New York."

Gould rose, still regaling, and went to the bar to refill his glass, not bothering to add ice. "That damned broad locked herself in, and I had to break down the door. Nearly broke my arm. . . ."

"What does Casa Dement mean?" Conan asked.

Marian looked up at him quizzically. "You haven't read *Stud*?"

He restrained himself to a simple "No."

She nodded. "Danny Dement was the protagonist."

"Danny Dement?" Conan was beyond restraining a laugh at that.

"I know, but Ravin's a brand-name author. He could call his hero Peter Pinafore and still have a bestseller." Then she added with unmasked cynicism, "They're all the same character, anyway. Men with more guts than sense, incredibly good luck, and cast-iron constitutions. And their gorgeous females seem to find them irresistible."

Conan watched Gould as he returned to the couch, glanced indifferently at his wife, then put on his glittering smile for Shelly while he rested one arm on her shoulder and she reached the limits of the couch. Savanna was still as stone; she didn't even seem to be breathing.

Conan observed, "They say writers write about the people they see in the mirror."

Marian considered that. "Ravin likes to play games. But he'll play one game too many someday. I don't know why Savanna's put up with him so long. I mean, she's not the *Blitz* bimbo with the heart of—"

The chime of the doorbell distracted her. Conan automatically looked at his watch: 9:05.

"Who the hell is that?" Gould muttered. He made his way a little unsteadily to the door, while Shelly took the opportunity to escape the couch and move around behind the settee. When Gould opened the door, he loosed a bark of a laugh and said, "I'll be damned!"

Then a feminine voice, the words becoming intelligible only as the woman entered the foyer: ". . . on my way to L.A., but I thought I'd just take a little detour. Couldn't call. You're not listed."

Gould had his arm around the woman's waist as they stepped down into the living room, and he said sardonically, "Look who's here!"

Conan heard Marian's gasp, her whispered "I can't believe it."

Neither, apparently, could Justine, who rose, heavy-lidded eyes riveted on the new arrival. Her husband also rose, reaching for Justine's hand in silence.

Fashionably, almost unpleasantly thin, the woman projected a taut, muscular energy. Her cruelly elegant, high-heeled shoes gave her at least a six-inch advantage over Gould, and she wore them with ease, as if they were entirely comfortable. She pushed back the cornsilk hair that curled under just short of brushing her shoulders, looked around the room, and seemed to find what she was searching for when her gaze met Savanna Barany's. Savanna's fair skin reddened, and she held her glass in a grip that should have broken the delicate stem.

For a split second the woman's face, which had at first glance struck Conan with its attractiveness, turned tense and ugly. It was an arresting face: narrow, with slanted shadows under high cheekbones, amber eyes set deep under pale brows, a mouth that was too large, yet mobile and expressive. While Gould helped her out of her tan raincoat and took the beige leather handbag with its oversize gold buckle, she shaped a smile and explained, "I had to talk to Billy Majian about a book he's taken an option on, and I just thought I'd pop up here and see you. I never realized it'd take so long to

get here. Thank God Baysea has that helicopter shuttle.''
Under the coat, she wore an impeccable beige linen dress,
and around her shoulders she had draped a brown and ochre
paisley scarf that startled Conan, because among the gifts he
had brought home from England for various friends and relatives was a silk scarf intended for his aunt Dolly that was
virtually identical to the one that now graced this woman's
shoulders.

Gould waved an arm vaguely. "I think you know everybody. Oh—this is Shelly Gage, news anchor at KEEN-TV in
Portland. Dana Semenov, editor-in-chief at Nystrom, Incor-
porated. And this is . . . uh, Conan. He runs a bookshop.
A very dangerous bookshop.''

Dana Semenov smiled pleasantly at Shelly and seemed to
dismiss her, but for Conan she had an assessing look, and
he wondered how she catalogued him. Definitely she was in
the habit of cataloguing people, and perhaps especially men;
it would be a survival tactic in the business world. And judging from the money invested in her clothes and hair, and the
tan that had not been acquired working in an office in Manhattan, she was quite successful in that world.

"A dangerous bookshop?" she asked. "That I must see."

Before Conan could respond, Gould cut in. "Wait'll you
hear how this man runs an autographing. But first let me get
you a drink." He started for the bar, nearly going down when
he misjudged the location of one of the stools. "Shit. Let's
see, it's white wine. Nothing stronger ever touches the lady's
lips. And lips that touch wine will *always*—"

Savanna's glass shattered on the hearth. She strode toward
the door to the deck, passing only a couple of feet from
Conan, and he could see that she was trembling.

"Hey!" Gould shouted. "Where the hell are *you* going?"

She thrust the door open. "Three in one day is too damned
many, Ravin!" And she ran across the deck and lawn toward
the beach stairs.

"Savanna! You bitch, come *back* here!"

She probably heard him—she had left the door open, and
his bellow was loud enough to be heard for blocks—but she

didn't pause. A moment later she disappeared down the stairway.

Gould seemed to become aware of the six people staring at him. He put on a cynical smile. "One thing that woman hates, it's being upstaged. Well, now . . . I got a nice little Oregon wine for you, Dana. Rex Hills Chardonnay. Where's that damn corkshrew? Ha! Cork*screw*. And screw *you*, Savanna, baby. Hey, anybody want another drink?"

The Laskys and Marian Rosenthal watched this display in silence, while Dana Semenov seemed oddly withdrawn, as if she had no part in it. A good poker face, Conan thought, another attribute that no doubt served her well in the business world. Shelly, he noted, seemed simply and transparently appalled.

Justine was the first to recover. She said in her quiet British accent, "Byron, darling, I'd like to go back to the Surf House. I'm tired."

He took her arm and started toward the door. "So am I. Marian?"

"I'm ready. Well, Conan, it was a pleasure. I'll try to stop by your bookshop before we leave."

He nodded absently while Shelly picked up her purse from the coffee table, smiled uneasily at Gould as she, too, headed for the door. "I'd better get back to Portland, Ravin. I've got to tape an interview at seven in the morning."

Conan was only a pace behind her, and Gould said loudly, "Hell, don't let a little fireworks scare you off. Hey!"

At the door, Byron Lasky turned, said wearily, "I'll talk to you tomorrow about those contracts, Ravin. Good night."

"To hell with the fucking contracts! And to hell with *you*! I don't *need* you, Byron. You know that, don't you? And if you don't, you'd fucking well better figure it out! There's agents under every damn rock in New York, and any one of them'd kill to have *me* for a client!"

Lasky stood pale, jaw clenched as if to contain any response to that, but his wife, who had to this point seemed possessed of unshakable calm, took a step toward Gould, her voice strained beyond recognition as she shouted, "You drunken bastard! Is this why you invited *her* here?" And she pointed at Dana Semenov. "So she could *gloat* while you—"

"Justine!" Byron said sharply, putting his arm around her. "Please, it doesn't matter. Come on. I'll deal with this later."

Her eyes met his, then she nodded, her composure restored as she turned away, and Lasky opened the doors for her.

Gould scurried out from behind the bar. "Justine, you bitch! Damn it, I made you, you and your fucking agency! I *made* you!"

"Oh, for God's sake, Ravin, let them go." That cool command came from Dana Semenov, who stood with her arms folded, studying Gould with a faint smile.

He glared at her, then abruptly relaxed and went behind the bar to fumble among the bottles. "They're gone, Dana. Gone!"

Marian hurriedly followed the Laskys out the door without a word, while Shelly grabbed Conan's arm and muttered, "Let's *go!*"

When Conan closed the double doors behind them, he heard Shelly's gusty sigh. It was fully dark now, and the wind was tingling with dew. The Laskys were getting into the gray Buick, and by the time Conan and Shelly reached her car, the Buick had already made the turnaround and headed north. Marian's white Buick was only a few seconds behind. Conan saw another car parked in front of the Ferrari: a maroon Skylark, probably another of Baysea's rentals.

"He's a real bastard, isn't he? Too bad." Shelly shuffled through her purse, adding, "*You* sure managed to stay out of the way."

"I told you not to expect any protection from me," Conan reminded her. "Besides, I wasn't sure you *wanted* protection."

She found her car keys and slid in behind the wheel. "Maybe I didn't at first. He really is a very attractive man, in spite of everything."

Conan said dryly, "His charms elude me, Shelly."

"Well, they would. You're a man. I mean, I can see through women just because I know all the moves, and I

don't understand why men fall all over themselves for somebody like Savanna Barany. I guess you can see through men
just because *you're* a man." Conan considered that philo-
sophical morsel without comment while she added, "Anyway, Conan, thanks for coming with me."

"Good night, Shelly." He closed her door, then frowned
at the crunch of gravel, looked north into approaching headlights, wondering who was driving up Dunlin Beach Road
this time of night. Not that it was so late. It wasn't yet nine-
thirty. He went to his car, glanced at the house, and saw
Dana Semenov pulling on her tan raincoat as she left the
porch.

A catalyst, and he wondered what she was catalyzing here.

He got into the XK-E as the approaching car passed. The
glare of headlights precluded his seeing into the car or seeing
it at all until it moved into the edges of Shelly's headlights.
A blue, fin-tailed 1959 Cadillac. It looked like Mrs. Carmody's vintage car. But it couldn't be. Mrs. Carmody's Cadillac actually was the kind of car that was only driven to
church on Sundays by a little old lady.

The Cadillac circled the turnaround, treating Conan to
another blinding glare, then accelerated past him with a hail
of gravel.

CHAPTER 5

The ring of the phone took the place of bagpipes in a dream in which Savanna Barany, wearing a Royal Stewart kilt, was executing a sword dance, toes pointed, red hair flying, but instead of crossed swords, she was tripping fantastically lightly amid crossed chain saws.

Conan sat up abruptly, trying to identify his own bedroom, the walls warm blue-gray, the Carl Hall bird-spirit looking back at him from across the room, and on his right the scrim curtains moving in the wind wafting through the open door onto the deck.

He let his breath out, then when the phone repeated its shrill summons, lunged for the side table. The clock on the control console read 8:10 A.M. The last time he remembered looking at it—just after he finished the book he'd started at the airport in Denver—the clock had read 3:20 A.M. He muttered a hello into the receiver.

"Mr. Flagg?" Beatrice Dobie's usually laconic voice was edged with alarm. "Mr. Flagg, you *know* I wouldn't call you at this time of the morning, especially when you must be worn-out from your trip, and especially after, well, after yesterday, and I really—"

"Miss Dobie, what's wrong?" He reached for the pack of cigarettes on the side table, shook one out, and put it between his lips.

"Well, I came to the shop early today. Didn't quite finish cleaning up yesterday, and . . . Mr. Flagg, the shop was *burglarized* last night."

"What?" The cigarette fell, bounced off the table to the floor.

"Yes! Somebody broke one of the panes on the north door so they could reach the inside lock. Did the same thing on your office door. And that one-way glass is *so* expensive."

"Is anything missing?"

"I haven't checked thoroughly yet, but the safe hadn't been opened, and we do have some rather valuable books in there. Oh—I didn't get a chance to tell you, but I found a first edition *History of Malheur County* while you were gone. At a garage sale, yet. And of course, there was a lot of cash from yesterday. I'd sold enough copies of *Stud* before the, uh, disturbance to cover the cost of the books. And the publicity—well, the bookshop can't afford television time like that."

Conan shook out another cigarette and got it lighted. "You don't think some potential customers might be put off at the possibility of running into the Oregon Chain Saw Massacre?"

"Oh, no, that just lends the shop a titillating air of danger."

"No doubt. Well, *I'm* titillated, Miss Dobie. *Is anything missing?*"

"Oh. Well, nothing important. Only Cady MacGill's chain saw."

Conan frowned at that. "Have you called Earl?"

"The first thing I did was call Chief Kleber. He said he'd be here by eight-thirty. Anyway, I'm sorry to bother you, and I don't suppose you really need to come to the shop, but I thought if I didn't tell you . . ."

Conan wondered if she expected him to ignore a break-in at the bookshop and just go back to sleep. "I'll be there in a few minutes."

He hung up, took a long drag on his cigarette while he listened to the soft rush of the surf. Cady's chain saw? The obvious conclusion was that Cady had decided to retrieve it. But it wasn't like him to resort to burglary. If Patrick and Mary MacGill had taught their rambunctious brood of three girls and three boys anything—and Conan was well aware that there was a great deal lacking in their education—it was the imperative to be respectable, law-abiding citizens.

Then Conan sighed, remembering the roaring chaos Cady had created yesterday with that damned chain saw.

He put out his cigarette, crossed to the bathroom, and stepped into the shower. Engulfed in flowing water and sea-colored light reflected from the tiles, he wondered if Angela MacGill had in fact been sleeping with Ravin Gould, and it seemed likely. Angie was a slightly spoiled young woman whose choices in reading matter at the bookshop revealed a fantasy life centered on Romance. With a capital R. She was intelligent enough to run her own bookkeeping and typing service, but her intelligence had never been challenged. Not when she was endowed with spun gold hair and a Miss America face and figure.

Conan turned off the water and reached for a towel. Silly fool, to be dazzled by Ravin Gould. But Shelly was probably right: Gould was very attractive to women. At least, to some women. Angie MacGill was exactly the kind of woman who would find him exceedingly attractive.

She was also Holliday Beach Police Chief Earl Kleber's oldest daughter. His fair-haired girl.

Conan drove the XK-E to the bookshop, although he usually walked the two and a half blocks. When he turned in to the parking lane, nearly every parking space was occupied, but that was only typical of August and nothing like yesterday's gridlock. At least twenty people gathered on the sidewalk in front of the bookshop, some at the north door, the rest at the main entrance toward the south end of the building, where they brazenly peered through the windows. Perhaps they were attracted by the two Holliday Beach Police Department cars. Conan found a parking space, and when he reached the shop, had to elbow his way to the south door where the CLOSED sign hung behind the glass panel, and when he took out his keys to unlock the door, had to explain repeatedly that the shop didn't open until ten, that he didn't know if there were any copies of *The Diamond Stud* left, and that the presence of the police had nothing to do with Ravin Gould or "that crazy logger," although he wasn't so sure of that.

Once inside the shop with the door locked behind him, he looked around the shadowy interior, finding as he always did a resonant satisfaction in the solid walls of books. Miss Dobie had done an admirable job of restoration. At a glance, only the broken bookshelves in the alcove area gave evidence of yesterday's absurd drama. As evidence of last night's drama, two policemen were dusting for fingerprints on the north door at the far end of the shop. Conan recognized Officer Joe Tasso and Sergeant Billy Todd. Tasso, dark and whip-lean, was new to Holliday Beach, but Billy Todd, tall and broad, red hair cropped short, was a native son and a habitué of the bookshop since childhood.

Conan looked down to find Meg weaving around his legs, delivering hoarse Siamese pronouncements. Apparently she had decided to forgive him his absence. He picked her up and massaged her back, and only then did he face Beatrice Dobie. She was standing in front of the counter across from the entrance. She said, a little grimly, "Good morning, Mr. Flagg."

"Good morning, Miss Dobie." He frowned at the door behind the counter, the door into his office. The PRIVATE sign was still there, but the door was beyond guaranteeing anyone's privacy now; the panel of one-way glass was gone except for a shark's tooth remnant in one corner. Someone was moving around inside the office.

"I assume that's Earl," Conan said.

Miss Dobie nodded and loosed a gusty sigh. "Mr. Flagg, if I'd had *any* idea what would happen—the autographing, I mean. It just seemed like such a *golden* opportunity. But all that glitters certainly isn't gold."

He countered with: "Well, live and learn. By the way, how did you talk Gould into it? He doesn't seem the type to be so generous with his presence for the sake of a historical landmark in a quaint little village.''

"Well, that was Angie's idea. She's typing his manuscripts, and—"

"And that's *all* she's doing for Ravin Gould!" That belligerent assertion came from Chief Earl Kleber as he crunched through the broken glass to take a stand outside the office door. He wasn't a big man, but he was broad-shouldered and trim in middle age, wearing his blue uniform well, his black hair showing only a few threads of white. And this morning, the set of his heavy jaw and the obdurate glint in his dark eyes made him particularly intimidating.

Conan put Meg down on the counter. "Good morning, Earl."

"You want to see it?" Kleber gestured toward the office. "Just don't touch anything. Billy and Joe haven't dusted in here yet. Miss Dobie says the safe's okay." Then to Miss Dobie, "Did you check the desk?"

"I was waiting for Mr. Flagg to do that."

Kleber followed Conan into the office, adding, "You won't find anything missing, Flagg."

So it was *Flagg*, not *Conan*. That was always an accurate barometer of Kleber's mood.

Other than the mirrored shards of glass littering the Kirman, Conan could see nothing out of place, except that the stacks of mail on the desk had been disarranged. He noted the ghostly traces of oil on the letters where the chain saw had lain, then went behind his desk and, using a pencil to hook the pulls, opened all the drawers.

At length, he straightened. "Nothing missing."

Kleber snorted. "I told you there wouldn't be. *Damn* that idiot! As if Angie hasn't had enough grief from Cady Mac-Gill all these years."

Conan raised an eyebrow. As far as he knew, Angie had been perfectly happy with her husband all these years. But then appearances—especially in a marriage—were often deceiving.

Conan asked, "You're assuming Cady is the burglar?"

"Who the hell else would want that damned saw? Who

the hell else would be stupid enough to commit a felony to get it? Giff Wills'll have a field day with this. Hell, there's no way I'll win that election now. I'll be damned lucky to keep my job here.''

Conan stared at him in confusion until he remembered the signs he'd seen advertising Earl Kleber as a candidate for county sheriff.

''Chief, what made you decide to run against Wills?''

Kleber shrugged. ''Maybe I just got tired of ol' Giff messing up nearly every case he got his hands on. Like that Labadee case. I gave him the evidence on a silver platter. Three of the missing coins in Bob Labadee's possession. And what'd Giff do? He *lost* the damn things!''

Conan decided it was the better part of valor not to comment on that, and finally Kleber added glumly, ''I've got an APB out on Cady. Of course, I had one out on him yesterday, but we didn't turn him up.''

''Is Gould pressing charges?''

''Not that I know of. *You're* the one should be pressing charges, considering the damage Cady did here, not to mention inciting a riot.''

''Yes, well, I thought I could work out something in the way of restitution once he cooled down. Chief, he's never gotten into this kind of trouble before, has he?''

Kleber frowned balefully, then admitted, ''Just a fight now and then at the Last Resort. But lately he's been doing a lot of heavy drinking. Damn! Angela could've married anybody she wanted. She could've gone to college, found herself a nice professional man. She could've been a teacher, like her . . . mother. But instead she has to pick that lunk, all muscle, including between his ears. Only good thing that's come of it is Michael.''

Nor did it seem valor would be served by any comment on Angie's choice of a marriage partner, nor her failure to follow in the footsteps of her mother, who had died when Angie was a child.

Conan asked, ''Where is Angie now?''

''My house. She and Michael stayed with me last night since—''

The ring of the phone on the desk interrupted him. Conan picked up the receiver. "Holliday Beach Book Shop."

"Conan? This is Dave Hight."

Sergeant David Hight was the Holliday Beach Police Department's daytime dispatcher. "Yes, Dave, what can I—"

"If the chief's there, tell him I just got a call from the Gould house. Ravin Gould's been murdered! Had his throat cut with a chain saw!"

Conan felt suddenly cold to the bone. He stared at the oil-stained letters, seemed to hear an echo of the whining roar of Cady's chain saw. Finally he remembered to hand the phone to Kleber. "It's Dave."

"Dave, what've you got?" Kleber listened, eyes reduced to slits, then snapped, "Call the M.E. in Westport. I'm going down to make sure there really is a body, and if there is, I'll seal off the scene. And by God, *I want Cady MacGill!*" He slammed the receiver down and nearly collided with Conan as he crunched through the broken glass out into the shop. "Joe! Billy!" he bellowed. "Come on, we've got a report of a murder. The Gould house, Dunlin Beach Road."

Miss Dobie emitted a strangled gasp. "The *Gould* house!"

Kleber nodded. "We've got to check it out. Don't open the shop or let anyone else in until Joe and Billy can finish dusting."

Miss Dobie was so aghast, she was almost at a loss for words. But she found them. "Chief, this is Sunday! A weekend! In August! We can't close the shop *today*!"

Conan said, "The shop will survive, Miss Dobie."

Her mouth went into a horizontal line that made her face even squarer, but her only comment was a prodigious sigh.

As Billy Todd lumbered the length of the shop, with Joe Tasso a pace behind, Kleber headed for the front door. Conan unlocked it for him and followed him outside, where Kleber glowered at the crowd staring unabashedly at them, then turned his glower on Conan. "Where do you think *you're* going?"

Mindful of the avid listeners, Conan answered, "I'm going where you are, Chief. Look, I was there last night."

"You were what? Oh, hell. All right, Flagg, just stay out of my way." And he stalked toward his car.

Conan ignored the questions asked of him by strangers as he strode to the XK-E. He was thinking about the grisly physical problem of cutting someone's throat with a chain saw. The problem was in cutting *only* the throat. A chain saw seemed more likely to remove the head altogether—along with limbs or any other parts of the body that happened to get in the way. It was not a weapon of finesse.

Had Cady MacGill wielded that saw? Conan still found it difficult to believe Cady was capable of burglary, much less a murder so hideous.

And where had Savanna Barany been while her husband was getting his throat cut with a chain saw?

CHAPTER 6

Conan ate the dust of the two Holliday Beach police cars down Dunlin Beach Road, and when they reached the Gould house, he parked behind them. The dust blew south, revealing two more parked cars: the rental Buicks he'd seen here last night. The Ferrari, he noted, was missing. Byron Lasky sat on the front fender of the gray Buick, with his wife and Marian Rosenthal standing on either side of him, all watching Kleber as he approached.

Conan arrived in time to hear Kleber, notebook in hand, ask the ashen-faced Lasky, "You say you're Gould's literary agent?"

If Lasky was aware of Conan, he gave no sign, nor did the women. Lasky answered, "Yes. Justine and I have an agency in New York."

Kleber asked for the address and phone number, consigned them to his notebook, then looked at Marian. "And you are, ma'am . . . ?"

"Marian Rosenthal, publicity director for Ravin's publisher."

When she supplied the address and phone number, Kleber wrote them down, then, "Where are you folks staying?"

"We're all at the Surf House," Marian answered.

"How long have you been in town?"

Again, it was Marian who answered. "Since Friday afternoon."

"Mr. Lasky, did you touch anything when you were in the house?"

"No. Well, except for the phone. I called the police and then Justine. I used the phone in the office. Ravin calls it his office. That's when I saw it had been ransacked, and all the manuscripts were gone." His voice went higher as he added, "His new book, Odyssey—all three drafts and the fourth he'd just started and his working notebooks—all of them *gone*!"

Justine reached for his hand. "Byron, please, you must stay calm."

Lasky nodded, but he was having a hard time of it.

Kleber said, "When you called us, you told the dispatcher that Mr. Gould had been killed with a chain saw."

"Yes," Lasky answered, nearly whispering. "It's there by the . . . couch. It's that logger's saw, the man who broke up the autographing yesterday."

Kleber's face went pale, but he didn't have time to question that.

"Chief?" Sergeant Todd stood at the open door of one of the patrol cars, the radio mike in his hand. "Chief, it's Dave. Says he's got to talk to you. It's important."

Kleber nodded and strode to the car. "You and Joe might as well start hanging the yellow ribbons," he said as he took the mike and perched on the edge of the driver's seat.

"Conan, how did you get mixed up in this thing?"

Conan turned, found Marian studying him over the top of her glasses. He shrugged. "Earl was at the bookshop when his dispatcher called about Gould. Someone broke into the shop last night and took Cady's chain saw. Mr. Lasky . . ." He waited until Lasky's distracted gaze focused on him. "You're sure the saw in the house is Cady's?"

"Yes, I'm sure. It's the same color and size. Damn it, I was there at your shop yesterday when that madman came after Ravin."

"It's just that I've known Cady since he was a kid," Conan

explained, "and he's never done anything . . . well, I find it hard to believe he's capable of murder."

Justine asked coolly, "Can one really know what another person is capable of?"

There was an undercurrent of rancor in that, but Conan didn't pursue it. Instead, he asked, "Where's Ms. Barany?"

"Portland," Lasky replied. "Thank God she wasn't here when . . ."

He couldn't go on, and Conan couldn't justify further prying. And it occurred to him that there was something beyond shock in Lasky's pallor, that he was ill. Seriously ill. Justine stood beside him, solicitous and protective, even if she wasn't at the moment touching him or looking at him. She was watching Billy Todd set long metal stakes along the front of the lot, while Joe Tasso followed with plastic tape to mark the boundaries of the crime scene, a yellow ribbon that symbolized a warning, not a hope for a return. Conan stared at the house and tried to imagine Ravin Gould dead. From here, it was an abstraction, even the means of death, however much it gripped the imagination.

Kleber's radio conversation with Dave Hight was short and apparently not sweet, judging by the set of Kleber's jaw as he left the patrol car. He paused for a few words with his men, then marched toward the Laskys and Marian, taking out his notebook as he approached. He squinted toward the house, asked, "Mr. Lasky, was the door open when you got here? What time was that, by the way?"

"About eight-thirty. The door wasn't open, but it was unlocked. I rang the bell first, and when no one answered, I tried the door."

"You don't have a key?"

"No. Why would I?"

Kleber didn't answer that. "Why did you want to see Mr. Gould?"

"I have some contracts to discuss with him, and he's been putting me off. Normally I wouldn't bother him so early. Ravin's a night owl. Works late and never gets to his typewriter before noon. But I thought this was the only way I'd ever pin him down. Of course, I knew he'd be upset because of Savanna, and I wanted to talk to him about that, too.''

"That would be his wife, Savanna Barany? Where is she now?''

"In Portland. Oh, God, I'll have to tell her—''

"We'll take care of that, Mr. Lasky. Why did she go to Portland?''

"They have a condo there. It's in a suburb, actually. Valley West. Savanna left Ravin last night. They had a sort of party earlier, and Ravin—well, he was drunk when we left, and Savanna said they had an argument. I guess it was the final straw. She plans to file for divorce.''

Kleber made a note of that. "Who was at this party?''

Lasky shook his head. "I . . . can't remember exactly.''

Justine answered the question in her precise British accent. "Byron and myself, Marian, a television reporter named Shelly Gage, and Mr. Flagg. Later, Dana Semenov arrived. She's an editor at Nystrom. A . . . friend of Ravin's.'' The inflection on *friend* was cold, hinting at something deeper than disapproval of Gould's relationship with Dana.

Kleber raised an eyebrow, but only asked for the correct spelling of Semenov and her present location. With an indifferent shrug, Justine replied, "I don't know. She said something about flying in from Portland on Baysea's helicopter shuttle.''

"With Dan Arno, probably. Okay, ma'am, do you know when Ms. Barany left the house last night?''

"I only know that she arrived at our suite at eleven. We were getting ready for bed, and I looked at my watch because I couldn't imagine who'd be knocking at our door so late.''

Lasky added, "She stopped to tell us she was leaving Ravin, and he was threatening to burn *Odyssey* because he didn't intend to let her get a cent out of it in a divorce settlement.''

"Then maybe that's why you didn't find the manuscripts this morning. Maybe he *did* burn them.''

"No!'' Lasky shook his head adamantly. "As soon as Savanna left last night, I drove down here to talk to him.''

"What time did you arrive?''

"Sometime between eleven-fifteen and eleven-thirty, I suppose."

"And you talked to Gould?"

"Not exactly. He was passed out on the couch where . . . where I found him this morning."

Conan grimaced. The chain saw's lack of finesse wouldn't be such a problem if the victim was unconscious.

"But Ravin was all right then," Lasky went on. "Snoring like a steam engine. I didn't see any reason to wake him. I doubt I could have. I went into the office to check the manuscripts, and they were all there. But this morning—the office looked like a hurricane had hit it. And the manuscripts are gone, every one of them!"

"Well, what are we dealing with here?" Kleber asked. "What do we look for with these, uh, manuscripts?"

Lasky took a deep breath. "There were three drafts plus the beginning of a fourth. I don't know how many pages the first three ran, but judging from past manuscripts, eight to nine hundred pages each. They were in typing paper boxes, two for each draft."

"Chief!" Again Todd and the radio were the source of distraction.

"What is it now, Billy?" Kleber asked irritably.

"Johnny and Elaine picked up Cady. He's at the station now."

Kleber smiled grimly. "Where was he?"

"At his house. Uh, Dave says Angie and Michael were there, too."

Kleber's smile vanished. He nodded, then checked his watch, and turned a cold eye on Conan. "Come on, Flagg. I've got to take a look inside the house."

Conan was so taken off guard by that invitation that Kleber was halfway up the flagstone walk before Conan caught up with him. The chief's warning at the bookshop had been unequivocal: "Stay out of my way." And now Kleber was inviting him—commanding him—to join him in viewing the crime scene?

Apparently recognizing Conan's confusion, Kleber

stopped when they reached the porch. "I need a witness," he said, as if that explained his aberrant behavior.

"To what?"

"To the fact that I'm not going to monkey with any evidence. My men might be called biased. You—well, you're better than nothing. I can't ask those people to come in here with me. They knew the guy, and Lasky looks like he's about to come apart at the seams already."

That didn't clarify the matter as far as Conan was concerned, but he decided that being better than nothing obligated him to some degree. And Kleber was already striding across the porch and into the house.

The double doors were ajar, and Conan had a clear image of Ravin Gould theatrically flinging them open with a smiling welcome to Casa Dement, a silly appellation that only now seemed prophetic.

In the foyer, Conan paused. The brass and glass table still offered its artful tidbits, the bottles on the bar stood ready. The coffee table had been pushed away from the couch, although the bouquet of orchids and ginger was still upright. There was a stale emptiness about the room; the smell of alcohol hung like smoke in the air.

And could he actually smell the pungent odor of gasoline? Perhaps. The chain saw, with its red motor housing, rested on the floor between the table and the couch. The blade pointed to the body.

James Ravin Gould lay with his head toward the windows, still wearing the white shirt and pants and the red handkerchief that had been stuffed with such careless artifice into the shirt pocket. His right arm had slipped off the couch, the hand palm up on the beige carpet. His head was tilted back as if to display the hideous, gaping wound under his chin. It seemed the site of a small explosion, skin, muscle, cartilage shredded, the ripped pillows and upholstery spattered with drops of blood and gobbets of foam rubber and flesh.

Kleber whispered, "Jesus . . ."

It took a certain mind-set to view this. Conan pulled in a long breath and let it out slowly as he walked toward the body, hands in his pockets, examining the carpet before him to make sure he didn't step on anything that might provide the criminalists with evidence. Kleber was only a pace behind him.

The horror of the wound didn't lessen with proximity. Yet there was something anomalous here. Conan said, "There's not enough blood."

Kleber stared at him. "What did you say?"

"There should be more blood. With the major veins and arteries in the neck cut, there should've been a rain of blood."

"Should've been, I'll give you that. So, what the hell happened?"

Conan studied the body carefully, holding on to his mindset. There were no other visible wounds. . . .

But something else was missing. "Earl, last night he was wearing a ring on his left hand. Turquoise and gold."

Kleber scribbled in his notebook. "You figure it was valuable?"

Conan remembered Marian Rosenthal's gasp when she saw that ring. "I doubt it was worth more than a few hundred dollars." Then he leaned closer to examine the handkerchief. On its clear carmine was a spot of a slightly darker, duller color. "Earl, give me your pen."

Kleber handed it to him. "What've you got?"

"I'm not sure." He used the top end of the pen to shift the red handkerchief, thus revealing a small hole in the shirt. The white cloth was gray around its bloody rim. Again using the pen, he lifted the shirt by the edge of the buttonhole panel, and beneath the hole was a red, circular hole in the skin.

Kleber said, "That's a *gunshot* wound."

"Small caliber, wouldn't you say?"

"Yes. The usual Saturday night special, probably."

"Looks like a contact wound. Point-blank into the heart." Conan stared at the small wound, wondering why it seemed more shocking than the terrible gash that had all but severed Gould's head.

Because this changed everything. Because *this* was the fatal wound.

Conan said softly, "He was dead when his throat was cut."

"What the *hell* is going on here?" Kleber demanded,

throwing up his hands helplessly. "Why shoot him good and dead, then—then do *that* to him? That stupid bastard!"

Conan straightened and faced Kleber. "You didn't know Gould well enough to call him a bastard, so I assume you're referring to Cady."

"Damn right, I am! Look at that saw."

Conan did, noting the smudges of oily fingerprints on the motor housing—Cady's prints, undoubtedly—and the small metal plate identifying the saw as belonging to C.M. He nodded. "It's Cady's saw. You expected that. But, damn it, Earl, do you really think Cady is capable of a murder this coldblooded, this . . . bizarre?"

Kleber stood motionless, gazing at the saw, the muscles in his jaw working. At length, his shoulders sagged. "No. I don't like Cady and never did, but I don't figure he'd do something like this. He's too damned thickheaded. But it doesn't matter what *I* think. Come on. I want to see this office Lasky was talking about. Where is it?"

"I don't know. Maybe up here."

Conan crossed to the opening to the left of the fireplace. No door, just two steps up to a room perhaps half the size of the living room. It was flooded with light from the windows on the south and west. Facing the west windows was a desk supporting a vintage electric typewriter. The hurricane Lasky had described was more of a whirlwind, but obviously someone had made a hurried search here. Books had been pulled off shelves, blank typing paper was scattered on the floor, the desk drawers had been emptied.

Kleber surveyed the room, then turned. "Well, somebody was damn sure looking for something. Come on, let's get out of here."

Conan gave the living room a last look as he followed Kleber to the front door. The fireplace, he noted, hadn't been used since it was last cleaned. And it seemed odd that he saw no evidence that Savanna Barany had ever occupied this room—except the broken champagne glass on the hearth. Of course, the house was a temporary residence, and no doubt she led a nomadic life. Still, he expected something beyond a memory: the memory of her husky voice in a recording of

"I Never Asked for Forever," the memory of Savanna in the Broadway production of *Blitz*, alone on a dark stage with a single spot lighting her exquisite face, her hair a flame in the darkness, and she had bound her listeners in breathless silence at the point of tears.

When they reached the porch, Kleber stopped and squinted past the yellow tapes. Todd and Tasso leaned against one of the patrols, chatting amiably, unconcerned. They hadn't seen what lay inside this house. Lasky, who had seen, slumped on the front seat of the gray Buick, while Justine and Marian waited in the backseat. And Conan considered the fact that Byron Lasky had not only found Gould's body, but had possibly been the last person to see him alive—if Gould had in fact been alive when Lasky left him.

Kleber eyed Conan speculatively, then finally seemed to come to a decision. He said, "I'll tell you what Dave was in such an all-fired hurry to talk to me about a little while ago. After he called me at your shop, he phoned the medical examiner in Westport, but Dr. Feingold wasn't in his office. On his way back from a drowning in Yachats. So Dave got him on his car radio. Damn it, I should've *told* Dave to keep this thing off the radio, but I figured he'd have the sense—" Kleber's teeth seemed to be grinding dangerously. "If some reporter happens to be listening to the police band . . . well, this isn't your run-of-the-mill murder. As soon as word gets out, we'll be hip-deep in reporters."

Conan said dryly, "The chamber of commerce people should love it."

Kleber gave him a baleful look. "Sure they will. So will Giff Wills."

"This is your jurisdiction, Earl. The sheriff hasn't any business in this case unless you ask for his assistance." Then, seeing the smoldering resentment in Kleber's eyes, Conan asked, "Or does he?"

"I guess Giff figures he does. That's what Dave radioed to tell me. Giff's on his way up here. And I might as well forget the election. My lunkhead son-in-law saw to that." Before Conan could object, Kleber added, "*Not* because I think he killed Gould. What the idiot did was rampage into your bookshop yesterday and threaten Gould with that chain saw in front of a hundred or so witnesses *plus* the TV camera. And now Gould's lying in there with his throat ripped open by the same saw. Yeah, I know the bullet wound complicates things, but that doesn't change the fact that it's Cady's saw by the body. And it doesn't change the fact that Giff damn sure won't let an opportunity like this pass him by. Can't you see the headlines? 'Police Chief's Son-in-law Murders Bestselling Author.' Giff's going to pin this murder on Cady any way he can just to make *me* look bad. Just to win a goddamn election!''

Conan considered that and found nothing in it he could argue. ''What are you going to do?''

''What the hell *can* I do? Not a damned thing. I'm going to turn this investigation over to Giff Wills like a lamb, because any court would call me biased, and that means any evidence I come up with is tainted. And that means Giff is going to have a free hand here, and I can't stop him. This election is history, so it doesn't matter anymore. Here's what matters: Giff is going to try to nail Cady with the murder, and God help me, I figure you're right for once. No way Cady'd shoot Gould first, then tear his throat out with his chain saw. That doesn't make any sense. Not even for a lunkhead like Cady MacGill.''

Again Conan waited, noting the reluctant set of the chief's mouth, and it was obvious what was coming next, but Conan gave him time to present it in his own terms.

Finally he did. ''There's no law against a policeman hiring a private investigator. I want to hire you to find out who murdered Ravin Gould.''

Conan folded his arms, aware of the constant murmur of the surf in the distance, of occasional stutters from the radios in the patrol cars. He understood how difficult it was for Earl Kleber to make that request, to admit his own helplessness.

But even if Kleber hadn't asked him to take the case, Conan knew there was no way anyone could keep him out of it. Unanswered questions made him profoundly uncomfortable.

''Earl, I'll do what I can.''

Kleber cleared his throat. ''I'll pay you. I'm not asking any favors.''

"We'll work that out later. I assume you don't want it broadcast to the world that I'm working for you."

"Hell, no!"

"Then maybe Angie should hire me—for appearances' sake."

Kleber nodded. "I'll talk to her." He paused, listening to the rumble of an approaching car, then said tightly, "That's either Dr. Feingold or Giff Wills. Come on. Can't stand around here gabbing."

CHAPTER 7

Conan followed Kleber down the flagstone walk, bending with him under the yellow tape. Justine Lasky was striding toward them, her posture imperious, her tone, when she spoke, controlled and crisp.

"Chief Kleber, how long must we wait here?"

"Ma'am, I'm afraid I, uh, don't have jurisdiction here. We're waiting for the sheriff."

She frowned, then looked around distractedly as a white station wagon slewed to a stop in a cloud of dust that overtook it and blew southward. Conan recognized the driver, whose profile was as distinctive as an Assyrian king's: Dr. Gregory Feingold.

Justine asked, "Is that the sheriff?"

"No, that's the medical examiner," Kleber replied. "Look, as long as you folks stay in town where the sheriff can reach you, I don't see any reason for you to wait out here in the sun."

"Thank you, Chief," she said with a sigh of relief. "We'll be at the Surf House if the sheriff wishes to speak to us." She started toward her car, then paused to add, "At least until the funeral arrangements are made. We will, of course, attend the services, wherever they may be.''

"Yes, ma'am. Just let the sheriff know before you leave town.''

She nodded and hurried away, while Kleber, with Conan in his wake, set out for the station wagon. By the time they reached it, Justine was already driving up Dunlin Beach Road in the gray Buick, with Marian in tandem at the wheel of the white Buick.

Feingold slid out from behind the driver's seat of the station wagon, peering through thick glasses at Kleber. "Chief, how are you?''

He didn't answer that. "I hear Giff is on his way.''

"Well, that's what he said. Conan! I wondered if you'd figure a way to get mixed up in this.''

"I'm just an innocent bystander. How are you, Greg?''

"Running a little ragged, actually. Summer. Business is brisk on the coast. By the way, Chief, Giff is bringing his crime scene team in.''

Conan asked, "His what?''

Kleber grimaced with disgust. "You haven't heard about Giff's shiny new crime scene team? Set the taxpayers back a bundle, and all he's got to show for it is a van with minimum equipment and two deputies to man it, and only one of 'em has any real training.''

Conan turned to Feingold. "Giff isn't calling in a State Police team?''

"He knows who the victim is, Conan, and he knows who the victim's wife is. He figures this'll give him more media coverage than he could buy in a lifetime. Ol' Giff isn't going to share any glory with the State Police—not with an election coming up.''

Kleber demanded, "He told you that?''

"I just read between the lines. I also read between the lines about who the main suspect is, and I'm sorry about that, Chief. One thing going for you, though, is he'll have to send all the material to the state crime lab for analysis.'' He pushed his glasses up on his imperial nose as he squinted northward. "Looks like the Marines are about to land.''

Out of a storm of dust, two tan sheriff's department cars rumbled into the turnaround, followed by a van of the same color marked with the same badge insignia and the words CRIME SCENE TEAM. As the dust settled, car doors opened, and the first to emerge was Sheriff Gifford Wills. Clad in a brown uniform, gun belt riding low under his belly, a tan Stetson covering his sparse blond hair, Wills strode toward Kleber.

But he wasn't alone. A young woman in a deputy's uniform got out of the passenger seat of his patrol and maintained a strict distance behind him of perhaps two paces. She was black, her café au lait skin unadorned with cosmetics, her Stetson aligned at a perfect horizontal over hair cut no-nonsense short. Her eyes were striking, large and slanted. Conan guessed she would be entirely captivating when she smiled. He guessed further that she seldom smiled on duty. No doubt she had trouble enough getting her male colleagues to take her seriously without calling attention to her very evident femininity.

Wills nodded at Feingold, then drawled, "Earl, how're you doin'?"

Kleber managed a curt "Fine," but he had a smile, however brief, for the deputy. "Morning, Deputy Jones."

"Hello, Chief," she said soberly, then pointedly surveyed Conan. He had the feeling she didn't miss much.

Kleber took the hint. "Conan, I guess you haven't met Deputy Neely Jones. Conan Flagg."

Neely Jones seemed a little surprised when Conan offered his hand and said, "I'm glad to meet you, Deputy. Neely? Was that originally Cornelia, by any chance?"

"Right. My aunt's name." She pronounced it *ahnt*. "Seemed a little too dignified for me. I figure I can always revert to Cornelia when I reach eighty." She had almost smiled with that, but with a glance at Wills, she reverted to her businesslike sobriety.

Wills eyed her obliquely, then hooked his thumbs in his gun belt and asked, "Well, Earl, what've you got here?"

Kleber gave him a succinct but full report, referring occasionally to his notes. The report did not, however, include his and Conan's examination of the body. Neely took out a notebook, and she wrote so quickly, Conan guessed she was using shorthand. Finally Wills nodded sagely, then turned to squint at the house. "Well, I better go have a look at the body. Come on, Neely. Dr. Feingold? You comin'?" Feingold nodded, and the three of them set out for the house.

Kleber sighed. "I'd give my eyeteeth to have Neely Jones on my force. Specialized in homicide investigation at the L.A. Police Academy, and Giff treats her like a combination stenographer and gofer."

"How long has she been putting up with him?" Conan asked. "And why?"

"Neely's been working for Giff for about a year, and I guess the why has to do with her boyfriend. He's a biologist at the Oceanographic Center in Westport." Kleber gave a short laugh. "Neely says she's Giff's bargain package. His token black and token woman, all in one."

Wills's look at the body was brief. He came out of the house, alone, moving noticeably faster than when he entered it, his usually florid face pasty. He paused to talk to his crime scene team, and they began hauling equipment into the house. Wills ambled over to Kleber and Conan, pushed his Stetson back, and shook his head, but his pale eyes were glinting with triumph. "That's the damnedest thing I ever seen. Earl, you got any idea who that chain saw belongs to?"

Kleber replied coolly, "We figure it must belong to Cady MacGill."

"MacGill?" The sheriff frowned, as if perplexed. "He any relation to the guy your daughter married?"

Kleber snapped, "He *is* the guy my daughter married." Then he added with some satisfaction: "We picked Cady up. He's at the station."

"Oh. Well, good work, Earl. Now, you know, we got a problem here. This *is* your jurisdiction, and normally this'd be your case, but—"

"I'm removing myself from this case," Kleber cut in. "It's all yours, Giff, and we both know why. The only reason I'm here now is because Byron Lasky called me, and I came out to secure the crime scene. And now that you're here, my men and I are leaving.''

He started to walk away, but Wills, obviously caught short, stuttered out, "Well—I mean, just—Earl, just a *minute*." Kleber turned, and Wills said, "Okay, but just remember, we gotta keep this thing off the radio. We don't want this gettin' out any sooner than we can help, or we'll have reporters and TV people all over the place.''

"Well, we certainly wouldn't want that, would we? *My* people have the word, Giff." And with that he stalked away to his patrol car, shouting orders to his men. Within thirty seconds, the two Holliday Beach police cars were heading north on Dunlin Beach Road. Wills glared after them, jaw thrust forward pugnaciously, and Conan decided that the time had come for an unobtrusive exit.

He made it to the XK-E, whose shining black finish had collected a great deal of the dust thrown up in the comings and goings here. And more dust was on its way. He frowned when he recognized the maroon Skylark that materialized out of the tan cloud, then he jogged into the turnaround to join Wills as he strode toward the car. "Sheriff, that's Dana Semenov. She was here at the party last night.''

"So?''

"So she was one of the last people to see Gould alive. She's a potential witness and maybe a suspect.''

Wills's snort of disgust was eloquent, but he held up a hand to stop Dana and went to the driver's side. She pushed her cornsilk hair back from her cheek with an impatient gesture. "Officer, what's going *on*?''

"It's sheriff, ma'am. There's been a death here, Ms. . . . Semenov. Is that your name?''

"A death?'' She stared at him, then opened the car door and got out, and for a moment it seemed she might bolt for the house. "Is it Ravin? What did he do? What happened?''

"I'm afraid Mr. Gould is dead, ma'am.'' While she digested that, Wills patted his pockets and finally came up with a pen and notebook. "I need your full name and address.''

Dana provided them, the words barely intelligible. Then she pleaded, "Officer, for God's sake, what *happened*?''

"It's sheriff, ma'am. Mr. Gould was murdered."

"What? Was it a burglary?"

"I don't figure it was, no, ma'am."

She sagged against the car. "This is . . . it's such a *shock*, Officer."

Wills grimaced irritably. "Lady, what's your relationship with the victim?"

"With Ravin? Well, we're friends. I've known Ravin and Savanna for years. I flew in last night for a quick visit, and I just came by this morning to say goodbye. I'm due in L.A. this afternoon." She looked at her watch and started to get back into her car. "Excuse me, Officer, I have to go. The helicopter shuttle leaves in—"

"It's sheriff," Wills repeated. "When was the last time you saw Gould alive? You *were* one of the last people to see him alive, weren't you?"

She flinched. "All I can tell you is that I dropped by to see Ravin and Savanna last night, and they had some guests. I left at the same time the other guests did—about nine-thirty—and drove back to Baysea. I had a drink in the bar, then I went to my room, and I didn't leave it. I was trying to sleep off my jet lag, and it wasn't easy. At one o'clock in the morning a bunch of drunks came staggering past my window and serenaded each other at the top of their lungs out in the parking area."

"Uh-huh." Wills nodded indifferently, his attention wandering. "Okay, I'll get a formal statement from you later. Maybe tomorrow."

"*Tomorrow?* Officer, are you out of your *mind*?"

Which was an error on her part, not only questioning his sanity, but persisting in calling him *officer*. Conan managed not to smile as Wills tipped back on his heels, eyes down to slits. "It's *sheriff*, lady, and I am *not* out of my mind. I'm investigating a *murder*. So stick around. I'll let you know when you can leave town." When she began sputtering in outrage, Wills added, "You got two choices: stick around, or I'll put you in the courthouse jail, where I can keep an eye on you."

Dana got into her car, the keys jangling with the shaking

of her hands as she started the motor. Then she looked at Conan suspiciously. "Your name is Flagg, isn't it? I thought you ran a bookshop. What're you doing here?"

"I was also one of the last people to see Gould alive, Ms. Semenov." Then he said casually, "By the way, there *was* something stolen: the manuscripts for Gould's next book. For *Odyssey.*"

He saw the suspicion freeze in Dana's amber eyes, and for a moment she couldn't seem to get her breath, and Conan considered that response recompense for risking the sheriff's ire.

She said bitterly, "Then it was probably *Byron* who stole them!"

"Why would he do that?"

"Because he—" She stopped to get herself under control, said coolly to Wills, "I'll be at Baysea, Officer." With that, she drove away, throwing up an explosion of gravel that forced Conan and Wills to step back out of the way.

Wills swore under his breath, then with one object of his annoyance gone, he turned on Conan. "Flagg, what the hell're you hangin' around for?"

"I was just pointing out a potential witness and suspect, Sheriff."

"Witness? Suspect?" Wills tore off the sheet on which he had written Dana's name and address, wadded it, and tossed it away. "Flagg, I don't need any witnesses, and I *got* the only suspect that matters."

"You mean Earl Kleber has him. Before you get too carried away, you'd better talk to Dr. Feingold." Conan looked past Wills and saw Feingold emerging from the house. "And here he comes. Goodbye, Sheriff." And he made his way to his car at a fast walk. Wills undoubtedly had more to say to him, but Dr. Feingold was heading in his direction, and he obviously had something to say to the sheriff.

As Conan drove down the dusty road, he lighted a cigarette and took a long drag, remembering that he'd had neither breakfast nor coffee this morning. Hell of a way to start a day.

Hell of a way to end a life.

He knew that the image of Ravin Gould's body and that hideous wound would never fade from his memory. Nor would that small, carmine wound, the bullet hole.

It didn't make sense.

Ravin Gould had doubtless provided ample motivation for his murder. He had taken such obvious pleasure in antagonizing people. Playing games. And there were the missing manuscripts to consider.

But why kill Gould *twice*?

And it was interesting that Dana Semenov claimed to have known Gould and Savanna for *years*, yet she hadn't asked about Gould's widow.

CHAPTER 8

When he passed the bookshop, Conan noted that it was closed as per Kleber's orders, while the other shops along the block seemed to be doing a brisk business. But Miss Dobie was still on duty, as evidenced by the presence of her red Porsche in the parking lane. He wondered what she found to do within the darkened shop, other than fume at the loss of what she called a Prime-Time day. Probably she was restoring books to their proper places, no small task at any time of year. Some perverse law of human nature dictated that once a book was removed from a shelf, it was never returned to the same place.

But such perversities were not foremost in his mind. As he drove north on Highway 101, he was still mentally wrestling with the fact that Ravin Gould had been murdered twice. And wrestling with the missing manuscripts: somewhere around twenty-seven hundred sheets of manuscript. Plus the notebooks. Who had stolen them? Not Cady MacGill. Why would he? To destroy them as an act of revenge?

That seemed too intellectual for Cady. He didn't lack intelligence, but his thinking processes were direct and pragmatic. He had an innate grasp of mechanical function, and he could not only use but repair any machine, from chain saw to Cat. He grasped the physics of falling a tree in the same manner, and his skill at dropping a hundred-foot, ten-ton column of solid wood and putting it exactly where he wanted it was legend. But if asked to explain how he achieved that feat, he'd probably shrug his massive shoulders and say, "Well, it just works out that way."

No, Conan thought, Cady MacGill didn't steal the manuscripts any more than he coolly shot Gould in the heart before administering that spectacularly unkindest cut to the throat with his own chain saw.

But the theft of the manuscripts and the murder *must* be related.

"Oh, hell."

He realized he was almost upon the junction where he should turn off to the police station. He squealed into a right turn, dodged potholes for two blocks, then turned left into the parking area in front of the concrete-block building that housed Holliday Beach's twelve-person police force. The station, and the radio antenna on its roof, had been given a new coat of paint this summer: pale blue with white trim.

Inside the station, Conan found Sergeant Dave Hight sitting behind the counter near the front door, arms folded over his thick torso, the fluorescent lights reflected on his bald head. He said, "Hi, Conan."

"Hello, Dave. Is the chief . . ." He noted Hight's worried frown and followed the direction of his gaze to the glass-paneled door on the east wall. Kleber's office. The chief was standing behind his desk, shoulders hunched with tension, and on the other side of the desk Angie MacGill stood, head bowed, waiflike in jeans and an oversize shirt that was probably one of Cady's.

Kleber's words weren't intelligible through the door, except for one phrase: "What would your mother have said?" It was then that Kleber looked out through the glass and saw Conan. He said something to Angie, and she nodded and left the office. She closed the door, staring at Conan, then ran to him and grasped his arms with small, strong hands.

"Conan, I've got to *talk* to you. *Please*, Conan!"

He nodded. "All right, Angie. Where?"

She apparently expected more resistance. "Well, we can use the interrogation room." She struck out toward the corridor leading to the back of the building, with Conan behind her, and once they were inside the small, windowless room, she sank into one of the metal chairs at the table and wailed, "Oh, this is all *my* fault. If it hadn't been for—I mean, Cady wouldn't have . . ." Her pretty face was so contorted, Conan expected a howl of anguish. But none came. She only repeated hopelessly, "It's all my *fault*. . . ."

"Why?" Conan sat down in the chair on the other side of the table. "Because you were sleeping with Ravin Gould?"

Perhaps that was less than tactful, but Conan needed a cup of coffee. He needed breakfast. He did not need Angie's *mea culpa*.

Her blue eyes went wide, then she looked down, nodded. "It seems so dumb now, but . . . oh, he was so sweet, so kind and gentle."

Conan took his cigarettes out of his shirt pocket, and while he lighted one, tried to imagine Ravin Gould as sweet or kind and gentle.

"Angie, did you tell your father about you and Gould?"

Her face reddened, and tears began to flow as freely as raindrops. "Ye-es. No! I mean, he—he guessed, sort of. And I couldn't lie to Dad. I never could." For a moment, she seemed mildly annoyed at that, and the flow ebbed. She found a Kleenex in her jeans pocket and discreetly blew her nose, then the enormity of her dilemma came back to her, and she pleaded, "Conan, you've *got* to help Cady. You're his only *hope*. And you're Dad's only hope, too. He told me you promised to investigate the murder for him, but he wants everybody to think I hired you. But, Conan, *I* want to hire you for myself. I mean, for Cady. I can pay you. It might take a while, but—"

"You can't afford me, so save your money for a lawyer. Cady's going to need a good one."

"Oh, I already called Herb Latimer. I was his secretary, you know and he said I could work out his fee over—well, as long as it takes."

"Herb isn't exactly experienced at criminal law. Look, I know Marcus Fitch. I'll call him and see if—"

"Marcus Fitch?" Her mouth dropped open. "I'd never be able to pay *his* fee if I worked for him the rest of my life. And Herb is a good lawyer. I know because I went to the courthouse with him on nearly every case he had for four years."

Conan flicked the ash off his cigarette into the dented metal ashtray on the table. "Angie, did Earl tell you why Giff Wills wants to see Cady convicted?"

"Yes, but I thought—"

"You thought Herb's connections with the good-ol'-boys network might help Cady?"

"Well, I figured they couldn't hurt!"

"Yes, they could. Herb will find it difficult, to say the least, to put up a real fight for Cady because that would jeopardize his position with the network. Whatever happens to Cady, Herb still has to practice law in this county. So you'd better reconsider your decision about Marc Fitch. He doesn't *always* charge an arm and a leg for his services." Just ninety-nine percent of the time, Conan added to himself.

Angie produced a resigned sigh. "Okay, Conan, whatever you say."

"I'll call Marc as soon as possible. Now, I have a couple of questions for you. When was the last time you saw Cady yesterday?"

She tried for an air of nonchalance, but only succeeded in looking sly. "Cady was at home with me all last night."

"Is that what you told Herb?"

"Well, yes. I mean, it's the *truth*."

Conan took a slow drag on his cigarette, letting the smoke out as he gazed up at the ceiling. "It's not nice to lie to your lawyer—*or* to the PI who wants to save your husband from a murder conviction. And I know already where *you* were last night. Earl said you and Michael spent the night at his house."

Her attempted nonchalance crumbled, and she seemed ready for another rain of tears, but apparently read something in his face that induced her to restrain them. "Conan, I didn't see Cady at all after I left the bookshop yesterday. When I got home, he wasn't there. It was, I don't know, maybe three or four in the afternoon when Michael and I went over to Dad's house.''

Conan grimaced. ''But you went back to your house this morning. You were there when Cady was arrested, weren't you?''

''Yes. Oh, it was awful—''

''I'm sure it was. When did you get home, and was Cady there?''

''About eleven. And Cady was lying on our bed with his boots on, sound asleep and smelling like a brewery! If he'd *only* lay off the beer, maybe—'' She stopped, perhaps realizing how petulant that sounded.

''Did he tell you when he came home?''

''No. We . . . didn't get a chance to talk about that before Johnny and Elaine came to arrest him.''

Conan put out his cigarette and rose, reminding himself that he hadn't expected much of an interview with Angie. He certainly hadn't gotten much. ''Angie, if you think of anything that might help, call me.''

''Okay, Conan.''

He opened the door for her, and as they walked down the corridor, he said, ''Until—or if—I can talk Marc Fitch into taking the case, make sure Herb Latimer's here whenever Giff questions Cady.''

''Dad'll see to that, but I don't know how Herb'll feel about having another lawyer—''

''Oh, I think he'll be delighted to throw this case in another lawyer's lap.'' They had reached the front counter, where Sergeant Hight was taking a report from two tourists whose car had been broken into. Conan said, ''Angie, go home and try to relax. I'll talk to you later.''

She nodded, managed a murmured ''Thanks, Conan,'' then with her eyes reddening for another downpour, hurried out the front door.

Conan went to the counter and, when the tourists had departed, said, ''Dave, I need to talk to Cady.''

''Sorry, Conan.'' Hight didn't look up from the form he

was filling out. "I've got my orders—damn." He turned to the radio console, commanded by a disembodied but peremptory voice. Conan waited.

And listened. The call was from the Sheriff's Department dispatcher in Westport, and the gist of it was that two men who had been residing in the county jail awaiting trial for felony murder had escaped. Hight beckoned frantically to Kleber, and the chief came out of his office to hear the sheriff's dispatcher explain that the felons were armed and dangerous, and Sheriff Wills was asking every law officer in the county, plus the Highway Patrol, to join the manhunt.

When Hight signed off, Kleber asked, "Where's Johnny and Elaine?"

"Out on their regular patrol. Well, right now they're having lunch."

"Get hold of them and tell them to head down to Westport and report to Giff. Better send Joe and Billy, too. Damn it, how the hell could two guys break out of that jail? When that bond issue passed, Giff said that jail would be escape-proof. Just like Alcatraz." He turned to Conan, asked wearily, "What do you want, Conan?"

"I want to talk to Cady. And before you say no, you should know that Angie hired me to investigate Gould's murder."

"Did she, now? Well, she's of age. She can do anything she wants, as long as it's not against the law. But I can't let you see Cady till Giff has a chance at him. And yes, we'll make sure Herb is on hand when Giff gets around to him. Don't know when that'll be." Kleber smiled uncharitably. "I figure Giff has his hands full right now."

Conan nodded, satisfied, as Kleber was, that Hight had gotten the message that Angie had hired Conan, and that Hight would, if he ran true to form, pass on the news to anyone who was in the least interested. Conan was thinking about coffee and breakfast when he turned away from the counter, or perhaps it would be lunch by now.

But he was destined to go hungry and caffeineless for a while longer. The front door opened, and Marian Rosenthal stood propping it with one hand, a determined set to her mouth. She fixed her gaze on Kleber and demanded, "Have you talked to Savanna yet? Has anybody bothered to tell her that her husband is *dead*?''

When that question met with a shocked silence, Marian sighed and approached Kleber. ''Chief, it's been a bad day for everybody, and actually I don't know Savanna very well or even like her very much, but I think that when she's notified, she should have somebody she knows there, not just a stranger taking notes of everything she says.''

Kleber said earnestly, ''You're right, Mrs. Rosenthal. The trouble is, I'm out of this case. It's in Sheriff Wills's hands. Now, if you'll excuse me, I've got a lot of work to attend to.'' And with that, he retreated to his office and closed the door behind him, but not before he gave Conan a meaningful glance.

Conan didn't need the glance. While Marian was catching her breath for a rebuttal to someone, Conan said, ''The sheriff is occupied with another crisis at the moment, and I guess you and I are as close to friends as Savanna has around here, so maybe it's up to us to tell her about her husband.''

Marian nodded. ''Then let's get at it. Why don't you ride with me? Justine gave me directions and a map.''

Conan almost balked at being without his own car, but two things made him reconsider. First, the drive to Portland—rather, to Valley West, or whatever the suburb was called—would give him an opportunity to question Marian, who was in a position to provide background information. She might even qualify as a suspect, if she couldn't explain why she had been so stunned by the ring Gould had worn last night, the ring that was missing from his body this morning.

Second, Savanna would have to return to Holliday Beach to deal with the myriad decisions inevitable with the death of a spouse. Maybe she'd need a driver, and she could certainly provide background information.

And Savanna Barany might also qualify as a suspect. Conan could neither forget nor dismiss the smoldering hatred in her eyes last night when she left the party.

He offered Marian his arm and headed for the door. ''Let's go.''

CHAPTER 9

The drive from Holliday Beach to Portland was beautiful in any season, but Conan never enjoyed it in August when Oregon's highways were clogged with wagon trains of RVs and campers. Nor did he enjoy being a passenger under any circumstance, especially not when Marian Rosenthal drove like a New Yorker accustomed to taking taxis.

Conan kept his safety belt fastened and tried not to look at the road ahead of him any more than necessary, while he considered how he might casually introduce the subject of Gould's murder, but in the end, *he* didn't have to do the introducing. When Marian turned off Highway 101 and headed east, she honked at a log truck that had the temerity to block her way, then as she gunned past its roaring length, asked, "Conan, are you a good judge of character?"

He studied the forest flashing past on his right, swallowing hard before he could answer. "Sometimes. Why do you ask?"

"Well, I was just wondering about Ravin's murder. You said you didn't think that logger was capable of murder."

"Not of *this* murder."

"Damn! Where did that pickup come from? Anyway, I think there's more to Ravin's murder than meets the eye."

Nothing met Conan's eyes at the moment because they were squeezed shut, but when he felt no crushing impact, he asked, "What makes you say that?"

"The manuscripts. I mean, the fact that they're missing."

"If Gould was on the fourth draft—well, are you sure he had the first three drafts here with him?"

"That's what Byron said. He saw them Friday."

"Didn't Gould keep copies somewhere else?"

"I doubt it. Writers always make copies of the final manuscripts, but not the early drafts. Well, they might if they use computers. It's so easy that way. But Ravin refused to modernize beyond an old electric typewriter. I'm surprised he wasn't still using a manual. To him that would be . . . I don't know. Macho, I guess. Road construction! Why can't they construct the roads in the winter?"

While the Buick chattered over a stretch of gravel, Conan replied, "Because they lose too many backhoes in the mud once the rains start. Have you ready *Odyssey*?"

"Me? No way. Ravin never let *anybody* read his manuscripts."

Conan silently wondered if someone wanted to make sure these manuscripts would never be read in the future. He wondered aloud, "Would any of those drafts be publishable?"

"There are publishers who'd print a grocery list if it had Ravin's name on it, and any reputable publisher would turn handsprings for that third draft. Ravin was a careful craftsman, actually, and I'm sure the third draft would be publishable with some line editing."

"I assume it would be quite valuable?"

She gave that her throaty laugh. "Valuable? James Ravin Gould's last book? His autobiographical novel? It'd be worth *millions*."

"Is that why Byron Lasky is so shaken about their disappearance?"

She concentrated on swerving past a flagger waving a sign that read SLOW. "Well, I think that's just reflex. Byron didn't have a contract with Ravin. That's not so unusual between agents and writers. And it means if—since Ravin is dead, Byron has no claim on *Odyssey*.''

Conan stared at the bumper sticker on the pickup ahead of them: GOD SAID IT, I BELIEVE IT, AND THAT'S THE END OF IT. They came to the end of the construction and lurched onto blacktop again, and it was something of a relief that the already thick traffic had backed up at the bottleneck of the road construction so that the Buick was caught in a blessedly slow-moving, bumper-to-bumper line sedately winding the curves as the highway climbed toward the crest of the Coast Range.

''Marian, you said Gould never signed a contract for a book until it was finished. Does that put *Odyssey* in public domain now?''

''No, the copyright was his from the moment he typed the first word. That's the way the law works. The only way anybody can publish any manuscript is to sign a contract with the author. Writers and publishers talk about *buying* or *selling* manuscripts, but that's just jargon. What really happens is a publisher contracts with the author—or his heir, in this case—for the right to publish a manuscript in exchange for a small percentage of the retail sales of the book.''

''And the agent negotiates the terms of the contract with the publisher in exchange for a percentage of the writer's percentage?'' Then at Marian's nod, ''What happens to the agent if the writer dies?''

Her eyes went to suspicious slits. ''You mean what happens to Byron and Justine now that Ravin is dead? They'll go on taking their percentage on the sales of any of Ravin's books they negotiated the contracts for, but any unfinished manuscripts—well, they're out of luck.''

''Wouldn't they also have been out of luck if Gould had decided to go to another agent? Last night he threatened to do exactly that.''

''Oh, that wasn't the first time Ravin threatened to dump Byron and Justine. It was just one of his power games. Or the booze talking.''

''Marian, I know the Laskys are your friends, but that threat is a possible motive for murder for both of them.''

The car wobbled unnervingly as she turned to stare at him. "That's crazy! Anyway, can you imagine either of them handling that chain saw? They wouldn't even know how to start the thing."

"That's not so difficult to figure out, and Cady's a handy scapegoat."

"Damn it, I've known these people for years, and they aren't even remotely capable of murder."

The tension was as taut as a vibrating violin string, but a moment later Marian laughed, damping it, and, to Conan's relief, focused her attention again on the road. "What is it with you, Conan? I mean, are you just normally nosy or what?"

Conan hesitated, finally deciding that if he didn't tell her why he was asking so many questions now, she might find out from someone else later and feel betrayed. A betrayed witness tends to bitter silence. And a guilty suspect wouldn't reveal anything to anyway.

He said, "I'm a licensed private investigator, and Angela MacGill hired me to find out who murdered Gould, since she believes her husband is innocent. So do I. *Marian, you can't pass here!*"

She swerved back into her lane. "Why not?"

Conan lowered his hands from their braced position on the dashboard. He didn't try to explain that passing on a curve on a hill on a narrow mountain road was not a good idea. He simply said, "The solid yellow line. It's Oregon law. You can't pass where there's a yellow line."

"There's been a yellow line for miles. I thought that was how they marked the center line here. Well, so you're a PI. I'll be damned." She studied him obliquely, and he couldn't read her reaction with any assurance. Finally she shook her head. "You know, I don't think I'm as surprised as I should be. Somehow you don't seem the type to spend all your time running a small-town bookshop. So that's why you're worried about Byron and Justine's motive for killing Ravin. Well, I guess you can't leave any suspects unturned."

"I'm afraid not. Do you object to helping me turn a few?"

"No, not unless you've got your heart set on pinning this murder on Byron and Justine."

"I just want to pin it on whoever did it. What can you tell me about Dana Semenov, Saturday night's catalyst?"

"Dana?" Marian wrinkled her nose. "She's a catalyst, all right. Well, Dana is typical of what I call the Yaffies—young, ambitious females. She grew up poor. Parents immigrated from Russia, I think. Always had a great sense of timing, and she's good at coordinating production, promotion, and sales. She started as an editorial assistant at Winfield and Ryder about ten years ago. I don't know offhand how many publishers she's worked for. At least four. That's not unusual these days, but every time she changed houses, she climbed a rung higher up the ladder. And she has a reputation as a big game hunter."

"Is that related to a headhunter?" Conan asked, quite coolly, he thought, in view of the fact that as the stream of traffic picked up speed, Marian did, too, and she seemed to believe that at fifty miles an hour, she *could* stop within ten feet if the car ahead of her braked suddenly.

"In a way. Dana's main claim to fame is the marketable authors she brought into her publisher's stables. I mean, we're talking brand-name authors, people who write books with legs."

"But she didn't succeed in bringing Ravin Gould into her stable."

"No, and it's not her stable. Nystrom, Inc's. Of course, it works out to the same thing. Every thoroughbred she rides into the winning circle makes her share of the purse that much bigger. She's editor-in-chief now, but I doubt she intends to stop there. She's aiming for the top rungs. Associate publisher, maybe, or even publisher."

"So, to pursue your mixed metaphors, would bringing *Odyssey* into Nystrom's stable boost her to the top rungs?"

"Damn right, it would. She's been after Ravin for years, and I think she almost had him with *Stud*. Or maybe he was just playing with her. Ravin enjoys having a tall, streamlined blonde on his arm—and probably in his bed—when he comes to New York." She grimaced. "I keep forgetting to put him in past tense. Well, a passing lane. Finally!"

As the highway widened to three lanes, Marian shot out into the center lane—oblivious to the tanker truck barreling along in the same lane behind her—and floorboarded the Buick past one car after another. Conan could only stare, paralyzed, as the highway narrowed again, and Marian managed to whip around one last camper, horn blaring a warning to the hapless driver of the car in the oncoming lane.

When Conan got his breath again, he asked, "Didn't Savanna go with Gould on his trips to New York?"

"Sometimes. Quite a lot before they were married. He liked to show her off. Short man's syndrome. He always picked beautiful women who were taller than he was, either as lovers or wives. Like Erin Chelsey. She was a model. Six feet tall. His second wife."

"How many wives has he had?"

Marian hesitated, then said indifferently, "Well, three, I think. Who knows?"

"Did Dana want to be number four—or who knows?"

"Maybe. If that's what it took to get Ravin and *Odyssey*."

"Why did she come to Holliday Beach last night? To harness Gould and *Odyssey*?"

"Why else?"

"It just seemed bad timing," Conan said, bracing himself as Marian squealed around another turn too fast. "I mean, since the Laskys are here. I didn't notice any great affection between them."

Marian loosed her big laugh. "There's a lot of history behind that. When Byron first met Justine, she was editor-in-chief at CCG."

"Yes, you told me about that. She was fired, wasn't she?"

"Right. And guess who took her job."

"Dana Semenov?"

"None other. Dana wasn't exactly gracious about it, either, which was her mistake. She managed to antagonize Ravin's agent. But an agent doesn't have the last word. If Ravin wanted to switch to Nystrom, he could, so Dana was going after him and bypassing Byron. And I'm damned sure she didn't know Byron and Justine were here when she *dropped in* last night.''

"What happens to Dana now? I mean, it's too late to bring Gould into Nystrom's stable, and it's possible *Odyssey* has been destroyed.''

"Well, it looks bad for one Yaffie. The word on Publishers Row is it's been a long time since she brought in a winner, and in this business—any business, I suppose—when you get near the top of the ladder, you don't just step down a rung or so. You fall. All the way to the bottom.''

"And this young, ambitious female wouldn't take the fall well?''

"I think she'd rather die." Marian turned to study him, curiosity glinting in her eyes. "Speaking of suspects, what about me?''

Conan nodded, managing a nonchalant air when he said, "This next curve is known among the locals as the widow-maker." Marian laughed at that, but she did slow down enough to make it through the long, flat curve without taking to the air. Conan said, "All right, what *about* you, Marian? What would your motive be?''

"Mm. Well, I don't know. I got along fine with Ravin, mainly because he didn't consider me either desirable or a threat. Nor was he a threat to *me*. I am not, thanks to Jacob, in need of money. Or this job. I love it, but I'm due to retire in two years, and what I'm looking forward to is time to spend with Jacob at the farm—he'll be retiring then, too—or visiting my grandchildren or getting serious about my roses.''

"So much for motive. At least, for any you're willing to divulge." Conan considered asking her about the ring, but decided to hold that in reserve. "What about means? You heard Gould recounting his epic encounter with Cady at the bookshop.''

"*Ad nauseam*. And I saw it on TV.''

"Then you might've known where to find Cady's chain saw.''

"I knew it was at your bookshop.''

Conan left the means at that, omitting any reference to the bullet wound. "Which brings us to opportunity. What did you do after you left Gould's house about nine-thirty Saturday night?''

"You sound like one of those cop shows. Well, I drove back to the Surf House and spent the evening in the lounge. They have a combo that plays the old Forties songs, and I stayed till closing time. That's two-thirty, isn't it? And when I got to my suite, I called Jacob and woke him up to tell him how much I miss him. Five-thirty in the morning in New York, but nostalgia does that to me. We talked about half an hour, and I assume that's registered in somebody's computer.''

"No doubt. All right, Marian, let's get back to the missing manuscripts. Who would benefit from possessing or destroying them?''

"Not me, and I know Byron and Justine would never destroy them, and I don't see how they'd benefit from possessing them.''

"Of course, spite or revenge is a possibility.''

"Then maybe you should ask Savanna about that.''

He sent Marian a sharp look. "Disposing of the manuscripts would be costly spite or revenge for her—assuming she *is* Gould's heir.''

"What if she's not? And what if she *knows* she's not?'' Marian tempered that with a smile, then, "As for Dana, I doubt she'd destroy the manuscripts—hope springs eternal— and it wouldn't benefit her to steal them. She'd still have to negotiate with Ravin's heir, and if that's Savanna, well, there's a lot of history there, too. Dana wouldn't have a snowball's chance in hell getting Savanna to sign a contract.''

"Uh, Marian, that car is signaling for a right turn.''

"Mm? Damn!'' She hit the brakes, and Conan felt the shoulder strap snap tight across his chest. How Marian escaped the collision that seemed inevitable, Conan would never know. When he opened his eyes, she was speeding blithely along to catch up with another camper. "Don't you have any other suspects?'' she asked.

Conan reached into his shirt pocket for his cigarettes, forgetting to ask Marian if she minded before he lighted one. He inhaled and waited for his nerves to cease quivering before he managed a reply to her question. "Gould was a stranger in Holliday Beach. Who knew him well enough to have a motive to kill him or steal the manuscripts?"

"I have no idea, but Ravin was *born* here, after all."

"But he was twelve years old when . . ."

Conan stopped, hearing yet again that sardonic singsong: *Doctor, lawyer, po-lice chief* . . .

They were past the crest of the Coast Range, and the curves and dips were smoothing out. "Marian, there's a restaurant called Emmy's Kitchen about a mile ahead. I'd like a cup of coffee and something to take the place of the breakfast I missed." And with any luck, he could convince her that he should drive the rest of the way. After all, she didn't know the Portland area as well as he did, and she'd have to do the navigating from Justine's notes.

And if she still objected?

He took another calming puff on his cigarette and wondered how long it would take him to hitchhike back to Holliday Beach.

CHAPTER 10

Marian Rosenthal made a better navigator than a driver, and to Conan's relief, she had acquiesced to the former role without argument. Guided by Justine Lasky's notes, Marian directed them to the suburb of Valley West without incident or even one wrong turn.

Valley West sprawled rawly across low hills, and Conan found it inordinately annoying. These constructions, with their nouveau eclectic architecture, occupied some of the richest farmland in the world. Year by year, acre by acre, the huge Willamette Valley—the promised land at the end of the Oregon Trail—was being inundated by ticky-tack like an alien fungus. Doubtless the residents of Valley West didn't see their community in that light. They were probably proud of its obsessively neat parkways and mousse-smooth streets, its small airport, its golf course cunningly dubbed St. Andrews West, its ostentatious homes surrounded by perfect lawns and spindly trees planted to replace the bulldozed native trees. Marian directed him past the stucco and glass and neon shopping mall with its multiplex cinema, told him to turn in to a street two blocks beyond, and there a sign announced that they had found THE EYRIE: CONDOMINIUMS FOR THE UPWARD BOUND.

Conan glared at the clusters of three-story, bastardized New England saltboxes sided in aluminum in precious pastels. He checked his watch. Two-fifteen. In the summer traffic, the trip had taken three hours, when two and a quarter should have sufficed. But then, he reminded himself, the three hours included the half-hour stop for lunch.

As he turned in to a paved circle fronting a lavender saltbox cluster, which another sign proclaimed to be Peregrine Court, he saw the yellow Ferrari among the foreshortened Cadillacs and silver BMWs. There was a parking place next to the Ferrari, and Conan drove into it.

"Savanna seems to be home," he said. "At least, the Ferrari's here. I didn't notice the California plates last night. Where in California?"

"San Francisco," Marian replied as she stowed Justine's notes in her purse. "Ravin had a town house in San Francisco, a beach house in Honolulu, and an apartment in Manhattan, but he always called this place home. Strange, when he hardly ever stayed here."

"Shelly said he liked to think of himself as a native son of Oregon. Marian, doesn't it seem odd to you that a man who could afford so many upscale residences and a woman of Savanna's fame and temperament would live without even a servant in sight, much less the sort of entourage you'd expect?"

"It may be odd, but that's the way Ravin liked it. Don't worry, they didn't have to fend for themselves around the house. It's just that Ravin wouldn't put up with any full-time servants. He hired people to come in and do whatever work was necessary, then get out from underfoot. And he never put up with an entourage of any sort. He said he couldn't work in a crowd."

"How did Savanna feel about that kind of isolation?"

"I don't suppose she liked it. I'm damn sure she wasn't used to it. Savanna needs people around her. Well. . ." Marian took a deep breath as she opened the car door. "I'm not looking forward to this."

Conan nodded, wondering what Savanna Barany's reaction to her husband's death would be. Not the usual grieving widow's, he was sure.

A sidewalk bordered in potted yellow mums led them to

a small lobby. There, flanked by Audubon reproductions, an elevator waited. Conan punched the button for the third floor. They emerged into a skylighted corridor and found the door marked 3C, where he pressed the doorbell, and finally a bolt snapped back, and the door opened.

And he was reminded that Savanna Barany had once been billed as the sexiest woman in the world. A tabloid columnist had coined the phrase after Savanna's spectacular Broadway debut in *Blitz*. She had been compared to Garbo, Dietrich, and Monroe, and in her presence, it was impossible to attribute her legendary allure simply to hype.

She wore no makeup and very little in the way of clothing: a pink spandex unitard, leather jazz shoes, and calf-high leg warmers. Her hair was twisted into a knot at the crown of her head, but wisps escaped to lie damp on her forehead and neck. She was breathing hard, and Conan was aware of the subtle scent of her flushed skin. She had obviously been exercising, and no doubt it was a daily drill and a hard one. He had seen her dance. She didn't seem disconcerted at being discovered in the scant attire appropriate to that drill. Conan had met this attitude before in performers. They regarded their bodies with concerned detachment, as a sculptor might a fine set of chisels whose shape and efficacy were to be admired, whose edges were to be kept razor-sharp.

She gave him a welcoming smile. "Conan! This is a surprise. Marian? What are you doing *here*?"

Marian said, "This isn't a casual visit, Savanna. I've got to talk to you about something."

Her purposeful tone erased Savanna's smile. "Come on in."

She led them down a hallway past two closed doors, from one of which came the beat of music with a heavy percussion line, and on to the living room. A white brick fireplace, whose fake logs were dusted with wispy ashes, was flanked by windows that rose from the floor to culminate in spoked arches. The walls were white, the furniture glass, chrome, and pale blue leather. A bookshelf displayed Ravin Gould's ten titles in their American and a variety of foreign editions.

Savanna picked up an orange towel from the back of the couch, and the towel, her bright pink suit, her copper hair, seemed accents chosen to complement the decor. She said, "I'm sorry I can't offer you coffee. I don't drink it myself, so I forget to keep any on hand here." Then with a wave toward a glass-fronted chest in one corner, "But Ravin always keeps the bar fully stocked, if you'd like something."

Marian shook her head as she sat at the edge of an armchair, and Conan remained standing, his back to the fireplace. Savanna seated herself on the arm of the couch, watching them curiously. "I suppose Ravin sent you. What did he tell you? That I stole the Ferrari?"

Marian replied, "No, he didn't . . . send us. Nobody did. I expect the police will be around later, but I didn't think you should hear this from a stranger. Savanna, Ravin was killed last night."

"He was *what*?" Savanna seemed ready to laugh at the sheer incredibility of those words. Then she shook her head. "Killed? Ravin?"

Marian nodded. "Yes."

Savanna's gaze was fixed on Marian's face, and apparently she found the verification she sought in it. She rose and crossed to one of the windows, stood looking out, motionless, molded in light, like an exquisite Tiffany figurine in subtly tinted frosted glass.

"*Damn* him!" She turned, her sensual mouth spoiled and petulant now. "I have the car, so he couldn't go out and wreck it. I suppose he ODed on that damn Scotch. Not on coke or any other drug. They weren't macho enough. Booze was the only *manly* drug."

Conan said, "He didn't overdose on anything." A pause, while he made sure he had her full attention. "He was murdered."

Again her first impulse seemed to be laughter, but the impulse was never realized. She made her way back to the couch, slumped into its cushions as if her knees were giving way.

"Murdered." It wasn't a question so much as a testing of the word to see what it sounded like, felt like. Dry-eyed, unblinking, she held the orange towel in cramped fists, and in the distance, the bass notes of the music thudded incessantly like an exhausted heartbeat. At length she looked up at Conan, asked, "What happened? Was it a burglary?"

"Not the usual kind of burglary. The only thing missing is the manuscripts for *Odyssey*. Of course, you'll have to check the house—"

"The manuscripts? They're *gone*?" She gazed at Conan for a long span of seconds, and this time she did laugh, but there was a hint of hysteria in it. "He *said* he'd burn them, but I didn't believe him. That'd be like burning his own child. Except he never had any children. Oh, that bastard! How could he *die*? How could he—" The words were choked off behind the trembling hand she pressed to her mouth.

Conan sat down on the couch beside her, and she took his hand, perhaps because it was near, and she needed something to hold on to.

"I don't—I don't *understand* this!"

The pressure of her hand on his intensified, but her eyes remained dry. Conan had seen this face streaked with tears for a fictitious grief on a stage where the lights made the tears jewels on her cheeks. But she allowed herself no tears now. She said, "Tell me what happened. I've got to *know*."

Conan glanced at Marian, but she seemed to have nothing more to say. He turned to Savanna. "I don't know what happened except your husband was . . . his throat was cut with a chain saw. Byron Lasky found him this morning at the beach house."

Her hand jerked out of his, and her face drained of color. "A chain saw? Oh, my *God*! But that's impossible. It doesn't make *sense*!"

Conan waited silently. He couldn't deny that, nor could he find any words that would help her make sense of it. Marian rose, moved toward them, asked, "Savanna, can we call somebody? I mean, if you have friends here in Portland . . ."

"Maggie. Maggie Herndon. She and Rich live in Three-A." Then she shook her head. "But they're gone today. Went hiking on Mount Hood. It's okay. I'll be all right. Conan, was it that logger?"

"Well, the police have Cady in custody."

"You know, I could understand about yesterday. I thought

he just meant to scare Ravin with that chain saw, and Ravin deserved it. He *was* sleeping with his wife. She was only one of a long, long string of women. That's why last night I reached the end of *my* string. It was just too much, and I don't have to live with—'' She stopped, seemed to remember that now there was no question of her living with her husband's infidelities. "I called my lawyer in L.A. this morning. Told him to start the wheels turning for a divorce. . . ."

Conan asked, "What happened last night, Savanna? I mean, after you left the party?" He wondered if she would take exception to that question from a virtual stranger, but she only shrugged.

"You mean after Dana broke up the party? That bitch, she couldn't have picked a worse time! Dana was one of Ravin's lovers, too. Yes, I knew about it. I knew about all his women. He saw to that. And I knew the real reason she showed up last night, and it wasn't just to drop in on old friends. Friends! She wanted *Odyssey*. But Ravin made sure she wouldn't have it. Oh, that's . . . funny."

Frowning, Conan asked, "How did your husband make sure she wouldn't have it?"

"Well, he burned the manuscripts, didn't he? I mean, you said—"

"No, he didn't burn them. Apparently someone stole them."

For a moment, she was silenced, then she asked, "But why?"

"I understand *Odyssey* would be worth a great deal to a publisher, even in its unfinished state."

"But nobody can publish it without a contract with Ravin."

"Or his heir?"

Savanna hesitated, finally admitted, "I guess so."

"Are you Ravin Gould's heir?"

"I don't know. I don't even know if Ravin made a will. Probably not. He thought he'd live forever. And I guess . . . I thought he would, too." She stared out the window for a moment, then turned her distracted gaze on Conan.

"What did you—oh, you wanted to know what happened after I left the party? Well, I went down to the beach to cool off. I suppose I was gone half an hour. When I came back, everybody had left. Ravin was drunk and ready to fight, and I gave him his fight. For a while, at least.''

Marian was still standing near them, arms folded, and her glance at Conan was cool, almost calculating, as she said, ''Savanna, there's something you should know about Conan. He's a private investigator, and he's working for that logger.''

Conan restrained his annoyance, wondering why Marian had chosen to apprise Savanna of that fact now. As a warning? But Savanna only smiled at him. She seemed ingenuously pleased.

''So that's why you're asking all the questions. Am I a suspect? Yes, I suppose I'd have to be.'' She laughed, an ironic laugh that ended in a sigh.

Conan said, ''I *am* working for Cady MacGill, but what I'm after is the truth. Do you mind answering my questions?''

''I'm not sure.'' She studied him intently, then smiled. ''No, I don't mind. Besides, I suppose the police will be asking the same questions.''

''Possibly. Was this fight with your husband violent?''

''You mean did he hit me? No. He has, though. I did *Blitz* in Honolulu a couple of months ago, and opening night I went on with a black eye.'' She pulled her legs up, wrapped her arms around her knees as if she were cold. ''Last night we just yelled at each other. I started packing. I told him I was leaving him, and he said he'd see me rot in hell before he paid me anything in a divorce settlement. I told him I didn't *want* anything from him, but he was sure I was going to rack him up for a big settlement. Well, his second wife did. Anyway, when I walked out the front door, he swore he'd burn *Odyssey* before he let *me* have a cent out of it. *I* didn't care if he burned it, but I thought I should let Byron know what was going on, so I stopped by the Surf House.''

Conan nodded. ''About what time was that?''

''I don't know. Oh—I remember Justine asked if I didn't realize how late it was, and she told me *exactly* how late it was. Eleven o'clock. I only stayed long enough to tell them I was leaving Ravin, and he was threatening to burn *Odyssey*. I don't know what Byron did about it.'' She looked up at Marian. ''Did he do anything?''

Conan didn't give Marian a chance to answer that. He asked, "Did you drive straight from the Surf House here?"

"Of course."

"You didn't stop anywhere along the way?"

"No."

"What time did you arrive?"

"One-twenty. I wouldn't have known that time, either, except when I got here—well, I *had* to talk to somebody. I was on the edge of . . . something. I don't know what. Anyway, I went straight to Maggie."

"That's Maggie Herndon?"

"Yes. Ravin and I didn't spend a lot of time here, but the Herndons were always, well, like the folks back in Georgia. Neighborly. To them, we were just neighbors. I liked that. Ravin didn't." She straightened her legs, crossed them, the suspended foot, with its dancer's arch, moving nervously, in synch with silence now; the thud of the music had stopped. "This last month while Ravin was working on his book, I came into Portland at least once a week. I'm sorry, Conan, but there's not much going on in your little town. Definitely no place to do any serious shopping. Anyway, Saturdays Maggie and I'd go downtown to shop and have lunch and talk. I don't have many women friends, you know."

"And last night—early this morning—you talked with Maggie?"

"Yes. Both of them. When Rich came to the door in his pajamas, I realized it wasn't a fit time to go visiting, and I looked at my watch and saw it was twenty after one. But they didn't seem to mind. Took me in and let me cry on their shoulders. I think it was about two when I left them." Then she frowned. "Will the police question Maggie and Rich? I mean, I don't know why they should be bothered with this thing."

Conan said noncommittally, "They'll probably have to make a statement." At least he *hoped* Giff Wills would demand a statement of the Herndons, knowing full well that it was unlikely.

Savanna swallowed as if her mouth had gone dry. "I'll have to go back to Holliday Beach . . . make arrangements. Oh, God, I don't know what I'm supposed to *do*. I've never been through anything like this before.'' Her eyes glinted with tears, but she shook her head, denying them. ''I won't go back to that house. I swore I'd *never* go back.''

''Well, I doubt you *can* go back to the house today,'' Conan said. ''Not until the police are finished with it.''

''Oh. What about Byron and Justine? Marian, are they still in Holliday Beach?''

''Yes. We're staying for the . . . well, until you decide on the funeral arrangements.''

Savanna grimaced, then asked, ''Is Dana still in Holliday Beach?''

Conan answered, ''Yes, the sheriff asked her to stay in town.''

''Then I can stay at the Surf House. Dana's at Baysea.'' Savanna rose, draping the towel around her shoulders. ''Conan, has any of this leaked to the press yet?''

''Sheriff Wills seems to be trying to keep a lid on it, but I doubt any lid will hold long, considering that the principles in this case are what you might call household names.''

''You mean somebody still remembers *my* name?'' she asked with a hint of bitterness.

Conan rose. ''Would you like me to drive you back to the beach?''

She looked up at him, her eyes luminous. ''Yes, I'd like that. I'll just take a shower and get a few things packed. Excuse me.''

Before she reached the hall, Conan asked, ''Do you know when the Herndons will be back?''

''No. Probably not before dark, though.'' She paused, then, ''You're a very kind man, Conan. I'm . . . grateful. You, too, Marian. Thanks for coming.'' She disappeared down the hall, and Conan heard a door close.

Marian made a waving motion, a mocking effort to get Conan's attention, and he realized he had been staring at the empty hall. She said, ''Well, I've done my duty, so I'll head back to Holliday Beach.''

He nodded. ''I'll walk you to your car.''

''You really *are* a gentleman, aren't you? Maybe that was my second good deed. Bringing you along, I mean. Savanna much prefers male company. And you don't need to walk me anywhere."

He settled for walking her to the front door, and when he opened it for her, she looked up over the top of her glasses at him. "Have you added Savanna to your list of suspects?"

"That depends on what the Herndons say about what time it was when she knocked on their door. I mean, Byron Lasky saw Gould alive at about eleven-thirty. If Savanna arrived at the Herndon's at one-twenty, that only leaves an hour and fifty minutes for the drive from Holliday Beach. It just took us two and a half hours, not counting the stop at Emmy's Kitchen. I don't think anyone could drive that road in an hour and fifty minutes, not even in a Ferrari, and that allows no time to commit the murder, and certainly none to break into the bookshop for Cady's chain saw."

Marian winced at that. "Well, good luck, Conan. With Savanna in the middle of this, you're going to need it."

With that, she headed for the elevator, and Conan closed the door, wondering how he was going to find out what the Herndons had to say. He had reduced his options to zero when he offered to drive Savanna to Holliday Beach. Now he couldn't simply wait until the Herndons returned and hope they'd answer his questions.

But perhaps he had a hole card.

He found a wall phone in the kitchen, a small space decorated in black and white and designed for devotees of microwave cuisine. He listened for the distant murmur of running water, then got out his phone credit card and punched a Salem number.

Getting through to Steve Travers took a while. His official title was Chief of Detectives for the Salem Division of the Oregon State Police, but Conan knew him from childhood. They had grown up on adjoining ranches near Pendleton, ridden fence together in bone-chilling winters and searing summers, baled hay, rounded up strays, and branded calves together.

He answered tersely: "Travers."

"Flagg," Conan countered. "I haven't much time now—"

"But you need a favor. Something to do with the Gould case?"

"The police grapevine works fast."

"Well, I had a call from Greg Feingold, and I figured I'd better check with Earl. That's off the record. All the way off."

"Then you know the situation with Giff Wills and Earl."

"Yeah. That damnfool Wills. I was hoping Earl would knock that Stetson off his head this election. Anyway, what's the favor?"

Conan explained the favor, but Steve hesitated at so blatantly meddling in another law officer's case, even one he regarded as a damnfool. Conan said, "All I ask is that you call the Herndons. I want what they say on record with someone official, and I doubt Giff Wills will bother to talk to them."

"Okay, I'll see what I can find out," Steve said with a gusty sigh. "But I want to know what's going on with this case. We'll stay out of it if we can, but if Giff messes up, he'll be doing it on network TV, and that leaves all of us spitting dust."

"I know, Steve. I'll call you tonight." Conan hung up and went into the living room. The sound of running water had stopped, and there was something he wanted to check before Savanna reappeared: an anomaly that had bothered him from the moment he first entered the room.

He crossed to the fireplace, knelt in front of it, and frowned at the arrangement of fake logs hiding the gas jets. In August, Savanna hadn't needed this ersatz fire for heat. Yet something had been burned here, and probably last night. The condo was impeccably clean otherwise, which could no doubt be attributed to a cleaning service, people hired, as Marian had put it, to come in, do the necessary work, then get out from underfoot, and in this case, it was most likely done discreetly in the owners' absence. This fireplace had undoubtedly been as clean as the rest of the condo at two in the morning when Savanna arrived.

The ashes lay atop the logs. Paper ashes. But some of them had fallen behind the logs. There was just enough room for him to get his head and shoulders into the fireplace to see a few white, uncharred fragments. He was well aware that what he was doing might be construed as tampering with evidence, and he salved his conscience by removing only one of the fragments, leaving at least three smaller ones.

It was a strip about three inches by eight and a half inches, the width of a sheet of typing paper. The top three inches of a sheet of typing paper, in fact. In the upper left corner was typed the words "ODYSSEY/Gould." In the upper right corner was a number: 241. Then after a space of about an inch, three partial lines of type ending in an irregular, charred edge:

rustle of satin sheets, like snakes writhing toward couplin
Jimmy like he'd taken a load of buckshot in the gut
Anna and Mayley, moaning and panti

Conan felt a little like he, too, had taken a load of buckshot. He went into the kitchen with the fragment, and after opening a few drawers, found a plastic bag. He placed the paper in the bag, then washed the soot off his hands and put the bag in his billfold.

He returned to the living room, stared into the fireplace. Part of *Odyssey* had been burned here, but there weren't enough ashes to account for more than a few pages. If Savanna had stolen all the drafts and the notebooks, why had she burned only a few pages? And why would she steal or destroy any of them? And if she *did* steal or destroy them, did that mean she had also murdered her husband?

He realized he didn't want to believe that, and his reluctance disturbed him. There was no reason for it. At least, no excuse for it.

Conan heard the door open in the hall, and Savanna came out into the living room and put a small, white leather suitcase down by the couch. She was wearing the peacock blue dress he'd first seen her in, her eyes masked with dark glasses. The small, rectangular purse hanging from her shoulder by a narrow strap was also of white leather. A memory that had been lurking in the recesses of his mind since he saw the bullet wound in Gould's chest abruptly coalesced into an image. It was the size and shape of this purse that brought the memory into focus. The color was wrong. Orange. It should be orange. Yesterday, while Cady was wreaking havoc with his chain saw,

Conan had caught a glimpse of an orange purse on the floor, and among its scattered contents was something he identified at the moment as a small, semiautomatic pistol.

But it *had* been a brief glimpse under thoroughly distracting conditions. Besides, he couldn't even be sure the orange purse was Savanna's.

She said, "Well, I guess I'm ready to go."

He picked up her suitcase and followed her out of the condo, and when they reached the Ferrari, she handed him the keys, apparently unconcerned about whether he had any experience driving a car of this kind. He slid into the driver's seat and took a moment to find his way around the controls before he started the engine, noting that the gas gauge registered three-quarters full.

"This thing must get good mileage," he said.

She laughed. "It gets lousy mileage. Ravin didn't buy it for its mileage. He always said he grew up dirt-poor, and now that he was rich, he intended to have the best and most beautiful of everything."

Conan wondered if she thought that in Ravin Gould's mind, the best and most beautiful included her.

He left the Eyrie behind with no regrets and had just turned onto the main thoroughfare in front of the shopping mall when he saw the flash of colored lights blinking atop an approaching car. The vehicles ahead of him dutifully pulled over. Conan followed suit and watched a Taft County sheriff's patrol car pass, followed by a KEEN-TV van with its red, white, and blue stripes.

He recognized Sheriff Gifford Wills at the wheel of the patrol car, but the sheriff didn't even glance in the direction of the yellow Ferrari. Deputy Neely Jones was again riding shotgun, and Conan was sure she saw the Ferrari. For a moment, she seemed to look straight at Conan. But apparently she didn't say anything. At least, nothing stopped the forward progress of the small, self-important caravan.

Conan didn't entirely succeed at restraining his smile.

CHAPTER 11

Savanna Barany did not remain silent on the drive to Holliday Beach, but neither did she talk about Ravin Gould or his death. Conan listened, occasionally making noncommittal comments, part of his mind focused on managing an unfamiliar car in the Sunday afternoon traffic, another part conscious of the hot summer wind, the gold of harvested wheat and hay fields, the elusive scent of Savanna's perfume.

She lounged in the bucket seat, the wind whipping her hair to abandoned disorder, and it didn't seem to matter to her. Yet he knew she was as aware of the sensuousness of her windblown hair as he was. And with the same self-awareness, she had embellished herself with earrings of cascading gold rods that he almost expected to ring like wind chimes, with pale lipstick that enhanced the soft curves of her lips, with eye shadow and mascara that intensified her magnificent eyes, although she only let him see them when he glanced at her in profile. Her sunglasses were an opaque mask when she turned full face.

What she talked about, with a faint Southern accent slipping through, was growing up in Atlanta, where she was born Sarah Lee Barany. That name, of course, had to go. It

sounded too much like a frozen pastry, and she changed it
when she was fourteen. She talked about her father, Dr. Talbot Barany, an orthopedic surgeon—a true Southern gentleman, she called him—about her mother, Melanie Lee, and
her brother, Tal, who was now a gynecologist in Memphis.

And Conan listened between the words and recognized a
childhood spent in the gracious surroundings that only money
could buy, where, thanks to ubiquitous servants—only one
of whose names she seemed to remember—the big, antebel-
lum house was always immaculately clean, meals always appeared punctually, served on china and crystal, and
fashionable clothes always hung ready in her closet. It was a
childhood in which a beautiful, talented little girl was the
focus of her father's doting devotion, her older brother's af-
fectionate solicitude, and her mother's surrogate ambition.

Melanie Lee Barany did all the things made possible by
wealth and social position to nurture her daughter's potential:
lessons in dancing, acting, singing, modeling, and when Savanna was only sixteen, the lead in a local production of
Annie Get Your Gun. At eighteen, Savanna went to New
York, where she had the best training available, and by the
time she was twenty-one, she had appeared in minor roles
in five Broadway shows, although none survived more than
a week. Then, at twenty-two, she was cast as understudy
for the role of Mona Fatale in *Blitz.* A storybook story, it
seemed: the star felled by stomach flu opening night, the
understudy going on, and—*voilà!*—a new star, a virtual su-
pernova, was born. *Blitz* was still a fixture on Broadway, but
Savanna left the cast after a year and a half to pursue her
destiny in Hollywood.

Conan knew her destiny there included the role of the
ruthless heroine in the film version of Ravin Gould's *The
Locusts.* That was undoubtedly where she met Gould, who
wrote the screenplay. But she wasn't willing now to talk about
her life beyond *Blitz,* and by the time they passed the crest
of the Coast Range, she had lapsed into silence.

Conan didn't break the silence, not until they reached Holliday Beach's city limits. "My car's at the police station,
Savanna, and I can have the dispatcher call Westport to see

if the sheriff wants to talk to you today.'' Conan was well aware that the sheriff was probably at this moment fuming along the Portland highway on his way back from a fruitless search for Savanna Barany at the Eyrie, but Conan intended to go through the motions so Wills would have nothing to complain about.

Savanna asked, ''Who do I talk to about . . . you know, about the body? I mean, I've got to make arrangements for the funeral.''

''It'll be up to the medical examiner to release the body. That's one problem you don't have to worry about today.''

She turned her opaque black stare on him. ''Conan, how long will I have to stay here?''

''I don't know. That'll be up to Sheriff Wills.''

''But I'm supposed to meet Booth Kettering in L.A. on Tuesday. I called my agent this morning, and she says Booth has an option on the film rights for *Blitz*, and he's lining up the cast *now*.''

Conan responded flatly. ''Unfortunately, Savanna, murder has a way of disrupting everyone's best-laid plans.''

She turned away, teeth pressed into her lower lip, and he was on the verge of an apology for that tactless reminder, but she nodded and said, ''I've never been involved in a murder, Conan. I don't know my lines for this scene.''

He signaled for a left turn, and when he reached the Holliday Beach police station, turned in to the parking area, which was empty now except for his XK-E. Before he pulled the key out of the ignition, he automatically checked the gas gauge. ''Savanna, you'll have to buy gas before you go very far. You're almost on empty now.''

''I'll take care of it,'' she said indifferently.

''Just don't forget. I'll be back in a few minutes.''

Inside the station, he found Sergeant Dave Hight at the counter reading a copy of *The Police Gazette*. Conan glanced up at the wall clock. Five-thirty, and the station was quiet. The Sunday evening lull, Kleber called it, when the weekend tourists were already on their way home, and the locals were either settling in for an early night with Monday morning facing them, or hadn't yet had enough to drink to cause trouble. Kleber's door was closed, but he was still at his desk, and he wasn't alone. He was talking with Kara Arno, the physical education teacher at the high school. Kara imparted to her drab surroundings a flavor of the exotic, with her hair in beaded cornrows, her long legs encased in ochre slacks, her belted blouse printed with a bold pattern of vermilion and umber. And Kara was particularly exotic in Holliday Beach, where she was one of only a handful of blacks.

Hight put his magazine aside. "Hi, Conan. What can I do for you?"

"Well, you can call Giff Wills and tell him Savanna Barany is here, and if he wants to talk to her now, I'll drive her down to Westport."

"She's here? Savanna Barany?" Hight seemed to come to attention, his bald head going pink. "You brought her from Portland? Damn, that must've been quite a ride."

Conan shrugged. "The traffic was terrible."

"With Savanna Barany in the same car, you were worried about the traffic?"

"Dave, did you expect the tires to melt?"

He sighed. "Something like that."

"They seem to be intact. Now, maybe you'd better make that call."

"Call? Oh. Sure." He turned and picked up the phone on the communication console behind him and began dialing.

Conan asked, "How's Cady?"

"Well, he spent most of the day nursing the worst hangover I've ever seen. He's okay now."

"Did the sheriff get around to questioning him?"

"Yeah, a few hours ago. Don't worry, Herb Latimer sat in on it. The chief saw to that." Then into the phone, "Hey, Lonnie, this is Dave Hight. Tell the sheriff Savanna Barany is here in Holliday Beach, and if he wants, she'll come down and—"

Conan waited through the silence while Lonnie undoubtedly explained that Wills was not at the courthouse and why. He looked into Kleber's office again, saw that the chief was also on the phone, while Kara Arno restlessly paced the room.

"Sorry, Conan, but Giff's out of town," Hight said, covering the mouthpiece with one hand. "Lonnie didn't say where."

"Maybe he's still out chasing escaped felons."

"No, those guys are back in custody. They stole a car and headed south, but they stopped for a cup of coffee at Beulah's in Yachats. Seems a couple of State Patrol guys had the same idea at the same time. You want to leave a message with Lonnie?"

"Yes. Tell him Ms. Barany came prepared to give Sheriff Wills a statement. If and when the sheriff decides he should deign to talk to the widow of the murder victim, she'll be at the Surf House."

Hight relayed that message word for word, apparently enjoying himself. At least he was smiling when he hung up. But his smile vanished when Conan asked, "Why is Kara Arno here?"

"Well, Dan's gone missing."

"Missing?"

"Yeah. Somewhere between Portland and Baysea. Dan flew choppers for four years in Nam and came through without a scratch, and Lord knows how many times he's made that shuttle run. But he didn't come home from this last one."

Conan felt an emptiness under his ribs. He didn't know Dan Arno well, but he admired his ambition because it was tempered with a sense of humor. Perhaps that was how Arno survived four years in Vietnam and kept himself mentally whole in the years after. And perhaps his stability could also be attributed to the woman waiting in Kleber's office for someone to tell her if her husband had survived one of thousands of helicopter flights from Portland to Baysea Resort's airfield.

Conan said. "I hope . . . well, maybe there's still a chance that he'll walk out of the mountains."

"Yeah. Maybe so," Hight agreed with no conviction. "Oh—I almost forgot. The chief says he's done with the bookshop. You can open it up tomorrow."

"Miss Dobie will be overjoyed. The bookshop is always closed on Mondays anyway. Dave, I need to talk to Cady."

"Well, the trouble is, Giff left orders that nobody was to talk to him except his lawyer till Giff gives the word. The chief said to go along with that. Said he didn't want to give Giff any grounds for grousing."

Conan started for the front door. "I'll be back tomorrow, Dave."

When Conan closed the door behind him, he saw Savanna leaning against the Ferrari, pushing back her wind-caught hair with one hand. He said, "Ferrari should hire you to show off their cars."

"Well, if they made me a decent offer," she retorted, her stance becoming a purposeful pose, "I'd do it in a minute. So, what's our next stop? The sheriff's office?"

"No. The sheriff was called out of town. You'll be hearing from him, but probably not till tomorrow. I guess the next stop for you is the Surf House. By the way, I know the owners of the restaurant there, and they treat me very nicely. Would you like to have dinner with me?"

She took off her sunglasses to study him. "Well, I have a problem when I eat in public places, Conan. People still recognize me, and that can be a hassle. And I'm not really looking forward to a room-service dinner. You know, I *can* cook, and you must have a kitchen."

"Yes, I have a kitchen," he admitted with a wry smile. And he understood what she was asking. She wasn't yet ready to be alone, and apparently the Laskys' or Marian's company didn't appeal to her. He reached into his pants pocket for his key ring, took off the key to his front door, and gave her directions for finding the house, then added, "Don't start cooking till I get there."

"Thanks, Conan." She leaned forward to leave a kiss on his cheek, but before he could respond in any way, she opened the car door and slid behind the wheel.

"Savanna, I hope you make it to L.A. for that appointment with Booth Kettering. No one else can do Mona Fatale justice."

She laughed as she started the motor. "Be careful, Conan. I could learn to love a man who says things like that."

CHAPTER 12

"It has to do with the way the atmosphere breaks up the sunlight into its component colors, like a rainbow. That puts a blue or green rim at the top of the sun, and the atmosphere magnifies it. . . ." Conan sighed and gave up his attempt to explain the green flash they had just watched. Savanna was listening to him, but not to what he was saying.

She sat across from him at the circular redwood table on the deck fronting his house. The table was cluttered with the remains of their meal. He had averted any culinary attempts on her part by bringing dinner from the Surf House: Dungeness crab Louis, sourdough garlic bread, and a Knudsen Erath Chardonnay. The salads were served in bowls as big as half a basketball, yet Savanna had demolished hers to the last shred of lettuce with unabashed gusto. But throughout the meal, she didn't once speak, even obliquely, about her husband or his murder. Now she sat holding a glass of wine, and the sunset fired her hair, deepened the violet in her blue eyes.

Conan took time to light a cigarette. "You know, Savanna, I have a job of work to do. I can't ignore it, and neither can you."

102

"Oh, I can try." She studied him with her eyes hooded. "So you really are a PI? How did you ever get into something like that?"

"I did a stint with G-2. Army intelligence. And yes, I know that's a contradiction in terms, but I had an unusual CO. I just didn't feel I should waste all that training."

"Is this what you do for a living?"

"Fortunately I don't have to depend on it for a living."

"Then why do you do it?"

Conan shrugged. "Because it's there. Something like that."

"And that logger is your client? What's his name?"

"Cady MacGill."

"But he . . . he killed Ravin." A pause while she searched Conan's face. "Didn't he?"

Conan took a puff on his cigarette, watched the wind catch the smoke. "Cady didn't kill him, Savanna."

"How can you be so sure?"

"Cady has many shortcomings, including a capacity for violence, but only the kind of violence acceptable to his code of ethics, which is limited to killing animals in the name of sport, or a brawl now and then at the Last Resort. Gould's murder was far too complicated for him."

Savanna rose and went to the railing, stood staring at the calm, summer sea. Conan watched her and waited.

Finally she turned. "Conan, I believe you. I mean, about Cady MacGill. But if *he* didn't kill Ravin, for God's sake, who *did*?"

"I don't know."

"Do you think *I* did?"

"I said I don't know who killed him."

"But I'm a suspect." She nodded absently. "I can understand that, considering how I felt about him, and I suppose I'll be his heir—unless he *did* make a will and left everything to the Old Machos' Home."

"Do you know if he had a lawyer?"

"Yes. Marvin Wanner. His office is in San Francisco."

"He might know if Gould left a will. One thing I must

ask you, Savanna. You own a gun, don't you? A small automatic?"

"Me?" She regarded him with a doubtful half-smile. "I *hate* guns. Even prop guns. I had to use one in *The Locusts*. Gave me the shivers."

Conan didn't pursue that subject. "What about the missing manuscripts. Do you have any idea why anyone would steal them?"

"No, but *if* I'm Ravin's heir, that should ease your mind about me. I mean, if I killed him, why would I steal the manuscripts? If I'm his heir, *I* can sign the contracts. And collect the royalties. Of course, I don't know whether it was at a point where it could be published."

"You haven't read it?"

She laughed. "*Nobody* read his manuscripts."

"And you never took a quick look when he wasn't around?"

She gave Conan an oblique smile. "Well, I did once when I first knew him. He was working on *Stud*. But he caught me and went into a rage over it. As for *Odyssey* . . . well, I just didn't give a damn by then."

"You don't have any idea what *Odyssey* is about?"

"Only that he called it an autobiographical novel. The story of James Ravin Gould, you know, as if the world was just waiting to hear all the boring details of his life."

"It's always amazing what the world is waiting to hear, Savanna. Didn't he keep a copy of his latest draft somewhere for safekeeping?"

"I don't know. Why all the questions about the manuscripts?"

He rose, joined her at the railing, and looked out at the gold-laced sea. "Because they were stolen from the scene of a murder. The question is, was that an act of spite or revenge, or was there something in the manuscripts that someone didn't want the world to hear about?"

"Well, *I* don't know what it was. And I don't care. I don't care if the manuscripts are ever found. I don't even care if anybody ever figures out who killed him. I just don't *care*!" There was a chilling anger in that, but a moment later her eyes filled with the first tears Conan had seen her shed. "I loved him. Once upon a time, I loved him more than I ever loved anybody. But I got over that long ago. And now I want to get on with my life. Do you know I haven't had a movie offer in two years? And when I did *Blitz* in Hawaii, that was a local production, and half the cast were amateurs. I just did it because I was going crazy sitting around waiting on Ravin like some cozy little housewife. He liked for me to be *handy* whenever he called, and he made sure I *stayed* handy. It wasn't till six months after I married him that I realized what he was doing, and it didn't stop then."

Conan frowned. "What do you mean? What *was* he doing?"

"He was making sure I never worked again. I don't know how many phone messages I didn't get because he got to them first. He even told people I'd retired, and I lost one agent because of him. And he kept telling me he couldn't stand to be separated from me, that he *loved* me." Her eyes closed, tears escaping to streak her cheeks. "And you know, I . . . I kept *believing* him . . . ."

Conan restrained the impulse to take her in his arms, to comfort her like a hurt child. He wasn't sure he trusted himself. What he felt now in the face of her aching bitterness was as irrational as his response to a moving passage of music; it reached into the ancient brain beneath the veneer of rationality.

He asked, "How long were you married to Gould?"

She took a deep breath, hurriedly wiped her cheeks. "Nearly three years. It would've been three years in October."

"Gould never had any children?"

"Well, not by any of his four wives. God knows, *I* wanted a baby. At first, anyway."

"His *four* wives?" Marian Rosenthal had mentioned three wives. Still, she hadn't been sure of the number.

"I was number four," Savanna said bitterly. "That should've told me something. The first was Julie something. Sanzio? That was back in what Ravin called his flower-child period.

Then after the money started rolling in, Julie got lost in the shuffle, and he married Erin Chelsey.''

''The model.''

''Yes. That was her only talent, from what I hear, looking good in clothes. Well, maybe she looked good out of them, too. Six feet tall with red hair down to her buns.'' Savanna ran her fingers through her own hair, her laugh caustic. ''I think Ravin had a thing for tall women with red hair. I don't know about his first wife, but I'm five ten, and Allison was about the same height, and she had red hair, too. Auburn, really.''

Conan frowned, taking a puff on his cigarette. ''Allison?''

''Didn't Marian tell you?'' Savanna's eyes narrowed, a knowing smile shadowing her lips. ''Allison Rosenthal. Marian's daughter.''

Conan realized he was holding his breath. He flicked the ash from his cigarette into the salal below the deck. ''No, Marian didn't tell me.''

''Well, I can understand why she wouldn't want to talk about it.''

''Why?''

''Because Allison died. That was about five years ago.''

''How did she die?''

''A car accident.'' Savanna looked up at him with a direct, almost challenging gaze. ''Ravin was driving. They'd been to Marian and Jacob's place on Long Island for dinner. It happened on the drive back to the apartment in Manhattan. Ravin lost control. Hit a garbage truck.''

''Was he drunk?''

''Marian always claimed he was, but the blood tests they did at the hospital got lost somehow. He wasn't even cited.''

''He was injured?''

She nodded. ''Concussion, broken ribs, broken arm.'' She turned to look out at the sea, going gray now as the light faded. ''Poor Marian, she took it so hard. I mean, Allison was the only one of her children who wanted to go into publishing. She was an editorial assistant or something when she met Ravin, and I guess she was a really sweet person. I was surprised when Marian came here with the Laskys. They're good friends, I know, but Marian has hardly spoken to Ravin since Allison died, except when she had to, and then it was all business.''

For a while Conan remained silent, absorbing that, then he looked at his watch, went back to the table to put out his cigarette. "It's after eight, Savanna. Did you call the Surf House?"

She admitted with a show of reluctance, "No, I didn't."

"I'll call them, but you may have trouble getting a room this late."

She followed him to the sliding glass door into the living room, and when he turned on the lights, she strolled idly to the concert grand, the centerpiece of the room, shining ebony black against the plum reds and deep blues of a Lilahan carpet. "Do you play?" she asked.

"Not really. I sometimes enjoy hearing the sound of this piano." He hoped she wouldn't ask to play the Bösendorfer, although he had no doubt that as a child, she had studied piano. But there was only one person whom he afforded that privilege willingly, and she was on a concert tour in Japan.

Savanna looked at him with her head tilted to one side. "Conan, I don't want to spend the night in a motel. Not *this* night. I don't want to be alone, I don't want to be with strangers, and I don't want to be with Byron or Justine or Marian. All we ever had in common was Ravin."

She said nothing more, but her alternatives were obvious: she couldn't stay at the Dunlin Beach house tonight, and she didn't know anyone else in Holliday Beach.

Except Conan Flagg.

"I have a guest room upstairs," he said. "You're welcome to it."

"I'd be very grateful, Conan."

There were no innuendos in that. He crossed to the spiral staircase beyond the piano. "Come on, I'll show you the room."

She followed him up the stairs, and when he reached the balcony, he went into the room on the south end and flicked on the light. She paused inside the door. "It's very nice."

Conan had gone to some trouble to make this room nice,

although it was seldom occupied. It had the west-facing windows that were *de rigueur* for every room in his house. The colors were cool earth tones inspired by the reproduction over the bed: O'Keeffe's *Black Iris*. It was the only reproduction in the house. The original was locked in a museum, beyond his reach and means, and he had to satisfy himself with this facsimile.

He said, "I'll get your suitcase. Where are your car keys?"

"Downstairs on the bar. Thanks, Conan."

He only shrugged as he left the room. When he reached her car, he considered moving it into the garage. The Ferrari was highly visible identification. Then he got her small suitcase out of the passenger seat footwell, annoyed at himself. Whose business was it where she spent the night? And why should he feel uncomfortable about having this attractive and perhaps vulnerable woman in his house?

He knew all too well that if he thought about it, he'd find many answers to that last question.

She was by the stereo console in the north end of the living room studying the titles in his tape library when he returned. He took her suitcase up to the guest room, and as he descended the staircase, said, "Savanna, I have to make some phone calls."

She turned, smiled faintly at him. "You don't have to entertain me, Conan. Is it all right if I put some music on?" Then, perhaps interpreting his hesitation—correctly—as reluctance to let anyone else operate his stereo system, she added, "I'll be *very* careful."

He laughed. "Have at it. Would you like some coffee?"

"No. I don't drink coffee. I get an allergic reaction, even with decaffeinated. Go on, now. Take care of your calls. I'm okay."

He finally nodded. "I'll be in the library."

When he closed the library door and settled in the chair behind the desk, he lighted a cigarette and stared at the phone, trying to refocus his thoughts, and realized he hadn't checked his answering machine since he came home. He turned it on at the same moment the room speakers burst forth with the emphatic opening chords of *The Sleeping Beauty*, and he smiled. He wouldn't have ventured a guess at what music Savanna might choose, but the Tchaikovsky didn't surprise him.

There were few messages; only a handful of people knew this unlisted number. Two calls from his aunt Dolly Flagg, one expressing forbearing amazement that he hadn't told her he was going to England, another inviting him to a family reunion at the Ten-Mile Ranch over the Labor Day weekend. "I've asked Marge Hirsch's niece. Such a lovely girl, and a bookworm, just like you." That message he would ignore. Then three calls from his cousin Avery Flagg, who had— willingly enough—assumed the burden of managing the Ten-Mile when Conan chose to depart the dry solitude of Eastern Oregon. Avery's messages detailed his problems with importing sheep from New Zealand, which Conan would also ignore. He had long ago made clear his feelings about running sheep on the Ten-Mile. That arid land wouldn't stand up to it.

Another message was only a few hours old: Shelly Gage asking him to call her. She'd heard a rumor that Ravin Gould had died or been killed. That was another message he had no intention of answering.

Finally he pulled the phone toward him, punched a number, and turned his chair to watch the last glow of color fading at the horizon. Miss Beatrice Dobie answered on the second ring.

"Miss Dobie, I thought you'd like to know that Earl has finished his investigation of the break-in."

He heard a sarcastic "Ha! His investigation left a lot to be desired, if you ask me. But what about Ravin Gould? Was he really murdered?"

"Yes, but that's classified information for the time being."

"Oh, of course. You're working on the case? I heard Earl has Cady MacGill in custody. Is he your client?"

"Angie hired me to do what I can on Cady's behalf. And that's all I can say now. I just wanted to tell you about the shop."

"I suppose Earl says we can *open* tomorrow. He closes us

up on a Prime-Time Sunday, then says it's all right to open on *Monday*."

"Life is inherently unfair, Miss Dobie."

"Yes. Well, Hi Hitchcock is coming tomorrow to repair the doors and that bookshelf, so I might as well keep the shop open. I'll be there anyway. I suppose you'll be . . . otherwise occupied?"

"I suppose I will, but I'll stop in if I can. Good night, Miss Dobie."

"Good night, Mr. Flagg. And good luck."

He hung up, listened for a moment to the sparkling harp entroit to the *adagio pas d'action*, then turned on the desk lamp, opened his address book to the Fs, and punched a number. After seven rings, he heard an impatient "Fitch, here. Who the *hell* is this?"

Conan laughed at that curt greeting. Marcus Fitch was a man who relished his anomalous existence, a man whose bearing commanded respect, a man with a penchant for expensive cars and impeccably tailored suits, a black man who had fought his way out of the unbarred prison of poverty and prejudice into which he had been born. And Marcus Fitch was the best criminal lawyer Conan knew.

"Conan Flagg is who the hell, Marc."

"Ah, my favorite semi-native American. Conan, I know you folks down at the coast live a quiet life far from the madding crowd and madding clocks and calendars, but let me tell you something: This is what is known in the real world as the *weekend*. Not much left of it, I admit, but I'm here in the sanctuary of my home enjoying the last moments of my weekend with an intelligent and lovely lady who will soon share my life—two weeks of it, anyway—in Majorca, and we are *not* amused at having our sharing interrupted."

Conan offered no apology beyond "I sympathize, Marc, but business before pleasure. I have a client for you."

"No! Absolutely not! I'm leaving in two days for a well-deserved vacation, and I will not be conned into taking on one of your clients. Besides, they're usually charity cases."

"And *you* are usually the recipient of the charity. You've

heard of a writer named Ravin Gould? Married to Savanna Barany?''

A brief silence, then: ''Who *hasn't* heard of them? Incidentally, I enjoyed your live-action show on TV last night.''

Conan took a puff on his cigarette, blew smoke out impatiently. ''Yes, I'm sure you did. And that's a good introduction to your client.''

''Ravin Gould? Or dare I dream it—La Barany?''

''Not Gould. He was murdered last night, Marc. Your client is the man who's now in custody as suspect number one: Cady MacGill.''

''The guy who was going to cut Gould's bleeps off?'' Fitch laughed heartily. ''So, did he?''

''No. But somebody nearly cut Gould's head off with Cady's chain saw. *After* shooting him in the heart.''

''Damn, Conan, that's weird.''

''Is it weird enough to induce you to delay your vacation?''

A long sigh. ''It's weird enough. Where's my client being held?''

''Right here in quiet, unclocked, uncalendared Holliday Beach. By the way, Cady is Earl Kleber's son-in-law.''

''Now, that is *really* weird. Look, I have to be in court tomorrow morning, but I'll be down in the afternoon. About three. Okay?''

''Okay, Marc.'' Fitch hung up without further ado, and Conan paused for a drag on his cigarette before he punched another number.

Steve Travers answered as if he'd been waiting by the phone. ''Conan, you're late. I figured you'd be calling before six.''

''And ruin my dinner? Did you talk to the Herndons?''

''Well, I talked to Mr. Herndon—just call me Rich, he says—and I had Jeff Kaw do a quick background check. Nice, squeaky-clean, yuppie couple. Both in their thirties and second marriages. No children. He's a stockbroker, she's an executive at the Port of Portland. They're so credible, it gives you goose bumps.''

Conan leaned back in his chair. ''Well, when you recover

from your chills of ecstasy, will you tell me what just-call-
me-Rich said?''

"He corroborated Savanna's time of arrival at the condo.
One-twenty. And about six-thirty this morning when they
left for their trek on Mount Hood, they saw the Ferrari parked
outside.''

Conan closed his eyes, surprised at the intensity of his
relief. "Thanks, Steve.''

"Looks like Savanna's off the hook. At least, she is if that
literary agent—what's his name?''

"Byron Lasky. He said he saw Gould alive at about eleven-
thirty.''

"Right. And even in a Ferrari, she couldn't drive from
Holliday Beach to Valley West in an hour and fifty minutes.''

"Minus the time necessary to kill Gould. Besides, it's
likely Savanna made a stop on the way, although she said she
didn't. I drove her back to Holliday Beach in the Ferrari, and
the gas gauge read three-quarters full when we left the condo.
I know she didn't drive from here to Valley West on a quarter
of a tank of gas. She probably had to stop near Mac-
Minnville. I watched the gauge today, and it was another
quarter down about there.''

Steve said dryly, "Glad to see you're not totally dazzled
by Gould's sexy widow. You're still managing a little detective work.''

Conan laughed. "Yes, I am dazzled, Steve. I'm only human.''

"Glad to hear that, too.''

"What else did Rich have to say?''

"Just that Savanna was nearly hysterical when she arrived.
They took her in and talked to her—or let her talk—till she
calmed down. They said she left their condo about two. They
didn't check on her in the morning. Not at six-thirty.''

"Neighborly of them. By the way, Shelly Gage left a message on my answering machine. She's been hearing rumors
about Gould's death.''

Steve's sigh was audible. "She's not the only one. We've
been getting a lot of flak from the press, but good ol' Giff
has scheduled a press conference at the Taft County Court-

house at eight tomorrow morning. He won't have the autopsy or any of the lab reports by then. I don't know how he expects to answer any questions.''

"Giff's a politician. He can answer questions for hours without answering a single question.''

"Yeah. Well, keep me up-to-date.''

"I will, Steve. Thanks.'' Conan cradled the receiver and sat motionless in the pool of light cast by the desk lamp. He could no longer see the surf, nor even hear the breakers turning, not over the music that filled the room, filled the house, just as Savanna Barany's presence filled it. He thought of the Dunlin Beach house, of the condo in Portland, places she had lived but left no imprint upon. There was something fey and ephemeral about her, yet any space she occupied, she dominated.

He tapped the ash from his cigarette into the ashtray, focusing his attention on the music. The overture from *Romeo and Juliet.*

At length, he turned on the answering machine again, rewinding until he came to Shelly's message. Then he punched the phone number she had left, waited for her brisk "Hello?''

"Shelly, this is Conan Flagg.''

"Thank God you called, Conan. What's going *on* down there?''

"No comment, Shelly, but there'll be a press conference—''

She cut in irritably. "Yes, I know about that, but—''

"And you know I can't jeopardize my good relations with the police by telling you anything now.''

"How good are your relations with Gifford Wills, anyway? That old blowhard! Do you know what he did to me this afternoon?''

Conan could guess, but he played straight man. "What did he do?''

"He called me at the studios, said he's on his way to notify Savanna Barany of the death of her husband, and he figured it might be a newsworthy event. Something like that. So I pull a crew off another story, and we follow Giff out to the

Gould condo in Valley West, and guess what? Nobody's home. He could've at least called ahead.''

''Giff isn't in the habit of such courtesies.''

''I noticed, but before I was through with him, he got the message that he'd damn well better not send me on any more wild-goose chases. Okay, so why are you calling me?''

''Oh, I was just wondering about the videotape of yesterday's donnybrook at the bookshop.''

A pause, then: ''You want to see the tape?''

''If possible. The unedited version.''

''It'll cost you, Conan.''

''Yes, I thought it would. What?''

''An exclusive interview.''

Conan grimaced. ''Maybe I'll ask Sheriff Wills to subpoena the tape. I have a feeling he wouldn't mind hassling you a bit.''

''Oh, damn you. Okay, then maybe you'll just think kindly of me when this is over, and maybe you'll let me have first crack at it?''

''That I can promise. The kindly thoughts, at least. And yes, I'll give you first crack at whatever I'm in a position to offer. Deal?''

Shelly laughed. ''Do I have a choice? Okay, I'll see what's available and send you a copy.''

''Can I play it on a VCR? And can you get it to me tomorrow?''

''That's what I like about you, Conan. You're so much into high tech. Yes, you can play it on a VCR, and yes, I can get it to you tomorrow if I can find somebody to bring it down.''

''Do you know Marcus Fitch?''

''Dandy Marc Fitch? Sure.''

''Send the tape to him. He's coming to Holliday Beach tomorrow.''

''Who's he representing?''

''You'll have to ask him.''

''Right. Just remember, Conan—you owe me.''

''I'll remember. Good night, Shelly.''

When he hung up, he frowned at the phone, well aware

that there was nothing more he could do now. He put out his cigarette, rubbed his eyes, wondering if he would sleep tonight. At length, he came to his feet, took a last look into the corner where the *Knight* offered the rose of love and the butterfly of hope, then turned out the light and made his way to the door.

The living room was empty and dark, yet he had the sense of something waiting in the shadows. A ghost of a fragrance, a ghost of . . . what? He looked up at the balcony. There was no light within the open door of the guest room. The only light was the dim glow coming from his bedroom at the north end of the balcony.

He went up the stairs, approached his door hesitantly, and finally entered. The light on the bedside table was on, and Savanna stood at the open door onto the deck, the scrim curtains blowing around her, her bare feet sinking into the winter-sea-hued carpet as she turned to face him. Her white nightgown clung lightly to her body, the bodice cut in a deep curve within which the sweet contours of her breasts weren't so much confined as confirmed.

He recognized the music: the opening *moderato* from *Swan Lake*.

Conan, whose feelings at the moment were anything but moderated, thought: *this is ridiculous*. But he couldn't manage a laugh.

She moved toward him as silently as the wind, surrounded him—or so it seemed—with her perfume. Her eyes, hooded and dark, were fixed on his. She stood before him, not quite touching him, yet he thought he could feel the warmth of her skin.

Dazzled, he thought, yes, I am dazzled. And I am indeed only human.

But he held his hands at his sides, even when she reached out and lightly ran her fingers over the planes of his face, as if she were blind, seeing by touch.

And finally he spoke her name. "Savanna . . . "

She withdrew her hand, and there was in her smile an equivocal poignancy. Her voice was husky, almost a whisper. "Ravin once called me a frigid slut masquerading as Aphrodite."

He felt the words like a slap in the face, as she must have when she first heard them. But he didn't speak. She had more to say.

"For a long time, Conan, I wondered if he wasn't right. Yet I was faithful to him. He never believed that, and I don't expect you to believe it, either, but it doesn't matter. Now I'm free. *Not* because he's dead. Maybe I just don't understand that yet. I'm free because I set myself free. I walked out on him. I left him. And I'm *free*."

"I doubt that, Savanna. Not yet."

She laughed softly. "Oh, you're wrong. But you're a man of honor, aren't you? Conan, I can't offer love. I'm not even sure I know what love is anymore. But I think *you* know, and that's why I can trust you."

Perhaps that trust set *him* free. He cupped her face in his hands, saw his skin bronze against her ivory cheeks, and he leaned toward her, closed his eyes at the gentle shock of her mouth against his. And the music he wanted to hear at this moment was a song freighted with sadness and ambiguous surprise.

I never asked for forever . . . only for today . . . .

CHAPTER 13

The phone rang—for the second morning in a row—at eight-ten.

But on this morning, Conan was already awake. He was sitting up in bed smoking a cigarette while he watched Savanna Barany sleep. He caught the phone in midring. "Yes?"

"Conan? This is Angie. Dad said he cleared it with Giff for me to see Cady. And you, too. I mean, I knew you'd want to talk to him."

Savanna stirred, the sheet twisting around her legs as she turned, propped herself on her elbows. Her hair spilled over her shoulders, and she smiled sleepily, like a child waking up on a birthday.

Conan said into the phone, "Of course I want to talk to him. When can I see him?" He gently brushed Savanna's hair back, and she kissed him at the curve of his jaw, then rested her head on his shoulder, her arm across his body, ivory on bronze.

Angie said, "Ten-thirty. I'll meet you at the station. Okay?" A short silence, then: "Conan?"

"Mm? Yes, I'll be there. By the way, I called Marc Fitch.

He *will* take Cady as a client. He'll be here this afternoon about three o'clock."

"Oh, Conan! Oh, that's terrific! Oh, you're *wonderful*!"

Savanna heard that. The decibel level was so high, she couldn't avoid hearing it, and she did a nice mime impression of Angie in a state of enthusiasm. Conan said, "Angie, I'll see you at the station," and hung up before she could hear his laughter.

Savanna said, "I gather that was little Angela."

"Yes," Conan replied as he put out his cigarette. "My client's wife."

The reminder was intentional, but Savanna didn't seem ready to accept it. With a feathery touch, she traced the scar that angled from his right clavicle to the eighth rib on his left side, where it ended in an inch-long cicatrix. "How did you ever get so scarred up, Conan?"

"From walking in dark alleys." He leaned toward her, bemused still and again by the perfection of her face. But when he kissed her, his lips were closed, and he put a cast of finality in it.

She looked at him and at length nodded. "I was right about you."

"About what about me?"

"I can trust you." She turned toward the windows. "Well, like they say, this is the first day of the rest of my life. I suppose I should check in to the Surf House. They ought to have a vacancy this time of day."

Conan didn't offer his house for another night. Last night he had sensed fear and loneliness beneath the veneer of indifference to her husband's death. And she'd had something to prove. But if she hadn't proved it now, she never would.

She left the bed, combing through her hair with her fingers as she walked to the bath. "By the way, is there a dining room in this hotel? Somewhere a girl could get some breakfast?"

"Yes, ma'am. Downstairs." He rose, found his robe on the floor at the end of the bed. "Scrambled eggs all right? The chef at this hotel is rather limited in his repertoire."

She laughed. "Oh, I wouldn't say that."

* * *

The kitchen alcove was an angled goldfish bowl of glass, and Conan had offered to lower the shades, but Savanna didn't seem concerned about being recognized by the tourists who paraded across the access to the beach, although she chose the chair on the north side of the table that put her back to the parade. She had downed two eggs and an English muffin and now was lavishing a second muffin with Mrs. Early's wild blackberry jam. Conan sat across the table from her with a mug of coffee and a cigarette, tolerating her silence until at length she finished the muffin, then turned to look out at the bank of fog on the horizon.

She said, "I guess I'll have to do something about arranging the funeral. I think . . . maybe I'll call my mother."

Conan nodded. "It'll be easier for your parents if they hear about Gould's death from you—before it becomes the lead story on the evening news. Sheriff Wills scheduled a press conference this morning."

There was an equivocal intensity in her eyes at that. "I knew it wouldn't last. You know, the privacy. Or maybe just . . ."

"A time when you could still deny it?"

"Maybe. Those damn reporters. 'How does it *feel* to find out your husband had his throat . . .' " She closed her eyes, breath caught, then sighed. "But it'll be over and forgotten by next year. That's what Daddy always used to say."

"Did your parents know you were considering a divorce?"

"No. I suppose that'll be out, too. Daddy hated Ravin from the moment they met. That was in Atlanta before the wedding. It was a big production, and Mama loved it. She loved Ravin, too. She thought he was *charming*. Most women thought that when they first met him."

Conan took a long drag on his cigarette. "Did you?"

"Oh, Conan, I was like a high school girl over Ravin." Her laugh was laced with bitterness. "And the first year I knew him, when we were just living together, it was lovely. I never should've married him, though. That was when things started to go bad."

Conan rose and went to the coffeepot to refill his mug. "Yet you stayed with him, through mostly thin, it seems."

"Very thin." The reply was almost curt, and Conan felt as if a door had slammed shut between them. He didn't try to open it.

He tested his coffee. "Damn!" he muttered, but not because the coffee was too hot. He was looking out the windows over the sink into the beach access, and he recognized the battered old Plymouth that pulled up in front of the house, recognized the elderly woman who got out of the passenger side, then with a wave to her husband, headed for Conan's front door. He said, "Mrs. Early."

Savanna only shrugged, and a moment later the front doorbell rang. Conan went out into the hall to open the door, and Mrs. Early, her aureole of white hair crushed under a scarf, bustled in.

"Well, hello, Mr. Flagg. Heard you was home, so I figgered I better come around for my reg'lar Monday stint. Say, did you hear 'bout that writer feller? Ravin Gould? It was on the radio this mornin'."

"Yes, Mrs. Early, I know, but—"

"And a sheriff's deppity stopped by to talk to me yesterday. Took my fingerprints."

"*Your* fingerprints?"

Conan didn't get an answer to that. Savanna came out into the hall, and Mrs. Early's mouth fell open on an unaccustomed silence until at length she breathed, "Miz Barany!"

"How are you, Mrs. Early?"

"You've met, then?" Conan asked irritably.

"Of course," Savanna replied. "Mrs. Early has been cooking and cleaning for us since we arrived in Holliday Beach."

"Oh, Miz Barany, I was so sorry to hear 'bout your husband." Mrs. Early remembered to put on a sympathetic expression with her condolences, but the effect was skewed by the suspicious glances she sent from Conan to Savanna and back again.

Savanna said soberly, "Thank you, Mrs. Early." Then with a quick breath, as if bracing herself, "I'd better get my things. This is going to be a long day." She turned and started for the living room and the stairs, leaving Mrs. Early with her mouth again open.

Conan asked, "Would you like a cup of coffee, Mrs. Early?"

"Mm? Oh. Don't mind if I do."

He returned to the kitchen, poured her a mug of coffee while she settled in a chair at the table and lighted a Camel, holding it curled in her hand. "Well, I wouldn't've said nothing 'bout Mr. Gould if I'd known Miz Barany was here. Nice lady, seems like. Not stuck up a-tall."

Conan sat down across from her. "I suppose the sheriff wanted your fingerprints for elimination."

"That's what Deppity Jones said. You know, I never had my fingerprints took before. S'pose they'll keep 'em on file somewhere?"

Conan smiled. "Well, in case they do, you'll have to wear gloves if you ever resort to burglary."

"Why, Mr. Flagg!" She gave that a laugh, then sobered as she added, "I heard Chief Kleber has Cady MacGill in jail. You just never know about people. They say he used his chain saw on poor Mr. Gould, and he was such a nice man."

Apparently Ravin Gould's attraction to women had no age limit.

"Did you hear that on the radio, Mrs. Early? About the chain saw?"

"More'r less." She emitted a puff of smoke. "Giff Wills just said Mr. Gould'd been murdered, and a chain saw belongin' to Cady was there next to the body. Is it true, Mr. Flagg? Did Cady slice up poor Mr. Gould like so much cordwood?"

Conan flinched. *"No."*

"Well, somethin' strange went on down there Saturday night."

Conan didn't comment on that. He heard footsteps in the hallway and rose as Savanna came to the door, suitcase in hand. She said, "I'd better be going. Goodbye, Mrs. Early."

"Bye, Miz Barany. Sure sorry 'bout Mr. Gould."

Conan took Savanna's suitcase and accompanied her to

the Ferrari. Her dark glasses went on as soon as she left the house, but Conan noticed a couple on their way to the beach staring curiously at her. She got into the car and lowered the window.

He asked, "Will you be all right, Savanna?"

"Oh, I'm a tough little broad, you know." She laughed and reached for his hand. "But if . . . well, I hope this isn't goodbye forever."

"No. Not forever." And he added to himself, *I never asked for forever*.

At 9:45 the Holliday Beach Book Shop was open, and Hi Hitchcock—the proverbial jack-of-all-trades and quick at none—was repairing the north door at his usual leisurely pace.

The shop was crowded even for August. Conan retreated to his office, and while Meg made herself comfortable on his lap, he stared at the mail accumulated on his desk, but he was thinking about Marian Rosenthal, whose daughter had not only been married to Ravin Gould, but had died perhaps as a result of his negligence. Why *had* Marian come to Holliday Beach? On business? To discuss with Gould publicity for a book he hadn't finished and that Harkness hadn't contracted for? Conan reached for the telephone and dialed directory assistance, asked for New York City, and eventually got the number for the Harkness editorial offices. It was the lunch hour in New York, but he assumed someone would be tending the telephones.

A voice that sounded as if it belonged to a young man fresh out of high school, but who may have been an editor, for all Conan knew, answered. "HarknessCronin'n'ComnymayIhelpyou?"

Conan assumed he had the correct number and replied, "I'd like to speak with Marian Rosenthal."

"Wha'depar'ment?"

"Publicity."

Conan was then treated to a recording of "Autumn Leaves," but it was cut off in midchromatic with "Sorry-she'snotavailableonvacation."

"On vacation?" But the representative of Harkness-Cronin'n'Comny had hung up. Conan shrugged as he followed suit. On vacation. He stroked Meg's back and said, "Very interesting, Duchess."

Then, with a sigh, he began sorting through the mail. The empty window on the office door provided no barrier to the distraction of customers at the counter, where Miss Dobie manned the cash register. Some had rental books jacketed in brown paper to return or check out, but in this summer season, most had purchases, many of which, he noted, were copies of *The Diamond Stud*.

There were a few locals among the customers. The Daimler sisters, asking when the latest Danielle Steele would be out in paperback. Olaf Svensen, muttering about the short salmon season, which he blamed on "them fool preservationists." Mrs. Carmody, frail and powdered, her hair the color of pale apricots, dithering over the purchase of a book. She was the owner of the blue '59 Cadillac parked outside the south door, and Conan frowned, remembering the car he'd seen on Dunlin Beach Road Saturday night.

Mrs. Carmody placed a book on the counter. "It's for Doc Spenser," she said to Miss Dobie. "He likes books on Oregon history, and I wondered, do you know if he has this one?"

Miss Dobie studied the book. "If he does, he didn't get it here."

"I'll take it, then. It's a belated birthday gift. I didn't find out till too late that his birthday was Saturday. He's such a dear man."

Conan tuned out the rest of the conversation, threw more junk mail into the wastepaper basket. When he had reduced the piles on his desk to no more than thirty letters, bills, and invoices that needed immediate attention—which they weren't likely to get—he checked his watch, saw that it was five minutes after ten, and rose, moving Meg to the desk. She responded with an inscrutable Siamese yowl and refused to stay put, leaving the desk in disarray with her departing leap. Conan followed her out into the shop, where Miss Dobie perched on a stool behind the counter, enjoying a lull in the stream of customers.

She said, "Well . . . I guess the cat's out of the bag now."

He blinked. "Meg?"

"Oh, Mr. Flagg, *you* know what I mean. Didn't you hear the news on the radio this morning?"

"Giff Wills's press conference? No, I didn't bother to turn it on."

"Well, you didn't miss much. I mean, he talked a lot, but he didn't say much. But, Mr. Flagg, what's happening? I mean, with Ravin Gould's murder? Who killed him if Cady didn't?"

"Miss Dobie, your faith in Cady is touching. So is your faith in me, if you think I have an answer to that."

"What about Savanna Barany?"

Startled, he asked, "What about her?"

"Well . . . *cherchez la femme*. And she certainly is a *femme*. A *femme fatale*." Miss Dobie smiled smugly as she added, "As in Mona Fatale, one might say."

"One might." He started for the door, but stopped when he saw a red-white-and-blue striped van outside. KEEN-TV, The Eyes of Portland, were again focused on Holliday Beach, and no doubt this was only the first wave of a flood of reporters.

"Miss Dobie, close the shop. I'm leaving now while I still can."

She was on her feet, eyes glittering. "Oh, Mr. Flagg, don't be silly. We've already lost one Prime-Time day. Go on, I'll take care of them."

"It's on your head!" And with that, he was out the door, its bells jangling discordantly as he sprinted for his car.

CHAPTER 14

Conan reached the police station fifteen minutes before the appointed hour of ten-thirty and before Angie MacGill, but not before five representatives of the third estate. They were, however, on their way out, encouraged by a belligerent Sergeant Hight. Inside the station, Conan only had time to exchange greetings with Hight before Kleber's door was flung open, and Byron Lasky emerged, his tie loose, eyes shadowed with fatigue. He frowned at Conan as if trying to remember who he was.

Conan identified himself and asked, "What's wrong, Mr. Lasky?"

"I can't get anybody to *understand*!" He ran both hands through his thin hair. "Those manuscripts, the best novel Ravin ever wrote, just vanished off the face of the Earth! And where's that police chief? I've been waiting for over an *hour*."

Conan glanced into Kleber's empty office as he offered, "The investigation has just begun, Mr. Lask—"

"And that sheriff, all *he* can say is maybe they'll turn up! *Turn up*, like lost dogs!"

The front door opened, and Lasky spun around, perhaps

125

expecting Kleber, but the new arrivals were Angie and her son. Blond, blue-eyed, and freckled, Michael had inherited his mother's coloring and his father's size, and at eight he was already as tall as the average ten-year-old. He approached Conan with a grin and a loud "Mom says you're gonna get Dad outa jail."

Conan glanced irritably at Angie as he reassured Michael. "I'm going to *try*, Michael. That's all I can do. How are you, Angie?"

"Better than yesterday," she said, managing a smile. And she looked better, with her hair combed and curled, her lips colored a pink that matched her summery dress. She turned to Sergeant Hight. "Dave, Dad said I could talk to Cady. Conan, too."

Sergeant Hight picked up the interoffice phone. "He told me, Angie. I'll have Charlie bring him to the interrogation room."

Lasky listened in silence to this exchange, and now he demanded of Conan, "You're going to talk to MacGill? I was told *nobody* could talk to him."

Before Conan could get a word out, Angie said coolly, "I get to talk to Cady because I'm his *wife*. And Conan is a private investigator, and Cady's his *client*."

Conan sighed, while Lasky blinked at him, repeated, "Private investigator . . ." He seemed about to ask a question, but changed his mind and hurriedly made his way out the door.

"Who was *that*?" Angie asked.

"Byron Lasky, Gould's literary agent," Conan replied absently.

"Oh. Yes, Ravin talked about—" She looked at her son. "Come on, Michael, let's go see Dad."

Conan said, "If you don't mind waiting a few minutes, I'd prefer to talk to Cady first."

"Why?" she demanded. "You think we're going to cook up some sort of story between us?" When Conan didn't respond, her righteous indignation gave way to a sigh of resignation. "Okay. Well, Michael, I guess we'll just have to wait a little longer to see your dad."

Conan ignored the accusation in that and walked down the hall to the door of the interrogation room, where Officer Charlie Olin was on guard. Charlie was the oldest member of the Holliday Beach police force, a man known for unwavering devotion to his duty, limited as it was to taking care of the jail's occupants. He opened the door for Conan, then closed it behind him, and Conan heard the snap of the lock.

Like Alice after swallowing the potion, Cady seemed too big for the small room. He wore the same faded plaid shirt, red suspenders, Levi's frayed at the hem, and scuffed boots in which he'd made his dramatic appearance at the bookshop Saturday, and now he seemed as faded, frayed, and scuffed as his attire, hair curling black and unruly around his face, blue eyes bloodshot, jaw dark with two days growth of beard. He was smiling in hopeful anticipation, but the hope seemed to collapse when he recognized Conan.

"Where's Angel and Mike?"

Conan went to one of the chairs at the bleak metal table. "They're outside, Cady. I just need to ask you a few questions first."

Cady eyed Conan suspiciously and went to the chair on the opposite side of the table, swung his leg over it as if he were mounting a horse, and said, "Herb Latimer told me you're *investigating* this thing."

"Yes. You have a new lawyer, by the way. Marcus Fitch. He's a friend of mine, and he's also one of the best criminal lawyers in the state. He's coming down to talk to you this afternoon."

Cady seemed confused at that. "How much is this best criminal lawyer going to cost me?"

"I have no idea, Cady, and that's the least of your problems." Conan lit a cigarette, taking his time about it before he asked, "How did you find out about Angie and Gould?"

Cady glowered from under his eyebrows. "*She* told me! Saturday morning. Angel and me, well, we was . . . having a fight."

"About Gould?"

"No. That was before I even knew about that bastard. We

got into a fight because I figure Mike needs a little brother or sister. It's not natural, letting a kid grow up by himself. Angel and me'd been through that before, but this time she flew mad. I never seen her so mad. Said she nearly died when Mike was born. Well, maybe she had a hard time, but she was nowhere near dying. Then she started in about how *Ravin* wouldn't ask her to go through that again or give up her *career*. Career! Hell, it's just typing and figuring accounts, and I told her so. And that's when she told *me* about her and that little shit, just throwing it in my face, and damn it, a man can't *take* that! You gotta *do* something!''

Conan nodded through an exhalation of smoke. "Well, you definitely *did* something."

"Yeah." Cady sighed. "I swear to God, I only meant to scare him."

"So, after your stunning television debut, what did you do?"

His massive shoulders shifted in a shrug. "I went home first, but I couldn't—I didn't want to stay there. I mean, I didn't want to be there when Angie came home. I mean, I just . . . well, I just couldn't talk to her, not right then. So I told Mike to go over to the Jamisons', and I—well, I went down to the Last Resort. But Abie said the police had been there looking for me. Sam and Travis was there and—"

"Who?"

"Sam Lowder and Travis Wheeler. Sam's a faller, too, and Travis is a Cat skinner. Known 'em for years. Anyway, Sam says why don't we pick up a case of beer and go over to his house. So we did."

Conan waited. "Then what?" he asked finally.

"Then nothin'. We just sat around and talked, the three of us."

"And drank beer."

Cady tipped his chair back, ignoring its groan. "Yeah. Then about four in the afternoon, Billy Todd came by asking about me, but Sam told him he hadn't seen me. And later—I don't exactly know when it was, but it was after dark—Sam and Travis took me home. Don't remember much about that, 'cept Angel and Mike were gone. Nobody home."

"Where was your car?"

"Don't have a car. Chevy pickup. I left it down at the Last Resort when we went to Sam's. I guess one of the guys drove it to my house when they took me home. It was in the driveway this morning."

"And what did you do when you got home?"

He loosed a bark of a laugh. "Passed out. The guys put me to bed. Don't remember a thing after my head hit the pillow."

Conan inhaled on his cigarette, and he didn't envy Marc Fitch this client. "So, you can't account for your time after your friends left you, and you had transportation handy."

"I was passed out, damn it!"

"But you can't prove that. Unless Sam or Travis stayed with you the rest of the night." And while Cady shook his head, Conan said, "I'm almost afraid to ask, but do you own a small handgun?"

"You mean one of those little popguns? Hell, no. Sheriff Wills asked me that. How come?"

"Because Ravin Gould was shot in the heart—*before* he nearly lost his head to your chain saw."

Cady's mouth went slack. "Hey, now, that . . . that's weird."

"Yes, *weird* seems to be the consensus. Did you happen to read any of Gould's manuscripts while Angie was working on them?"

"Course not. I never go into her office. She doesn't like me or Mike bothering her in there."

Conan nodded. "Cady, is there anything else I should know?"

He pulled in a deep breath, letting it out in a weary sigh. "No. I guess I'm in real trouble, aren't I?"

"Yes, I guess you are."

"But I didn't kill that bastard, I swear it!"

"I believe you." Conan crushed out his cigarette and rose. "Marc Fitch will be here about three, and you'd damn well better tell him everything he wants to know and do exactly what he says."

Cady bristled at that, but finally said almost meekly, "Okay."

"And by the way, I still expect you to pay for the damage you did at the bookshop."

"I'll make good on it," he insisted. "Somehow."

Conan went to the door and knocked, and when Charlie opened it, Angie and Michael were waiting outside. Conan said, "Angie, you can go in now," then walked away from her and the questions she was so obviously champing at the bit to ask. He heard the boisterous sounds of Cady's greetings before Charlie again closed and locked the door.

Kleber was at the front desk conferring with Dave Hight, while Billy Todd was at the entrance, using his bulk and boyishly honest manner to convince a covey of reporters that they were not welcome. Conan reached the counter in time to hear the chief say to Hight, "We'll pass the hat here. Dan helped us out with his chopper so many times. Damn. After four years in Nam, and now this. Makes you wonder. . . ." But Kleber apparently wasn't willing to verbalize his wondering.

Conan asked, "Dan Arno? Is that who you're talking about?"

Kleber turned, jaw muscles bunched. "Dan got himself killed. Routine trip back from Portland early Sunday morning, and he crashed on Spirit Mountain over near Grande Ronde. I just got back from telling Kara. The kids were home. Dan Junior's just starting high school this fall, and Noele . . . she's only ten years old."

Conan was willing to wonder about what Kleber wouldn't enunciate: about the role of blind luck in human affairs. But he didn't voice his musings, knowing Kleber to be a churchgoing man who firmly believed there *was* a purpose in events and lives.

"If you're passing the hat, I'll add something," Conan said as he pulled his billfold out of his back pocket. Then he frowned, finding a total of twenty-one dollars in it. "After I go to the bank," he amended.

Kleber nodded. "I figure Kara can use anything you can

spare. Odd, though, Dan had already started passing the hat, so to speak.''

''What do you mean?''

''Well, Dom Kouros from the NATSB called me about Dan. He said they found nearly eight hundred dollars cash on him. Must've been getting some extra runs in. Kara said they'd been saving up for a vacation in Hawaii.'' He glanced back toward the interrogation room, asked, ''You get anything useful out of Cady?''

''Not really. By the way, Marc Fitch will be arriving this afternoon.''

''Yeah, Angela told me. Well, Fitch is going to have a hell of a time pulling *this* one out of the fire.''

Conan only nodded as he headed for the door.

CHAPTER 15

The Taft Bank had been among the first businesses to move into the new shopping mall at the north end of town, and Conan left his accounts with them in spite of his resentment for the mall with its blandly anonymous design. It seemed to say, smugly, that the quaint little village of Holliday Beach was acquiring Progress. The next thing, Conan thought bleakly, would be a McDonald's.

He drove into the parking lot, which in summer was much like playing bumper cars, and as he neared the bank, he saw a car backing out of a slot in front of it: a yellow Ferrari.

It was Savanna, but she turned and drove away from him, apparently without noticing him.

He swung into the empty slot, and when he entered the beferned interior of the bank, a young woman stood ready at her window with a smile. "Hi, Conan. How was your trip to England?"

"Delightful, Ellie." He took a check out of his billfold, began filling in the spaces. "Wasn't that Savanna Barany I saw leaving the bank?"

"Sure was. She and Mr. Gould opened an account here,

you know. She came in to close it and clear out their safety
deposit box.''

Conan stared at Ellie. ''Did she take anything out of the
box?''

''I don't know. I mean, I'm not supposed to watch what
people do when they get into their boxes. Of course, I usually
don't handle that anyway, but Marie's out to lunch.''

''You haven't heard about Ravin Gould?''

Ellie hesitated, then: ''Well, I heard he'd been murdered.''

Conan finished writing out his check. No doubt Ellie would
find out soon enough that the IRS frowned on survivors
opening safety deposit boxes before its agents had a chance
to inventory the contents. ''If you'll just cash this for me,
Ellie. And may I have an envelope?''

Conan drove back to the police station, wondering why it
should bother him that Savanna had cleared out the checking
account and safety deposit box. To her it would be a perfectly
reasonable thing to do, since she didn't plan to stay in Holliday Beach any longer than necessary. She'd had no experience with the legal aftermath of death, nor, he was sure,
any direct dealings with the IRS. Such details would be handled for her by agents, accountants, or lawyers.

When Conan returned to the Holliday Beach Police Station,
Sergeant Hight was at the counter consuming a chocolate-
iced doughnut with a mug of coffee. The door into Kleber's
office was open, and the chief was laboriously pecking out a
report on a typewriter.

Conan handed Hight an envelope. ''This is for Kara. Has
Angie left yet?''

Hight nodded as he licked chocolate off his fingers. ''Said
she had to take Michael down to the grade school. They're
running a summer soccer clinic for the kids. I guess Mike's
one of their stars. Damn!''

That expletive was in response to the tan patrol car that
had pulled into the parking area outside.

''Chief!'' Hight hollered. ''It's Giff Wills.''

And it was indeed Sheriff Gifford Wills who emerged from

the driver's side, adjusted his Stetson, and headed for the entrance, while Deputy Neely Jones followed at her usual ironically respectful distance.

Kleber rose to look out his own window, then, swearing volubly, went to his office door and closed it, after which he returned to his desk to pound at the hapless typewriter, while Dave Hight hid the remains of the doughnut in a drawer under the counter and napkined his mouth and hands. Wills strode into the station, every step marked with the leathery squeak of his gun belt. Deputy Neely Jones was right behind him, ramrod-straight, soberly businesslike. She didn't squeak.

Wills nodded at Hight. "Mornin', Dave." He looked into Kleber's office, but the chief was assiduously beating the typewriter to death.

Hight asked, "What can I do for you, Sheriff?"

"I want to talk to MacGill, have him check his statement."

Conan leaned on the end of the counter and said, "Not without his lawyer present, Sheriff."

Wills stared at Conan, as if seeing him for the first time. "This is none of your business, Flagg."

The sheriff usually put on a show of friendliness for Conan in their occasional encounters. But not today. Conan said, "Yes, it *is* my business, because Cady MacGill is my client."

"Your client?" Wills's face turned a blotchy pink. "I should've seen *that* coming. Okay, you can sit in while I talk to him. Damn it, I just want him to go over his statement before he signs it."

"Unfortunately, I'm not a lawyer. By the way, Cady's hired a new lawyer. He'll be here this afternoon. Marcus Fitch."

At that, Conan caught a twitch of a smile escaping Neely Jones's careful control. She met Conan's eyes, then looked away. The sheriff's response was less controlled. It was a bellowed "Marcus Fitch! What the hell're you trying to do, Flagg? Make a circus out of this thing?"

"Anyone accused of a crime is entitled to the best legal counsel available. Have you talked to Ms. Barany yet?"

The sheriff's blood pressure was obviously rising dangerously. "I *would've* talked to her if I could've *found* her!"

"Lonnie didn't give you my message? She was ready to make a statement yesterday, but you weren't available. Anyway, she's staying at the Surf House. Oh—you might want to question her neighbors at the condo in Valley West, Rich and Maggie Herndon. They may be able to establish an alibi for her."

Wills snorted. "Waste of time checking *her* alibi. We got the man we want, right here in Earl Kleber's jail. His own son-in-law!"

Conan heard Dave Hight's hissing intake of breath, but kept his gaze fixed on Wills. "There's still the little problem of the actual murder weapon. Cady doesn't own a handgun."

"So he says."

"Sheriff, I can imagine Cady with an arsenal of rifles and shotguns, but *not* a small-caliber handgun."

"I can imagine Cady MacGill with damn near anything!"

"But you haven't found the gun."

"No, but I sure as hell will!" He reached into his breast pocket and pulled out a folded document, waved it under Conan's nose. "This here's a search warrant, Flagg, for Cady MacGill's house and vehicles."

Another hiss from Hight, but Conan only nodded, finding nothing surprising in Wills's alacrity at obtaining a search warrant. Conan asked, "Does the warrant include the missing manuscripts? They could be worth millions."

"You been talking to that literary agent. Yes, the warrant includes the manuscripts."

"Well, I'm glad to hear that, Sheriff. Do you have warrants for the other suspects?"

Neely Jones's eyes flashed as she looked at her boss, and Conan surmised the answer to that question was a bone of contention between them. But Wills wasn't aware of her disapproval. He braced both hands on the counter and leaned close to Conan. "*What* other suspects? Who else left his chain saw next to the body?"

"But the question is, who *shot* Gould? There are a number of people who might have pulled the trigger. Savanna Barany, for instance, if her alibi doesn't hold up. Byron and Justine Lasky, Marian Rosenthal, Dana Semenov.''

"Who the hell're all *those* people?'' Wills demanded irritably.

"People who were at Ravin Gould's little party Saturday night. People who might have wanted him dead.'' Conan wasn't sure that was true of Dana Semenov, but he saw no reason to exclude her.

"How the hell do *you* know if any of these—''

"I've been on this case twenty-four hours, Sheriff. I've been asking questions. And here's a question you should ask of our esteemed district attorney: Ask Owen Culpepper how he'll feel if the defense brings up all these potential suspects in court, and you haven't raised a finger to eliminate them. All Marc Fitch has to do is prove reasonable doubt, and five other suspects will make casting reasonable doubt a piece of cake.''

Wills leaned closer, his face no more than a foot from Conan's. "Flagg, you just don't understand how juries think. One look at the autopsy pictures of Gould's body, one look at MacGill's chain saw lying next to the body, one look at the videotape those TV people took at your bookshop Saturday, and Fitch won't be able to raise enough reasonable doubt to save MacGill's ass if there was *twenty* suspects.''

Conan could think of no response to that, so he changed the subject: "Have you found out if Gould left a will?''

The sheriff drew back, blinked. "Well . . . no, not yet, but we're working on it.''

"You've talked to his lawyer?''

"I, uh, Neely, didn't you call that lawyer like I told you?''

No doubt it would have been more politic for Neely Jones to back up her boss's lie, but either she was too honest or simply too annoyed to do so. "No, sir,'' she said crisply. "I wasn't given the lawyer's name.''

Wills sent her a searing squint, but before he could speak, Conan put in: "I'm sure Ms. Barany can provide the name, Sheriff.'' Conan might have provided it himself, but he saw no reason to make things easier for Wills.

After a suspicious glare, Wills seemed to become aware

of the search warrant he still held crumpled in one beefy hand, and his mouth slid into an unpleasant grin. "Well, Flagg, since I can't talk to Cady till his fancy lawyer gets here, guess I might as well serve this search warrant." Abruptly he about-faced and headed for the door. "Come on, Neely. We'll radio Sonny on the way down to MacGill's house."

Neely followed Wills out the door, but before it closed, she glanced back at Conan with an unmistakably questioning look. He nodded, realizing that her silent question was: *are you coming?*

He went to the door, smiling faintly. Had he found an ally of sorts in Giff Wills's ranks?

CHAPTER 16

The MacGill house faced an unpaved street east of Highway 101. It was a modest structure about twenty years old, sided in pale green with a brown composition roof. The yard was fenced, but obviously its owners weren't gardeners; the lawn was yellowing with August, and the nasturtiums had escaped the beds flanking the front door. There was no garage, but two vehicles were parked in a driveway at the side of the house: a red Chevy pickup and an aged, once blue Honda.

When Conan arrived, Sheriff Wills had already planted his patrol in front of the MacGills' gate. He and Neely were at the gate, waiting, but not for Conan. At least Wills had nothing but a scowl for him when he parked across the street. As Conan got out of his car, another Sheriff's Department patrol drove up and parked behind him.

Conan recognized the deputy behind the wheel: Sonny Hoffsted, a cadaverously lean man who had been with the Sheriff's Department since before Wills was first elected three terms ago. As Conan started across the street, Hoffsted emerged from his car, yawning expansively, and joined him. "How you doin', Conan?"

"Not bad enough to complain, Sonny. Long night?"

"Yeah. Had to transport a prisoner to Gilliam County."

When they reached the gate, Hoffsted touched the brim of his Stetson. "Morning, Sheriff. Deputy Jones."

Wills nodded, ignoring Conan. "Sonny, what we're looking for is some manuscripts for a book named . . ." He had to check the search warrant. "Named *Odyssey*. The other thing we're looking for is a small handgun, probably twenty-two caliber."

Sonny Hoffsted was not a man to waste words. He only nodded, and Wills opened the gate and led the way to the quiet house. The front door was open, but the aluminum-framed screen was closed. He knocked, and within seconds, Angie appeared behind the screen. She examined the official deputation waiting on the stoop, one eyebrow going up when she saw Conan standing behind them.

"Well, have you come to arrest me, too, Sheriff?" she asked.

"I've got a search warrant here, Angie," Wills said irritably. He offered the warrant, and she opened the screen enough to prop it with her hip while she scanned the document.

Finally she looked past Wills to Conan. "What about this, Conan?"

He shrugged. "There's nothing you can do to stop him, Angie."

She stood aside, and Wills, the deputies, and Conan filed into the living room, a comfortably prosaic room with its overstuffed couch cluttered with comic books and plastic aliens and dinosaurs. Judge Wapner was dispensing Solomonic justice from the television.

Wills made a fast tour of the house, then returned to pass out assignments. He would begin in Angie and Cady's bedroom, Hoffsted would take Michael's room, and Neely would take the kitchen. And Angie could go on with her project in the kitchen. "Looks like you got a real nice potata salad going, Angie." She ignored that overture, and Wills didn't add that Neely was to watch her to make sure she didn't dispose of any evidence. Conan had no doubt that Angie understood that as well as Neely did. Angie was, after all, a policeman's daughter.

Finally Wills recognized Conan's presence. "Flagg, don't you have nothing better to do than hang around here?"

"No, Sheriff, can't think of a thing."

"I'll just bet you can't. Well, you stick with me. I want you where I can keep an eye on you."

Since Conan was equally determined to keep an eye on Wills, he only nodded and followed him as he strode through an arch to the right of the front door that gave access to a hallway on which four doors opened. The room at the front of the house was undoubtedly Angie's office. Conan caught a glimpse of file cabinets. The next was Michael's room, wallpapered in Trail Blazer posters. Next was a bathroom, and at the end of the hall, a bedroom. The furnishings there were Sears Ornate, the color scheme brown and beige, except for a quilted bedspread covered with pink flowers. Angie's influence, no doubt. Cady's influence was evident in the gun rack over the chest of drawers. Two shotguns and three rifles, one with telescopic sights.

Conan stood in the doorway and watched Wills attack the room with frenzied thoroughness, leaving behind a chaos of emptied drawers, boxes with their contents strewn on the floor, clothing heaped at the bottom of the closet, the bed a tangle. But Wills was doomed to disappointment, and after twenty minutes, he was apparently beginning to recognize that possibility, and his temper flared when Sonny Hoffsted came in to report that he'd found nothing in Michael's room or in the bathroom, and should he start in Angie's office?

Wills was on his knees pawing through a drawer full of Angie's lingerie. "Damn it, get on with it, Sonny!"

Ten minutes later, Wills gave up on the bedroom, passed Conan as if he didn't exist, and stormed into the office. Conan followed him. Hoffsted was peering into a file cabinet, lamenting, "Well, I never seen a manuscript, Giff. Makes it hard to know what I'm looking for."

"The gun!" Wills snapped. "Forget the damned manuscripts. It's that gun we're after." Then seeing Conan at the door, he demanded, "What do *you* want?"

Conan shrugged. "You told me to stick with you."

"Sonny, I'll be in the living room. Come on, Flagg."

While Wills began wreaking havoc in the living room, with Donahue and an avid audience arguing the fine points of date rape as background, Conan took up a position at the kitchen door. Neely was on a stepstool checking the contents of the cupboard over the refrigerator, and Angie was standing at the kitchen table stirring mayonnaise into a bowl of potato salad with vigorous strokes that suggested she might prefer to put the wooden spoon to better use. She nodded at Conan, then glared into the living room. "What's he *doing* in there?"

Neely climbed down from the stepstool, shaking her head. "That's just Hurricane Giff, Angie."

Wills's search of the living room was also fruitless, as were Neely's and Hoffsted's searches. Finally Wills stood at the kitchen door and shouted, "The garage! Come on, Sonny."

"Sheriff, we don't *have* a garage," Angie pointed out.

He glowered at her as if she were personally responsible for the missing garage, then gestured toward a closed door. "What's in there?"

It was Neely who answered, "It's a utility room, sir. I've already—"

But Wills wasn't listening. "Let's go, Sonny."

Hoffsted dutifully went, and for a few minutes the sounds of havoc in the wreaking were audible. Angie beat at the potato salad, said bitterly, "Neely, it's too bad you can't teach Giff how to do a search. Look at this kitchen, Conan. You'd hardly know she'd been here."

Neely laughed. "Well, I don't think anybody's likely to teach Giff anything." The she sobered abruptly as Wills and Hoffsted emerged from the utility room.

Wills crossed to the back door, gazed out at a weedy lawn where a swing set and inflatable wading pool in the shade of a willow tree were all that was visible to the fence lines. Wills said, "He probably buried the damn thing. Or threw it in the ocean. Or maybe *you* got rid of it, Angie. You had plenty of time. But if you think this is going to get MacGill off the hook, you've got another think coming!"

Angie gripped the potato-salad-smeared spoon like a bludgeon, her wide blue eyes startling against her flushed skin. "Giff Wills, it's *you* that's got another think coming! You didn't find one thing to prove Cady killed Ravin, did you? *Did* you?"

Wills eyed the shaking spoon and sidled toward the living room. "Just because I didn't find anything doesn't mean there's nothing to *find*!"

"Oh! You—you—" Angie moved menacingly toward him, sputtering incoherently, and Wills went pale as he backed into the living room, with Angie in hot pursuit, while Neely and Hoffsted turned eyes heavenward and hurried after him. But suddenly Angie halted, distracted by the chaos Wills had left in the wake of his search. From the television, a frizzy-haired woman insisted, "Some men just don't know when to stop."

Angie screeched, "What *happened* here?"

"Now, Angie," Wills began, one hand raised, palm out, presumably in a gesture of peace. "Angie, just calm down—"

"Calm down! It looks like a bull elephant was let loose in here, and *I just got through cleaning house*!"

She lunged for Wills, and Conan grabbed her around the waist, for which he was rewarded with a dollop of potato salad in his right eye, while Wills about-faced and ran for the front door, with Neely and Hoffsted right behind him. As they tumbled out onto the stoop, the spoon hurtled through the air, but before it could connect with Wills's head, Hoffsted slammed the screen door shut, and the spoon and its gelatinous burden collided with the screen with a mushy twang, stuck for a long moment, then clattered to the floor.

Angie let out a long, heartrending wail and burst into tears.

Conan put an arm around her shoulders, and when he heard the departing roar of Wills's patrol car, followed by the quieter rumble of Hoffsted's, he led her back to the kitchen, settled her in one of the chairs at the table, and found a paper towel to wipe away the potato salad adorning his face. By the time he pulled up another chair and sat down, her tears had run their course. She dabbed at her reddened eyes with a Kleenex. "Oh, I *hate* this! Every time I get mad, I start crying."

Conan nodded. "Well, you had provocation enough."

His sympathy almost started a new bout of weeping, but she firmed her quivering lips and went to the sink to splash water on her face. When she returned to her chair, she seemed in control of herself.

"Angie, has anyone told you that Gould's manuscripts—all three drafts plus his working notebooks—are missing?"

"What?" She sniffed and blinked, then shook her head. "No, nobody told me. Neely asked if I had copies or printouts. But I don't. All I have is the first forty pages of the fourth draft on disk. That envelope I took to the bookshop Saturday when . . ." She looked down at her hands knotted in her lap. "That was the printout of those pages."

"What happened to them?"

"I . . . well, I tore them up when I got home from the bookshop."

Conan frowned. "Why so few pages? Was that just what you happened to grab at the moment?"

"That was all I had right then. The way Ravin worked, he'd go over a chapter or two and mark it up—and sometimes I could hardly read it when he got through—then he'd give me a bunch of pages to type, anywhere from thirty to a hundred at a time."

"How did he give them to you?"

"He'd call me, and I'd . . . go down to his house to pick them up and bring him whatever I'd been working on."

No doubt those exchanges were made when Savanna was in Portland shopping or otherwise occupied outside the house.

"Angie, did you type any of the third draft?"

"Oh, yes. All of it."

"*All* of it? But you didn't keep a copy of any sort?"

Her eyes widened. "Me? Oh Ravin would've killed me if I kept copies of any of it. Of course, while I was working I made backup disks, but when I finished the third draft, he asked for the original disks—there were two of them—and told me to erase the backups."

Conan leaned toward her. "*Did* you erase them?"

"Yes. That was just last week."

He sagged back in his chair. "Do you know what Gould did with the original disks?"

"No. Weren't they at his house?"

"Apparently not. Were they marked?"

"Oh, yes. With Ravin's name and the title of the book."

Conan nodded. If the disks were well marked, Neely or one of Giff's crime scene team would have found them. Of course, it was possible that whoever stole the manuscripts also stole the disks. If they were at the house. And Conan was thinking about the safety deposit box Savanna had cleared out.

"Angie, do you still have the disks you erased?"

"Yes. I started the fourth draft on one of them. Well, they were already marked with Ravin's name, so I just put them aside for him."

"Is there any way you can . . . unerase them?"

She shook her head. "No. At least, *I* can't. I guess maybe it could be done if you had the right programs and you really knew what you were doing, but I'm not much of an expert when it comes to computers."

"You didn't erase the forty pages of the last draft?"

"Not yet."

"Can you give me a printout?"

"Sure." She rose, led him to her office. The small room had been intended as a bedroom, but now it was furnished with file cabinets, shelves of accounting manuals and printed forms, and a computer. There was a tiny, rainbow-striped apple on the front, but otherwise it and its accoutrements were a neutral beige, and he wondered if computer manufacturers hadn't early on paraphrased Henry Ford and said, "You can paint them any color you like as long as it's beige."

Angie looked around the office and breathed a sigh of relief. "Sonny must've searched this room. Thank goodness Giff didn't get at it, or I wouldn't be able to find anything for a week." She patted the computer as if to reassure herself that it was still intact, then had another fond pat for the machine next to it, which Conan assumed was a small copier until Angie said, "This is my pride and joy. It's a laser printer. Awfully expensive, but it puts out fabulous copy. Looks like it was printed, and my clients like that, even if it's just office accounts. Here, I'll run off those pages for you."

While Conan watched with the daunted amazement of one in the presence of arcane skill, she turned on switches, and the screen lighted, then she opened a small file filled with three-and-a-half-inch plastic squares bearing stickers on which she had written identifying notes. She slid one into a slot, waited while the machine made discreet, electronic burps, then when symbols enclosed in rectangles appeared on the screen, she manipulated a palm-sized box and, magically, lines of words appeared. Then another rectangle, more manipulation, after which she rose, leaving the machine to its own devices. The printer began softly whining as typed pages emerged from a slot on top.

But forty pages did not a manuscript make. "Would you be willing to part with the disks you erased?" Conan asked. "Maybe I can find an expert who can recover that third draft."

In fact, he had in mind an expert who could recover the third draft if anyone could. Manny Chavez, who lived in a log house fifty miles south in the Coast Range, a house furnished primarily with Manny's toys, his computers, on which he sometimes produced games, but more often industrial-strength computer programs that had made him a millionaire. Not that Manny had ever aspired to wealth. It just seemed to happen to him, and one of the beneficiaries of that happenstance was The Earth Conservancy, which was how Conan had first met him.

Angie took a tremulous breath. "I promised Ravin I'd never let anybody read his manuscript or even talk to anybody about it. But that doesn't matter anymore, does it?"

"No. What do you remember about the third draft? About the story."

"Not much," Angie replied, frowning. "The trouble is, when you're trying to figure out all the little notes and arrows and mark-outs, it's hard to keep track of what you're typing. What it really means, you know. And besides, I worked on it in bunches in between a lot of typing and accounting for other people.''

"But you must remember something about it." At least, he fervently hoped so.

"It was about a guy named Jimmy Silver. Funny name, I thought. It was the story of his life, except it wasn't told straight through."

"Gould used flashbacks, then?" And when she only looked at him blankly, he said, "Never mind. Go on."

"Well, this Jimmy Silver was a writer, and he traveled a lot and got into all kinds of trouble. He was into drugs in California, but that was back when they were doing stuff like LSD. He was a draft dodger, too, but they never caught him. Or did they? He *was* in jail for a while. In Texas, I think. Or maybe Alaska. And wherever he went, he kept meeting these gorgeous women and, well, going to bed with them. Ravin was . . . kind of specific about that. Sometimes I'd be sitting at my Mac just *blushing*. But sometimes when he wrote about places he'd been, it was beautiful. Made you feel like you were right there."

"Did Jimmy Silver spend any time on the Oregon coast? In Holliday Beach?"

"The Oregon coast, yes, but there wasn't anything about Holliday Beach. He grew up in a town called Forsuch Beach. Only, half the time Ravin spelled it Forsook. I asked him about that, and he said it was supposed to be spelled Forsuch, but it was pronounced Forsook." She shook her head at that evidence of creative inconsistency.

"What can you remember about that part of the story?"

"Oh, I don't know, Conan. I mean, it was scattered through everything else." A long sigh, then, "I remember Jimmy's father was a logger and a real lowlife. Treated Jimmy and his mother like dirt."

"Can you remember anything about the mother?"

"I can't even remember what *name* Ravin used for her. Something terrible happened to her, I think, but that was later. Of course, something terrible happened to nearly everybody. People got beat up or shot or knifed in just about every chapter."

"What about the father?"

"He got killed, too. Or maybe *he* killed somebody. Or did he just get run out of town? I'm sorry, Conan, I can't remember anything else. Like I said, I saw it in pieces, and I wasn't reading it like a book, and it was so confusing, the way he wrote it."

Conan stared at the lines of words on the screen. If the writer had been less paranoid, if the typist had been more attentive . . .

But at least there was still some hope. The erased disks. He understood only vaguely how information was encoded on those disks. For all he knew, once it was electronically erased, it was gone forever.

Manny Chavez would know—assuming Conan could get his attention long enough to ask the question.

"Angie, did you ever hear Gould use the phrase 'Doctor, lawyer, po-lice chief'?"

"No. Police chief? Could that mean Dad?"

"I don't know."

The printer swished out one last page, then stopped, waiting with machine patience to be commanded into action again. Angie picked up the sheets, and Conan asked, "May I see one of those?"

"Sure." She handed him a page, and he had to agree that the laser printer put out beautiful copy. It did not, however, produce copy at all like the manuscript fragment he'd found in the fireplace at the Eyrie. This was a sans serif type, for one thing.

"Will this thing print in different typefaces, Angie?"

"You mean fonts? Yes, I have eight different fonts, but most of the time I use Geneva. That's what this one is called."

He returned the page to her. "You used Geneva on the third draft?"

"Yes. I think it looks nice. Sort of modern-looking." She found a paper clip to fasten the sheets together and gave them to him.

"Thanks, Angie. Oh—the disks?"

"I almost forgot." She turned to the computer, maneuvered the small box, and a moment later a disk spewed out of its slot, then she flipped through the file and came up with another. "Here. Oh, Conan, I hope you will find what you're looking for on them."

"I hope so, too, Angie. I hope what I'm looking for is still there."

As Conan walked to his car, he checked his watch: one-fifteen. If he hurried, he could drive down to Manny Chavez's house and get back by the time Marcus Fitch arrived at the police station.

Conan slid behind the wheel of the XK-E. Maybe he could write a note, tie the disks to a rock, and throw them into Manny's house. The front door would probably be open.

It would also be guarded by Skookum, a massive black dog whose throaty baying always sent atavistic tingles down Conan's spine. It wasn't that he didn't like dogs. He had grown up around ranch dogs, and some of them had been close friends. But Skookum wasn't an ordinary dog. He was a husky-wolf mix. A mistake, Manny agreed, and not of his making. Nor had Skookum's former owners ultimately found such toying with wild genes a good idea, since Skookum decided their three-year-old daughter didn't understand her place in the pack hierarchy and enforced the lesson with a nip to her head that nearly blinded her. Skookum had been destined for the gas chamber when Manny rescued him.

Conan patted the disks in his pocket and started the motor. Skookum was really a marshmallow, Manny insisted, as long as you understood the rules.

CHAPTER 17

Conan sat on the XK-E's fender and watched Marcus Fitch, debonair in an off-white silk suit with a blue-gray shirt and tie, emerge from the police station to face a bevy of reporters armed with Nikons, video cameras, and tape recorders. He answered their questions with quotable flair, giving them everything they thought they wanted, yet revealing nothing they didn't already know.

It was a few minutes after four, and Conan had been waiting outside the station nearly half an hour. The trip to Manny Chavez's isolated log house had taken longer than he expected, but today he was lucky. He actually exchanged words with Manny, who was taking a break, sharing his lunch of a peanut butter sandwich with Skookum on his front porch. Skookum was downright mellow—due perhaps to the pacifying effect of the peanut butter, which had stuck to the roof of his mouth and kept that fanged orifice occupied—while Manny was almost talkative. He studied the disks Conan gave him, nodded through his explanation of the importance of recovering the data on them, then asked, "You want a printout?"

"Yes, of course I do. I mean, if it's possible."

Manny finished his sandwich, wiped his hands on his Greenpeace T-shirt, then rose and headed for his front door. "This'll take a while."

"How long?"

Manny shrugged as he disappeared into the shadows of his house, and Conan thought he heard him say, "I'll bring it to you."

Conan hadn't pursued the matter. Skookum's mouth was at last free, and he displayed his formidable canines and emitted a low growl, at which point Conan had decided the time had come for a cautious retreat to his car.

Now he straightened as the reporters finally dispersed, and Marcus Fitch sauntered over to him, looking down on him with hooded eyes. "Conan, you definitely owe me for this one."

"For all the free publicity? I'd think you owe *me*, Marc. You've seen your client?"

"Yes, the Incredible Hulk. And incredibly short on information. Conan, I want to know what the hell's going on here. Buy me a drink at the Surf House, and you can tell me all about it." And he strode toward his silver Rolls-Royce.

Conan drove to the Surf House in Fitch's wake, joining the southbound traffic on Highway 101, where the Rolls commanded a certain degree of deference. When Conan passed the bookshop, he noted that the KEEN-TV van had departed, only to be replaced by two more from rival Portland stations. Three blocks south of the bookshop, he followed Fitch through a right turn onto a gravel road that wound through a residential area to Front Street. A left turn there, and Conan caught glimpses of the sea between houses, and, farther south, between motels and condominiums. The Surf House was one of the oldest of the motels, and over the years it had added a restaurant, bar, swimming pool, tennis courts, shops, and more rooms in three-story blocks facing the beach, until at length it called itself a *resort*.

When Conan followed Fitch into the main parking lot, the office was besieged by a crowd armed with cameras, and now Conan knew where the KEEN-TV van had gone. Fitch found a parking space within a few feet of the covered walkway that led past the swimming pool to the restaurant entrance, while Conan had to tour the lot three times to find a spot, and that spot was at the far north end. As he began the trek back to the restaurant, he angled over to the walk fronting the newest units—or suites, as the discreet signs on the doors designated them. Savanna no doubt occupied one of them. He couldn't imagine the Surf House putting her in any of the older, more plebeian units. But apparently the reporters hadn't discovered her exact location. The only person he saw near the suites was a dark-haired woman in a loose white dress who was walking toward him through the parking lot. She was at least seven months pregnant, her gait flatfooted and swaying.

Conan shifted his attention to the resort office, saw another television van turn in from the street, this one from a Seattle station, and he wondered why the tragedies of the rich and famous were so fascinating to those who were neither. Perhaps it was a need to find out if their household gods bled when cut.

"Hello, Conan."

He stopped, startled, saw the pregnant woman a few paces away.

"Savanna."

She laughed, ran to him, and took his arm. "Oh, Conan, I *did* fool you, didn't I?"

He could only laugh with her and agree. "Damn right, you did."

And now he realized that the black hair was only a wig that on close examination would fool no one, nor would the padding under her dress. This disguise depended on distance. And skilled acting. The posture and gait had been entirely convincing. He touched the shiny fake hair. "Where did you find this?"

"Oh, I always keep it with me. Never know when it's going to come in handy." She glanced toward the office where yet another van—this one from Vancouver, B.C.—had arrived. "Come on, let's get inside."

She took a key out of her big straw purse as she led the way to Suite 115. Once inside the sitting room, she tossed the purse on a glass-topped table, swept off the black wig, shaking out her flaming hair, then pulled up her dress, unabashedly displaying her dancer's legs, untied the white sash that held the pillow, and flung the pillow on the couch. "Oh, you can't imagine how hot that thing gets. But it works."

"Very well, in fact. How are you, Savanna?"

She shrugged, her ebullient mood fading as she tied the sash around her waist and smoothed her dress, then crossed to the sliding glass door on the west wall, opened it to let the sound and the wind of the sea into the room. "I'm okay, Conan. I went to the local funeral home today. Nice couple running it. I made arrangements to have Ravin's body cremated, but I didn't know what to tell them about . . ." She turned to face Conan. "Ravin said he didn't have any family left here in Holliday Beach, but if any of his people are buried here . . . well, I think he should be buried with them."

Conan didn't know how to meet the plea in her eyes except to say, "I'll try to find out about his family."

"Thank you, Conan."

He nodded, then: "I was on my way to meet someone in the bar."

"Oh, do you have to leave now?"

"Yes, unfortunately." He paused, trying to read the shift in her mood, the veiled excitement in her eyes. "Savanna, you look like a kid who's just seen Santa Claus."

"Maybe I have," she replied with an enigmatic smile. "Lainey called me—Lainey Dixon, my agent—and she said Booth Kettering wants to talk to me about *Blitz*." Then, as if she were revealing a secret she could no longer contain, she added, "He's coming up to see me! Tonight!"

"Coming here?"

"Yes! Thank *God* you've got an airfield in this burg. He and Lainey are flying up in his plane, and she says he's ready to talk *contract*. Conan, this is—it's a new beginning for me! I'm coming back to *life*."

She was radiant, and Conan felt the warmth of her happiness as a tangible sensation. "Well, Kettering knows a perfect match when he sees one. Mona Fatale is yours, Savanna, and always will be."

She said in her best cockney. " 'Ow, dearie, yew'll turn me 'ead w' that kinda tolk!''

He pressed the palm of her hand to his lips, then turned and crossed to the door. ''Good luck tonight, Savanna.''

''Thanks, Conan. You know, I think *you're* my good luck.''

The Ebb Tide Lounge occupied the northeast corner of the restaurant. Its architect seemed to think drinkers were less likely to demand an ocean view than diners, and had given them a view of the swimming pool. Max Heinz, who could pass for an ex-boxer, although he'd never been one, was bartending, managing the summer crowd with the ease of long experience. When Conan came in, Max glanced up from pouring liquor with deceptive abandon and called out, ''Conan! I thought you were hibernating for the summer.''

''Well, I was wakened early this year. The usual for me, Max.''

Conan hadn't ordered a drink here for months, but Max would remember his usual. He had a bartender's memory. Conan found Marc Fitch at a table in the corner to the left of the entrance with *his* usual, Chivas rocks. He wasn't alone. Marian Rosenthal looked up from her whiskey sour when Conan joined them.

''Hi, Conan.'' Then she leaned toward him. ''That Max is amazing. When Marc walked in, Max told me, 'That's Cady MacGill's lawyer.' ''

Conan raised an eyebrow, but didn't speculate about how Max Heinz had learned that. Bartenders seemed to osmose information out of the air. ''How are you, Marian?''

''Weary, but it's after business hours in New York, so there's nothing more I can do today.''

Fitch flashed his spectacular smile. ''Except delight the benighted natives. Conan, Marian thinks I should write my autobiography.''

She laughed at that. ''I said he was telegenic, and I wished he'd written a book because he'd be so easy to promote.''

Max arrived at the table with Conan's Old Forester rocks. ''Marc tells me this round is on you.''

Conan nodded. "Marian, can I include you in that?"

"No, thanks. I'm just waiting for Justine and Byron. We're going to have an early dinner."

Max returned to the bar, and Conan asked, "What's made you so weary, Marian?"

"Trying to do my job from three thousand miles away." She sighed. "You know, there are times I wonder how I justify what I do."

"What do you mean?"

"Well, it seems . . . ironic that when a man dies in a very unpleasant fashion . . . he's suddenly worth his weight in gold. Harkness is going back to press with *Stud*. They're ordering an initial run of a *million* copies. And the average hardbound is lucky to sell ten thousand. Anyway, I have to organize a new promotion campaign."

Conan said casually, "That certainly puts a crimp in your vacation."

She stared at him, then managed a laugh. "What made you think I'm on *vacation*? By the way, I gather nobody's found the manuscripts."

"No, not yet."

"Poor Estes." Then she explained, "Estes Baruch. He's Harkness's CEO since we got conglomerated."

"Conglomerated? Even Harkness, the Great American Publisher?"

"American? We're part of a German conglomerate now. But the management is still American. Estes has been in the business forty years, but he's going to have a coronary over this. He'd sell his soul for *Odyssey* right now."

Conan glanced at Fitch, who was sipping his Scotch with his eyes half-closed, apparently tuned out of the conversation, but listening, Conan knew, to every word.

Conan said to Marian, "Byron Lasky seems in a mood to sell his soul for *Odyssey*, too. I saw him at the police station this morning." Her only response was a raised eyebrow, and Conan added, "Didn't you say he had no contract with Gould and no legal claim on *Odyssey*?"

"Well . . . yes, but Byron believes in his authors. I've seen him work for years to get a first novel published when he knew it wouldn't make enough money to cover the cost of his messenger service."

Conan let that non sequitur pass. "Is Lasky seriously ill?"

"I think so," she replied with a grimace and a sigh. "He won't talk about it, and neither will Justine, but a year ago Byron had a thick head of hair any man his age would envy. And now look at him."

"Chemotherapy or radiation, possibly?"

"That occurred to me. But I don't think it's any of my business."

"Nor mine?" Conan nodded, but he could still wonder privately how a possibly terminal illness might affect a person's attitudes. What's a life sentence or even the death penalty to a man who may be dying?

It was at that moment that Marian raised her right hand to push her glasses up, and Conan felt as if that hand had just connected with his solar plexus. Still, he managed to keep his face under control and even smile as he said, "That's a beautiful ring, Marian."

And it was beautiful: a wide band of turquoise inlaid with gold in a pattern of thick curves. It was the ring he had seen on Ravin Gould's hand Saturday night, the ring that had elicited a gasp of surprise from Marian when she saw it then. The ring that had not been on Gould's hand when Conan saw his body Sunday morning.

Her first response to his comment was an abortive attempt to put her hand and the ring out of sight, but apparently she thought better of that and spread her fingers as she looked down at the ring. "Thank you. It's a favorite of mine. Jacob gave it to me."

Now that he had a closer look, Conan realized that the odd shapes inlaid in gold were letters. Hebrew letters. "The design spells out a Hebrew word, doesn't it?"

"As a matter of fact, yes. *Ahava*." Then she glanced toward the bar, and her patent attempt to change the subject wasn't surprising. "Conan, there's something I wanted to tell you. Probably doesn't mean a thing, but see that elderly man at the far end of the bar? The one in the brown suit?"

Conan decided to leave the change of subject unchallenged. He turned, saw Doc Spenser, a nearly empty rocks glass clutched in one hand, sitting at the bar where it made a right angle to butt against the north wall. His plastic-rimmed glasses were crooked, and he sported a bandage on his right thumb, which wasn't unusual; in Doc's normal state of inebriation, he was a constant risk to himself around anything sharp.

Conan nodded. "What about him, Marian?"

"Well, Saturday afternoon after the brouhaha at the bookshop, I was here talking to Max. Of course, Max had heard all about it, and at the time . . . well, it just seemed funny. That man heard us talking and introduced himself. Doc Severinson? No, he plays trumpet."

"Dr. Maurice Spenser, but he likes to be called Doc. He was the first physician in this area, and I think he said something about knowing *Jimmy* Gould."

"He told me that," Marian said, "and he seemed fascinated with Ravin's new book. He kept asking me if I'd read it. And I kept telling him I hadn't, and I was sure nobody else had, either."

Conan sipped at his bourbon. "What else was he fascinated with?"

"Nothing, really. He left after a few minutes. It just seemed . . . odd, but it probably doesn't mean a thing."

"Probably not." Conan rose. "But I need to talk to him, anyway." He crossed the room and sat down on the empty stool next to Doc, who looked around at him, eyes unfocused and puffy. "Doc, how are you?"

He offered a mellowed smile. "Fine, Conan. Damn sure will be nice when Labor Day comes, won't it? All these strangers."

"Only a few more days, Doc. I understand you knew Ravin Gould's family." Then when the doctor frowned and raised his glass to empty it, Conan added, "You knew him as Jimmy."

Doc's glass hit the bar with a thump, which was as likely indicative of the fogginess of his vision as his state of mind. "Sure, I knew his family. Weren't many people around here I *didn't* know back then. I was the town *doctor*. Don't much remember Jimmy. He was just a kid when he and his mother moved away. That was after Tom left her."

"Tom? Jimmy's father?"

"Yeah. Damn. My glass is empty."

With some qualms, Conan took the hint and signaled Max to bring Doc another drink. Not that it would make any difference whether or not Conan provided the Scotch. If Doc wanted more, he would have it, and his capacity was legend.

Doc squinted into space and said, "Tom's folks lived in Westport. The old man was a logger, too. Tom settled here after he married Loretta. Maiden name was Ravin. That's where Jimmy got that name. She came from Portland, met Tom during the war."

Max brought his drink with a cheerful "Here you go, Doc," then added under his breath to Conan, "That's six since two." He returned to the other end of the bar to fill more orders.

If Doc heard that tally of his drinks, he gave no sign, only raising his glass and taking a swallow before he peered at Conan suspiciously, asked, "Why're you interested in the Goulds?"

"Jimmy's wife is making the funeral arrangements. She thought if any of his family are buried here, he should be buried with them."

"Oh. Well, Tom's folks are buried in Westport, and Loretta died in Portland. But Jimmy had a little sister. Marilyn. Red hair and blue eyes, just like her mother. She was only five when Loretta brought her to me burning up with fever. Polio. Everybody's forgotten about polio, and it wasn't that long ago when kids were dying right and left. Little children, crippled and dying." Doc seemed on the verge of tears.

Conan asked, "Marilyn was among the casualties?"

"Yes, rest her soul. She's buried in Crestview Cemetery, and maybe it'd be right, having Jimmy buried there, too. He really loved his little sister. But everybody did, she was so pretty and bright. Just like her mother. Poor Loretta. Don't think she was more'n eighteen when she married Tom. Might not've, if she'd been old enough to know better."

"Why not?"

"Because if . . ." Doc stopped, his eyes closing to slits as he downed half his drink in one swallow. "That was a long time ago. I'm going home. Too damn many strangers." He dismounted from his stool and with beleaguered dignity made his way to the entrance.

Max was taking advantage of a lull in orders to inventory the bottles behind the bar. He came over to Conan. "What'd you do to the old man? Never seen him leave anything in his glass before."

"I don't really know what I did, Max. By the way, were you on duty Saturday night?"

"Yes. I usually pull a double shift on Saturdays."

"The lady with Marc . . ."

"Marian Rosenthal?" Max asked. "What about her?"

"Do you remember seeing her here after, say, ten o'clock?"

Max picked up Doc's glass and wiped the bar with the towel that always seemed to be ready in his left hand. "She was here, Conan, but I can't be sure of the time. I do know she was still here at closing time."

"But you can't say whether she was here all the time from ten until two-thirty?"

"Nope. Saturday nights are always busy in the summer. I can keep my eye on people I think might make trouble, but Marian wasn't the troublemaking type. I just remember she seemed to be having a real good time. Liked the music."

"So she said. Do you know Byron and Justine Lasky?"

"Sure. Perrier twists and *very* dry martinis."

Conan smiled at that. "Did you see either of them Saturday night?"

"Not here. But I saw Mrs. Lasky. I took a cigarette break about midnight, and when it's not raining, I like to go over to that spot on the walk between the pool and the new suites. Kind of out of the wind, and I can see the ocean from there. As it happens, I get a good view of the front of the suites from there, too, and I saw Mrs. Lasky leave the building and go to her car and drive off. The walk's lit up at night, so I was sure it was her. She's the kind of woman you remember."

"She was alone?"

"Right. That seemed strange. I mean, she and her husband are like Siamese twins, you know. Always together."

"Did you see her return?"

Max laughed. "Hey, Conan, I was lucky to get *one* break Saturday night." His eyes narrowed as he looked toward the entrance. "Damn, speak of the devil. Or angels, for all I know."

Justine and Byron Lasky had just walked into the bar. Marian hailed them, and Conan watched while she introduced them to Marc, who rose and offered Justine a courtly bow. Byron Lasky seemed entirely recovered from the near panic Conan had seen this morning, and Justine, her exotic coloring enhanced with a scarlet blouse and white slacks, was smiling graciously. They did not, however, sit down, and Marian rose, seemed ready to leave, then began rummaging around in her big canvas purse.

Conan crossed to the table, arriving just as she took something out of the purse and started to hand it to Justine, but, perhaps distracted by Conan, dropped it. "Oh, damn . . ."

He leaned down to retrieve it. An amber plastic pill bottle. He managed to read three words on its label before he handed it to Marian: *Byron Lasky* and *Nembutal*.

Marian said, "Oh, thanks, Conan. Here, Justine, I'd better get these back to you before I forget."

Justine slipped the bottle into her slacks pocket, her smile cool as she faced Conan. "Mr. Flagg, how nice to see you again. I didn't realize earlier that we were in the presence of a genuine private investigator."

Byron offered a smile that, unlike his wife's, seemed quite sincere. "I hope that's not something you didn't want bandied about, Mr. Flagg."

"Well, it seems to invite bandying."

"I'm sure it does." Lasky's smile turned ragged around the edges as he asked, "Do you know if anyone has found the manuscripts?"

"No, not yet, Mr. Lasky."

Marian cut in, "Conan, what do you recommend for dinner here? I'm famished. Must be the sea air."

"Well, I like the stuffed sole, but I've never had a bad meal here."

That served as a signal for hurried—and it seemed to Conan nervous—leave-takings, and within a minute Marian and the Laskys had disappeared to seek a window table in the dining room.

Conan resumed his chair and his drink, while Fitch watched him with the intent patience of a cobra. He said, "Conan, I'll forgive you for dallying around while I sit here in miserable ignorance, because I find your Manhattan friends most interesting, and because I know bartenders are perhaps the best sources of information on Earth. But what about the old man? Did he offer a revelation?"

"No. Damn, I have to find out what *Odyssey* was about, Marc."

"Maybe you should look in a bookshop. Like your own. What kind of bookshop doesn't have at least one copy of Homer?"

"Not that *Odyssey*. Gould's last book. The manuscripts are missing."

Fitch reached for his Chivas. "Ah. Now we're getting down to the case on the docket. *Talk* to me, Conan. Tell me everything you know."

Conan talked to Fitch and answered his questions for half an hour, and finally Fitch seemed mollified, if not satisfied. There were too many gaps in Conan's knowledge to satisfy either of them.

At length, Fitch rose, glanced at his diamond-encrusted watch. "I've got another court gig in the morning, but I'll be back here tomorrow afternoon for MacGill's bail hearing. Not that any Taft County judge is likely to grant my client bail, but one must try. After all, that's what I'm getting paid for. Isn't it, Conan?"

Conan laughed as he walked with Fitch out into the entry hall. "Well, Angie said she was willing to work out your fee. I'm sure you could use a little help around the office."

"Are you talking about MacGill's ever-loving Angel?"

"Of course. She was Herb Latimer's secretary for four years. Almost his legal secretary, she says."

"An *almost* legal secretary trained by Herb Latimer?" Fitch pushed open the outside door, staring back at Conan. "Surely you jest!"

"Not at all. By the way, you were supposed to bring a package from Shelly Gage today."

"Well, unfortunately, I came to Holliday Beach straight from the Multnomah County Courthouse. I called my secretary on my car phone, and she told me about the lovely Shelly's visit, and yes, she did leave a package." They had reached Fitch's Rolls-Royce, and he unlocked the door and slid in behind the wheel. "What's in it?"

"I'll tell you about it tomorrow." He was not in a mood for more of Fitch's comments on his television appearance. "Just bring the package."

Fitch began backing out of the parking place without bothering to look behind him. Miraculously, he didn't hit the passing station wagon and its vacationing family, complete with at least four children and a cocker spaniel.

"Not to worry, Conan, I'll bring it. And then you will damn well reveal the contents of that package."

CHAPTER 18

Conan stood at the bar at the south end of his living room, a hand still resting on the telephone. It had been a one-sided conversation, Savanna bubbling on about Booth Kettering's imminent arrival, about the myriad calls and offers her agent had reported, about people she referred to by first names, whom he guessed he should recognize, but didn't. She was, as his father might have said, wound up like a ten-cent clock. Conan offered occasional comments so she'd know he was still on the line, but he wondered if she needed that. Perhaps. Her farewell had been equivocal: "Conan, oh, you sweet man, don't forget me."

As if she didn't know very well how impossible that would be.

He hadn't asked Savanna about her visit to the bank. He told himself he couldn't be sure Gould *had* put the original disks of the third draft in the safety deposit box.

Behind the bar, the lights in the cases that displayed Conan's collection of jade prayer wheels had automatically switched on as the last light faded on the horizon. He poured an Old Forester rocks and took it with him into the library. On the desk lay a plastic envelope containing the scrap of manuscript he had taken from the fireplace at the Gould condo, a legal pad and several sheets of notes, plus the first forty pages of Gould's fourth draft.

Conan sat down at the desk, lighted a cigarette, took a sip of bourbon, and thus fortified, picked up the manuscript. Ravin Gould's hook, his immortal first line, was: "My father was a fucking bastard." Conan groaned, but read on hopefully. Gould did not, however, amplify that lead in this chapter, which took place when Jimmy Silver, down to his last dollar and last toke, was living in an empty warehouse in New Orleans, where he not only found a willing and exotic fifteen-year-old girl to bed down, but was graphically beaten by the nymphet's pimp, and while lying bleeding in the rain, had a full-blown epiphany.

All this in forty pages. And none of it told Conan anything about Jimmy Silver's formative years in Forsuch Beach.

Conan grimaced as he tossed the manuscript aside. But there were other questions whose answers might be more accessible. He went to a shelf near the corner where the *Knight* brooded, pulled a book off the shelf, and took it to the desk. It was a Hebrew-English Dictionary.

All he had to go on was the sound of the word Marian Rosenthal had said was inlaid on the ring, and it took a while to translate the sound into a word: *ahava*. He had no doubt this was the word she intended. The dictionary translated *ahava* into the English word *love*.

Had Jacob Rosenthal given that ring to his wife? It didn't seem likely in view of the fact that it had been on Ravin Gould's hand Saturday night only a few hours before he was murdered.

It seemed far more likely that the ring had belonged to Gould's third wife, the daughter Marian still grieved.

Allison Rosenthal Gould.

Conan wrote *ahava* on the yellow page headed *Marian*.

He turned to another page, one headed *Dana*. There were few entries there. After a moment, he opened a drawer and pulled out a local phone book, found the listing for *Baysea Resort, motel office*. When he punched the number, a voice both young and feminine answered with "Baysea Resort, this is Tiffany."

Conan thought: *of course it is*. Aloud he said, "Yes, ma'am, this is Conan Flagg, and I'm investigating the murder of Ravin Gould."

There was a sharp "Oh" from Tiffany before she asked, "What can I do for you, Officer?"

Conan let the *officer* stand. "I'm checking a witness statement, ma'am. Was a Ms. Dana Semenov registered there last Saturday night?"

"Well, let me check . . ." Conan heard the click of computer keys, then Tiffany said, "Here she is. Room 1003 in the top tier. She's still registered, you know."

"Yes, ma'am. The witness claims there was a commotion in the top tier about one o'clock Sunday morning. Some intoxicated persons were singing loudly in the parking area. Did your office receive any complaints from other customers that would verify that claim?"

"Oh, yes, we got lots of complaints. Frank—he's the manager—went up with the security man, you know, but by the time they got there, the people had gone to their rooms and passed out. I mean, that's what Frank said probably happened."

"How many complaints did you have?"

"Let's see, there's a form I have to fill out if—oh, yeah, here it is. One, two . . . uh, five units called in. You want their names? They all checked out, you know, but we have the names and addresses."

"No, that won't be necessary at this time, but I'd appreciate it if you didn't destroy the list until you hear from me."

"Oh, I wouldn't do that anyway. Everybody who stays here, you know, goes on our mailing list."

"Was one of those complaints from room 1003?"

Tiffany took a moment to check her forms, then replied cheerfully, "Nope. No complaint from 1003."

When Conan hung up, he wrote: *Five complaints, none from Dana*, after the notation *Singing drunks—1:00 A.M.* And he wondered if Dana had actually heard the inebriated car-

olers or had been told about them the next morning by one
of the complainers.

His next call also went to Baysea, this one to the Orca
Lounge, where he learned that the bartender on duty tonight,
one Dion Lake, had also been on duty Saturday night. Yes,
he remembered a tall, attractive blonde. He *always* remembered tall, attractive blondes, although this one was maybe
a little thin-shanked. Vodka, ice-cold and straight up. He
even knew her name, because she paid her tab with an American Express card. Dana Something. The accounting department could find it. They had all the charge card slips.

Conan asked, "Can you remember approximately when
this Dana arrived and when she left?"

Dion had to think about that. "Well, she must've come in
about ten-thirty. I didn't go on till ten, and it wasn't long
after that when this bim—uh, this lady came in and sat down
at a table in the corner. All by herself, but she wasn't interested in company. When I was delivering a round to the next
table, I heard her tell one guy to bugger off. Said she was
expecting somebody."

Conan made a note on Dana's sheet. "Did that somebody
appear?"

"Nope. A little while later, she left."

"Can you be more specific about the time?"

"Hey, it was a Saturday night. We were busy. I'd say it
was maybe eleven-thirty when she left. Could've been later,
I don't know."

Conan thanked Dion and hung up, made a notation on
Dana's sheet, then picked up the plastic envelope and studied the manuscript fragment. Was it something that Gould
had deleted from the third draft? If so, why had Savanna
burned it?

And why didn't he just ask her?

Because, he reminded himself, staring into the corner at
the *Knight*, it wasn't always wise to reveal evidence to a
suspect.

Was Savanna Barany still a suspect?

Conan put the envelope aside and lighted another cigarette

before he again reached for the telephone. This was a long-distance call. It went to Steve Travers in Salem.

He found Steve at home, apparently watching a baseball game. "Okay, Conan, it's the seventh-inning stretch, so what's going on down there?"

"If you really want to know, it'll be a long stretch."

Steve sighed. "Well, it's a lousy game anyway."

"By the way, is the Oregon State Police's official policy still to give Giff Wills his head?"

"Right. But we're keeping a tight rein on him. He just doesn't know it yet. In fact, we've been taking care of a few details for him, just in case he forgets."

"Details like what?"

"Like a search of the Gould condo. But before I start spilling all my beans, I want to hear what you've got to say for yourself."

Conan had a lot to say for himself. He referred occasionally to his notes, sometimes adding a question as it occurred to him. Yet when he had finished his account, it seemed pitifully devoid of substance.

Steve, however, was impressed enough to say, "It'll do for a start."

"It damn well better." Conan picked up his glass, noting that the ice had melted down to transparent pebbles. "So now it's your turn. What about the autopsy?"

"It's done. We had the body sent to the state M.E.'s lab, and Dan Reuben did the autopsy himself. He faxed me a copy of the report. Just a minute, let me get my briefcase." There was a silence, then after a minute or so, a rustle of papers. "Okay, Dan says the cause of death was a twenty-two caliber bullet fired into the heart at point-blank range, probably from a small handgun. If the gun ever turns up, he extracted the bullet for ballistics. Time of death, between 11:00 P.M. and 2:00 A.M., give or take an hour or so."

"When did Gould get his throat so crudely cut?"

"*After* he was shot. That's as far as Dan would commit himself. He says it's hard to pin down the time on a post-mortem wound."

"What else did he come up with?"

"A blood alcohol content high enough to kill some people in itself. Other than that, nothing. No marks on the body to indicate a struggle."

"Which might mean that when Gould was shot, he was unconscious due to his high Bruichladdich content?"

"High what content?"

"Bruichladdich. It's a single-malt Scotch. Gould's poison of choice."

"Well, he wasn't alert enough to fight back when somebody pulled a gun on him." Steve hesitated, then, "Damn it, why would somebody shoot him dead, then go to the trouble of nearly cutting off his head? Why take the extra risk of breaking into your bookshop to steal the chain saw?"

"Maybe it was symbolic, Steve." Conan blew a lopsided smoke ring while he waited for the predictable explosion.

"Symbolic! You mean a satanist killing, like Gould was some sort of sacrificial lamb? Who ever heard of sacrificing a lamb—or goat or virgin or whatever—with a chain saw?"

"Well, Taft County does have a few satanists in its wide lunatic fringe, but I'll admit a chain saw is an unwieldy tool for a sacrificial coup. Did Giff's crime scene team turn up anything at the murder scene? They sent everything to the OSP Crime Lab, didn't they?"

"Yes, and I've got an inventory and a report on that, too. Giff's men picked up some glass fragments sifting through the stuff off the carpets in the living room and office, and they match the glass from your shop."

"Not exactly a revelation. Steve, did anyone find any computer disks in the house? I think they'd have noticed, since the disks were marked with Gould's name and *Odyssey*."

"Let's see . . . no, nothing here about computer disks."

"What about fingerprints on the saw?"

"There were plenty, including yours, but the rest were MacGill's. Interesting thing, though, the lab guys found a fragment of something caught in the chain. Maybe plastic or rubber. They're working on it."

Conan frowned as he took a swallow of watered-down whiskey. "Anything else at the scene?"

"Not a hell of a lot. All the fingerprints check out with people who had good reason to be in the house. No tracks outside or tire prints, since it's been so dry. No sign of breaking and entering. Of course, Earl said Byron Lasky wasn't sure whether he locked the door after his visit Saturday night. And if he didn't—hell, anybody could've walked in there. A perfect stranger, for all we know."

"A perfect stranger with a motive to murder Ravin Gould?"

"From what I hear about Gould, there might be hundreds of people who wanted him dead, and anybody could drive in and out of Holliday Beach without leaving a trace. Even if they flew in, they'd land at Baysea's airfield, which isn't exactly Portland International. Most of the time there's nobody there, except when the helicopter shuttle picks up or delivers passengers."

Conan took a drag on his cigarette, thinking of Kara Arno and her two children, wondering how they were playing out the hand that fate had so indifferently dealt them. "Well, you've lost one possible witness at the Baysea airfield."

"You mean the pilot? Earl told me about him. Arno helped us find a homicide suspect in the Coast Range a couple years back. Damn, you know, that . . . well, I get nervous with coincidences. And yes, I know they happen all the time."

"What do you mean by coincidences?"

"That pilot crashing Saturday night—the night of Gould's murder."

Conan's cigarette scattered a shower of parks when he dropped it on the floor. He leaned down to pick it up and crushed it out in the ashtray. "Saturday night? Earl told me Arno crashed on *Sunday*."

"Actually it *was* Sunday. Sometime after three in the morning."

Conan felt a shiver of excitement, yet it faded in moments. Before he got mystic about this juxtaposition of events, of deaths, he had to find some connection between them stronger than their timing.

"Steve, do you have a report on the Gould condo?"

"Yes. I sent Jeff Kaw up to take care of the search. He

got an official statement from the Herndons, too. I looked it over. They hadn't changed their story.''

''What about the condo?''

''No sign of the gun or the manuscripts. Jeff said it looked about as lived in as a hotel room. Except he found some charred scraps of paper in the fireplace. Real strange, you not noticing them.''

Conan smiled at the sarcasm in that. ''Glad to hear somebody got to them before the cleaning crew came in.''

''Yeah, well, the lab's working on—damn! Look at that sucker go!''

''What sucker?''

''The ball! Canseco just hit a home run—with two men on!''

''All right, Steve, I can take a hint. Call me if anything interesting turns up.''

''Mm? Oh, sure, Conan.'' And Steve hung up without further ado.

Conan leaned back in his chair and rubbed his eyes, then again read through his notes, irritably noting all the question marks. He read them again, hoping inspiration would hit so he could strike out some of those marks. Instead, he found himself adding more question marks.

At length he reached for the phone again.

After six rings, Earl Kleber answered irritably, ''This had damn well better be a real emergency.''

Conan looked at his watch: eleven-fifteen. And Earl Kleber believed in rising at the crack of dawn. ''Well, not exactly, Earl.''

''Flagg?'' Kleber groaned. ''What the hell do you want?''

''Can you get me more information on Dan Arno's crash?''

Another groan, then: ''Probably, but for God's sake, *why*?''

Conan thought, *so I can get to sleep tonight*. He said, ''I'm not sure, Earl. Maybe it's just that coincidences make me nervous.''

''Right. Tomorrow, Flagg. *Maybe*.'' And he hung up.

CHAPTER 19

At eight-forty Tuesday morning, Conan found the parking lot at the Surf House swarming with vehicles displaying newspaper, magazine, radio, and television logos. He parked on the street, noting the crowd outside Savanna's suite. The hounds had run her to earth.

Five of the hounds were waiting to use the phone booth near the restaurant. Conan went to the office and found the two pay phones there occupied by more reporters reeling off stories. But he had the advantage of knowing the clerk, Helen Day, who was among the bookshop's most loyal customers. She let him use the phone behind the counter. The voice that answered his call wasn't Savanna's, but when he identified himself, Savanna was on the line in a matter of seconds.

"Conan! Oh, Conan, where *are* you?"

"In the Surf House office, and I'm at your service. Besides, Giff said you wouldn't go to the beach house without an escort."

A sigh, then, "I just can't face that place alone."

"Who's your telephone receptionist?"

"Oh, that's Lainey. Booth had to fly back last night, but, oh, Conan, this thing is bigger than I ever *dreamed*. I mean,

170

what he wants to do with *Blitz*—special effects and Dolby sound and Belikova for the choreography. It's going to be incredible!''

Conan saw one of the reporters eyeing him curiously. "You deserve nothing less. Now, how do you want to manage your departure?''

"I'll just *walk* out, that's all. I'm sick of hiding, and Lainey says I should get it over with. Let them see me, anyway, and take some pictures. So just drive over and honk twice.''

Conan retrieved his car and, as instructed, honked as he neared Savanna's suite, and she emerged, soberly attired in a simple cotton dress of black with black-rimmed sunglasses, to meet her clamoring public, which included fans and the curious as well as the media. The woman at her side sported a fluorescent sundress and a tangled pouf of dark hair that nearly hid her face. Lainey Dixon, no doubt. Conan pushed through the crowd and a din of shouted questions and whining shutters until he reached Savanna, then he began elbowing a path back to the car. She clung to his arm as she parried the verbal barrages fired at her. "Please . . . that's all I can tell you now . . . I just don't know. . . .''

Lainey Dixon remained at the door, shouted, "I'll answer any questions I can,'' but got few takers. Savanna's entourage stayed with her, moving as one wriggling, noisy mass. Conan helped her into the XK-E, hurried to the driver's side, slammed the door on more questions, then revved the motor to a warning roar as he drove forward, and the multimouthed creature divided, coalesced again behind the car. Once out of the parking lot, he turned north on Front Street, checking his rearview mirror, and he wasn't surprised to see that some of the reporters had resorted to their vehicles.

"Savanna, we're being followed. Do you want me to lose them?''

She laughed, a sound inimical to her sober attitude to this point. She looked out the back window, said gleefully, "I'll bet you *can't*.''

It was a game to her, but Conan was willing to play. He accelerated for breathing room, then turned off Front Street, careened along a zigzag course through familiar back streets, reached the highway, and spurted across it in the path of an oncoming log truck, and all the while Savanna laughed with the abandon of a child on a roller coaster. But one van managed to stick with them. Conan made a squealing left turn, sped north on a residential street, then after five blocks, swung hard right, while Savanna gasped and fell against him. Two more blocks, then another right turn, and when he came out of it and gunned the Jaguar south, she was still laughing.

Foothills Boulevard Road, named in hope by the founders of the village, was only a graveled byway with few houses along it. He managed to hit forty briefly on this stretch, then braked for a left turn and slowed to a reasonable ten miles an hour on the narrow lane that wound to the top of a hill and Crestview Cemetery.

He doubted Savanna had seen the sign that would have warned her of their destination. When she realized where she was, she lost any inclination to laughter. He stopped and got out of the car to listen for the van, but heard nothing. He opened Savanna's door, and she took off her sunglasses as she emerged, gazing up at the ancient Sitka spruces at whose roots the gravestones huddled. The silence here had nothing to do with the slabs of marble and granite. The trees owned this silence.

"Oh, Conan, this is *beautiful*," she whispered.

"You asked if any of your husband's family were buried in Holliday Beach. Only one. His sister, Marilyn. She died of polio."

"Oh, yes, now I remember. Ravin told me about her. He said when she died, it was the first grief he'd ever felt . . . and the worst."

Conan saw tears in her eyes as she bent to pick a Queen Anne's lace blossom, studied its delicate fretwork, then again looked around her. "This is where he'll be buried," she said. "That's why you brought me here, isn't it? You knew this is where Ravin should be buried."

Conan didn't deny that, yet if he'd had any motive in bringing her here—other than eluding the van—it was to shake her out of her stage persona and perhaps to remind her of something she seemed to constantly forget: that her husband had been murdered.

But he wondered what he would find beneath her stage persona. She was still wearing it, and it fitted her so exquisitely, he had to ask himself if it should—or could—be put aside.

"Conan? What is it? Oh . . ." She reached for his hand. "Is somebody you loved buried here?"

That was true, in fact, but he only smiled and opened the car door for her. "We'd better get down to Dunlin Beach. The sheriff is waiting."

Toward the end of Dunlin Beach Road, a white Highway Patrol car blocked the road, the patrolman standing guard in front of this erstwhile barrier. He didn't stop them. Gazing raptly at Savanna, he waved them around. There was barely enough space at the side of the road for Conan to clear the patrol car, and he winced at the scrape of pine branches along the XK-E's side.

When they reached the house, Giff Wills was waiting by his car. He hurried to the XK-E to offer Savanna a hand out. "Thanks for coming, Ms. Barany," he said in an atypically hushed, awestruck tone.

"I guess I had to face it sooner or later," she said, regarding the house with patent dread. When Wills started up the flagstone path, she took Conan's arm, her grip tightening as they approached the front door. There she paused, then resolutely marched inside.

"All I need to know," Wills said, "is whether anything's missing."

She wrinkled her nose as she stepped down into the living room. "My God, the buffet's still here. Couldn't somebody clean up that food?"

But she didn't seem to expect an answer. She was staring at the couch, at the torn and bloody pillows. She said nothing, instead began a survey of the house. Conan accompanied her, with Wills like a shadow a few paces behind. She began with the kitchen, glanced indifferently at the detritus of Saturday night's party. She was equally indifferent—

although it seemed more studied—when she led the way into the master bedroom, with its pseudotropical decor and king-size water bed and the hot tub on the adjoining patio. In the walk-in closet, she touched a man's leather coat, then turned, went into the bath. Towels and clothing had been left where they fell.

She retreated from the bedroom, crossed the living room without looking at the couch, and went into the office, where she gazed for some time at the typewriter.

Conan asked, "Savanna, do you mind if I use this typewriter?"

She looked at him curiously. "No, I don't mind."

Wills, Conan was sure, *did* mind, but couldn't seem to think of a reason to stop him. Conan took a blank sheet of paper from the box at the back of the desk, typed out two alphabets, one lowercase, the other in capitals, then folded the paper and put it in his shirt pocket.

By then, Savanna had moved on to the bedroom that opened off the office, and when he joined her there, with Wills serving sentry at the door, Conan saw that the room had been converted into an exercise room, furnished with a stationary bicycle, a rowing machine, and a racklike arrangement that no doubt converted to a number of excruciating uses. "Ravin wouldn't let me put in a barre," she said. "He kept saying we were just renting. . . ."

At length she returned to the living room. Again she didn't look at the couch. "Nothing's missing, Sheriff. You know, I've got to get this cleaned up before I go. Is it all right if I have Mrs. Early in tomorrow?"

"That'll be okay, Ms. Barany. We're done with the house."

"And are you finished with *me*? I want to schedule the funeral for Thursday morning, and I promised my agent I'd be in L.A. by Thursday night. Sheriff, it's vitally important."

Wills seemed to go limp under the full wattage of her appealing gaze. "We'll, ma'am, I don't see any reason why you can't leave. We should have this thing wrapped up by tomorrow."

Conan managed not to groan aloud, but he couldn't quite stomach Wills's warm-pudding grin while Savanna offered her gratitude. He cut in, "By the way, Savanna, have you heard from your husband's lawyer?"

"No. I don't know why I would. He wasn't *my* lawyer."

"But he might know if Gould made a will."

The sheriff frowned balefully at that, and Savanna said indifferently, "Well, I haven't heard from him." She looked around the room and shivered. "Conan, I'd like to get out of here."

He nodded. "Sheriff?"

"Mm? That's fine. Uh, Ms. Barany, I was wondering . . ." He took his notebook out of his breast pocket, and while Savanna smiled sympathetically, he asked, "Could I have your autograph?"

Conan watched her write: "Best wishes to Giff Wills, the nicest sheriff I've ever known." And probably the *only* sheriff she'd ever known, Conan thought, as she signed her name with a dramatic flourish.

At the Surf House, the reporters had either left in frustration or taken a coffee break. There were a number of marked cars and vans in the parking lot, but no one was waiting at Savanna's door. Conan stopped the XK-E there and turned to face her. She hadn't spoken since they left the Dunlin Beach house.

"Savanna?"

She sighed. "It's just that house. Conan, come see me this evening. I mean, just to have dinner and talk."

"Won't you and Lainey have plenty to talk about?"

"She's leaving in a couple of hours."

"All right, Savanna. I'll call you later."

"Don't forget." She leaned toward him, and he closed his eyes, finding in the scent of her perfume, the softness of her lips, a poignant echo. Then she pulled away, got out of the car, and hurried to her suite.

Conan took a deep breath and began patrolling the parking lot for an empty slot. It was nearly eleven. As good a time as any for an early lunch. Or late breakfast. He'd only had time for a cup of coffee this morning after Wills phoned him for escort duty.

He found a parking place, made his way to the restaurant, walked down the hall past the bar, then descended five slate steps into the dining room, where the hundred-foot arc of windows offered a stunning panorama, and nothing stood between the viewer and the horizon but miles of sea. The dining room was crowded, even for August, the noise level daunting, but Tilda Capek Tally, slender and Dresden-delicate, was an oasis of graceful calm. She was serving as hostess today.

"Conan, it's good to see you. Brian said he'd heard you were back and hard at work. At least, that's the gossip." Then with a soft laugh, "But the gossip is not always to be believed."

"In this case, you can believe it, Tilda."

"Then I wish you good luck. Are you having lunch? Good, I have a window table." She led him to a small table in the northwest corner where he would have a view not only of the beach, but north to the distant Lands End Point. He seated himself to face that view, while Tilda handed him a menu before departing. He made a leisurely study of the menu and had decided on the razor clams for which the restaurant was justly famous when a movement caught his eye.

This vista included an oblique view of the west façade of the building that housed the new suites, and a figure had appeared on one of the first-floor balconies: a woman in yellow slacks and blouse, her hair hidden under a straw hat, her eyes hidden by black-rimmed sunglasses. A big straw purse was slung over her shoulder. She looked down at the beach, which was at least ten feet below her; the railings on the first-floor balconies were built on top of a concrete sea-wall. There was, of course, an easy access to the beach: the ramp south of the restaurant. But this woman apparently didn't want an easy access. She swung her legs over the railing and dropped into the sand, landing without losing her footing, then set off northward at a casual stroll.

Savanna. Had she taken this precipitous route to the beach simply to avoid being seen by the reporters?

Savanna's ambling course took her close to the water's edge, where she seemed to find various flotsam and jetsam to examine. The beach was well populated, some of the beachgoers having chosen a spot to make a temporary home furnished with folding chairs, picnic baskets, and coolers, while others vicariously took to the sky with kites glowing like stained glass in the sun, and still others jogged or ran with stoic determination. The less determined were content to simply walk in solitude or in groups, and dogs of every size and kind lounged, played, jogged, ran, or walked along with their human alphas.

"Have you decided what you'd like, Mr. Flagg?"

Conan looked up at the waitress, then shook his head. "Not yet."

She tapped her pencil against her order pad. "Okay. I'll be back."

Savanna had stopped, stood facing the sea. He studied the people around her, fixing finally on another woman—she was also carrying a large purse—walking toward Savanna from the south. The woman had neglected to cover her hair. Her cornsilk blonde hair.

Dana Semenov.

Savanna watched Dana as she approached, and neither seemed pleased at this encounter, although it couldn't by any stretch of the imagination be accidental. They both stood stiffly, arms folded, yet no more than two feet separated them. They talked briefly, then Dana took a manila envelope from her purse, gave it to Savanna, and it disappeared into Savanna's purse. At that point, Dana began walking briskly back toward the resort and, no doubt, the ramp south of the restaurant. Savanna walked north, maintaining her casual pace.

Conan watched Savanna until she turned toward the bank. There was a public beach access there that would take her to Front Street, and a three-block walk would bring her back to her suite.

With a sigh of regret, he put the thought of lightly crusted razor clams, tender enough to cut with a fork, out of his mind and left the table, passing the startled Tilda on his way up the steps to the entry hall. Outside the restaurant, he angled north and east through the parking lot to reach Front Street. He noted that a cluster of reporters had again gathered around Savanna's suite.

On Front Street, he sighted Savanna before she did him, but when she was half a block away, she paused, then hurried toward him. She didn't remove her sunglasses, but she was smiling. "Conan, I finally found a way to get out of my suite without any of them seeing me."

"Rather a dangerous way, going over the seawall. There might've been a log or a broken bottle buried in the sand where you landed."

"You *saw* me?"

"Yes, I was in the restaurant. I also saw your meeting with Dana."

She sobered, and her voice went husky. "You were *spying* on me."

"Actually, I had nothing more nefarious in mind than lunch. What's in that envelope she gave you?"

"Oh, for God's sake, as if that's any business of yours."

"When two of the suspects in a murder meet clandestinely, I have to wonder about it."

"So wonder all you like!" And she strode past him.

He fell in step with her. "By the way, there's a collection of reporters at your door."

She stopped. Then her chin came up, and she set out again.

And he kept pace with her. "Savanna, you know I'm investigating your husband's murder, and I can't just look the other way—"

"But I damn well didn't know you still thought I was a *suspect*! Conan, I trusted you. I thought you trusted me. I thought you . . ." And again she stopped, turned away from him.

He said quietly, "It's hard to trust you when you set up a secret meeting with someone you've led me to believe you despise."

Savanna faced him, but the dark lenses made her expression unreadable. "I *do* despise Dana. But in any kind of business, you've got to deal with people whether you like them or not. What she gave me was a contract to show Lai-

ney. Dana called me yesterday and said Nystrom wants to
publish my autobiography. They want a kiss-and-tell book,
but I don't care. She says they'll hire a ghostwriter and have
it on the shelves in a month, and she guarantees it'll be a
best-seller. And Nystrom is offering a four-million-dollar advance.''

Conan raised an eyebrow. "Is this to be a hardbound
book?''

"Yes, of course.''

"A hardbound on the shelves in a month. Well, congratulations, and I'm sure you won't mind letting me see the
contract.''

"What?'' She seemed appalled at the suggestion. "No!
Damn it, it's none of your business. Now, just leave me alone.
I've had enough of this stupid investigation, and I've had
enough of *you*!'' And she again set off for the Surf House,
pausing only once to aim a Parthian shot: "Don't bother
trying to call me. You won't get through!''

Conan didn't attempt a reply, but simply watched her walk
away from him. Finally he followed, but he was on his way
to his car, and his thoughts were focused on Dana Semenov,
who had now become a player in this game, one to be taken
seriously.

If in fact the manilia envelope had contained a contract,
there would be a copy somewhere. Possibly in Dana's room
at Baysea.

Conan seldom indulged in illegal searches, not only because they *were* illegal, but because he was too jealous of his
own privacy to invade anyone else's without some qualms.

But there were occasions when he had no choice.

CHAPTER 20

Past Sitka Bay, Highway 101 cut through a dense stand of wind-bent jack pines for a mile before a billboard-sized sign announced the entrance to Baysea Resort, and Conan turned right onto a paved road that struck out toward the sea. He was driving his faithful blue Vanagon. When he had stopped by his house for the van, a vehicle Dana Semenov was unlikely to recognize, he had also clothed himself in a manner that was unlikely to attract attention when he picked the lock on Dana's room in broad daylight: a tan coverall with *Henry* embroidered in red on the pocket, a billed cap, and dark glasses. On the passenger seat was an old wooden toolbox with screwdrivers, hammers, and wrenches plainly visible. What wasn't visible was the only tools he would actually need: a set of lock picks in a leather case. Of course, all this subterfuge might be in vain if Dana had decided to spend the day in her room.

Baysea had leveled a small forest to accommodate their resort, but they had left enough trees standing to provide a shadowed lane along this approach. Where the trees ended, Conan looked down on Baysea Resort, laid out before him in all its boxy glory. The motel units were arranged in two-story clusters tiered up the slope, landscaped with pines pruned like Westminster Dog Show poodles.

He knew Dana's room number and its location, thanks to the helpful Tiffany, so he turned right into the parking area east of the first block of units, noting that the maroon Skylark was not, to his relief, in front of 1003, then he drove down to the parking area for the tier below and found an empty slot for the Vanagon. He looked up at the west façade of the first tier, noting that each room was provided with a minuscule balcony. With his toolbox in hand, he walked around to the door of 1003, knocked—just in case—then after a few minutes of painstaking manipulation, opened the lock.

The room was large, its accoutrements styled in hotel/ motel provincial. There were two big windows, one facing inland toward the trees, the other facing the sea, but the drapes were closed on both views. He opened the east drapes about two feet, crossed to the west drapes and opened them a similar span, opened the sliding door to the balcony, left his toolbox there, then went to work.

His initial survey was disappointing. There were no papers visible on any flat surface, nor did he see a briefcase, and he couldn't believe that Dana Semenov traveled without a briefcase.

He opened her suitcase, which rested on the shelf at the end of a long, screwed-to-the-wall arrangement of desk and chest of drawers, and found that Dana had a penchant for lacy lingerie, which surprised him. Most of the jewelry in the velvet case was gold, and all of tasteful quality, which didn't surprise him. There was a jar of Yuban instant decaffeinated coffee. He opened it, sniffed at its contents. Apparently it contained exactly what was advertised on the label. It was half-full, and Dana probably carried it only for emergency use. On the table near the west window were the remains of a room-service meal, including a thermos carafe. Conan closed the suitcase and crossed to the table to unscrew the top of the carafe and determine that it contained a cup or so of still warm coffee. He wondered how many of these carafes Baysea lost to theft. It was handsomely designed, made of satin-finished steel with a red enamel cap. Dana's lunch had been a spare meal: a salad dressed with lemon juice, Rykrisp, coffee, and water. Perhaps this was how she maintained her fashionably emaciated figure.

Conan's eyes narrowed. There were *two* water glasses on the tray. He leaned close to examine the glasses. Both had lipstick on the rims, and both were pale pink, but one was a warmer hue.

He crossed to the east window to make sure the Skylark wasn't heaving into view, then went back to the desk/chest and opened the drawers. Except for the usual phone book, stationery, and Gideon Bible, the drawers were empty. Then he checked under the bed and lifted the mattress, and as he was restoring the bedclothes, he thought absently that Baysea was stingy with its pillows. There were only three where he would expect four. He opened the drawers of the bedside tables, then turned to the closet and knelt at the open door to run his fingers across the soles of Dana's shoes in the futile hope of finding glass fragments visible to his naked eye or tangible to his naked fingertip.

There were only two pairs of shoes: sandals with thin, interlaced straps, and high-heeled, beige pumps. Dana was traveling light. A black satin robe and a lacy nightgown hung in the closet along with a pair of white slacks, a green silk blouse, a white linen jacket, the beige dress she'd worn Saturday night, and a raincoat. But this coat was pale blue, and he remembered that the coat she wore when she made her entrance at Gould's house was tan. It didn't seem likely that she would be wearing it now, not with the temperature rising to a sizzling—for the coast, at least—eighty degrees, and why would she bring two coats on this trip when she had packed so few clothes otherwise?

And something else was missing: the paisley scarf Conan remembered so clearly from Saturday night because it was the twin of the one he'd bought in London for Aunt Dolly.

He almost missed the navy canvas flight bag in the darkness at the back of the closet. It was empty, except for an outside pocket. He unzipped it and found a folded map. A map of Portland and environs. He spread it out on the end of the bed. There were no marks on it.

Why would Dana want a map of Portland?

Conan heard the soft rumble of a car motor and went to the window, breathing a sigh of relief as a white Lincoln with an elderly couple in the front seat passed.

He folded the map, slipped it into the side pocket of the flight bag, and returned the bag to the closet. Next, he went into the bathroom, pushed back the shower curtain, then checked the wastebasket, and went so far as to take the lid off the back of the toilet and look inside. There were no drawers, no other hiding places. Conan studied the bottles and jars by the sink, noting that Dana's choices in perfume were White Linen and Obsession. In a leather cosmetic bag he found a plastic pill bottle. He read the label, and one eyebrow shot up. Nembutal.

Nembutal seemed to be popular in the Big Apple. But then, he was well aware that Nembutal was popular anywhere in this country. Dana apparently had some trouble sleeping. There were only ten capsules left out of a prescription for fifty, and it had been filled a week ago. But maybe she hadn't brought along the full prescription.

Again he heard the rumble of a motor, and crossed to the east windows, and when he looked out, abruptly pulled his head back. The Skylark was approaching, and it was already close enough so that he could be sure it was Dana at the wheel.

He didn't try to restore the drape to its original position, but sprinted across the room to the west window, picked up the toolbox and slid the door shut, paused only long enough to see if anyone was in the parking lot below, and when he saw no one, vaulted the balcony railing. Then, controlling the urge to run for the Vanagon, he slowed to a casual walk as he made his way down the grassy slope to the asphalt. When he reached the van, he put the toolbox behind the driver's seat, swung in, and drove to the north end of the parking lot and around to the top tier's parking area.

Dana was unlocking her door. She was wearing no coat, nor was she wearing the paisley scarf. Her ensemble consisted of khaki-colored slacks and a sleeveless white blouse.

Slung over one shoulder was a pale blue leather purse, at her feet was a slim, dark briefcase.

Conan drove sedately past her as she unlocked her door, picked up the briefcase, and let herself in. She glanced once in his direction before the door closed.

He irritably tossed his cap on the seat beside him, then sighed, reminding himself that he shouldn't expect much of any search.

But, he added to himself, he could damn well hope.

CHAPTER 21

Conan stopped at his house to leave the Vanagon, his coveralls, and toolbox, and since he had lost his enthusiasm for razor clams at the Surf House, but recognized his tendency to irritability when hungry, he prepared himself a peanut butter sandwich. And thought of Skookum. And of Manny Chavez. But there was no way to find out what progress Manny had made on the erased disks short of driving to the log house and risking an encounter with Skookum with his mouth free.

Conan chose instead to go to the Holliday Beach Police Station.

It was one-thirty when he reached the station and found Sergeant Hight mediating a dispute between a hirsute man in floral-print shorts, and a couple approaching middle age ungracefully, accompanied by a teenage boy who held a boom box against his ear while the thumps and shrieks of the music drowned everyone's arguments, and finally Hight roared, "Turn that thing off or I'll cite you for disturbing the peace!"

The music stopped, but not the high-decibel disagreement. Conan saw Giff Wills in Kleber's office and invited himself in, closing the door to damp the bedlam. Kleber was at his desk, with Wills, his Stetson tipped back on his head, fists on his hips, standing to one side, both facing the man in the chair in front of the desk. All three turned, and Wills seemed inclined to order Conan out, but perhaps remembered that this wasn't his office to do the ordering out of, and Kleber seemed almost glad to see him: "Conan, I've been trying to get hold of you."

"Well, I've been . . . busy, Earl. Hello, Sheriff."

Wills emitted a noncommittal grunt, while the visitor, a rangy man with dust-colored hair and sage-colored eyes, rose, squinted at Conan, and asked, "Where the hell've you been, Conan? Sleepin' in again?"

"Sure, Steve. Figured you guys could maintain law and order without me for a while."

Steve Travers laughed and put out his hand to shake Conan's, as always revealing more in his handclasp than he ever did in words. "Well, you might as well pull up a chair. Got what you might call some developments you'll be interested in."

"Developments to explain your sudden appearance in Holliday Beach?" Conan asked, as he brought a chair to the desk and sat down next to Steve.

"That, too."

Wills deposited one ham on Kleber's desk, folded his arms belligerently, but remained silent, unwilling, it seemed, to question the judgment of an Oregon State Police Chief of Detectives in discussing police business with the likes of Conan Flagg.

Kleber was equally willing, however. He said soberly, "Conan, you wanted more information about Dan Arno's crash. Well, now it's a murder investigation, and the National Air Transportation Safety Board turned it over to the OSP."

For a moment Conan could only stare at Kleber, too stunned to speak, and it was then that he became aware of the object in the plastic sack on Kleber's desk: a thermos carafe made of satin-finished steel with a red screw top. Finally he asked, "Have you told Kara?"

"Yes. Steve and I just got back from her house a little while ago."

Conan indicated the carafe, asked Steve, "Does this explain why Arno crashed on Spirit Mountain?"

"Part of it. Arno was drugged."

"With what?"

"Nembutal. It was dissolved in decaffeinated coffee in that carafe. It was found in the cockpit."

"Nembutal?" Conan caught himself before he said anything more in Giff Wills's presence.

Steve nodded. "There was enough in the carafe to kill him if he drank the whole thing, but he didn't have to. He probably only drank about a cupful, and that was enough to put him to sleep."

And enough to cause an experienced pilot who had survived four years in Vietnam to slam into a mountain in Oregon.

Conan asked, "Any fingerprints on the carafe?"

"Arno's, of course," Steve said, "and some smudges and three good prints on the bottom. No ID yet, but we're checking them out."

"What did Kara tell you?"

"Well, let's see." Steve stretched forward to pick up a notebook from the desk, and flipped a few pages. "She said Arno got a call at ten-thirty Saturday night. He wrote the name down: Mrs. James Booth. Said she lived in Portland, but she was staying the weekend at their beach house, alone, and she'd had a call from St. Vincent's Hospital in Portland. Her husband was brought in with a heart attack. What she wanted was for Arno to fly her to Valley West Airport. It's not far from St. Vincent's. She offered him three hundred and fifty dollars."

Kleber put in, "Kara says that Jetranger took three passengers, and on a normal run Dan charged a hundred bucks apiece."

"Right," Steve went on, "so Arno told Mrs. Booth okay, and she said she'd meet him at the Baysea airfield at midnight."

"Why the delay?" Conan wondered aloud. "At ten-thirty

her husband was in the midst of a heart attack, but she didn't want to leave until midnight?''

Steve shrugged. ''If she explained that to Arno, he didn't explain it to his wife. I don't figure there *was* an explanation. We checked with St. Vincent's. Nobody named James Booth was admitted with a heart attack Saturday night. Anyway, Arno left his house at eleven-thirty.''

''Did he take this carafe with him?''

''No. Mrs. Arno said she's never seen it before. But they're not that hard to come by. Made in Seattle, and we called the manufacturer. They gave us a long list of motels and hotels in Oregon that use them, including four in Holliday Beach: the Surf House, Riley's Bed and Breakfast, Baysea Resort, and the Beachside Motel. On top of that, you can buy one just like it at any K Mart or Fred Meyer.''

''Damn. Was this sort of off-hours run unusual for Arno?''

''Not according to Mrs. Arno,'' Steve replied, turning a page in his notebook, ''and she wasn't worried about this one. She went to bed, then about three woke up and saw he wasn't back, so she called Valley West Airport. They told her Arno'd had to wait for another fare, but the fare backed out, and he took off just before three. It's a forty-minute flight from Portland, and when he didn't show up by four, Mrs. Arno called Valley West again, and they notified the NATSB.''

Conan turned to Kleber. ''Earl, didn't you say Arno had nearly eight hundred dollars on him when his body was found?''

Kleber nodded, and Steve explained, ''We figure part of it was from this Mrs. Booth and most of the rest from the second fare—the woman who backed out.''

''Does she have a name?''

''The name she gave was Mrs. Sarah Talbot, but we haven't had time to track her down.'' Steve turned more pages. ''So back to Mrs. Booth. As far as we know, nobody was at the Baysea airfield when she arrived except Arno. He phoned Valley West at midnight to give them his ETA and flight plan, and arrived there on schedule at twelve-forty.

Mrs. Booth called a cab from the office. I talked to the lady on the night shift in the office. Name is Connie Stein.''

Conan asked, ''Did she get a good look at Mrs. Booth?''

''Yes, but she didn't pay much attention to her. Middle-aged, gray hair in a bun, light-colored raincoat and walking shoes. *Maybe* she had a suitcase, maybe not. She went outside to wait for the cab. It arrived in about ten minutes. No, we haven't checked the cab companies yet.''

''When did the second woman—Sarah Talbot—enter the picture?''

Steve again referred to his notebook. ''Connie Stein says she got a phone call at 1:05 A.M. from the Talbot woman. Said she had to get to Holliday Beach that night, and Connie told her Arno was about to take off. Mrs. Talbot said she'd pay him three hundred bucks to wait and fly her to Holliday Beach. So Connie called the hangar, and Arno said he'd wait. Mrs. Talbot arrived about 2:45 A.M. Came by cab. Connie said maybe she had a small cloth bag, but she wasn't sure. She said Mrs. Talbot was between thirty and forty, wearing high heels, a tan raincoat, and a beige purse with a big buckle on it. Black hair, what she could see of it. She had on a scarf.''

Conan raised an eyebrow. ''What did it look like?''

''Let's see . . . here it is. Brown with some sort of pattern. Connie said she couldn't see much of the woman's face. She had on sunglasses.''

''At nearly three in the morning?''

''Right. But we have another witness to that, a lineman name of J. C. Lawson. He saw her when she went out to the pad where Arno was waiting by his chopper. He was passing the time talking to Lawson. He says Mrs. Talbot got into the chopper with Arno, then she started crying and carrying on, and after a minute or so she got out and ran back to the office. Connie says she called a cab and waited for it outside. Arno told Lawson the woman had been planning on leaving her husband to meet her lover in Holliday Beach, but she got cold feet. We figure she let Arno keep the three hundred she promised to pay him.''

Conan asked, ''Did she give him the carafe?''

"Well, Lawson said after she left, he saw what he called a thermos—we haven't shown him this one yet—on the seat next to Arno, and he was drinking from a cup he keeps in the chopper. Arno took off then. That was about three o'clock. And that's all we know so far."

Conan only nodded, staring at the plastic-shrouded carafe, and Kleber said, "Okay, Conan, why were you so interested in Arno's murder? You think it has something to do with Gould's?"

Conan hesitated, but finally answered, "I don't know."

Wills had been listening with steadily decreasing patience, and now he rose. "Earl, by God, you're really reaching. How the hell could this have anything to do with Gould's killing?"

Steve Travers's sage gray eyes slid toward Wills, and his cool, assessing gaze was enough to silence the sheriff. Then Steve drawled, "Speaking of the Gould killing, Giff, remember I told you there was a fragment of material caught in Cady's chain saw?"

Wills glanced at Conan, then nodded. "What about it, Chief?"

"Well, the lab identified it. Latex. Like they use in surgical gloves."

Conan leaned forward. "Surgical gloves? That might explain why the only prints on the saw were Cady's and mine."

"There's another way to explain MacGill's prints, Flagg," Wills said truculently. "Saturday morning he threatened to *kill* Gould with that same saw."

Conan didn't remind Wills that Cady hadn't actually threatened to kill Gould, but to cut off a particular portion of his anatomy, nor did he remind Wills that Gould had died of a bullet wound, nor point out how unlikely it was that Cady would use surgical gloves to avoid leaving his prints on the saw without wiping off the prints he'd already left there. Conan was not at the moment thinking about the prints on the saw. He said, "Steve, those three unidentified prints on that carafe . . . maybe you should check them against the elimination prints from the people involved in Gould's murder."

Steve studied Conan curiously. "Worth a try."

"Flagg, you're reaching farther'n Earl here," Wills said with a snort of disgust. "You ask me, there's no mystery about Arno's murder. You dig deeper, and you're going to turn up his wife."

"Giff, for God's sake, that's crazy!" Kleber burst out.

"Maybe. Maybe not. I always say, when a husband gets murdered, you better take a good look at the wife."

Kleber's eyes were down to crackling slits. "Is that where you're looking in the Gould murder?"

Wills glared at him, then for a moment turned thoughtful. That didn't last, however. He started for the door. "The Gould murder is an altogether different case, Earl. Now I gotta get to work. Can't stand around here reaching for straws."

Conan waited until Wills had reached the door before he asked, "By the way, Sheriff, have you found out yet if Gould left a will?"

Wills seemed to freeze, then he retorted, "If he did, his lawyer didn't draw it up for him. Ain't that right, Chief Travers?" And with that he made his exit, slamming the door behind him.

Kleber winced. "Ol' Giff's going to shake that glass out before this case is over."

Steve only laughed as he reached into his breast pocket. "Funny you should ask Giff about the will, Conan."

"What's funny about it? Giff's damn sure not going to let me see Gould's will if he finds it."

"Yes, but you've got a friend in high places." With a Cheshire cat grin, Steve handed Conan a folded sheet of paper, and another to Kleber. "Giff'll get a copy, too. I'll fax it to him when I get back to Salem. But Giff's been such a pain in the backside, I figured I'd let you guys have first go at it."

Conan looked at the sheet of paper, and it jolted him to his feet. "For God's sake, Steve, this is Gould's will!"

Steve smiled benignly. "Sure looks like it. And Giff's right: Gould's lawyer didn't draw it up or know anything about it. The SFPD found the original in a safety deposit box in a San Francisco bank. Holographic, but legal. And the handwriting checked out.''

Conan hungrily read the words scrawled with such seeming carelessness, despite the serious purpose of the document. The notary public's stamp was as incongruous as a diamond brooch on a faded sweatshirt. The will was dated nearly three years ago, and its provisions were simple. All Gould's assets, including future income from his books, he bequeathed to his present wife, Savanna Barany, with the exception of $500,000 to his first wife, Julie Sanzio, identified as a professor of biology at the University of Oregon.

"Maybe someone should be questioning Julie Sanzio," Conan said.

"We checked her out," Steve said. "Right now Dr. Sanzio is in Costa Rica on a field trip, and she's been in the university's field headquarters in San José since she broke her ankle a week ago. Fell out of a tree. You got to that last paragraph yet?''

Kleber had, apparently. He muttered, "Well, I'll be damned . . .''

Conan had also reached the final paragraph, and he read it with a sensation of rising hackles. James Ravin Gould, in sound mind, had written: "Full control of my literary estate shall remain in the hands of Byron Lasky of the Lasky Literary Agency. I want Byron Lasky to continue in his present capacity, at his present ten percent commission, as long as any book of mine remains in print anywhere in the world.''

Kleber recovered enough to say: "Maybe this explains why Lasky's in such a stew for somebody to find those lost manuscripts.''

"*If* he knew about this will," Conan noted as he folded his copy and put it in his shirt pocket. "Gould didn't tell his lawyer about it, nor Savanna, apparently. Would he tell Lasky?''

Both Kleber and Steve were spared speculation on that point by the jangle of the phone. Kleber reached for it, asked, "What is it, Dave?" Then after a nod, he handed the receiver to Conan. "For you. Miss Dobie.''

Miss Dobie's first words were "If that strange young man

ever brings that dog into this shop again, I can't be responsible for my actions! He *terrified* Meg!''

Conan asked cautiously, ''Was this a large, black dog who looks like a wolf?''

''Yes! And he said he was a friend of yours!''

''Skookum?''

Miss Dobie sighed audibly. ''That strange young man! Anyway, he left a package here for you. He said you wanted it, whatever it is.''

''A package? *Yes*, I want it. I'll be there in five minutes!'' He hung up, started for the door. ''I'll talk to both of you later.''

''What the hell lit a fire under *you*?'' Kleber asked.

But Conan was already gone, the glass rattling as he slammed the door.

Miss Dobie was concluding a sale when Conan flung the bookshop's door open and demanded, ''Where is it?''

She cocked her thumb toward his office without looking up from counting change for a young woman with a baby strapped to her back. The baby began wailing the moment Conan entered the shop.

He made no apologies but went straight to his office, and there on the floor by his desk was a carton about a cubic foot in dimension. Since Conan was expecting something closer to the size of a couple of reams of typing paper, this carton gave him pause. He was given further pause when he picked it up to put it on the desk.

''Damn!''

Behind him, Miss Dobie laughed, not charitably. ''Heavy, isn't it?''

Conan decided she deserved any satisfaction that barb might provide after encountering Manny Chavez and Skookum without prior warning. ''Where's Meg?''

''Upstairs sulking on the top shelf of the Philosophy section. What in the world is in that box?''

''Ravin Gould's last book,'' Conan replied, ''if Manny the *wunderkind* and his magic computers had any luck.'' He opened the carton and tried to lift out the first sheet, but the second and third followed. It was fanfold paper, the edges punctured with regularly spaced holes, and judging from the height of this boxed pile, there were at least four reams altogether. He tore off the first sheet and groaned, "Oh, my God."

The print was pale dot matrix, and on the left half of the sheet were nine columns of numbers, seven digits in the first, four in the others. Down the center of the page was another column a little over an inch wide, each line beginning and ending with a colon to form a tenuous border, but at least there were words in this column. They were broken at random at the end of each short line, but Conan deciphered with some satisfaction the words:

```
                    :My father was a f:
                    : ucking  bastard. :
```

"This is *it*, Miss Dobie. Manny came through."

She peered at the sheet. "But with what?"

"That," Conan replied as he lifted the carton, "is what I have to find out."

CHAPTER 22

It was two-thirty in the afternoon when Conan hauled the printout to his library. He left it on the floor behind his desk and opened the sliding glass door on the south wall; the small patio was shaded with pines that cooled the air, and on this relentlessly sunny day, the library's west windows had collected more heat than he found comfortable. Then he went to the living room to put a tape on the stereo—he decided to listen to all nine Beethoven symphonies as accompaniment for this reading marathon—then to the kitchen for a mug of coffee, then back to the library, where he settled in the chair behind the desk.

But he wasn't yet ready to begin reading. He took two sheets of paper from his pocket and unfolded them. One was Ravin Gould's will. The other was the sample from Gould's typewriter. He reached into a drawer for the envelope containing the fragment from the Eyrie's fireplace, and smiled. The type matched.

Which still didn't explain why Savanna had burned part of Gould's manuscript.

Conan lighted a cigarette, turned his chair to face the car-

ton on the floor, then, with a sigh, picked up the top sheet
and began to read.

The format made that difficult enough, and as Angie had
hinted, *Odyssey* was a labyrinth of flashbacks. At any point
in the story, Jimmy Silver might be reminded of something
that had happened in his childhood. And Gould had fixed on
one event in Jimmy's childhood as the focus of suspense,
teased the reader with intimations and scattered incidents
establishing the context for it. After the first hour and first
four hundred pages, it was clear to Conan that Gould didn't
intend to fully reveal that event until near the end of the
manuscript.

And thus Conan, who once promised himself he would
never waste a moment on a Ravin Gould novel, spent the
long afternoon doggedly reading, or at least skimming, each
dot-matrixed page in search of that crucial event, because it
might also be crucial to Gould's murder.

At 6:45, with the second movement of the *Ninth*, the *Molto
vivace*, just beginning, he dropped the final page on the pile
that had accumulated on the floor, and the thick brass chords
and hoofbeat thuds of the timpani paced his thoughts. He
had never before been aware of the passionate irony in this
movement.

Now he understood that sardonic "Doctor, lawyer, police chief."

But there was more he didn't understand.

For one thing, why, when Gould devoted a long chapter
to each of his first three wives, did he ignore his fourth? He
had fictionalized the names; for instance, using Alice Rose
for Allison Rosenthal, whom he treated with atypical kind-
ness, even romanticizing her. Rather, romanticizing Jimmy
Silver's grief at her death. But there was no character Conan
could equate with Savanna, except one who was represented
by no more than a name, Anna Vas, a device Conan found
cloyingly cute. He also found the name mentioned only once,
and that as a guest at a bacchanalian party at best-selling
author Jimmy Silver's Hawaiian mansion.

And why was there no mention of the character Mayley,
who appeared in the fragment from the fireplace?

And why was there no Chapter 11?

Conan opened the local phone book, found the MacGill number, and reached for the control console on his desk to lower the volume on the music. When he punched the number, it was Angie who answered.

He said, "Angie, I have a printout from those disks."

"Conan, that's incredible! Did you find what you're looking for?"

"Possibly. But there's no chapter eleven in this printout. The question is, was the chapter lost in an electronic cul-de-sac, or did Gould inadvertently misnumber a chapter, or what?"

"Oh, I remember about that. There *wasn't* any chapter eleven. I asked Ravin if I should change the chapter and page numbers, and he just said to stet it. That means let it stand."

"He offered no explanation, I suppose."

"No. He never offered me *any* explanations."

"Thanks, Angie." Conan cradled the phone, turned up the volume, savoring the lyric theme and lush strings of the third movement, before he added yet another question to his notes.

Abruptly he realized he was no longer alone and sprang to his feet, then let his breath out in a shudder of relief when he saw Marcus Fitch lounging at the patio door, a white paper sack in each hand.

"I brought sustenance," Fitch shouted. "Will corned beef do?"

Conan turned down the music. "Anything will do. Thanks, Marc."

Fitch handed him one of the sacks and pulled a chair up to the other side of the desk. While Conan delved into his sack, found a thick sandwich and a vanilla milk shake, Fitch said, "I wasn't sure about the milk shake, but it sounded good after an afternoon in the sweltering halls of the Taft County Courthouse."

Conan tasted his milk shake. "Haven't had one of these for years. Reminds me of the soda fountain in the old drugstore in Pendleton."

"Reminds me of the Dairy Queen across the street from

my high school. The parking lot behind it was dubbed the *candy store*, as I remember. Incidentally, my client is again enjoying Earl's hospitality. The judge denied bail. And what in God's name is that pile of paper?''

Conan didn't answer until he had finished chewing a mouthful of sandwich. ''A printout—of sorts—of Ravin Gould's last masterpiece.''

''Ah. You've read it?''

''I had no choice. It'll be another blockbuster, no doubt, which should make Savanna happy. And the Laskys.''

Fitch paused with his sandwich poised. ''How so?''

Conan pushed aside his notes and found the copy of Gould's will. He planed it across the desk to Fitch, then watched a wolfish grin light his face as he read it. ''I love it! Oh, Conan, my man, this is *lovely*!''

''It's also our little secret for the time being.''

Fitch nodded. ''I wonder if the redoubtable Gifford has confronted the Laskys with this yet.''

''Who knows? Oh—I stumbled on another piece of the puzzle today. Maybe it's a piece. Savanna had a meeting on the beach with Dana Semenov. Before they parted, Dana gave her a manila envelope.''

''What was in it?''

''Savanna says a contract for a book deal with Nystrom. They want to publish her autobiography. With a four-million-dollar advance.''

''Damn, I'm in the wrong business. I should've turned my talents to authorship.''

Conan laughed. ''I have a writer friend who told me the average writer in this country makes less than ten thousand a year. If you're in it for the money, you might as well go to Vegas. The odds are better.''

''You think the deal for La Barany's autobiography is legitimate?''

Conan looked toward the corner where the *Knight* haunted the shadows. ''It could be. Part of it, anyway.''

''Was there anything about Savanna in Gould's opus?''

''She was conspicuous by her absence.''

''Any sign of the Laskys or anyone else we know?''

"Only Byron, possibly, in a very minor role. And Marian was transfigured into a young, voluptuous blonde who made Jimmy Silver's author's tours sexual as well as public relations marathons."

"Flirting with libel, wasn't he? What else did you find in that pile?"

Conan absently stirred his milk shake with the straw. "Marc, there was one key event in Jimmy Silver's life, and it happened in his childhood in Forsuch Beach."

"Does that translate to Gould's childhood in Holliday Beach?"

"I think it does. Gould's father was a logger named Tom. Jimmy Silver's father was a logger named Tim. Gould's mother had red hair and blue eyes, and her name was Loretta. Jimmy's mother, also redheaded and blue-eyed, was named Laura. Anyway, Gould characterizes Tim Silver as a heavy drinker when his family was destitute, a gambler and cardsharp who cheated, a womanizer who slept with his best friends' wives, who beat and raped his own wife, and who occasionally beat his son. Yet it seems Tim Silver was a man of mesmeric charm. No one in Forsuch Beach realized what a bastard he was. Then when Jimmy was twelve, Tim disappeared."

Fitch started on the second half of his sandwich. "Sounds like a story with a happy ending."

"Oh, that's only the beginning. Laura thought he'd deserted her, and by this time she was a basket case. She and Jimmy moved in with her parents in Portland, and it was all downhill from there. She died at forty-five of asphyxiation when she choked on a piece of food. This was in a motel room rented by a man who signed in as John Smith."

Fitch raised an eyebrow. "That's how one writes a bestseller?"

"That's how Ravin Gould wrote a so-called autobiographical novel."

"Was that the key event in his life—his mother's death?"

Faintly Conan heard the magnificent chorus of the "Ode to Joy," but resisted the urge to turn up the volume. "No.

That happened years after he left Forsuch Beach. The key event was his *father's* death.''

''I thought the father disappeared.''

''Permanently, it seems. The trouble is, I don't know how much poetic license Gould took, or how much *Odyssey* and reality have in common.'' Conan pushed his chair back and rose. ''Marc, I'm going to the bookshop. Maybe I can find out a little about the reality.''

''Before you rush off so precipitously . . .'' Fitch reached into his sack and removed a flat, rectangular package wrapped in brown paper. ''From the lovely Shelly Gage.'' Then as Conan took the package, Fitch added, ''Judging by the size and source, that can only be a videotape. A tape of what?''

''Of the unexpurgated version of the Oregon Chain Saw Massacre.'' Conan hesitated, hefting the tape, then put it on the desk. ''But it can wait. Marc, are you going back to Portland tonight?''

''No, I'm staying in your fair village.''

''You're welcome to my guest room.''

''A gracious offer, my friend, but I prefer lodgings with room service. I've made a reservation at the Surf House. Have you any objection to my perusing that literary master-piece?''

Conan laughed as he went to the glass door to close and lock it. ''You're welcome to it. By the way, try using the front door next time.''

''I *did* try.'' Fitch began transferring the fanfolded pile from the floor to the box. ''Apparently your eardrums were too numbed with Beethoven to register the doorbell. *Now* what?''

That was in response to the ring of the phone. Conan reached for the receiver. ''Yes, what is it?'' he asked impa-tiently.

''Earl Kleber is what it is,'' came the response. ''I've got an interesting piece of news for you.''

''I'm interested, then.''

''It seems Giff Wills dropped by to see Byron and Justine Lasky a couple of hours ago.''

"To tell them about Gould's will? Well, at least that means he's recognized the possibility that Cady isn't the only viable suspect."

"Sort of. Giff's come up with a new theory. He figures Cady and the Laskys were working together. Some sort of conspiracy. Anyway, when he showed the Laskys the fax of the will, they both swore up and down they didn't even know Gould had made a will. Then after Giff left, they checked out of the Surf House and just plain disappeared."

"Disappeared? When?"

"About half an hour ago. Giff told Helen Day at the office to let him know if they did anything unusual, and they did, so she did. It was Justine who did the checking out. Helen said she didn't see Byron in the car. Anyway, Giff called me because he put out an APB on them."

"Did he check Baysea's helicopter shuttle?"

"Yes. They didn't leave town on the shuttle. In fact, they didn't turn in their rental car at Baysea. Giff figures they headed for Canada."

Conan ran a hand through his hair. "Earl, what about Marian Rosenthal? Did she make a run for the border, too?"

"Well, I sent Billy over to the Surf House, and she's not there. Neither is her car. But she didn't check out, so maybe she's just gone shopping. I called Baysea, and she didn't take the shuttle, either."

"Let me know if anyone finds any of them. And thanks, Earl."

When Conan hung up, Fitch was leaning toward him, long arms braced on the desk. "If anyone finds *whom*?"

Conan gave him the gist of Kleber's news, and Fitch straightened, his teeth gleaming white against his umber skin. "I think there's light at the end of MacGill's tunnel after all."

Conan nodded, and he was almost envious. Marc Fitch's obligations were met with the shadow of a doubt. His own obligations wouldn't be met until he knew who murdered Gould. Not once, but twice.

But Ravin Gould had been a storyteller, and he'd had one last tale to tell.

CHAPTER 23

It was Holliday Beach's version of low-cost housing. The apartment building had once been a motel, a stark row of ten units, all under one roof. In daylight, the wood siding was pale yellow, but at night in Conan's headlights, it seemed gray. Nine o'clock, and most of the windows were dark, but light glowed behind the curtains of number five. When Conan knocked on the door, he heard a thump and a shuffling, then the porch light went on, and Dr. Maurice Spenser opened the door, squinting at him through his plastic-rimmed glasses.

Conan said, "Hello, Doc. May I come in?"

"Conan? Well, sure, come on in."

He motioned Conan into a small living room where the yellow light from a brass table lamp shone on walls papered in a faded floral print. Against the left wall slumped a couch upholstered in worn, gray velour; the matching armchair was backed to the far wall near the wood stove. There were two doors on the right wall opening into a tiny kitchen and a bedroom. Conan knew Doc had lived here for ten years, yet the apartment still had the look of a motel unit, perhaps because there was so little evidence that anyone had occupied it for any length of time: on a corner shelf, a few books; by the bedroom door, a glassed photograph of the old covered bridge over the Sitka River; and on the side table by the armchair, directly under the lamp, a silver-framed snapshot of a young woman with pale hair styled in a page boy typical of the Forties.

There was also an overflowing ashtray on the side table along with two bottles of Scotch. The one labeled Bruichladdich was nearly empty; the other, with the Monarch label, hadn't been opened.

"Well, this is an unexpected pleasure," Doc said. "Can I offer you a drink?" He went to the table, coming between it and Conan, and removed both bottles, took them with him to the kitchen.

"Yes, thanks." And while Doc opened cupboards and rattled glasses in the kitchen, Conan checked the wood stove. It was overflowing with gossamer ashes.

Doc returned with two glasses, both four fingers up with undiluted Scotch, sans ice. He handed Conan one of the glasses. "Have a seat."

Conan chose the couch, leaving the armchair to Doc, who put his glass on the side table and sank into the chair. He wore his gray suit and vest, white shirt, and tie. His collar was unbuttoned, the tie loose. He was, Conan realized, thoroughly drunk, yet there was no slurring in his speech, no uncertainty in his movements.

Conan asked, "What happened to your thumb?"

Doc frowned at the frayed bandage on his right thumb. "Oh, I cut it with a paring knife. Guess I ought to put on a new bandage. Like they say, Doctor, heal thyself."

Conan gave that a polite smile, then looked up at the photograph of the covered bridge. "I suppose you crossed that bridge many a time."

Doc smiled, drank sparingly of his Scotch. "I first crossed that bridge in a '44 model Studebaker. And I watched them tear it down when they widened the highway in 1948."

"You've seen a lot of history here."

"Seen most of Holliday Beach's history. Weren't more than three hundred people when I came. That was right after the War. I was a medical corpsman in France and Italy. Anyway, I was the town's first doctor, and the only one for a long time. I figure I delivered half the population of the town, and I knew them all, watched them grow up. Outlived some. It *meant* something back then to be the town doctor."

Conan tasted his Scotch; it was the Monarch. He indicated the photograph on the table. "Is that Beth?"

"Yes," Doc said huskily. "Beth Neary. She taught at the grade school here. I'd spent two years trying to put broken boys back together, and Beth . . . she was like sunshine after a storm."

"She was still a young woman when she died, wasn't she?"

Doc looked at Conan sharply, then took time to light a cigarette. His hands were shaking slightly. "She was thirty-two. Died in childbirth. So did the baby. My . . . son."

There was the weight of grief in the silence that followed, of tears spilled and always ready to be spilled again. Conan saw the wedding ring on the bony, parchment-skinned hand that held the Scotch. Doc raised the glass, took another swallow, visibly gathering himself.

"Conan, you seem to know a lot of Holliday Beach history."

"Yes, well, I just spent some time at the bookshop reading *The History of Taft County*. You're featured prominently in it."

Doc puffed out a veil of smoke. "Well, like I said, I've been around a long time."

"You've been retired for quite a while, haven't you?"

"About thirteen years. By then, we had half a dozen doctors here, and now we've got the hospital. I figured the town didn't need me so much anymore."

Conan nodded, well aware that the real reason Doc retired from medicine was in his hand now.

"Doc, I understand you and Mrs. Carmody have become very close."

"Who told you that? Mrs. Carmody and I are good friends, that's all. Known her for years. Knew her husband, too."

"Well, in a small town, people always gossip. I suppose

it's because they've seen you driving Mrs. Carmody's old Cadillac.''

Doc went stiff with alarm. ''Hope the police never get wind of that. I, uh, lost my driver's license a few years back. My eyes, you know. Can't see well enough at night.''

Conan didn't challenge that rationalization. ''But Mrs. Carmody loans you her car sometimes, doesn't she?''

''Well, just for emergencies or special occasions.''

''Special occasions like Saturday night? By the way, I should wish you a belated happy birthday.''

Doc's eyes narrowed suspiciously. ''My birthday's not till October.''

''Why would Mrs. Carmody think your birthday was Saturday?''

''Well, I . . . I guess she just got confused.''

''Not Mrs. Carmody. You *told* her it was your birthday, didn't you? Probably told her some friends were giving a party in your honor. She'd be happy to loan you her car for an occasion like that.''

''If she said that, she's full of beans! I was right here at home Saturday night. *All* night.''

''Doc, I saw Mrs. Carmody's car on Dunlin Beach Road about nine-thirty Saturday night. I was just leaving Ravin Gould's house.''

Doc resorted to his whiskey before he could attempt a nonchalant ''You must've seen somebody else in a Cadillac.''

''Yes, there must be any number of blue 1959 Cadillacs around. You knew Tom and Loretta Gould, of course.''

''No, I mean, I . . . I don't remember them.''

''You did yesterday. Doc, there's a photograph in the *History* taken in 1950 at a Christmas party. You were dancing with Loretta Gould, and Beth with Tom, and you'd all stopped to mug for the camera. Another man was making a show of cutting in on you and Loretta. The caption identified him as Deputy Sheriff Raymond Wherry, nicknamed Ox.''

Doc's skin assumed a waxy cast, but he managed a smile as he admitted, ''Could be. We used to have lots of community dances here.''

"Tell me about Tom Gould."

"Why? What's he got to do with anything?"

"Well, his son was murdered Saturday night."

"Earl's got Cady MacGill in jail. Always was hotheaded, but I can understand it, what he did. I mean, when you find out a man's been sleeping with your wife . . ."

"I don't think Cady murdered Gould."

"No?" Doc raised his cigarette to his lips, took a puff. "Why not?"

"The police found a fragment of material caught in the chain on Cady's saw. The same material surgical gloves are made of." Conan leaned back into the sagging cushions. "If Cady used surgical gloves to avoid leaving fingerprints, why didn't he wipe the saw clean first? His prints are all over it. Anyway, I doubt it would occur to him to use surgical gloves. But it might occur to a doctor."

Doc surged forward in his chair, scattering cigarette ashes on his vest. He brushed them off hastily, crushed out the cigarette. "What do you really want? What's any of this got to do with *me*?"

"Everything, Doc. Are you willing to let Cady be convicted for a murder he didn't commit?"

"How do *I* know whether he committed it or not?"

Conan said distinctly, "Doctor, lawyer, po-lice chief. When Ravin Gould spoke those words, I thought he was looking at me, and that didn't make sense. But you were standing next to me at that moment. He saw you in the crowd and recognized you, and those words were meant for you and only you."

"I don't know what you're talking about," Doc retorted staunchly.

"*You're* the doctor. The police chief—well, Gould took some liberty with the truth to paraphrase the old rhyme. The police chief was actually a deputy sheriff. Ox Wherry. I don't know who the lawyer was. The *History* provided several possibilities, but not enough information for me to be sure of any one of them."

"I don't know what you're *talking* about!" Doc repeated stubbornly.

"Of course you do." Conan took another bitter sip of whiskey. "You should clean out that stove more often. It's a fire hazard."

"Damn it, I don't figure that's any concern of yours."

"It depends on what you burned in that stove. I think the crime lab can easily establish that those are paper ashes. Nearly three thousands sheets of paper, in fact. It must've taken a long time to burn all those manuscripts and the notebooks." Doc seemed to retreat, turtlelike, into himself, and Conan added, "And then there's that bottle of Bruichladdich you whisked into the kitchen when I arrived."

"What bottle . . . oh, yes. Well, I guess I should've offered you some, but most people don't like single-malt Scotch."

"Where did you get it, Doc?"

He attempted a shrug. "Down at the liquor store. Where else?"

"Not at an Oregon liquor store. I called George at our liquor store. He says the Oregon Liquor Control Commission doesn't list Bruichladdich, and if they don't list a brand, you can't buy it in this state. But Bruichladdich was Gould's poison of choice, and he could afford to bring in his own, and he did. There were a number of fifths of Bruichladdich at the Dunlin Beach house Saturday night."

Doc's mouth thinned into a defiant line, and Conan played his ace. "Did you know Angie MacGill was typing Gould's manuscripts?"

The defiant line slackened. "I . . . don't believe that."

"She typed the entire third draft of *Odyssey*. On a computer, which means every word was preserved on disks. Doc, I just finished reading a printout of that third draft, and everybody *was* there, just as Gould promised: doctor, lawyer, po-lice chief."

Doc closed his eyes, and it seemed that life was draining out of his body, leaving him inert, empty. But finally he roused himself enough to say, "He didn't care who he hurt, no more 'n his father did. And his father hurt *him*, too. You'd think he'd just let the dead past bury itself."

"Ravin Gould was not a generous man. I've read his version of Tom Gould's murder. Do you want to tell me yours?"

Doc laboriously got to his feet and made his way to the kitchen. Conan waited, and when Doc returned, he had two empty glasses and the fifth of Bruichladdich. He put the glasses on the coffee table in front of the couch, carefully poured the remaining Scotch into them, left one for Conan, and with the other, slumped into his chair. There was about him a pendent calm; perhaps it was resignation. He said, "Might as well finish this off. I took two bottles, but this's all that's left."

Conan tasted the Scotch, heavy with the earthy scent of peat, while he watched Doc savor a sparing sip, then, "Okay, Conan. I'll tell you my version of Tom's murder. Funny, I never thought of it that way. It was more like an accident. And he brought it on himself, the bastard. He *deserved* it." Doc's eyes squeezed shut, then he sighed. "Jimmy got it mostly right, what happened that Saturday night out at Cam's cabin."

"Cam?" Conan reviewed the list of possibilities garnered from *The History of Taft County.* "Camden Yates? He was the lawyer?"

"Yes. The four of us, Tom, me, Cam Yates, and Ox Wherry, used to meet Saturday nights for poker at this cabin Cam owned north of town. I didn't go every Saturday. Couldn't afford it, really, and like I said, I was the only doctor in town. So they'd have other guys in sometimes, but the four of us, we were the regulars."

"Did Beth know about your nights out with the boys?"

"Yes. She said I deserved a night out now and then. But she didn't know—not to begin with—what went on at that cabin sometimes. Damn it, I was a young man, and it didn't seem . . . wrong. Not in those days. There was always a lot of liquor, and the stakes were always high. Higher than I should've been playing for. And sometimes . . . well, Cam had plenty of money. Been a county commissioner besides his law practice. Sometimes he'd bring . . . girls to the poker parties." He paused, finally shrugged. "What the hell, they were whores."

"But on the Saturday in question, there were no *girls* present?"

"No. Just Cam and Ox and me. And Tom Gould. Good ol' Tom, the war hero. He liked people to think he'd been a hero. I got to where I never believed a word he said. But you know . . ." Doc shook his head, frowning. "When he and Loretta first came to Holliday Beach, Tom seemed like such a fine young man. But he was laid up for six months with a broken leg, and him with a wife and two kids to support. Then he lost one of the kids. Marilyn. I don't really know what happened to Tom, but he just gradually went bad. The drinking was the worst of it, and he had a hell of a temper. And the gambling. He was good at cards. As it turned out, he was good at cheating, too. Cam Yates had his suspicions early on, but the rest of us didn't believe him. Not till that Saturday night. As for Cam, gambling was . . . well, you could call it an addiction. He lost a lot of money to Tom. In Reno, too, I guess. Cam had money, but at the rate he was losing it, he was courting bankruptcy."

"And that was Yates's motive?" Conan asked. "That Tom was cheating him into financial disaster?"

"Motive?" Doc sipped at his whiskey and seemed to consider the word as he did the earthy taste of the Scotch. "Yes, I guess you could say that. Not just the money, but the cheating. That rankled with Cam."

"And Ox Wherry's motive?"

"Well, I didn't find out about that till . . . afterward. Ox was a big man with a short fuse. One night he arrested a guy at the Lo-Tide Tavern and took him out to his patrol car. Tom was at the Lo-Tide that night. Followed them outside, but Ox didn't see him. The guy gave Ox some trouble, and Ox got mad. Hit him one time too many. Killed him."

"And Tom used that to blackmail Ox?"

"I guess so."

Conan leaned forward. "What was *your* motive?"

"If you read Jimmy Gould's story, you know," Doc said bitterly. "Except it wasn't like he told it. Damn it, Beth never—" He stopped to get himself under control, then, "Tom wrote Beth a letter, but he didn't sign his name, the bastard. *A friend*, that's how he signed it. He told her if she knew what went on at those Saturday night poker games, she'd never want to see me again. Liquor, high-stakes games. Girls. He really laid it on about the girls. She didn't show me the letter till a week later. Said I had to know. I had to understand, or we'd never be able to forgive each other. And she told me . . . well, the day that letter arrived, Tom came to see her in the afternoon while I was gone. Smooth as silk, she said, so gentle and kind. And she was so hurt about what she'd read in that letter, she . . .'' Doc couldn't seem to finish that.

Conan didn't ask him to. Ravin Gould had spelled it out in *Odyssey*. ''Didn't mean a damn thing to Tom, except he knew what it'd do to me. He liked to watch people squirm. That bastard hurt Beth so bad, she never got over it, and all so he could watch *me* squirm.''

''Yet you still played cards with him?''

''Only once. I don't know why I went to the cabin that Saturday night. Maybe I thought I had the guts. . . .'' He shook his head and went on: ''None of us knew Jimmy Gould was watching us. He said in his book it wasn't the first night he followed Tom to the cabin and watched through the window. Well, it seemed like things went wrong from the first that night. We were all drinking too much, especially Cam Yates. If anybody started it, Cam did. He caught Tom cheating, caught him red-handed. And Tom just *laughed* at him. Laughed at all of us, said we were a bunch of stupid suckers. Cam roared up out of his chair and threw a right hook across the table. I remember . . .'' Doc stopped, eyes focused inward.

Conan had to ask. ''What, Doc? What do you remember?''

''The way Tom looked just before Cam's fist hit his face. For the first time as long as I'd known Tom, he was *afraid*. I think right then he knew what was coming, knew he was about to die. Then Ox and I both waded in with both fists and whatever came to hand, and everything just seemed to explode. It's a wonder we didn't all end up burned to death, because the only light we had was a kerosene lamp hanging from the ceiling, but somehow nobody knocked it down. Well, I suppose the whole thing was over in a minute or so. Tom was lying on the floor in his own blood with his skull caved in and his face so beat up, you couldn't tell who he was. And all I could think of was, Tom Gould wasn't ever going to hurt anybody again.''

Conan took a deep breath, finding it necessary to clear his throat before asking: ''What did you do with the body?''

''We took it in Ox's pickup east into the hills. Plenty of places up there to bury a body, and they don't last long in this climate. Then we all went home. Beth wondered why my clothes and hands were so torn and bloody, and I told her I fell into a ditch when I went out to answer the call of nature. Don't know if she believed me. Things were never really right between us after that. And two years later, she was dead.'' Conan felt the despair in the long sigh that echoed in this anonymous room where Doc Spenser seemed only a transient visitor.

At length, Doc took a swallow of Scotch. ''A week after Tom died—after we killed him—Cam saw to it that his cabin burned to the ground. Everybody figured it was a vagrant holing up in the cabin started the fire. As for Tom, everybody figured he'd deserted his wife and boy. I didn't see much of Cam or Ox after that.''

''What happened to them? Are they still alive?''

Doc finished his whiskey, put the glass down carefully. ''I'm the only survivor. Cam did all right for a while. A few years afterward, he ran for district judge and won the seat. Then about 1965, he had a bad stroke. Totally paralyzed, couldn't even talk. He spent five years in a nursing home dying. Ox didn't last as long as Cam, but it was faster for him. He was elected sheriff, but a few months after he was sworn in, somebody got the drop on him with a shotgun. Blew the top of his head off. Maybe you'd call that poetic justice for both of them. I figure it's just the luck of the draw. It doesn't matter how hard you try or how smart you are, it's the cards you draw that count.''

Conan might agree with that philosophy to a point, except for the negligence in it. But he wasn't here to argue philosophy. "Doc, was Ravin Gould's arrival in Holliday Beach just another card dealt to you?"

Doc grimaced. "That bastard was no better 'n his father. I saw that at the bookshop. Doctor, lawyer, po-lice chief. And that talk about his *autobiographical* novel. Yes, he recognized me, and he was watching me squirm. *I* was this town's first doctor. That *meant* something. And Beth . . . nobody knew about Tom and Beth, but I figured if he knew about the murder, he knew about that, too. I couldn't let him drag her name through his kind of filth. I read one of his books once. Filth! And he was going to tell the world about me, about my Beth. I couldn't let him *do* that!"

"So, to preserve your reputation and your wife's, you were willing not only to kill Gould, but to see Cady convicted of murder."

"Cady *could've* killed him. He damn well wanted to. *You* saw that."

For a moment, that incredible rationalization left Conan speechless. Finally he said, "You talked to Marian Rosenthal Saturday afternoon. Was that to satisfy yourself that no one had read Gould's manuscript?"

"That woman at the Surf House? Yes. She told me Gould never let *anybody* read his manuscripts till he was finished with them."

"What happened Saturday night, Doc?"

He brooded for a moment, then with a shrug began, "After I talked to that woman, I started making my plans. I called on Mrs. Carmody, and yes, I told her a friend was giving me a birthday party, so could I borrow her car. And I did drive down Dunlin Beach Road around nine-thirty. Just scouting the place. Then I drove back to Holliday Beach and parked up a side street near the bookshop and waited till midnight. I used Mrs. Carmody's tire iron to break into the shop to get the chain saw, then I drove back to Dunlin Beach. Didn't see a car at the house, and I was glad about that. Guess I hadn't figured out what I'd do about Jimmy's wife. Had a ski mask to cover my face, but thank the Lord, she was gone. You know, it was just like everything'd been laid out for me. The front door was even unlocked." Doc's mouth twisted in a sardonic smile. "And Jimmy Gould—he was passed out on the couch. Didn't hear me come in, didn't even wake up when I got that damned saw started. Had a little trouble with it." He held up his bandaged thumb. "And with all that racket, Jimmy just lay there, too drunk to hear. He looked so much like his father. Chip off the old block, even if Tom was such a bastard to him. That's what I'll never understand, 'specially after what I read in those manuscripts. Tom beat his wife and beat his boy, yet his boy grew up to be just like him. Just as mean."

Doc seemed ready to lapse into another dark silence, and Conan had to prompt him. "So you cut his throat with the chain saw."

"Yes." His breath caught, his bony hands closed into fists. "Oh, damn, I guess I never thought about what that saw would do. Didn't matter. It was fast."

"And when it was done?"

"I went to the room where he worked. Found those boxes with his manuscripts. Hell, he'd written enough for four or five books. And the notebooks, the ones he'd marked *Odyssey*. Took 'em all out to the car."

"Along with a couple of fifths of Bruichladdich?"

"Well, didn't seem like I should let 'em go to waste." Doc tried a laugh, but it degenerated into a sound closer to a sob. "It was . . . terrible, what I had to do. But I *had* to do it, and I *did* it. And I had the same feeling looking down at him with his throat gaping open that I did when I looked down at Tom Gould lying in his own blood on the floor of that cabin. I thought, he's not ever going to hurt anybody again."

"Then you came home and burned all the manuscripts, all the notes, and thought the door Ravin Gould had opened was safely locked."

Doc stared at the wood stove. "You were right. It took a long time."

"Yes, I was right." Conan pulled in a deep breath; he felt suddenly claustrophobic in this room. "Doc, how much Scotch had you put down before you cut Gould's throat? I assume you had a few drinks at the Surf House in the afternoon. Then you came home to work out your so-called plan, and that probably required a few more drinks. Then you waited in Mrs. Carmody's car until midnight before you broke into the shop. You had company, didn't you, in the shape of a fifth of Monarch?''

"I don't see how that's any of *your* business."

Conan laughed bitterly. "I'm trying to understand how anyone could undertake a murder with such incredible ineptitude."

"Maybe I was just lucky. The cards fell right. Maybe that's the way they were *meant* to fall."

Conan rose, went to the telephone on the stand by the door. "Don't invest this act of arrogant stupidity with divine purpose. That's more than I can take." He started dialing, while Doc stared at him numbly.

Earl Kleber answered after only two rings, and Conan said, "Earl, meet me at the police station as soon as you can get there. You'd better roust Giff out, too."

"What've you got, Conan?"

"The man who cut Ravin Gould's throat."

"I'll be there in ten minutes."

When Conan hung up, he looked at Doc, and the old man pulled himself to his feet and surveyed the room. Finally he picked up the photograph of his wife, removed it from its frame, and slipped it into his breast pocket. "I'm ready."

CHAPTER 24

It was nearly midnight by the time Doc Spenser had recapitulated his story for Earl Kleber and Giff Wills. The tape recorder hummed on Kleber's desk, and the old man was pale, forehead shining with sweat. The chief had offered to call another doctor, but Doc refused. He also refused Kleber's offer to call a lawyer before he answered any questions. It didn't matter, he said. Nothing he did now mattered.

Doc concluded his story with the hours spent burning Ravin Gould's manuscripts page by page. "It was like seeing the past turn to ashes."

Conan stood at the window, looking out at the street in the pink glow of a streetlight. The houses beyond the potholed asphalt were dark, their occupants no doubt peacefully asleep. He turned, and Kleber glanced up at him from behind his desk, sighed, and again focused his attention on Doc. The sheriff had throughout the confession slouched in a chair at one end of the desk, eyes locked in a squint, mouth sagging open, which might have been due to weariness or simple dismay. He rose now, frowning. "Doc, what'd you do with the gun?"

Doc looked up at Wills blankly. "What gun?"

Kleber leaned forward. "Doc, you *do* own a gun, don't you? A small twenty-two?"

"Earl, I never owned a gun in my life."

"Damn it, Doc," Wills said irritably, "you've already confessed to murdering Gould. You might as well tell us the whole story."

"I *told* you the whole story. That's all there is to tell, all there is left. . . ." And he seemed on the edge of tears. "Damn, I need a drink."

"We'll make you as comfortable as we can here," Kleber assured him, "but that's one thing we can't supply."

Wills eyed Conan. "Did he tell you anything he hasn't told us?"

"Nothing."

"You didn't ask about the gun?"

"I thought I should leave that to you." Conan smiled fleetingly at Wills's raised eyebrow, the annoyance in the set of his jaw.

"Yeah." The sheriff turned to Doc. "Will you swear you never owned a gun, that you didn't take a gun with you Saturday night when you went to Gould's house to kill him?"

Doc pressed his stiffly curled hands to his eyes. "No! No! I told you, I don't own a gun, I don't know anything *about* a gun!"

Wills shook his head. "Well, Earl, I guess you can book him."

"What's the charge?" Kleber asked. "We can forget Tom Gould's murder. Witnesses are all dead, crime scene burned to the ground forty years ago, and the body—if anybody knew where to find it—is probably nothing but mulch. We can't even prove there *was* a murder."

"But I—I told you," Doc insisted. "I *confessed*."

"Doesn't mean a thing by itself," Kleber said. "People confess to crimes they never committed all the time. So what does that leave, Giff? Mutilation of a corpse?"

Wills emitted a grunt of disgust, and Doc half rose from his chair, sank back into it. "Mutilation of . . . What are you saying, Earl?"

"Doc, if you didn't shoot Gould—"

"Shoot him? No, of course I didn't *shoot* him."

"But somebody else did. He was dead when you went at him with that chain saw. You murdered a dead man."

Doc stared at Kleber, and Conan wondered how much he understood of what the chief had told him. Enough, it seemed. He sat with his bony hands clasped and began weeping in devastating silence. Earl came around the desk, helped him to his feet. "We're going to have to book you. Look, I've got to call Herb. He's your lawyer, isn't he?"

"I don't want Herb. I don't want anybody. Just take me wherever I'm supposed to go. . . ."

Kleber led him out to the front desk, and within a few minutes another officer appeared and took the old man in hand. Kleber returned to his office, slumped wearily into his chair. "I wonder if Doc'll last the night. And I wonder what Culpepper *will* charge him with."

"Besides mutilation of a corpse?" Conan went to the chair Doc had vacated and lighted a cigarette, feeling the ache of tension in his shoulders as he inhaled.

Wills said, "That's a legitimate charge, Flagg."

Conan looked at him. "Yes, I know. Sheriff, it seems to me this blows the case against Cady out of the water."

Wills scowled, arms folded across his chest. "Maybe. I'll have to talk to Owen tomorrow." And with that he headed for the door, apparently ready to depart without another word nor even a glance at Kleber.

Conan stopped him with: "Have you had any luck tracking down the Laskys?"

"No!" And the door slammed behind him, rattling the glass.

Kleber only laughed. "Ol' Giff seems a bit put out." Then he sobered. "You did one hell of a job, Conan. May take Giff a while to admit it, but the case against Cady MacGill is closed."

Conan nodded as he exhaled a veil of smoke. "And we still don't know who murdered Ravin Gould."

"No, but that's not what you hired on for. All I asked was for you to clear Cady."

"Yes, well, I have a problem with loose ends."

Kleber sighed. "Okay, so who's left? The Laskys?"

"And Marian Rosenthal and Dana Semenov." Then he added reluctantly: "And Savanna Barany."

"You think *she's* a suspect?" Kleber tilted back in his chair. "But if you believe the Laskys and the Herndons, there wasn't time for her to kill Gould after eleven-thirty and still arrive at the Eyrie at one-twenty, even if she *didn't* have to steal the chain saw."

"You're assuming she *drove* to Portland."

"You think she made the trip by helicopter? But what about her car? If she flew to Valley West, how did her car get parked outside her condo by six-thirty in the morning when the Herndons left on their hiking trip?" He paused, then, "Have you checked the bus schedules?"

Conan leaned forward to tap the ash from his cigarette into the green glass ashtray on Kleber's desk. "Two buses from Portland come through here every day: one at three in the afternoon and another at six-thirty in the morning. Even if she took the bus that arrives at six-thirty, that wouldn't explain how she got her car parked in front of the condo at approximately the same time."

Kleber shrugged. "So, what are you worried about? How about the Laskys? Gould's will adds a little spice there."

"And Byron may be fighting a losing battle with cancer, and besides that, they love each other profoundly. A volatile combination. Then there's Dana Semenov, who wanted *Odyssey* desperately. Yesterday I was sure she had no motive, because it didn't seem likely killing Gould would get her any closer to *Odyssey*, but I'm not so sure of that now. His heir can sign a contract. Then there's Marian Rosenthal, whose daughter was married to Gould and died in a car accident probably caused by his drunkenness."

Conan took a puff on his cigarette, watched the smoke dissipate, and it seemed his speculations had just as much substance. He crushed it out in the ashtray as he rose. "Earl, I still have something to take care of tonight."

"Conan, it's half past midnight."

"And the night is young yet. I'll talk to you tomorrow."

* * *

When Conan reached his house, he poured himself a cup of leftover coffee and went to the library. The coffee had little to recommend it but caffeine, which was why he tolerated it. He drank it while he made a phone call to Marc Fitch informing him of Doc Spenser's confession. For that news, Marc forgave Conan for waking him at this ungodly hour and promised to be at the Taft County Courthouse tomorrow morning when it opened to secure Cady's release.

Conan made a second call, this one to Steve Travers, who was no more pleased than Fitch to be summoned from sleep at this hour, not until Conan told him the reason for the rude awakening. Steve's response had been: "Well, that clears the air a little."

A little, Conan conceded, but the air was far from crystalline.

When he hung up, he unwrapped the videotape and found a note: *Conan, you owe me!—Shelly.*

For a moment he held the black box, feeling a paralyzing reluctance to find out what was inside it. But finally he took it to the VCR, slid it into the slot, found the remote control, and pressed *play*.

The show began with exterior shots of the bookshop and the gridlock outside, cut to the interior and the alcove stage, with a long study of Savanna. In the brilliant light, she was electric, preternaturally alive. Then the camera shifted to Gould and his flashing, cynical smile. Conan fast-forwarded to the point where Angie made her appearance. The sound pickup was vague against the background noise from the crowd, but Gould's "Goddamn it, stop that camera!" came through. But the cameraman didn't stop, and it was then that Cady's chain saw became audible. It sounded as tinny as a toy, and Conan was reminded of the crackling whir of a rattlesnake. No audio reproduction he had ever heard caught the overtones of menace in that sound, either.

Again Conan fast-forwarded through the riot, Cady's confrontations with Gould and with Conan, and Cady's subsequent exit. Conan returned to normal speed as the camera shifted back to Gould. When Gould grabbed Savanna's arm,

Conan moved the tape backward, then forward, then stopped it.

Savanna was kneeling, sweeping the spilled contents into an orange purse, her extended hand frozen over a small, silvery object.

The image was blurred, but there was no way he could doubt what he saw.

A small handgun.

And he remembered Savanna when she came to him asking for proof of something vital to her. *I'm not sure I know what love is, but I think you do. That's why I can trust you.*

He was rigid with anger. She could trust him? Of course she could. She made sure of that.

Then the anger faded, and he felt an enervating weariness. Savanna had undoubtedly believed every word she said. At least, at the moment she spoke. That was her extraordinary talent, whether speaking or singing. She believed every word, felt it to her soul, at the moment. Whoever she might be, at the moment. And she could make an audience of strangers believe every word, feel it to *their* souls.

Conan punched *rewind*, waited for the VCR to click off, then took the tape back to the desk, and it occurred to him that he might be overcompensating for his failed objectivity. Yes, Savanna had a motive for murder in Gould's philandering and his sabotage of her career. Yet she had another option open to her: divorce. Of course, he couldn't explain why she hadn't exercised that option sooner. As for the means—the gun—he had no proof that the gun in her purse Saturday morning was the one that fired the fatal shot, or that she had fired it.

He couldn't even be sure she had opportunity, not when the squeaky-clean Herndons swore that the Ferrari was parked in front of the Eyrie at six-thirty in the morning.

If Savanna had parked it there, she did not have opportunity.

He took his car keys out of his pocket as he left the library and walked down the hall to the utility room and through it to the garage.

It was a beautiful night for a drive.

CHAPTER 25

A glow of light to the east presaged the town of Mac-Minnville. Between sporadic chains of headlights from oncoming traffic, Conan looked out on either side of the highway and saw distant lights of farmhouses set against the gray velvet of fields and soft blacks of oak-forested hills. It was 2:00 A.M. when he reached the city limits of Mac-Minnville, a small, prosperous town that in daylight would be bustling with traffic, but now its dark streets echoed with emptiness.

He passed two filling stations on the outskirts of town, both closed. The third was open, an island of light. Conan drove up to the rank of pumps nearest the station, watching a young man clad in a red and white MacMinnville High School jacket jog out to the XK-E. Conan got out of the car, leaned on the door. "Can you tell me if there are any other gas stations around MacMinnville open this time of night?"

The young man had the wholesome, freckled look of a Norman Rockwell illustration. "Well, if you don't have an Arco card, we'll take Visa."

"No, that's not the problem." Conan got out his wallet, flashed his private investigator's license. "I need some information about someone who bought gas at a station in Mac early Sunday morning.''

The youth examined the license, then grinned. ''You came to the right place. This is the only station open after midnight around here.''

''I'm Conan Flagg, by the way. And yes, I also need some gas.''

''Bobby Gallagher. What does this car take? Leaded?''

''Unleaded. I had a converter installed.''

''Yeah? Man, she is really *awesome*.'' Bobby pulled the nozzle out of its slot and began filling the Jaguar. ''Wish my dad could see her. He collects antique cars.''

Conan had never thought of the XK-E as an antique, but he let that pass. ''Bobby, were you on duty Sunday morning?''

''From midnight to eight. I've been working graveyard all summer. It'll pay my tuition at Linfield this fall. So who're you looking for?''

Conan had a newspaper clipping of Savanna Barany. He took it out of his shirt pocket, but didn't unfold it yet. ''I'm looking for the driver of a yellow Ferrari.''

Bobby nodded. ''Sure, I remember that car. California plates.''

''You got the license number?''

''Nope. Just happened to notice the plates. It was a cash sale.''

''What can you tell me about the driver?''

He shrugged wide shoulders. ''Well, not much, really. It was a woman. Probably good-looking, but it was hard to tell.''

''What do you mean?''

''She was wearing sunglasses. It was really weird, you know. In the middle of the night, this woman is wearing sunglasses. And she had a scarf on her head tied under her chin.''

''What did the scarf look like?''

''Oh, I don't know. Dark, I think, with some sort of pattern. Anyway, the woman had black hair, what I could see of it.''

Conan waited until Bobby topped off the tank, withdrew the nozzle, and clanked it back into the pump. "What was she wearing?"

"A raincoat. Light color, maybe tan. And she had a purse on the passenger seat. It was tan, too, with a buckle on it."

Conan showed him the clipping. "That's Savanna Barany," Bobby said. "Hey, you must be working on that murder down on the coast."

Conan nodded. "Was this the woman in the Ferrari?"

"Savanna Barany? No way. Well . . . I don't think so." He squinted at the clipping. "Maybe so, and she was incognito, or whatever. But, you know, with the sunglasses and all, it's hard to say."

"Do you know what time it was when the woman stopped here?"

"Yeah. One o'clock. I've got a TV in the station, and I like to watch the Thrilltime movie on channel eleven. It always starts at one, and I remember the titles had just come on when this woman drove in."

"Is there anything else you can tell me about her?"

"Well, no. Except she asked for her change in quarters."

"Quarters?" Conan felt an adrenaline rush that translated into a sensation of cold on his skin. "Did she say why?"

"Nope. Didn't say any more than she just had to, you know."

Conan extracted a fifty-dollar bill from his wallet. "Thanks, Bobby. This is for the gas. Anything left over is for your tuition fund."

By three o'clock, Conan was on the beach below the house, walking in the wet sand at the edge of the waves, barefoot and savoring the chill of the water when it surged around his ankles. Moonlight transformed the dry sand into dimpled pewter, gleamed on curling breakers, made distances equivocal so that the lights of boats on the horizon seemed close, like static fireflies ready to be caught and held in his palm.

The sound of the breakers, the rush of water toward him, the murmur of its retreat, was hypnotic, yet it never produced in him anything like somnolence. It always seemed to wake some center of perception beyond the reasoning mind. It was like music, perhaps because it was one of the sources of music.

And there was a song that repeated itself endlessly in his memory: *I never asked for forever . . . I only wanted today . . . I never asked for your soul . . . I only wanted your heart . . . for today, for today. . . .*

CHAPTER 26

At dawn, the wind shifted fitfully to the southwest, but it brought no promise of rain, only fog that gave the air a moist chill and hushed the rush of breaking waves. From the deck off his bedroom, isolated in a pocket of perception limited to a few hundred feet, Conan watched the coming of the day, evident only in the gray light that pervaded the fog.

Wednesday. Five days since Ravin Gould was murdered. In his mind the days seemed to count themselves off like the tolling of a clock.

Finally he left the cocooned world of his deck and went inside to shower and dress. At a few minutes past seven, when he went down to the kitchen, the gray light was brighter, but the fog made the windows look frosted. He put the coffee on to drip while he prepared himself a hearty breakfast: bacon, eggs, and toast. It was a pale shadow of the ranch breakfasts he remembered from childhood, which often included freshly baked pies, but this breakfast served as a kind of ritual preparation that was on some irrational level satisfying.

He turned on the radio while he ate and heard a garbled account of Doc Spenser's arrest. Giff Wills had managed to take full credit, and nothing was said about what charges had

225

been brought against Doc or the fact that Gould was dead when Doc tried to kill him or that Cady had been exonerated. When the telephone rang, Conan willingly turned off the radio as he went to the wall phone by the kitchen door. "Hello?"

"Oh, Conan, I'm so glad you're there."

Savanna. He felt an equivocal urge to laugh. Her voice was warm, even intimate, the memory of their last parting apparently forgotten.

"Yes, Savanna, I'm here."

"I thought the fog might've taken you away on little kitten feet. Anyway, I've decided to check out of here and go to the beach house. Mrs. Early said she could clean it this morning. Maybe after that I can stand . . ." A sigh, then, "The reporters are camped on my doorstep, and I don't want them to know where I'm going. I've made arrangements for somebody to bring my car and luggage down later, but meanwhile . . . well, I need your escort and evasion service."

"I'll be there in about fifteen minutes."

"You're a doll, Conan. You really are." And with that she hung up.

He grimaced as he cradled the receiver, poured himself a mug of coffee, then went back to the telephone and punched a familiar number.

It was a harried Dave Hight who answered. "Holliday Beach Police—Billy, take care of that door! Uh, yes, who's calling?"

"Conan Flagg. I wanted to talk to Earl."

"Well, he's sort of busy right now, Conan."

"What's going on, Dave?"

"It's Doc Spenser. He had a heart attack. We called Nicky Heideger, and she ordered the ambulance. Just got here a few minutes ago."

"I didn't know Doc had a heart condition."

"Me, neither, but Nicky's his doctor. She says Doc knew about it, but he wouldn't let up on the booze. Says he's been trying to kill himself ever since Beth died."

Conan remembered a silver-framed photograph of a young woman with pale hair, a photograph that was the only thing

Doc took with him when he left the place where he had existed for ten years.

"Dave, I just wanted to ask Earl if anyone's found the Laskys or Marian Rosenthal yet."

"I doubt it. The chief didn't say anything about it this morning."

"Thanks. Tell Earl I'll talk to him later."

When Conan reached the Surf House, the reporters were indeed camped on Savanna's doorstep, and again he had to escort her through the clamoring crowd to the car, and again he had to run a tortuous evasion course to escape the journalists who took to their vehicles, and again Savanna, in a summery dress of snow white that made her seem a figure out of Watteau, laughed with delight all the while.

But the fog gave him an unfair advantage today, and he lost even the most serious pursuers after no more than five sudden changes in direction. When he turned south on 101, he took cover between two billboards of RVs, and Savanna said gleefully, "Conan, you're amazing!"

"Just part of the service, ma'am."

Her smile turned wistful. "You know, I'm going to miss you."

"Oh, you'll find someone else to chauffeur you through evasion courses. But that sounds like the beginning of a goodbye."

"I guess it is. I've scheduled the funeral for tomorrow morning at ten. I haven't told anybody about it. I don't want those media people making a circus of it. But I couldn't get hold of Marian yesterday afternoon, and the office told me the Laskys had checked out. I mean, I *did* intend to ask them to come to the funeral. And you, too."

Conan didn't comment on the Laskys' and Marian's absence. "I'll come if you want me to, but otherwise I don't think I belong there."

"I'd like you to come."

He glanced at her, then nodded. "All right, Savanna."

"And after the funeral . . . I'm leaving, Conan. I have no reason to stay here, and lots of reasons to go."

"Well, you have the sheriff's blessing," he said, trying not to sound too bitter about it. "Even if your husband's murder is still unsolved."

"But they arrested that old man, the doctor. I heard it on the radio this morning."

"Yes, they arrested him, but not for murder. Gould was already dead when Doc used the chain saw on him."

"What?" It came out in a husky whisper. "But they said— I mean, I . . . I thought the same man who shot him . . ." She lapsed into silence.

Conan left her to her silence. He understood it. She had believed nothing was left but the curtain calls.

The fog curdled thicker around Sitka Bay. He followed the taillights on the car ahead with a sense of motionlessness so real that he nearly missed the junction with Dunlin Beach Road, and catching the turn to the south fork of the road required some concentration. They had almost reached the house when Savanna broke her silence. Her chin came up defiantly as she declared, "I'm still leaving tomorrow. Lainey's scheduled a meeting with Booth, and I've *got* to be there. This is my *future*, Conan."

He only nodded as he parked in front of the house. Mrs. Early was waiting on the porch. In the fog, the house seemed an inexplicable fortress that didn't belong to the kind of stolid reality she represented.

He walked with Savanna to the porch, and she greeted Mrs. Early, slipping into a Southern accent with the pleasantries. But Conan was hard put not to stare at his housekeeper.

What held his attention was the scarf that confined her buoyant hair. It was silk with a paisley design in browns and ochres.

When Savanna unlocked the door, and the three of them entered the foyer, he made sure he was at hand to help Mrs. Early out of her coat, to take the scarf when she removed it, and say casually, "What a beautiful scarf, Mrs. Early." The label read *Bloomingdale's, New York*.

She beamed, fluffing her hair. "Well, I volunteer Tuesdays

down to the Humane Society Thrift Shop. Saw this when I come in yesterday and bought it right off.''

Savanna had gone on into the living room. "Mrs. Early, maybe your thrift store could use Ravin's clothes. I don't want to have to pack them up. This food . . .'' She wrinkled her nose at the stench of molding salmon and caviar. "Just throw it in the Disposall.''

Conan tuned out the remainder of Savanna's instructions. He hung Mrs. Early's coat in the closet on the left wall of the foyer and took a moment to examine the scarf, but there was no other label, no initials. When he closed the closet, he saw Savanna open the sliding door onto the deck. She glanced at him, then went out, leaving the door open, and while Mrs. Early began carting the stinking remains of the buffet to the kitchen, he followed Savanna.

She stood at the south end of the deck, her hair a beacon of color in the fog. On the beach below, waves materialized out of grayness with hollow sighs, but Savanna was facing the windows, staring into the room Gould had called his office. "Dead matter,'' she said absently.

"What?"

"This house, everything about it, it's like everything's been . . . used up. Dead matter.'' Then realizing Conan was in no way enlightened, she added: "After a book comes out, and the publisher doesn't need the manuscript anymore, they send it back to the author. They call it dead matter. Ravin always thought that was . . . funny. He used to say that's what he wanted carved on his tombstone.''

She turned to face Conan, and he wondered what she *would* order carved on James Ravin Gould's tombstone. A smile shadowed the curves of her lips as she said softly, "Conan, come *with* me.''

"Where? To Never-Never Land?"

She laughed. "Well, to La La Land, maybe.'' She took a step closer to him, pushed one hand through her luxuriant hair, and Conan recognized the calculation in that gesture. And recognized its efficacy.

"Why, Savanna? Why would you need me in La La Land?''

Another step closer, and her hands rested on his chest, she whispered, "I need you because you're honest. Because I can trust you."

He relaxed into her kiss, savored the coiled power of her body against his, and when she drew away, he touched her parted lips with his fingertips. "If you can trust me, I should be able to trust you."

"You *can* trust me, Conan." There was just enough chagrin in that.

"Why did you wait so long before you decided to divorce Gould?"

Her ivory skin colored exquisitely, her eyes went wide, as if he had slapped her. Then the long, dark lashes swept down. "That's none of your business. It's nobody's business but mine now."

"Savanna, nothing is sacred or private in a murder investigation."

"What went on between Ravin and me *is* private! I *won't* answer any more questions, and I won't . . ." Her anger dissipated as abruptly as it had come into existence, her breath came out in a sigh. "I just want to get back to my life. Oh, Conan, *this* is Never-Never Land."

He found himself holding her, felt her tremble with silent weeping. It was far more effective than wailing sobs would have been. When she pulled away from him, her eyes were red, her checks wet with tears.

"Conan, I meant it when I asked you to come with me."

"I know you did, Savanna."

"But you won't come."

"No."

She studied him intently, then said with teasing nonchalance, "Well, you had your chance. Maybe I *don't* need you. But it's been lovely having you around. Maybe I just don't want to give that up."

He smiled. "Maybe."

"I think I'll go to the beach and get out of Mrs. Early's way." Then as Conan accompanied her to the other end of the deck, she said, "Damn this fog. Tell Mrs. Early if I'm not back in an hour to send out the Coast Guard."

He watched her stride across the lawn to the stairs that would take her down to the beach. It was an image he'd remember, Savanna Barany in white, tossing her candescent hair as she moved into the fog. No doubt she expected him to remember it.

He went to the sliding door, ignoring a glimpse of Mrs. Early hurrying away from the kitchen windows. Inside the house, he found her at the sink rinsing plates and stacking them in the dishwasher.

"Mrs. Early, I'd like to ask you a favor."

"What's that, Mr. Flagg?" She turned off the water, wiped her hands on the towel sewn into the waistband of her apron.

"That scarf you bought at the Humane Society Thrift Shop, I'd like to buy it from you."

"Buy it?" Then she shrugged. "Tell you what, it cost me a dollar, but you can pay the thrift shop. I don't want nothing for it myself."

Conan had paid £50 for its twin at Harrods, and he doubted it had cost any less in dollars at Bloomingdale's. He restrained a laugh and said, "Thanks, Mrs. Early. It's not often you find something from Neiman-Marcus in a small-town thrift shop."

"Well, it wasn't from Neiman-Marcus, if that's what you're after. Bloomingdale's, it was. New York City."

"Yes, of course." And, satisfied that Mrs. Early could identify the scarf if necessary, he took his leave. "I'll get it from the closet as I go, and I'll stop by the thrift shop today."

"Okay, Mr. Flagg. Say, what d'you want that scarf for, anyway?"

But he was on his way to the front closet and could pretend he didn't hear that question.

CHAPTER 27

Conan considered himself fortunate to find a parking place only a block south of the Humane Society Thrift Shop. He walked the remaining distance along a sidewalk that was, despite the fog, crowded with tourists shivering in clothing meant for sunshine. The thrift shop, a dour little building amid garish tourist traps, occupied a corner on the east side of Highway 101 two blocks north of Holliday Bay. As Conan crossed a side street to the shop, he saw a big wooden bin against its south wall. The sign on the bin read "Donation Drop Box."

There were no displays in the windows, only a view of a dim interior. A bell heralded his entrance into a claustrophobic space cluttered with clothing, linens, crockery, glassware, toys, games, books, records, appliances, plastic icons. He made his way to the back of the shop, where Mrs. Iona Higgins beamed at him from behind the counter.

"Mr. Flagg! Well, what can I do for you?"

He took the folded scarf out of his pocket and put it on the counter with a five-dollar bill. "Mrs. Early bought this scarf here. She said she'd sell it to me on condition that the money went to the Humane Society."

Mrs. Higgins laughed and whisked the bill into a tackle box that served as a cash register. "Then I guess it's yours. That scarf came from Bloomingdale's in New York, you know. I saw it yesterday. There's usually a lot of things left in the drop box Monday when we're closed, so I always come in on Tuesdays to help sort them out."

"Then the scarf was left in the drop box sometime Monday?"

"Or Sunday after hours."

"Was there anything else from Bloomingdale's?"

She eyed him curiously. "Well, there *were* some other things from New York in the box, but not from Bloomie's. I get their catalogue at Christmas. Sort of fun, seeing how the other half lives. Anyway, there was a nice purse and a raincoat, both from Bonwit Teller."

He didn't try to restrain a smile of satisfaction as he returned the scarf to his pocket and asked, "May I see them?"

"Not the purse. Sold that to Mrs. Benton."

"Oh. Was it by any chance beige leather with a big gold buckle?"

"Sure was. How'd you know?"

"Lucky guess. Did you sell the raincoat?"

"Oh, no, it's still here." She came out from behind the counter and maneuvered her impressive girth neatly along the crowded aisles to a rack of women's clothing. Conan dodged a macramé plant holder, then waited while she searched the rack, the hangers squeaking as she pushed them aside. At length, she found a tan raincoat, checked the label, and handed it to him. "There you are. Bonwit Teller, New York."

There was no doubt in Conan's mind where he had first seen this coat. He felt inside the pockets, but they were empty. "Mrs. Higgins, do you often find clothes with New York labels in your drop box?"

"Never have before. We get some really nice things now and then, but they're more likely to be from stores in Portland."

"I'd like to buy this."

Mrs. Higgins raised an eyebrow. "Okay, that'll be six dollars."

She draped the coat over her arm and sidled back to the counter. Conan followed her, took a twenty from his billfold, and put it on the counter. "Six dollars for a coat that probably cost two hundred?"

"Didn't cost *us* anything," she said, taking the twenty. "People don't expect to pay a lot for what they find here, and six dollars will buy maybe ten pounds of dog or cat food. Let's see if I have change. . . ."

"Consider the change a donation. Now, what I'd like you to do is put the coat aside and keep it for me."

Her eyebrow shot up again. "Is this coat *evidence* or something?"

"I'm not sure. But just in case it is, I know it's in good hands."

As he left the shop, he wondered if the coat would ever become evidence in a legal sense. Certainly it was evidence in his mind.

It was after nine-thirty, yet the fog persisted, especially around Sitka Bay. Conan followed the taillights of the car ahead of him past the bay to the Baysea Resort junction. The stand of pines was transformed into a misty, mythical forest, and it seemed a long time before he emerged from it. He parked in front of Dana Semenov's room, and when he knocked on her door, heard an impatient, "Come in!" He did. The door was unlocked.

The drapes were drawn back, and on the floor by the bed, her suitcase and briefcase stood ready. Dana was sitting at the table by the west windows, one hand cupped over the mouthpiece of the phone.

She said irritably, "I thought you were room service." Then into the phone: "Yes, I'm holding. I've *been* holding for ten minutes. What? No, I will not settle for a flight through Phoenix. For God's sake, don't you have any direct routes to New York out of that burg?"

No doubt that *burg* was Portland, a city of a million people, counting its suburbs. Conan sat down in the chair across the table from Dana, his gaze fixing briefly on the manila envelope by the telephone.

Dana concluded her call with a curt, "No, I will *not* go on standby." She slammed the receiver down, then her long, manicured nails tapped against the plastic as she studied Conan.

He said casually, "I can recommend a travel agent in Portland. She'll get you a flight to New York if it's humanly possible. But I thought you were headed for Los Angeles."

"I *was* headed for L.A. but as you might've noticed, I've been stuck here for the last three days. I had to send my assistant. What's your travel agent's name?" She picked up a pen and pulled a notepad closer.

"Lisa Hartford, Trans-World Travel Agency." He provided the phone number, and as Dana's pen moved in quick, bold strokes, Conan added, "I think you should reconsider before you call her. Gould's murder hasn't been solved."

Dana lifted the receiver. "They arrested somebody. That doctor."

"Gould was already dead when Doc besottedly tried to kill him."

She stared at Conan, not so much shocked as suspicious. Then she shrugged, began punching numbers. "I'm as curious as anybody to find out who killed poor Ravin, but I can't sit here in the boonies waiting for an answer. Yes, may I speak to Lisa Hartford? And if the police don't like my leaving, they can damn well arrest me. That's the only way they'll keep me here. Ms. Hartford? You were recommended to me by Conan Flagg. He lives in—what? I see." She glanced at Conan, and he rose and went to the west window, putting his back to her to give her a semblance of privacy. He listened to her conversation, noting her businesslike tone more than the words; a tone that made it clear that she would brook no nonsense.

When she hung up, he returned to his chair, while she checked her watch. "Your friend says she'll call me back in fifteen minutes. Damn, I've got to catch the helicopter shuttle at twelve."

"Baysea found a replacement for Dan Arno?"

"Who?"

"The helicopter pilot who brought you here Saturday night. The pilot who was killed returning from another run to Portland early Sunday morning."

"He was killed? That's too bad."

"Yes, it is," Conan said flatly. "He left behind a wife who loved him and two children, Dan Junior, fifteen years old, and Noele, ten years old."

Dana leaned back and crossed her legs, regarding Conan with narrowed eyes. "That's too bad, too. Mr. Flagg, what do you want?"

"Some answers."

"To what questions?"

"Well, I'm interested in the publishing business. Your title is editor-in-chief, isn't it?"

"Yes, as a matter of fact."

"Sounds like a position of great responsibility. Is it difficult for a woman to reach that level in the publishing business?"

"Are you trying to bait me, Mr. Flagg?"

"No, just revealing my ignorance."

One eyebrow arched up. "Yes, it's difficult for a woman to reach that level in *any* business. I started at the bottom and fought my way up, and none of it came easy." There was an undercurrent of passion, even bitterness, in that.

"What's the criterion of success for an editor? Acquire or perish?"

She pushed her hair back from her cheek. "Yes, but I have a history of acquiring very well. I've acquired bestsellers—blockbusters—for every publisher I've worked for."

"What bestsellers have you acquired for Nystrom?"

"That is certainly none of your business."

"In other words, you can't name any bestsellers you've acquired for Nystrom. But maybe your superiors are willing to wait patiently until you come up with a blockbuster."

"You're out of line, Mr. Flagg," she said, leaning forward, leading with her chin. "And you can just leave—*now*."

Conan ignored that. "But if Nystrom isn't patient, what happens then? What happens if you can't deliver *Odyssey*?"

"You bastard!"

Her frustrated anger was answer enough, even though she had herself under control a moment later and managed a cool laugh. "Oh, Mr. Flagg, you *are* baiting me. Well, I would've loved to deliver *Odyssey* to Nystrom, but Ravin Gould wasn't the only writer in the sea, and the world won't come to an end if *Odyssey* is never published."

"In fact, the world might be a better place. But not *your* world." He smiled at her. "However, that's not a problem for you now. You're going back to New York in triumph with the contract for *Odyssey*, signed by Ravin Gould's widow and heir, in that manila envelope."

One hand moved abortively toward the envelope, then she laughed. "You're right, I do have a contract in here signed by Ravin's widow and heir—*for her autobiography*." Dana paused, enjoying herself, it seemed, then handed him the envelope. "See for yourself."

He called her bluff, realizing with a sinking sensation when he glanced through the contract that it was not a bluff. Nystrom, Inc., had indeed agreed to publish an autobiography, not yet titled, by Savanna Barany, said autobiography to be ghostwritten by an author chosen by Nystrom. The bottom line was that Nystrom was offering Savanna an advance against future royalties of $300,000.

Conan put the contract in the envelope, dropped it on the table. "*Touché*. Will you also let me see for myself what's in that briefcase?"

She surged to her feet. "That briefcase is *locked*," she said as she reached for the phone and punched a single number. "If you so much as touch it, I'll—" Her next words were spoken into the phone: "Just a moment, please." She covered the receiver, then, "I've got the office on the line, and I'll scream for help, I'll accuse you of rape or anything I have to, if you don't get out of here right now and leave me *alone*."

He held up his hands in a gesture of surrender. "I had no intention of touching the briefcase." He didn't need to now.

She gave him an unblinking scrutiny, then said into the

phone, "I'm sorry, I meant to call room service." When she hung up, she said distinctly, "*Goodbye*, Mr. Flagg."

He rose but made no move to leave, instead reaching into his pocket for the scarf. "You forgot you were in a small town when you disposed of this. Not much happens around here that someone doesn't find out about." He unfurled the scarf, let it fall on the table.

What he was seeking was there in her eyes: a flash of recognition.

But it was gone in a split second, and she gave him an arch laugh. "*Now* what? Have you taken to selling ladies' accessories? If so, this is very pretty, but it doesn't go with anything I have."

"It went very nicely with the tan raincoat you wore Saturday night. The one from Bonwit Teller. And the purse with the gold buckle. It was from Bonwit's, too. I suppose you were afraid someone might identify you by your clothes."

She stood frozen while he picked up the scarf. He went to the door, paused to look back at her. She hadn't moved.

"*Goodbye*, Ms. Semenov."

CHAPTER 28

"Good morning, Miss Dobie."

The bookshop was open when Conan arrived at ten-thirty, and Beatrice Dobie was at the cash register, while Meg lounged on the end of the counter grandly tolerating a cooing matron.

Miss Dobie said, "Good morning, Mr. Flagg," as she slipped two books into a sack and handed them to the matron's husband. Two copies of *The Diamond Stud*, Conan noted as he unlocked the office door.

The one-way glass had been restored, but he didn't close the door. He tossed the scarf on the desk, and when he sat down, Meg leapt into his lap and permitted him to massage her back. More mail had accumulated, but he ignored it for the memo written in Miss Dobie's fine, slanted hand: *Marc Fitch called. DA and Judge Lay agreed. Cady released this morning.*

"Mr. Fitch said something enigmatic about sunshine in the tunnel," Miss Dobie announced from the doorway. "And an even more enigmatic intimation about Sheriff Wills having a new bee in his Stetson."

Conan frowned. "Marc didn't explain that, I suppose."

"No." She looked out into the shop to be sure no customers were bearing down on the cash register, then, "There was another call. Well, actually, it wasn't just one call. She's been calling every five minutes since I opened, but she refused to leave a message. I just don't understand why young people never learn proper telephone etiquette. After all, they spend most of their adolescence on the phone. Of course, most young people these days never learn *any* kind of—"

"Miss Dobie!" Under other circumstances, Conan might have been willing to wait for her to reach her circumlocutory point, but not today. "Did this person have a name? A phone number? Anything?"

"No phone number. She said she didn't know how long she'd be at the same phone, and she made it plain that she really didn't want to give me her name, and if you ask me, the one she finally *did* give is an alias. She was obviously young, and it's not a young woman's name. Maybe her grandmother, but—"

"Miss Dobie, for God's sake!"

"Cornelia."

Cornelia. That could only be Deputy Neely Jones. "Did she say whether she'd call back?"

"No . . ." Miss Dobie apparently saw customers in the offing, and began retreating toward the cash register. "She didn't say, but I expect she will. Let me help you with those, ma'am."

Conan rubbed Meg under the chin. "Well, Duchess, I guess there's nothing to do but wait." And try to figure out what kind of bee Wills might have in his Stetson. Conan had made no progress at that when the phone rang. He lunged for it, and Meg, alarmed at the upheaval, leapt for safety, digging her claws in for a better takeoff.

"Ow! Holliday Beach Book Sh—"

"Conan? Thank God. Look, I need your help."

It was Neely Jones, and the anxiety in her voice made the back of his neck tingle. "Of course, Neely. What's wrong?"

"I've *got* to talk to Chief Kleber—and *soon*."

"Is he still at the hospital?"

"I don't *know* where he is. I haven't called the station. I can't talk to him on police lines. That's why I'm calling you. I was hoping you could get hold of him and arrange a meeting.''

"I'll find him. You can meet here at the bookshop. Okay?''

He heard her sigh, then, "I'll be there in half an hour.''

"Neely, what—'' But she had hung up. He muttered, "Damn,'' as he went to the door to close it, ignoring Miss Dobie's questioning glance. Then he returned to the phone and punched the number for the police station. To his relief, Kleber was there.

"Earl, this is Conan. I have something important to talk to you about. Here at the bookshop.''

"At the bookshop?'' Kleber asked doubtfully. "What is it?''

"I can't discuss it on the phone.''

A moment of silence, then, "Well, I've got something to talk to *you* about, too, Conan. I'll see you in a few minutes.''

Conan arranged two straight chairs on the other side of the desk, then stood at the door and watched Miss Dobie sell more copies of *The Diamond Stud* until finally Earl Kleber appeared at the shop entrance. Conan opened the office door for him and closed it behind him, ignoring another of Miss Dobie's silent queries. "Have a seat, Earl.''

The chief did, slapping a file folder down on the desk. "What's so all-fired important you couldn't come to the station to tell me about it?''

Conan sat down behind the desk. "Neely Jones wants to talk to you, and she insisted on privacy. I don't know what it's about, but from the way she sounded on the phone, I think you'd better listen.''

"Where is she?''

"On her way. From Westport, I suppose. She should be here in about twenty minutes. Earl, what about Doc?''

Kleber rubbed his eyes with one hand. "He's critical. Nicky says she wouldn't bet on his living to stand trial, especially since he doesn't *want* to live to stand trial or anything else.'' Conan didn't attempt a response to that, and Kleber absently fingered the paisley scarf. "What's this, lost and found?''

"In a way." He explained the scarf's recent history, adding that when it was found in the Humane Society's drop box, it had been accompanied by a tan raincoat and gold-buckled purse with Bonwit Teller labels.

"Okay, the odds are those clothes *do* belong to Dana Semenov," Kleber conceded. "So what?"

"So you have to wonder why Dana disposed of perfectly good clothes. Because she got tired of them suddenly? Or she has a passion for animals? Or because she was afraid someone might be able to identify them—and her?"

Kleber shrugged off those questions. "Well, if she wants to leave, nobody can stop her. Besides, it doesn't matter now."

Conan waited for him to explain that, but Kleber changed the subject with "The Laskys are still missing, but Marian Rosenthal showed up. I sent Billy to the Surf House this morning, and her car was in the lot, and there was a Do Not Disturb sign on her door."

"So she didn't make a run for the border after all. Earl, I had a cryptic, secondhand message from Marc Fitch. He was at the courthouse this morning. He got Cady released, by the way."

"I know. Angie told me all about it, and she thinks you're the greatest thing that's happened since Sam Spade."

Conan gave that a brief laugh. "Anyway, Marc said Giff has some sort of bee in his Stetson. And no, I can't explain that."

"Maybe I can," Kleber said grimly as he opened the file folder. "Steve Travers faxed me the latest reports on the Gould and Arno cases this morning. Transcripts of witness statements mostly."

"Anything from the cab drivers?"

"Yes." Kleber sorted through the papers in the folder until he found what he was looking for. "First, the cabbie who picked up Mrs. James Booth at Valley West Airport right after Dan Arno left her there. The cabbie logged her in at 12:55 A.M., and at 1:03, he dropped her at an apartment at 11522 Alderbrook Drive."

Conan reached into a desk drawer for a map of the Portland area, squinted at the fine print in search of the listing for Alderbrook Drive, and Kleber said casually, "If you're wondering how far the apartment is from the Gould condo, I already checked it. A little over a block. And nobody named Booth lives there."

Conan returned the map to the drawer. "What's your point? That Mrs. Booth is Savanna Barany?"

"Well . . . yes. The receptionist at the airport described Mrs. Booth as a middle-aged woman with gray hair, but we're dealing with an actress here. That would be a piece of cake for her."

Conan was remembering a pregnant woman walking across the Surf House parking lot, a woman he hadn't recognized until she was only a few feet away. "Yes, it would be easy for her. A little talcum and hair spray is all she'd need for the gray hair."

"You don't seem surprised."

"That Savanna was Mrs. James Booth? No. What about the cab that brought Sarah Talbot to the airport?"

Again Kleber shuffled papers. "Here it is. The driver said he picked up Mrs. Talbot at the mall in Valley West—and it's only about two blocks from the condo. She probably called the cab from a phone booth in the mall. The cabbie said she was waiting near a booth."

"Could he provide a description?"

"Sort of tall, black hair, thirty to thirty-five, wearing a tan raincoat and a scarf. He picked her up at 2:35 A.M. and left her at the airport ten minutes later. After she supposedly got cold feet in Arno's chopper, another cab picked her up and took her downtown to Union Station. Steve's people asked around at the station. Nobody on the late shift remembers her, and they probably would. No passenger trains were due for two hours, so the place was nearly empty."

"Union Station is only a short walk from the Greyhound Bus depot."

"Right. And a bus leaves for the coast at four in the morning. That's the one that arrives in Holliday Beach at six-thirty."

"In other words, you think Savanna was not only Mrs.

James Booth but also Mrs. Sarah Talbot? What about the squeaky-clean Herndons, who swore they saw the Ferrari parked at the Eyrie at six-thirty?''

"Well, maybe they're just overwhelmed at having somebody famous like Savanna Barany call them friends."

"But why would Savanna kill Dan Arno?"

"That's obvious," Kleber replied irritably. "To protect her alibi. She was afraid that once Dan got to thinking about it—like when he heard about Gould's murder—he'd realize who Mrs. James Booth really was."

Conan shook his head. "No, Earl, that's one thing she wouldn't worry about. She is above all an actress, and quite aware of her genius. It would never occur to Savanna Barany to doubt any role she played."

Kleber shrugged, his square jaw working. "Conan, some new evidence has turned up. That carafe, the one Arno drank the Nembutal-laced coffee out of . . ."

"What about it?"

"Remember, there were three fingerprints on the bottom?"

"Yes, I remember."

"And you were the one who suggested they should be checked against the elimination prints from the suspects in Gould's murder."

"Am I going to regret that suggestion?"

"I don't know. Anyway, the crime lab got a match."

Conan had to force himself to ask, "Whose prints are they?"

"Savanna Barany's."

Conan looked out the window, vaguely aware that there was a blue cast to the fog now, the sky coming through. Yet he felt as if something cold and opaque were enveloping him.

How did Savanna's fingerprints get on that carafe?

He took a long breath, realizing that the question he should be asking wasn't *how* Savanna's fingerprints got on the carafe, but *when*.

And *why*?

Rather, why were Savanna's prints *left* on the carafe?

"Oh, damn . . ."

Kleber asked, "Conan, what's wrong?"

He focused on Kleber, but he wasn't ready yet to answer that question. "What else is in that folder?"

"Well, another interesting item is that Saturday afternoon Savanna used the automatic teller at the Taft Bank to take a thousand dollars cash out of their joint account."

"And you think she paid Arno with that money?"

"Yes. And I think that Saturday night when Gould passed out from a near OD of scotch, Savanna drove to the Surf House and told Lasky that story about Gould burning his manuscripts. She knew that'd get him down to the beach house fast. But she didn't leave town then. She drove back to Dunlin Beach, hid her car—probably in one of the driveways along the road—and waited till she saw Lasky head for the house, then drive away. Then she went to the house, and *that's* when she shot Gould. Afterward, she put on her Mrs. Booth disguise and drove to the Baysea airfield. Forty minutes later, Dan Arno left her at Valley West Airport. She took a cab to that apartment on Alderbrook and walked the block to her condo. I figure it only took her a few minutes to call Valley West Airport as Mrs. Sarah Talbot and get rid of her disguise, then at one-twenty, she knocked on the Herndons' door."

Conan tapped his fingers on the arms of his chair. "The call from Sarah Talbot to the airport—are you sure it came from the Eyrie?"

"I couldn't find anything about that call in these reports, but it'll be easy to check." When Conan only nodded, Kleber went on. "I figure Savanna talked the Herndons into lying about seeing the Ferrari the next morning, then she went to her condo, made some coffee, and put it in that carafe with the Nembutal. I don't know where she got it, but it's not that hard to come by, and *her* fingerprints are on the carafe."

"Was there any coffee in the condo for her to make this deadly brew with? She's allergic to coffee, Earl. When Marian and I went to the condo Sunday, she apologized because she couldn't offer us any."

Kleber grimaced impatiently. ''I don't *know* about coffee in the condo, but it's not exactly hard to come by, either.''

''But did she have time to come by it?''

''Well, there's plenty of grocery stores open all night.'' Kleber rose and began pacing, even though the room was so small, it allowed him no more than two paces in any direction. ''Anyway, I figure Savanna put on another disguise—this one for Sarah Talbot—and walked to the mall, called a cab, and it took her to the airport. She did her cold feet act and left the carafe with Dan. And a cup of coffee must've sounded good to him right then. She knew it would. Then she called another cab to take her downtown to Union Station and walked to the bus station. The bus got her to Holliday Beach about six-thirty. This morning, I called the driver on that run. He lives in Eureka. He says he dropped off a female passenger at the Baysea junction, and his description tallies with Mrs. Talbot. She must've walked to the Ferrari at the airfield and drove back to Valley West. Probably got there about nine.''

Conan didn't respond to that. He was looking out the one-way glass. A blue pickup had pulled in on the other side of the parking lane. Neely Jones got out, crossed to the bookshop with a determined air that brought a car, which might have bluffed any other pedestrian into waiting, to a screeching halt. Conan opened the office door.

She was starchily uniformed, as usual, but she wasn't wearing a gun belt or badge. She marched into the shop, nodded to Miss Dobie, whose eyebrows were at full attention, then marched into the office, and when Conan closed the door, her breath came out as if she'd been holding it, and she announced, ''I've been *fired*!''

Conan stared at her, but after the initial shock, he didn't find it surprising that Neely and Giff Wills had come to a parting of the ways. Kleber waved at one of the straight chairs. ''Neely, you better sit down and tell us about it.''

''I've worked my butt off to satisfy Giff,'' she insisted as she seated herself, ''and damn it, I've been a good deputy.''

''Yes, I know you have.'' Kleber sat down in the other

chair, angling it to face her. "And I'd be happy to have you on *my* force any time."

She gave him one of her rare, glowing smiles. "Well, maybe if you win this election, I'll get my old job back."

"Not much chance of that. My winning, I mean. All right, Neely, what happened?"

"I told Giff I didn't like the way he did business. And that's what I have to talk to you about, Chief." She took a closer look at the folder on the desk. "Good. You've seen the latest reports. Is the one about the fingerprints in here?"

Kleber nodded. "Savanna Barany's? Yes."

"Well, that's what set Giff off. He was in his office waving these reports around when I came to work at seven this morning. He was talking to a couple of the guys, but the door was open, and I could hear every word from my desk. He said maybe he'd lost MacGill as a suspect, but this case was still going to win him the election. He said it'd get him all the TV coverage he could ever want, and the voters of Taft County wouldn't forget that *he* was the one who arrested Savanna Barany for the murder of her husband *and* Dan Arno."

Conan felt a queasy sensation in his stomach as he sank into his chair, and Kleber said, "I guess Giff came to the same conclusion I did. Which doesn't make me feel good about it." And he sketched for Neely the scenario he had just presented to Conan.

She nodded through it, and when he finished, she said, "That's it, and the DA rushed the case to the grand jury this morning. He had two clinchers. One, Savanna could leave the state at any moment, and probably would. Two, the fingerprints on the carafe."

Conan demanded, "He got an arrest warrant on that? Neely, what about the Herndons' testimony? What about the Laskys, who've made themselves so conspicuous by their absence? What about Bobby Gallagher? He works graveyard at the gas station in MacMinnville where a yellow Ferrari with California plates stopped for gas at one o'clock Sunday morning. And what about the phone call at 1:05 from Sarah Talbot to Valley West Airport? Where did it come from?"

"That's what I mean! That's what I asked Giff! Well, I

didn't know about the guy at the gas station. You know what Giff told me? None of that shit—his word—means a thing. She could've bought off the Herndons, or just charmed the hell out of them. And if the phone call didn't come from her condo, well, the phone company has been known to make mistakes. He'd probably get around that gas station attendant, too. Did the guy get a license number?'' When Conan shook his head, she went on: ''Giff says all a jury will see is the rich-bitch superstar thinking she can get away with murder. And those fingerprints. That's what will convict her. Now, I don't know whether she's guilty or not, but railroading her just to win an election isn't my idea of good police work.'' Neely caught her breath, then added, ''Chief, I know this might be called whistle-blowing, and I know exactly how popular that makes me, but damn it, I thought you had a right to know what Giff is up to.''

Kleber apparently found the crease of his blue pants in need of straightening, then he met Neely's intent gaze. ''Well, I guess it *is* whistle-blowing, but in this case I'm grateful. Trouble is, I don't see what I can do about it.''

Conan had listened to Neely with a sense of apprehension that became more oppressive with every word. He said bitterly, ''We have to do *something* about it, or someone *is* going to get away with murder. And possibly with another murder. Neely, do you know when Giff intends to serve the arrest warrant, or has he already?''

''Probably not. He wants to make sure the arrest gets plenty of press. When I left him, he was on the phone lining up TV coverage. In fact, he was talking to Shelly Gage, the woman who was here when—''

''Yes, I know Shelly.'' Conan grabbed the phone and dialed directory assistance, then the KEEN-TV studios in Portland, and finally reached the producer of the evening newscast, who at least knew where Shelly was.

''On her way down to Holliday Beach,'' he said. ''Something broke on the Gould murder case.''

''That's what I'm calling about, and I'm in Holliday Beach now,'' Conan replied. ''Have you any idea when she plans to arrive here?''

"She left at ten. Should be there about twelve-thirty. If you have any information about the story, I could call her on the van radio."

"I'll see her when she gets here. Thanks." Conan hung up and checked his watch as he rose: 11:35. "I'm going down to Dunlin Beach."

Kleber and Neely came to their feet voicing simultaneous objections, but Kleber was louder. "What the hell do you think you're doing, Flagg? Giving her fair warning?"

"No, I'm going to try to talk her into turning herself in to you."

"To me? Wait!" Kleber reached the door before Conan and stood poised to stop him by force if necessary. Then he relaxed, even smiled as he stepped aside. "Okay, Conan. Just be careful. The murder weapon is still missing. Maybe it's out to sea somewhere. But maybe it's not."

Conan nodded, and Kleber's atypical acquiescence didn't register at the moment. "I'll keep that in mind."

Miss Dobie sent him one of her questioning looks, but he missed it. He was out the door and running for the XK-E when she emitted a portentous sigh and rang up another sale for another copy of *The Diamond Stud*.

CHAPTER 29

By the time Conan turned onto Dunlin Beach Road, the fog had dissipated, and the sky was clear except for remnants of clouds hounded southward by the wind. When he reached the end of the road, he parked, got out of the car, and studied the secretive façade of the house. The front doors were open, but the house seemed no more welcoming for that. When he walked up the flagstone path, he could hear music: the sprightly "Underground Masque" chorus from *Blitz*, with its odd minor-key overtones.

In the foyer, he paused. The door onto the deck was also open, the air stringent and clean. The pillows on the couch had been arranged to cover the torn and bloody cushions where Ravin Gould had lain mutilated in death. Still in white, her magnificent hair loose, Savanna perched on a stool at the bar, a telephone receiver braced against her shoulder while she filled a tulip glass from a bottle of Dom Perignon. It was a one-sided conversation: He heard only a guarded "Of course I will." Then she abruptly put the bottle down. She had seen him.

She said into the phone, "Conan's here. I'll talk to you

later," and hung up, offering him a smile as he approached. "Conan, you've come back to me. Forever?"

He sat on a stool facing her, wondering who she'd been talking to. Dana Semenov, no doubt. And wondering at the subtle contours of her face, the shimmering light in her blue-violet eyes. "No, not forever."

Savanna put on an expression of desolation, then shrugged. "Well, have some champagne anyway." She reached over the bar for a glass, filled it, and handed it to him.

He asked, "What are you celebrating?"

"My freedom! My future! But most of all, getting *out* of here." She touched the rim of her glass to his. "Except . . . I truly will miss you."

That face was amazing, changing in a moment, and every new mood as true as the sky, the sea, the sunlight flooding the room. He tasted his champagne, asked, "Doesn't your celebration include the four-million-dollar advance you'll collect from Nystrom for *Odyssey*?"

She laughed, shaking a finger at him in mocking reproof. "*You* are a *very* stubborn man. I told you, that was for my autobiography."

"Oh, yes. The hardbound you said Nystrom was going to have on the shelves in a month. I don't know much about the publishing business, but I'm damned sure that would be one for *Guinness*."

"Did I say a month? Actually, I don't know how long it'll take."

"You don't even seem to know how much the advance is. There's quite a difference between three hundred thousand and four million."

"Oh, Conan, if you're going to be such a grouch, you can just go away. Nobody's going to rain on *my* parade today."

"I'm afraid I have no choice about raining on your parade."

"But you *do*, love." She leaned toward him with a heavy-lidded look of invitation. "You can celebrate *with* me."

"Are you sure your husband didn't leave a will?"

She sighed, put aside her coquettish persona. "Well, no-

body found one, did they? And they won't. I asked him once
if he'd made a will."

"When was that?"

"I don't know. A couple of years ago. *I'd* just made a will
leaving nearly everything I owned to him. He thought that
was funny. Said *he'd* never make a will. Let the survivors
fight over the spoils." She began humming along with the
raucous, bittersweet melody of a song called "Mona's
Theme."

Conan listened to Savanna's recorded voice, as amazed as
he had been when he first heard it at the convincing cockney
accent, the exuberant sexuality in it, the sheer, vivid alive-
ness.

"Savanna, he lied to you."

"Mm? What about? He lied about so many things."

"About his will. He made a will soon after he married
you. It was in a safety deposit box in San Francisco."

She stared at Conan. "I don't believe you!"

"I can show you a copy of it."

She put her glass down on the bar. "What did it say?"

"That you're his heir, except for a bequest to his first
wife."

"Oh . . . ." Her breath came out in a sigh.

"It also said that the Laskys are to continue as agents for
his literary estate, and they're to have complete control over
it. You get the royalties, minus the usual commission, but
they make the decisions."

She reached for her glass, hit it with her hand, and it tipped,
cracking its fragile rim, spilling out a froth of champagne.
"Damn!" Her chagrin seemed focused on the glass, and she
went around behind the bar for a towel to wipe up the spill,
then found another glass, filled it, and calmly drank from it.

Conan watched that performance in silence, then said
flatly, "That contract isn't worth the paper it's printed on."

"*What* contract? Is there anything in the will that says I
can't sell my own autobiography?"

"You know what contract I mean. The contract for *Odyssey.* You'll collect the royalties, but the Laskys will decide
who publishes it, and I leave it to you to predict whether

they'll choose Nystrom as long as Dana is editor-in-chief there.''

From the speakers Mona Fatale belted out her philosophy of life: *Make him laugh, make him sing, but never make him love you.*

And Savanna walked around the end of the bar, as unconcerned as a girl walking through a field of wildflowers on a summer day. "I told you, I haven't signed any contracts for *Odyssey*, so why should I worry who publishes it, as long as I get the royalties? I never wanted any of Ravin's money, but I'll take it. Why not? I earned it."

"Savanna, for God's sake, you have plenty to worry about, and one thing is that in a very short time, Sheriff Wills will be knocking at your door. He's coming here to arrest you. On *two* counts of murder."

He could believe the spectrum of emotions she displayed now was authentic: shock wavering into fear, then chagrin, and finally anger. She shouted like a fishwife, "You *bastard*! I *trusted* you!"

"You trusted me to fall blindly in love with you. That way I not only wouldn't be a threat to you, I'd be your informant."

"That's not *true*." Now she was all contrition. "I mean, I never said I loved you, but you understood that. I thought you did. Conan, I've never had to sell my body for anything, and I never *will*!"

He looked away from her, because the appeal in her eyes was too convincing. "I thought I *did* understand at the time. I didn't betray you to Giff, by the way. He came up with his own version of the truth."

Her eyes narrowed then she pushed herself up onto the stool, sat facing him. "And what *is* his own version?"

"I *do* make a good informant, don't I?" he asked with an oblique smile. Then he recounted the scenario that Earl Kleber had presented—the one that, according to Neely, Giff Wills had also embraced—while the music segued into a chorus singing "Rock of Ages" against the rumbling bass leitmotif for the V-2s. She didn't seem to hear it. She was intent on him, her face void of emotion, as if she were waiting for a cue.

The cue seemed to come at the point when Kleber speculated that she left the Herndons and went to her condo to brew the decaffeinated coffee and add the Nembutal. But her response was subtle: only a slight movement around her mouth suggesting a smile reined.

Conan withheld the vital element of the story, concluding with Savanna Barany, aka Mrs. Sarah Talbot, returning to the Eyrie in the Ferrari at nine in the morning. And Savanna laughed.

"Oh, Conan, don't tell me anybody *believes* all that. It's a crock, the whole thing. You know that."

"Do I? Unfortunately there's one piece of evidence I can't ignore, the one that guaranteed Giff an arrest warrant."

She didn't try nonchalance again, but waited breathlessly, lips parted. Conan said, "The carafe had been wiped clean. There were no fingerprints on it other than Arno's—except for three on the bottom. The police have identified them. Savanna, they're yours."

Again he recognized the authenticity of her emotions. She was too stunned to move, until finally she shivered, and when she spoke, the words came out in a whisper: "That's not possible. . . ."

"It's possible. And those prints will be the keystone of the DA's case against you." He took her hand, felt a brief resistance. "Savanna, you *know* how your prints got on that carafe."

"I don't even know what you're talking about." She put on an ironic smile as she withdrew her hand. "This whole thing is—well, it's ridiculous. *I* didn't kill . . . what was his name?"

Conan said irritably, "You know his name. You phoned him Saturday night to make arrangements for your flight to Portland."

"I told you, I did *not* kill that pilot!"

"I know you didn't."

That seemed to throw her off balance. Then tears gathered

in her eyes. "Oh, Conan, I *knew* you wouldn't believe I could kill anybody."

"I didn't say that. I said I know you didn't kill Dan Arno."

"But you *do* believe . . . what, Conan? Go on! *Say* it!"

"I believe you murdered your husband."

She twisted off the stool, took two strides away from him, then stopped, finding herself looking over the back of the couch at the pillows that hid the bloodstained cushions where Gould had died.

Conan said, "I believe you shot your husband, point-blank, in the heart with a twenty-two caliber handgun."

"How could I? I don't even own a gun. I *told* you that."

"So you did." He picked up his glass, but didn't drink from it, only watched the glitter of rising bubbles. "I saw the unedited videotape of the donnybrook at the bookshop Saturday. In the confusion, you dropped your purse—the orange one, remember?—and a gun fell out of it. A small automatic. Where is it now?"

"There *isn't* any gun," she insisted. "There never was!"

He studied her, aware of the sweet conviction in her voice purring from the speakers in beguiling harmonies with the male lead's tenor. *One more day to live . . . one more day to love . . .*

"Savanna, what I don't understand is why you didn't simply divorce him."

"I was *going* to divorce him."

"You went through some motions—*after* he was dead. But why didn't you divorce him sooner? You married him three years ago, and you told me you knew by the end of the first year it was a mistake. You also told me he was systematically sabotaging your career. Now, I can imagine some women staying with unhappy marriages for various reasons. The remnants of love. Hope. Fear. But you aren't like ordinary mortals, Savanna. You need a stage to make you whole, to keep you alive. You wouldn't have stayed with any man a week, much less over two years, once you realized he was coming between you and your stage. Why did you stay with Gould?"

She returned to the bar, sat beside Conan with her hands clasped in her lap, eyes downcast. "I told you why, but obviously you didn't believe me. I *loved* him, Conan."

He turned to face her. "The trouble with extraordinary talent is that it can be an obsession, and obsessions make you vulnerable. Gould enjoyed his power over you, didn't he? What was he blackmailing you with? Why did you have to kill him to gain your freedom?"

"He wasn't blackmailing me with anything, and I didn't *kill* him!"

"The irony is that in a way Gould passed on his power over you when he died. To Dana Semenov. I suppose she came here Saturday night at some inopportune moment and discovered you with Gould's body and the proverbial smoking gun. She was in the Baysea bar from about ten-thirty until eleven-thirty, and she was expecting someone. Maybe Gould promised to meet her there, and when he didn't come, she decided to drive by the house to find out why, or just to scout out the possibilities of seeing him alone. Maybe she heard the shot."

Savanna's tone was pointedly sarcastic now. "Conan, *you* should be the one writing books."

"This one would be nonfiction." He put his glass, still half-full of a wine of celebration, on the bar. "For whatever reason, Dana appeared at the crucial moment, and she had you in her power. You were Gould's heir and could sign the contracts—or so you both assumed. In exchange for *Odyssey*, she would not only remain silent about Gould's murder, she would become your accomplice. Is that when you loaned her your black wig? You were wearing it Monday afternoon when you arrived at the Surf House in your pregnant woman disguise. You'd been to see Dana at Baysea. Did she return the wig to you then?"

Savanna eyed him coolly. "This is *your* story, Conan."

"No. It's yours, Savanna. Someone was in Dana's room that afternoon. Someone wearing pale lipstick, who drank a glass of water; someone who purloined one of the pillows from the bed. And that morning, you took something out of your safety deposit box at the bank. The disks with the third draft of *Odyssey*. You gave them to Dana, and I'm sure as soon as you left, she went to the post office and sent them by express mail to Nystrom."

Savanna reached for the bottle and poured more champagne into her glass. "All I got out of the safety deposit box was some jewelry."

He ignored that. "You and Dana didn't have much time to make your plans. You had to meet Arno at the airfield at midnight, and Dana had to leave her car at Baysea first. I suppose you followed her in the Ferrari, maybe waited on the road while she parked her car outside her room. She went into the room and a few minutes later came out with a flight bag and a carafe of coffee. Did she tell you she needed the coffee for the long drive ahead of her? That was when you handled the carafe, wasn't it, probably just to put it out of the way somewhere. And that was when you gave her the map of Portland you kept in the car."

Cool sarcasm gave way to annoyance. "Conan, damn it, this isn't *funny* anymore."

"No, it isn't funny. Do you want to tell me the rest of it?"

"There *isn't* any rest of it!"

"Then I'll tell it. You and Dana drove to the airfield, where Arno was waiting for you. Rather, for Mrs. James Booth. When you arrived at Valley West Airport, you called a cab and gave the driver the address of an apartment a block from the Eyrie. The fact that you knew that address implies premeditation. On one of your trips to Portland to shop with Maggie Herndon, you noticed that conveniently located apartment and memorized the address. Of course, with your training, I'm sure you only had to see it once. Anyway, on Sunday morning, the cabbie left you at that apartment, then you walked—or probably ran—the block to your condo, where you got rid of your Mrs. Booth disguise, then presented yourself at your neighbors' door, thereby establishing the time of your arrival with two very credible witnesses."

"That *wasn't* why I went to talk to Maggie," she said, giving him a look of searing accusation. "And if I flew to Valley West by helicopter, how did my car end up parked at the condo early the next morning?"

"Magically, it seems, if you didn't stop anywhere along the way. That's what you told me. But the gas tank was three-quarters full when I drove you back to Holliday Beach Sunday afternoon."

"Maybe I *did* stop for gas. I was so hysterical, I don't remember."

"You were *never* hysterical," he said, shaking his head. "You don't remember stopping for gas because *you* didn't drive the Ferrari. *Dana* did. When she left you at the Baysea airfield, she drove the Ferrari to Portland, and she stopped for gas in MacMinnville. She asked for her change in quarters. My guess is she needed them to make a call at a phone booth, a long-distance call she didn't want on her credit card."

"You think she was calling *me*?"

"No. She was calling Valley West Airport—as Mrs. Sarah Talbot."

The wail of sirens startled him, and for a moment he thought Wills was approaching with a warning fanfare. But the wail came from the speakers and gradually merged into the jubilant "All Clear" chorus.

Conan glanced at his watch: twelve-twenty. He was running out of time, but he went on, chipping away at that impervious yet changeable façade: "Sometime after you left the Herndons, you probably went out and saw the Ferrari parked in front of the condo where Dana left it, and you breathed a sigh of relief. The rights to *Odyssey* were a small price to pay for the risk Dana was taking. I suppose you originally planned to leave the Ferrari at the Baysea airfield and return for it by bus yourself, but Dana assumed that task. She left the Ferrari at your door, then walked to the mall and called a cab. She was supposed to go straight to the bus station and take the first bus back to Holliday Beach. But she didn't, Savanna. You were sure your Mrs. Booth persona was entirely convincing, that Arno would never link Mrs. Booth to Savanna Barany, but Dana didn't have as much faith in your talent. *She* decided the only way to prevent Arno from identifying you was to see that he had a fatal accident. And, Savanna, she decided that *before* you left Holliday Beach.

When she left her car at Baysea and went into her room, she filled one of Baysea's carafes with instant, decaffeinated coffee. She carried a jar in her suitcase, and I suppose she made it with water from the tap. It would be hot enough. Hotels and motels usually set their water heaters unnecessarily high. Then she emptied some of her Nembutal capsules into the carafe. Her prescription for fifty capsules was filled a few days before she left New York, and there were only ten left on Monday.''

Savanna was staring into her glass, and she didn't seem to know what role to assume now. Conan leaned toward her, but her only response was to turn her head a few degrees away from him.

He said, ''The question is, did Dana intend to leave your prints on the carafe? I think she did. Now the sheriff is convinced he has a case against you for *both* murders. Only you. A jury might be lenient when it comes to Gould's murder, because he had a history of adultery and cruelty. But Arno's murder is too cold-blooded to arouse any sympathy for you. He was an innocent bystander, one with a wife and two children, who will undoubtedly be in the courtroom every day of your trial. Savanna, your *only* hope now is to go to Chief Kleber and make a voluntary statement. Tell him what really happened.''

For a long time, she didn't move, even to blink or breathe. Then her shoulders came back, and she had decided on her role. Conan recognized it as the role of maligned virtue.

''That's a fascinating story, Conan,'' she said archly. ''The only trouble is, the whole thing is a figment of your imagination.''

He came to his feet, suddenly consumed with anger, and so strong was the urge to pick her up bodily, to drag her kicking and screaming to the Holliday Beach police station, that he had to move away from her until he got his anger under control.

Finally he looked directly at her and said, ''There's something else you must understand: Dana is a very dangerous accomplice. Now that you've signed the contracts for *Odyssey*, you're only a liability to her. She set you up with those fingerprints so you'd be the prime suspect in both murders, but she can't afford to let you live to be arrested. You might tell the police the truth, and you might be believed.''

Savanna slipped off the stool, took a step toward him. ''I am *not* a liability to anybody, because you're *wrong*, damn it, and I won't—''

''I'm *not* wrong, and you *are* a liability to a woman who's already demonstrated her willingness to dispose of liabilities by murder. And you *are* in a legal noose. With a good lawyer, you might get off with a light sentence *if* you're only charged with Gould's murder. If you're charged with both murders—well, maybe you didn't know that in Oregon, aggravated murder carries a death penalty.''

Her eyes went wide and dark with fear, and the moment hung like a raindrop caught on a leaf. Conan said softly, ''Please, Savanna, talk to Earl Kleber. Tell him the *truth*.''

Then the moment was gone. ''I don't believe you! You're just trying to frighten me!''

Conan caught her arms, felt her trembling like a bird ready to take flight. He said, ''All right, Savanna, forget Earl for now. Just let me take you to my house, somewhere *safe*.''

''No! Let *go* of me! *Leave me alone!*''

A shadow of motion caught his eye, fixed his attention on the door onto the deck. Someone was standing there.

Dana Semenov.

He had just run out of time.

Her cornsilk hair was windblown, and she stood with her hips canted, like a model displaying the stylishly loose slacks and oversize jacket of white linen, the mint green blouse, the latticed white sandals.

But her sandals were crusted with sand, and what she held in her right hand was jarringly inappropriate to the ensemble.

He had asked Savanna where the gun was, even then doubting that she knew. Now they both knew. Sunlight glinted on the silvery barrel of the small automatic in Dana's hand. Her gloved hand. She was wearing leather driving gloves.

No one spoke or moved, not until Dana walked slowly toward them, stopping perhaps ten feet away, until she said, ''It's all right, Savanna. I won't let him hurt you.''

Savanna pulled away from him, ran to Dana as if she were an angel of mercy come to her rescue. "Dana, we've got to get out of here! That sheriff is coming to *arrest* me."

Conan felt a chill between his shoulder blades. Dana glanced at Savanna, then turned her unblinking gaze on him, and the circular void of the gun's barrel was no less menacing for its small size. At ten feet, a bullet fired from that gun could be as deadly, if not as destructive, as a .44 Magnum. He was dimly conscious of the music shifting in mood to the dark "Blitzkrieg" theme with its stalking, empty fifth chords.

Amber eyes narrowed speculatively, Dana said, "I suppose Savanna spilled her guts for you, Flagg. I knew she would."

Savanna stared at her, perhaps beginning to sense the deadly potentials here, and Conan stood poised, part of his mind calculating timing, distance, probabilities, another part battling the adrenaline rush that made his pulse pound, that urged him to reckless flight.

He yelled, "Savanna, get away from her!" and took a stride forward, but Dana reached out, hooked her left arm around Savanna's neck, and Savanna fell against her, then went rigid when she felt the muzzle of the gun jammed against her right temple.

He froze, hands loose at his sides; Savanna whimpered, "Conan . . ."

And Dana said flatly, "You can't change anything, Flagg."

Conan knew then that the decision had already been made. Dana had already designed Savanna's *suicide*. No doubt she had included him in her plan. Savanna had told her on the phone that he was here. And so Savanna Barany, having murdered two people, would suffer an attack of remorse and despair in the face of her imminent arrest. Conan Flagg would try to stop her, but in the struggle, she would shoot him, then turn the gun on herself.

Seven feet between him and Savanna and the gun at her head. And where the hell was Wills? All Conan asked was a distraction. Any kind of distraction . . .

"Dana," he said, "the police found Ravin Gould's will."

The gun remained pressed into the soft flesh at Savanna's

temple. "And I suppose you're going to tell me Savanna isn't his heir?"

"Oh, she's his heir. But there was another provision in the will."

"Of course. And what is it?"

"Another provision besides the bequest to his first wife—"

"Damn it, what *is* it?"

Conan took a deep breath, let it out slowly. "It has to do with Gould's literary estate."

"What *about* his literary estate?"

"Gould named Byron and Justine Lasky agents for his literary estate, and that includes any manuscripts not yet published. That includes *Odyssey*, Dana."

But she only laughed. "Sure. Good try, Flagg."

Savanna cried, "It's *true*, Dana!"

"Shut up! I'm not stupid!"

Her fingers flexed on the gun's grip, and Conan saw her swallow as if her mouth were dry. Perhaps killing didn't come so easily when she held the victim in her arms.

But Dana Semenov had gone too far to stop now. She would pull the trigger, and while Savanna lay dead at her feet, she would pull it again until Conan also lay dead. She would put the gun in Savanna's lifeless hand and press her index finger against the trigger to fire a random shot so that a test would show the expected powder residue.

And she would never even flinch.

Conan shouted, "Dana, she's left-handed!"

He knew that to be a lie, but Dana had to think about it, to realize that a small mistake of that nature might make the police wonder if an apparent suicide was murder.

And Savanna perhaps felt a slight change in the pressure of the gun, or perhaps she had simply reached a point of mindless desperation. She thrust her elbow hard into Dana's stomach, twisted away. With Dana's cry of chagrin, the gun went off, and Conan launched himself across the abyss of seven feet.

"Police! Freeze!"

Before he could complete the two strides that bridged the

abyss, Dana fired twice. Momentum carried him crashing into her, and his weight bore her down with a strangled cry that was cut off abruptly when her head thudded against the floor.

And it was only now that the shouted order registered. Police? He rolled away from Dana, found himself looking up at Earl Kleber. But even Kleber's presence was only a peripheral awareness.

"Savanna . . ." She lay in a motionless swirl of white, sunlight like fire on her bright hair, the right side of her face streaked with blood welling from the gash in her temple.

Kleber knelt beside her, fingers pressed to her throat. He nodded. "She's alive. You okay?"

Conan slumped with his elbows on his knees, panting with relief, and it seemed incredible that Dana had missed him with both shots. "I'm intact, Earl. She must be a lousy shot."

"Not that lousy. She winged Neely. Where's the damn phone?"

"On the bar." Conan turned to Neely, whose left sleeve from just below the shoulder was soaked with blood. She had Dana on her feet and handcuffed. Dana's eyes were glazed, blind, and she was offering no resistance.

Neely answered his silent query. "I'm okay," she said tightly. "For now, anyway."

He nodded and leaned over Savanna. She didn't seem to be breathing at all, yet when he held his fingers to her open lips, he could feel a faint, wavering warmth.

"The ambulance is on the way," Kleber said as he hung up the phone. "Just don't try to move her. Billy's on his way, too. Neely, you look a little green around the gills. You better arrest that woman and read her her rights while you're still on your feet."

Neely frowned. "Chief, she's *your* prisoner."

"Not the way I figure it. She's all yours, Officer."

Conan realized then that Neely was wearing a gun and a badge: a Holliday Beach Police Department badge.

Neely let her smile come through, but only briefly. She was all business when she asked, "What are the charges, Chief?"

"Well, I guess you can start with the attempted murder of Savanna Barany and assault on a police officer."

Conan took Savanna's hand and felt for a pulse, found it finally, slow, but strong. He said, "And the murder of Dan Arno and conspiracy in the murder of Ravin Gould."

"We'll get to that part later," Kleber said, nodding to Neely as she began the ritual of arrest. Dana listened in numb silence, but managed a clear "Yes" when Neely asked her if she understood her rights.

The wail of sirens didn't come from the speakers this time. Kleber said, "That's either the ambulance or Billy or . . ." He laughed as he headed for the door. "Come on, Conan. Neely, bring the prisoner. It just might be ol' Giff."

With some reluctance, Conan rose and left Savanna, followed Kleber and Neely, with Dana in tow, to the door. When they reached the porch, the air seemed to vibrate with an ominous rumble, a cloud of dust moved toward them until it enveloped the turnaround in a tan fog, and the rumble became a roar as a squadron of vehicles slewed to a stop. The first two were Taft County Sheriff's Department patrols, but the rest were a motley of vans, station wagons, sedans, and even a motorcycle, most marked with television, radio, and newspaper logos. Their occupants spilled out and poured toward the house.

This, Conan thought grimly, was a beachhead, even if the soldiers carried cameras and mikes instead of guns. And leading the clamoring charge, breaking though the yellow tape at a jouncing jog, was Sheriff Gifford Wills.

But when he had almost reached the porch, he came to a sudden halt. His troops stopped behind him like a wave hitting a breakwater. Wills glared at Neely and demanded, "What the hell're *you* doing here?"

Conan smiled as he retreated into the house to wait at Savanna's side for the ambulance. He held her hand, simply to assure himself of the life still warm in it, and listened to the music, to a rich, husky voice, fragile and sweet to bring tears to his eyes.

I never asked for forever. . . .

CHAPTER 30

After spending most of the afternoon at the Holliday Beach Police Station answering questions for various agencies of the law, as well as answering questions—as promised—for Shelly Gage, Conan didn't reach the North Taft County Hospital until nearly five o'clock.

The small, fifty-bed hospital hadn't been so crowded since the infamous twelve-car pileup on Highway 101 ten years ago. The corridors were full of reporters, plus an unusual number of visitors who decided this was a good day to visit friends or relatives who happened to be confined to the hospital, and even an unusual number of hospital personnel who decided this was a good day to put in extra time inventorying linen and bedpans, not to mention the hospital volunteers who found this a good day to bring cheer to the patients. Even the patients were amazingly ambulatory today, when there was a chance, however remote, of catching a glimpse of Savanna Barany.

With few exceptions, no one even came close to a glimpse.

Conan had had numerous updates during the afternoon on Savanna's condition. The bullet had grazed her skull, causing a concussion and some blood loss, but she would certainly recover. Thus when he arrived at the hospital, he didn't ask the harried staff about Savanna, but searched out Neely Jones's room. Deputy Sonny Hoffsted was posted outside. He smiled and waved Conan in.

Neely wasn't alone. On the other side of the bed stood a lithe young man of Oriental descent, who held her hand in a tender grasp. Neely seemed quite lively for someone who had recently had a bullet removed from her left arm, which was bandaged and restrained in a sling. The television set on the wall across from the bed was on, but the sound was muted while an inanely cheerful, middle-aged man with a bristly crewcut sold appliances.

Neely said, "Hi, Conan. I want you to meet a friend of mine." And she looked up with the secretive, revealing smile of love at the young man. "Jan Koto. He's a biologist at the Oceanographic Center." Then as Conan and Koto shook hands across her bed, she added, "Jan's from San Francisco, too. He's a rock climber and a brown belt in karate."

Koto laughed. "That's not a warning. Actually, Neely's better at karate than I am, but I can outclimb her any day on a good rock face."

Conan said, "You make a formidable team. Neely, how are you?"

"I feel terrific, and I don't see why I have to stay here tonight. The arm doesn't hurt at all."

"It will if you don't stay near a good supply of Demerol."

"Hey, it's about to start," Koto cut in as he snatched the remote control from the bedside table, and the energetic music loop that introduced KEEN-TV's Evening News rattled from the television.

The events in the quaint little village of Holliday Beach were the lead story, and Shelly Gage's face filled the screen as she began the saga, but she was displaced by the scene at the Gould house as Giff Wills led the charge, only to find Earl Kleber, a handcuffed Dana Semenov, and a bleeding Neely Jones on the porch. Behind them, Conan was retreating into the house.

And Giff Wills, pink-faced, shouted at his erstwhile deputy. "What the hell're *you* doing here?"

The cameras and mikes simultaneously shifted to Earl Kleber as he replied, ''Officer Jones was wounded in the course of arresting this woman for the attempted murder of Savanna Barany.''

If Wills had been smart, he would have simply faded into the crowd at that point. If he had spoken in less than a bellow that the mikes easily picked up in spite of the general hubbub, no one would have heard his chagrined, ''*Officer?* You're *my* deputy!''

Which gave Neely an opportunity to counter, ''You *fired* me! Remember?''

Then a cut to the arrival of the ambulance and Savanna's removal from the house on a stretcher; a cut to the hospital and a curt comment from the physician on duty in the emergency room, Dr. Nicole Heideger; then comments from DA Owen Culpepper and other official personages explaining in sound bites that Savanna was under arrest for the murder of Ravin Gould. Dana's role in the affair was obviously a source of confusion for both the interviewers and interviewees. Wills had the last word. When asked how it felt to have the deputy he had just fired solve this sensational case, his comment was, ''No damn comment!''

When it was over, and Koto muted the sound again, Neely frowned. ''What happened to Chief Kleber? They just ignored him.''

Conan said, ''You're more telegenic than Earl.'' And she had indeed been impressive, standing straight and unflinching, her sleeve drenched in blood, her prisoner firmly in hand. Dana had probably been close to shock, but in the video eye, she looked sullen and dangerous.

''At least,'' Koto said, ''Giff had his chance to make a real ass of himself on TV.'' Then he squeezed Neely's hand, gazed into her eyes. ''And you were incredible, Neely.''

Conan decided that he constituted a crowd here and was about to make an unobtrusive exit when the door swung open, and Dr. Nicole Heideger strode into the room, an attractive woman, somewhere in her forties, dark hair cut short, who had no time for cosmetics or fashion. She gave Conan a crooked smile. "Damn, it's refreshing not to have to patch *you* up with the other casualties."

"I find that rather refreshing myself. How are you, Nicky?"

"Today? Running my feet off. Hi, Jan. Okay, Neely, let's see what's going on here." And she began studying Neely's chart.

Neely said, "You were on TV, Dr. Heideger." Then she laughed. "The look you gave that reporter should've frozen the camera."

Nicky cast an annoyed glance at the television. "Every TV in the hospital is tuned to the news today. Usually it's Lawrence Welk or *Star Trek*. Even Mr. Lasky was watching the news, and he's from New York."

Both Conan and Neely came to attention, and Conan was first with "Who did you say, Nicky?"

She looked from one to the other in bewilderment. "Byron Lasky. He came in yesterday. Visiting from New York City."

"That idiot!" Neely burst out. "Conan, Giff was so sure the Laskys had made a break for Canada, he didn't even check with the hospitals."

Conan asked, "Nicky, what room is Lasky in, and can I talk to him?"

"No way. I'm trying to get him stabilized for a life flight to Portland. I don't want him talking to anybody except me and his wife."

"His wife is with him?"

"Yes. She's been with him round the clock."

"Was there a middle-aged woman with reddish hair—"

"Who sounds like Lauren Bacall? You mean Marian. Yes, she's been here most of the time, too. In fact, she was here just a few minutes ago." When Conan made a headlong dash for the door, Nicky called, "Conan!" waited until he stopped, then added, "Room thirty-nine."

"Thanks, Nicky."

Room thirty-nine was in the new wing, and its main corridor was blocked by a crowd of reporters, fans, and the curious. When Conan pushed his way through, he discovered that the crowd was restrained behind a barrier consisting of two large, armed State Patrol officers and the equally large and armed Sergeant Billy Todd.

Todd recognized him and waved him forward. "Hi, Conan. Ms. Barany said she wants to see you."

The crowd behind him clamored at the unfairness of it all, and Conan didn't explain to Todd that he hadn't come to this wing to see Savanna. He simply nodded and set off down the corridor.

A short distance past the barrier, the corridor made a sharp right turn, and just beyond it Conan was hailed by a familiar voice. "Conan, my man, I've been looking to hell and gone for you."

Marcus Fitch. He stood at the door of one of the rooms, talking to a nurse who gazed at him with a beguiling smile. As Conan approached, she hurried away, tossing her flaxen hair over her shoulders.

Conan cocked a thumb at the door. "I assume this is Savanna's room and you're here because she's your client."

"Your deductive powers are dazzling," Fitch replied with a tigerish grin.

"I won't ask how that came about. It seems all but inevitable."

"Kismet, no doubt. Conan, I'll need to discuss La Barany's case with you. At least I'd like to know if you're going to be a hostile witness."

"Probably not. Call me this evening, Marc."

"I will. Meanwhile . . ." He gestured toward the door. "She wants to see you."

Conan almost balked at the presumption that if Savanna wanted to see him, he *must* want to see her. But he had to admit that he *did* want to see her. To say goodbye? Perhaps.

Entering her room was like walking into a flower shop, with bouquets occupying every available flat surface, and even a few on the floor. Savanna was wearing an ordinary hospital gown, with a white patch of bandage extending from her right temple to above her ear, and she had lost some hair around the wound. Her right eye was swollen and turning purple, and she wore no makeup. And how, Conan wondered, did she still manage to look so beautiful?

She said huskily, "Oh, Conan, I'm so glad to see you."

He took the hand she offered, asked, "How's your head."

"Well, this is the worst headache *I* ever had, but they're keeping me doped up. Conan, I *had* to see you before they took me away. And they will. Tomorrow, probably, or the next day. I'll . . . be in jail."

That prediction had a distinctly melodramatic air, but he couldn't argue its likelihood. "I'm sorry, Savanna."

"You really are, aren't you?" she asked, and she seemed a little surprised. "Well, I suppose I might get out on bail or whatever. Anyway, I had to thank you, Conan. You saved my *life*."

"At the time, I was thinking very hard about my *own* life."

"Won't you accept even a little gratitude?"

"I'd rather accept some honesty."

For a moment, her eyes brimmed with tears, then she said softly, "That's not so easy, you know."

"I know."

"You want honesty?" She took a deep breath. "I'll tell you this: I'm not sorry I killed Ravin. I am sorry about Arno. And, Conan, I'm sorry you and I couldn't . . ." She let that hang, then called up a smile. "Nystrom *does* want my autobiography. Maybe it'll pay my legal fees."

"I understand you've found yourself an excellent lawyer."

"Marc? Oh, the man is *beautiful*! Friend of yours, isn't he?" Conan nodded, and she went on in a rush of enthusiasm. "Marc thinks he can get the charge reduced to manslaughter, and since Dana *did* try to kill me so I couldn't talk to the police, well, he thinks that'll make all the difference with a jury. He says I might not have to do any real time in prison at all. And, Conan, he's sure he can get a special dispensation—I forgot what he called it—so I can leave the state long enough to do *Blitz*. Booth says he can schedule the takes I'll be in and finish them in two months, and Marc says they'll never get around to the actual trial before that. And the publicity—I mean, this film is going to break box-office *records*." She paused, and perhaps it was something she read in Conan's eyes that dampened her ebullient mood.

Not accusation, not even doubt. Only a bittersweet amazement at finding himself in the presence of a phenomenon he couldn't quite grasp. He said, "You'll be magnificent." Then he pressed her hand to his lips as he might a letter from a long-lost passion. "Goodbye, Savanna."

"Conan . . ." For a moment, like a shadow, he saw in her exquisite eyes a baffled regret. Then it vanished, and she smiled, blew him a kiss. "I'll call you, Conan."

When the door swung shut behind him, he found the hall empty. He stood for a moment, hands thrust into his pockets, then started down the corridor in search of room thirty-nine.

Call him? He knew she wouldn't remember his name in a few weeks. And she had no concept of the world she was entering in the courtroom, in the sterile misery of a jail, or behind the walls of a prison, where the erstwhile superstar would find her talent and beauty meaningless in a subsociety structured by violence and despair.

Then he shook his head, an ironic laugh escaping him. With Marc Fitch defending her, with her acting ability, it was quite possible her rosy picture of her future was not at all unrealistic.

As he passed a window alcove furnished with four armchairs, a low table, and an assortment of old magazines, he stopped. A woman holding an open newspaper in front of her occupied one of the chairs. She lowered the paper, looked at him over the top of her glasses, and smiled. "Conan, if you're looking for Savanna's room, it's back that way."

"Actually, Marian, I'm looking for you and the Laskys."

"Well, you've found us." Marian Rosenthal nodded toward the room across the hall: room thirty-nine. "Justine's in there with Byron."

He sat down, asked, "What happened to Byron?"

"Justine said that sheriff came to their suite and told them about Ravin's will," she replied, dropping her newspaper on the table. "The man was convinced they knew about the will and had murdered Ravin. He wanted a confession then and there, and he was a real bastard about it. When he finally gave up and left, Byron collapsed. Hemorrhaging, that sort of thing. Justine called me, and we brought him here to the emergency room. We didn't know what else to do. He wasn't in any shape to fly back to his doctor in New York.''

"Did you know Giff's had an APB out for the Laskys—and you—ever since Justine checked out of the Surf House? But he was so sure you'd made a run for Canada, he neglected to check the local hospital.''

Marian laughed at that. "I guess I should go turn myself in.''

"Don't bother. Giff has trouble enough. How is Byron now?''

"Seems to be doing well, thank God. The doctor wants to transfer him to a hospital in Portland tomorrow. She keeps calling it Pill Hill.''

"Officially the University of Oregon Health Sciences Hospital. Don't worry, it's an excellent hospital.'' He hesitated hooking his arm over the back of the chair. "Marian, would you answer a few questions for me?''

"Why not? It's all kind of academic at this point, isn't it? By the way, Justine may have a question . . . well, it's something she wanted to talk to somebody about, and you may be the somebody. Anyway, what did you want to ask me?''

"About the ring.''

Marian caught her breath, but after a moment, she nodded. "Allison gave it to Ravin on their first anniversary. I helped her pick it out. *Ahava.* It means *love.* And that son of a bitch had to wear it Saturday night, knowing I'd be there. Oh, Ravin enjoyed his games.''

"How did it end up on your hand Monday afternoon?''

She laughed. "Damn, you have a good poker face. I didn't think you recognized it. Well, after the party broke up Saturday night, I didn't go straight to the Surf House. I turned off the highway and waited a couple of minutes, then drove back to Ravin's house. Savanna hadn't come up from the beach yet, and Ravin had passed out on the couch. And I took the ring. Stole it, actually, although somehow I felt I had a right to it.''

Conan looked out at the jack pines shading the window. "Why did you choose to spend your vacation here?"

"How did you know I was on vacation? Never mind. You're right, I did come here on vacation, but that ended when Ravin was murdered. I wasn't kidding when I said his books were suddenly worth their weight in gold. I should be in my office now, scrambling to finish a campaign to sell a million copies of *Stud*. Well, I've done what I can by phone, and I guess it's time my assistant had a real test."

"But you didn't come to Oregon solely to retrieve the ring."

She gave him a crooked smile. "No. I'd heard about Ravin's 'autobiographical' novel, and I wanted to find out what he said about Allison before the damn thing got published. So when Justine told me she and Byron were coming here to see Ravin, well, it seemed like a good time for a vacation on the Oregon coast."

"And your purpose in going back to the beach house Saturday night was to get a look at *Odyssey*—possibly *borrow* one of the drafts?"

"Yes. I knew Ravin, and I knew before we all left the party that he was just about at the point of passing out. He always got belligerent then. More than usual, that is. So I went back to the house hoping he'd reached that point. And he had. The door was unlocked, and Savanna was still on the beach. My golden opportunity, right?"

Conan nodded. "But one you missed, I assume."

"Right. First, I decided I had to have that ring. Then I was about to go into the office when I saw Savanna coming up the steps from the beach. And I panicked. I took my booty and ran. I don't think she even knew I'd been there. Anyway, I'm glad the damn manuscripts are lost. Except I'm sorry for Justine and Byron to lose their commission."

Conan turned in the chair, crossing one leg over the other. "*Odyssey* isn't lost. I think if the Laskys check with Nystrom, they'll find that Dana sent them two computer disks—Angie's disks from her typing of the third draft."

"Oh, no . . ." Marian stiffened, her mouth slack.

"You don't need to be concerned, Marian. I've read a

printout of the third draft. Gould treated Allison very kindly. His one true love, it seems. Actually, he concentrated more on his own trauma in recovering from the car accident and his overwhelming grief.''

"That bastard! Well, I suppose I should be relieved. And I am. Conan, I'm very grateful to you." She gave him a smile made wistful with memories of a daughter she still grieved, then pulled herself to her feet. "Well, you'd probably like to talk to Justine. I'll be back."

Conan heard Justine's voice as Marian opened and closed the door of room thirty-nine. He picked up the newspaper she had been reading: this morning's edition of *The Oregonian*. It was open to a two-page spread on the Gould murder made hopelessly out-of-date by this afternoon's events. Among the photographs, he noted one of Savanna getting into an XK-E with a man identified as Kevin Flogg. Another photograph showed Savanna as Mona Fatale in *Blitz*. Apparently the only photograph available of Cady was from his high school yearbook.

"I'm glad you found us, Mr. Flagg."

He looked up to see Justine Lasky, with Marian in her wake, emerging from room thirty-nine, Justine as perfectly groomed as ever, striking in a gray silk dress whose color matched her eyes. There was weariness in those eyes now, but the imperial chill had thawed.

Conan rose. "I hope Mr. Lasky is recovering well."

"Very well, all things considered." She and Marian seated themselves in adjoining chairs, and Conan saw that Justine was holding a Federal Express envelope. She put it on the table, then looked up at Conan. "Marian said you have some questions. I'll answer any I can."

Conan sat down, leaning forward to ask, "Where did you go Saturday night about midnight, Mrs. Lasky? I know you went somewhere. You were seen driving away from the Surf House."

"Is this simply to satisfy your curiosity, Mr. Flagg?

"Yes."

She smiled at that straightforward answer. "I should think you deserve that much. Actually, I went to Baysea. It was ill advised, to say the least, but I was so bitterly angry at Dana. She was trying to drive a wedge between Byron and Ravin, and Byron didn't need more anxiety. Besides, Dana and I . . . well, that's a long story. At any rate, my purpose was to have it out with her and to tell her that I intended to use my influence with other agents to boycott Nystrom. Fortunately, I was saved from my own folly. She wasn't in her room, nor in the bar.''

Conan asked, ''Her car was parked in front of her unit, wasn't it?''

''There *was* a maroon car directly in front of it, but frankly, I hadn't noticed what kind of car she was driving, so I didn't know whether it was hers or not. Eventually I gave up and returned to the Surf House, cooler, if not wiser. And no, I did not go near Ravin's house.''

''Thank you for assuaging my curiosity. A failing of mine, I'm told.''

''You're quite welcome,'' she said with a smile that faded as she reached for the Federal Express envelope. ''Mr. Flagg, there's a matter that Marian felt I should discuss with you, and I agree.''

Conan glanced at Marian, who remained attentive but silent. Justine seemed to need a moment to gather her resolve, then she began, ''Ravin was in New York about six months ago, and he left an envelope with Byron, rather melodramatically done up with sealing wax and with instructions that it was only to be opened in case of his death. On Monday, after the murder, Byron called the office and had the envelope Fed Exed to him. And this . . .'' She removed a manila envelope and handed it to Conan. ''This is what he found.''

Conan opened the envelope and took out a sheaf of manuscript pages. The running head read ''ODYSSEY/Gould,'' and the first page was marked CHAPTER 11.

''Oh, my God . . .'' he whispered.

Marian asked, ''What's wrong, Conan?''

''This chapter was missing from the third draft.'' He checked the numbers in the upper right corner. They made an unbroken sequence from page 218 to 247. He turned to 241 and found that the first three lines corresponded exactly with those on the fragment he had taken from the fireplace at the Eyrie.

He went back to the first page, skimmed the entire chapter, while Justine and Marian waited patiently. Most of the chapter dealt with Jimmy Silver's marriage to Anna Vas, star of stage, screen, et cetera, whom Gould blatantly described as "the sexiest woman in the world." Conan couldn't judge the accuracy of the events preceding the marriage, but he found it difficult to believe that Savanna had once been literally on her knees begging to be bedded by Gould. At that point, she had been at the height of her popularity, a superstar who had found her stage, and it was the world. She undoubtedly had her choice of willing partners, and she didn't need Ravin Gould to feed her ego.

Yet Gould characterized Anna Vas as a clinging vine who cast aside her career to spend every waking moment in Jimmy Silver's presence, who was irrationally jealous, even though Jimmy led a life of virtuous fidelity during the marriage.

But his resolve to virtue was shattered in the chapter's final scene—and the fragment from page 241 was part of this scene—when, after an author's tour, Jimmy returned a day early to his apartment in New York and found his wife in bed with someone else. With an actress named Mayley Harlette. The scene was described in vicious detail, and it was obvious that the author considered such relationships disgusting. Beyond that, he insinuated that this was Anna Vas's chosen means of sexual gratification. Jimmy Silver in his righteous chagrin called her a sham whore, a man-hating, man-eating dyke.

Conan said, "This is despicable."

Justine nodded. "Did you see the note on the last page?"

On the final page, the text ended halfway down the page, and on the blank half was written in a small, erratic hand, "Byron, if anything happens to me, I want this chapter included in *Odyssey* when it's published. And if you have any doubts about the last part, talk to Marletta Hayley, sometime actress, New York. Ask her about her roommate in the three months before *Blitz* hit the fan. JRG."

Conan tossed the pages on the table, feeling an anger he

knew was only a shadow of the rage Savanna had lived with since she read the chapter. And she *had* read it. She had burned one copy of it. She didn't know about the copy Gould had left with Byron Lasky.

This was how Gould had blackmailed her into submission while her career crumbled. If she was a good girl, he wouldn't include this chapter when he submitted *Odyssey* for publication. If she wasn't . . .

"Marian, you work in the ephemeral world of public popularity—what would happen to Savanna if this chapter was included when *Odyssey* is published?"

Marian took a deep breath. "Well, you know, there's not much stars can do these days to disillusion their fans to the point of turning against them. But this . . . maybe it's the last taboo. At least for somebody like Savanna, whose popularity is based so much on her sex appeal. I think it would've destroyed her."

"Apparently she thought so, too." He turned to Justine. "Mrs. Lasky, what are you going to do with this chapter?"

"Normally Byron and I would decide that together, but he's too ill to deal with this . . . this utter garbage now, and I'm simply too distracted to be objective about it. That's why I wanted to discuss it with you. I don't know, for instance, whether it might be considered evidence in Savanna's trial."

Conan swallowed the bitter laugh that was his first impulse. That chapter would be considered damning evidence, especially since it could be compared to the other burned fragments Steve Travers said were found in the condo's fireplace.

"Mrs. Lasky, you called this garbage. It's far worse than that. It was a knife in Savanna's back, and Gould relished twisting it. He had a sadist's eye for vulnerability, and he understood very well that Savanna Barany without a stage might as well be dead. In a sense, she was fighting for her life. And it was a battle to the death."

Justine pressed her fingers to her eyes and finally said, "You've put the matter into perspective very nicely. I can't honestly say I like Savanna, perhaps because she's so beautiful, so incredibly talented, and it seems that everything has come so easily to her. I suppose I'm jealous of that. But it is not my intention to make her suffer." Then she added, "*Nor* to serve as Ravin's henchman beyond the grave."

Marian loosed a whispering sigh. She said, "Justine, I think the place for that chapter is in the nearest fire."

Justine nodded and began to gather the pages and tap them together. "I think Byron would agree. Thank you, Mr. Flagg."

Conan rose. "I hope your husband's recovery continues, Mrs. Lasky. Marian, it's been a pleasure knowing you, in spite of the circumstances."

"Well, this has certainly been an interesting vacation. Next time you're in New York, plan to stay with Jacob and me at the farm."

He thanked her for the invitation, then turned and walked down the corridor, past Savanna's room and beyond through the crowd still clamoring at the entrance to the wing.

When at length the hospital doors closed behind him, he paused to look up at a sky of singing blue filled with towers of cumulus cloud, blue-gray beneath, ivory and snow white on their crowns.

"Good afternoon, Mr. Flagg."

His gaze shifted downward. Beatrice Dobie. She was carrying a bouquet of yellow chrysanthemums in a quart jar.

"Good afternoon, Miss Dobie."

"These are for Doc Spenser," she said, frowning into the mums.

Conan said, "Oh," hoping his embarrassment wasn't obvious. It hadn't occurred to him to ask about Doc while he was in the hospital.

"Mable Cranwoody is a candy striper, and she said the poor man doesn't know what's going on around him, but I thought . . . well, people sometimes feel things they don't actually react to. I mean, even when they're sick or unconscious. I remember my sister Liz when she—"

"Yes, a miraculous recovery. Is the shop battened down?"

"Mm? Well, it's after six, Mr. Flagg." Then her square face lighted with a secretive smile. "Incidentally, we set a record today. I mean, a record for the bookshop. As of closing time today, we sold *five hundred* copies of a book that perhaps you'd rather not hear the title of.''

"You mean, of course, *The Diamond Stud*."

She watched him, and when he didn't go into apoplexy, apparently decided it was safe to continue. "Subtracting freight and the cost of the autographing, we cleared a total of—" she paused for effect "—four thousand one hundred and fifty dollars. And forty-seven cents.''

"Amazing," Conan said, managing a suitably amazed expression.

She beamed proudly. "Well, yes, it is. And Cady came in today to make arrangements to pay for the damage he did. I had a list for him, and he promised to pay fifty dollars a month.''

"Miss Dobie, you have snatched profit from the jaws of disaster." Then he frowned. "But if you *ever* do anything like that behind my back again . . ." She looked so miserably contrite among the mums that he relented. "Well, just don't tell me about it.''

"Oh, Mr. Flagg, I've learned my lesson. Besides, I don't suppose we'll have another best-selling author in Holliday Beach very soon.''

"Especially not one who enhances the value of his books so dramatically by getting himself murdered. Anyway, I think you're due a vacation. And a bonus. About . . . four thousand one hundred and fifty dollars. And forty-seven cents.''

Her mouth fell open, then she recovered to sputter, "But, Mr. *Flagg*!''

"To do with as you see fit," he added, smiling benignly, "as long as not one cent of profit from a Ravin Gould book is returned to the Holliday Beach Book Shop.''

She made a huffing sound, and before she could manage any intelligible words, he set off across the parking lot toward the XK-E, calling over his shoulder, "The Galapagos, Miss Dobie. You always wanted to see the Galapagos.''

E P I L O G U E

On the first Wednesday in November, a sou'wester hit the Oregon coast with forty-mile-an-hour winds gusting to sixty, and, as of four-thirty in the afternoon, over three inches of pounding rain.

Conan Flagg found it most satisfactory.

He might ordinarily have watched the storm from his house, where he could see the wind-whipped ocean assaulting the shore, but there was no one else to mind the bookshop since Miss Dobie had—finally—departed on her vacation three weeks ago.

And so Conan sat on a stool by the cash register, which had registered only two sales since ten this morning, with the weekly *Holliday Beach Guardian* spread out on one end of the counter and Meg spread out on the other. The bookshop was empty, and the stereo in his office was at full volume, the Bach *Toccata and Fugue in D Minor* providing a suitable accompaniment to the rain slashing at the windows.

Meg was using the telephone for a headrest, and when it rang, she was startled into an easily translatable Siamese yowl of annoyance. She shifted an inch or so away from the offending instrument and gave Conan a strabismic glare as he reached for the receiver.

He wasn't startled by the ringing of the phone. He had been expecting the call, although Miss Dobie had steadfastly maintained that he wouldn't hear one word from her until she returned.

Still, yesterday had been election day.

"Holliday Beach Book—"

"Mr. Flagg, I'm calling from Guayaquil," Miss Dobie shouted, unnecessarily, since the line was quite clear. "We just sailed into port a little while ago."

"I hope the Galapagos lived up to your expectations."

"Oh, it was a fabulous trip. I shot twenty-nine rolls of film. But I just couldn't stand the suspense anymore. What about the election?"

Conan said blithely. "Well, the weather was perfect, and there was a good turnout. According to the *Guardian*, a fifty-one percent—"

"Mr. Flagg, please, I'm just interested in the results!"

"I have the newspaper right here." He turned to the front page. "Let's see, Frank Spanicek held on to his city council seat, but Harry Lufton lost to Jean Casper Davis. She must be Denny Casper's daughter. Judge Lay managed to hold on, too, but it was a squeaker."

"Mr. Flagg!" There was a definite edge in her tone.

And since Conan was feeling perverse, he replied, "You probably want to hear about the state races. Senator Hatwood won again, but he had to get out and dirty himself in the trenches this time, and Donny Jones lost quite thoroughly to—"

"Mr. Flagg, the *sheriff's* race! Who won the *sheriff's* race?"

Conan smiled at Meg, who was watching him intently, the tip of her tail twitching. "Well, Miss Dobie, there's good news and bad news, as they say."

A groan, then: "What's the bad news?"

"Earl Kleber lost by a little more than a hundred votes." Conan let Miss Dobie sputter awhile, then interrupted her with "The *good* news is, Giff Wills *also* lost. By about a thousand votes."

In the ensuing silence, Conan looked down at the headline under the *Guardian*'s masthead: SURPRISE WINNER IN SHERIFF'S RACE.

Miss Dobie shouted, "What *happened*, Mr. Flagg?"

"An unprecedented write-in campaign, spearheaded by Lydia Quigley, who is, of course, a force to be reckoned with, since she's active in every civic and/or women's organization in Taft County. And she had an excellent candidate to throw her considerable weight behind."

"Oh, you don't mean . . ." Miss Dobie all but giggled. "You don't mean the write-in candidate was . . ."

Since she couldn't seem to get the name out, Conan provided it: "Deputy Neely Jones."

Conan hoped Miss Dobie was making this call in the privacy of a hotel room, since if she was in a public place, her whoops of joy would make passersby assume she was either hysterical or drunk.

At length she calmed down and caught her breath. "But what about Chief Kleber? Is he terribly disappointed?"

"I talked to him last night, and he seemed relieved. Earl and Neely will be the finest law enforcement team Taft County ever had."

"Amen. Oh, I must send Neely a telegram of congratulations."

"But you'll be home in a day or so." When that met with a long silence, he asked, "Won't you?"

"Well . . . I thought maybe while I was in the neighborhood, so to speak, I might have a look at Machu Picchu. And there's an air tour of the Andes I heard about from a lovely gentleman I met on the ship."

Conan smiled and whispered to Meg, "The plot thickens." Meg flicked a velvet ear at him.

"I mean, since business is always slow this time of year, and Lord knows when I'll ever be in South America again . . ."

"Miss Dobie, go. With my blessings."

"I was hoping you'd feel that way. Oh—sorry, I have to

sign off now. Miguel, uh, Mr. Rivera is waiting for me. Thanks for the good news.''

Conan hung up, frowning. ''Meg, I may have made a serious error in sending Miss Dobie that close to the equator.''

Then he looked down at the *Guardian*. No. Miss Dobie would be back. She wouldn't be able to resist returning to see Taft County's good-ol'-boy network shaken to its foundations. He wondered idly what Giff Wills would do for a living now.

Open a real estate office, no doubt.

Meg stretched methodically and thoroughly, baring her teeth in a benign grimace of a yawn, then stalked across the newspaper to rub against Conan's arm with a hoarse, running commentary.

He took the hint. An early twilight had already activated the streetlights outside, and Meg's internal clock, which was linked directly to her stomach, was sounding an alarm. ''All right, Duchess. Time to close the shop. Come on, I'll serve your royal highness's dinner.''